MAGICAL LOVE

With a sprinkling of fairy dust and the wave of a wand, magical things can happen—but nothing is more magical than the power of love.

Don't miss the other books in the series!

Sea Spell
TESS FARRADAY

As a child, Beth fell into the churning sea, only to be lifted gently out by a dark-haired youth with a knowing, otherworldly smile—who then vanished into the mist. Somehow the young girl knew her elusive rescuer was a powerful, legendary selkie, who could become the love of her dreams . . .

Once Upon a Kiss
CLAIRE CROSS

For over a thousand years—so legend has it—the brambles have grown wild over the ruins of Dunhelm Castle. Many believed that the thorns were a sign that the castle was cursed, so no one dared to trespass—until an American hotelier decided to clear away the brambles himself, and found a mysterious slumbering beauty . . .

A Faerie Tale
GINNY REYES

According to legend, a faerie must perform a loving deed to earn her magic wand. So, too, must the leprechaun accomplish a special task before receiving his pot of gold. But the most mystical, magical challenge of all is . . . helping two mortals fall in love.

One Wish

C. J. CARD

JOVE BOOKS, NEW YORK

If you purchased this book without a cover, you should be aware that this book is stolen property. It was reported as "unsold and destroyed" to the publisher, and neither the author nor the publisher has received any payment for this "stripped book."

MAGICAL LOVE is a trademark of Berkley Publishing Corporation.

ONE WISH

A Jove Book / published by arrangement with
the author

PRINTING HISTORY
Jove edition / September 1998

All rights reserved.
Copyright © 1998 by Carol Card Otten.
This book may not be reproduced in whole
or in part, by mimeograph or any other means,
without permission. For information address:
The Berkley Publishing Group, a member of Penguin Putnam Inc.,
375 Hudson Street, New York, New York 10014.

The Penguin Putnam Inc. World Wide Web site address is
http://www.penguinputnam.com

ISBN: 0-515-12354-4

A JOVE BOOK®
Jove Books are published by The Berkley Publishing Group,
a member of Penguin Putnam Inc.,
375 Hudson Street, New York, New York 10014.
JOVE and the "J" design are trademarks belonging to
Jove Publications, Inc.

PRINTED IN THE UNITED STATES OF AMERICA

10 9 8 7 6 5 4 3 2 1

This book is dedicated to:

My agent, Karen Solem,
whose belief in me is inspiring;

My friends, "The Breakfast Club,"
Shirley Frye, Cheryl Herring, Maryanne Hofer,
Barbara Page, Barbara Schnieder, and Charlene Speice,
whose friendships I value;

and

My son, Stephen, a film major at UNLV
whose creative mind gave me the ending.

Thanks,

I love you all.

My Beloved Comes

You came to me just before
the Christians rang their bells.
The half-moon was rising
looking like an old man's eyebrow
or a delicate instep.

And although it was still night,
when you came, a rainbow
gleamed on the horizon,
showing as many colors
as a peacock's tail.

—Ibon Hozm (994–1063)

One Wish

Prologue

Ninj was weary.

Sprawled upon a bed of jewel-colored pillows, the once-great genie lay in utter desolation. Tears like flowing springs traced paths down his pale cheeks. *Men don't snivel,* an inner voice warned, *not men of your magical powers.* But that was then and not now. That was before he was imprisoned.

"My life is not worth camel dung!" he wailed to walls that were as iridescent as a butterfly's wings. He'd been enclosed in this prism of cut glass for so long, he doubted he would ever taste freedom again.

"A bellyache to the Sultana." His hand raked over the jewelless turban on his head before covering his traitorous lips. He glanced about nervously. Like the Sultan's harem, the walls had eyes and ears. Eyes and ears that betrayed.

"Forgive me, my Sultana," he begged. "I meant you no disrespect. It was the bad jinn who sentenced me here, not you. It was the trickster. The usurper, claiming Ninj was too old and his magic no longer good."

Sipping from a crystal goblet, Ninj sighed reflectively. "Most beautiful Sultana, we had such good times together—I miss those halcyon days. If you would but give me another chance to grant you your heart's greatest desire, I could make it happen. Then you could be the Sultan's favorite, and I could retire.''

Ninj knew his situation was hopeless, and anger soon replaced his bittersweet longings. In desperation he slung the drinking vessel against the wall. The vessel splintered, the glass glittering like diamonds against the kilim-covered floor.

"Master," he moaned, "where are you? I am waiting for your summons."

One

Miller Holbrook stood at the front window of his third-floor apartment on Thomas Jefferson Street, staring south toward the C & O Canal. If he stood at just the right angle, he could see a sliver of the sluggish green waterway and its sandy towpath that was alive with activity this morning.

Georgetown was the south terminus of the canal, and the boats departing now had earlier unloaded their cargo of Cumberland coal. Those same boats would make the return trip up the waterway loaded down with goods that had come into the Potomac seaport from all over the world. Everyone claimed that the railroads would be the death of the canal, but from Miller's vantage point above the busy comings and goings on the street below, the prediction seemed absurd.

In Miller's opinion, the impending arrival of his new landlady, Antonini Vassily's niece, was just as preposterous. A letter written in flowing, flowery script had arrived last week informing him of the lady's arrival today. What had Antonini been thinking when he had left his estate to a woman? And what if he and Miss Jenny Blake didn't get along?

Miller had lived in the building belonging to his old friend for so many years that the third-story apartment felt more like home than his parents' house in Charlottesville, Virginia, ever had.

Arriving in Georgetown seven years earlier to begin his teaching career at Georgetown College, Miller had rented rooms from the strange little man who owned the building and the shop on the first floor filled with curiosities. Miller had chosen the location not only because of its proximity to the trolley line, but also because he felt comfortable among the many ancient relics Antonini had collected. Soon Miller had become fast friends with his landlord, enjoying his company and the many intellectual conversations they shared.

He looked at the wooden floor where the bright sun sketched the window and his shadow. In the rectangle of golden light, Antonini's cat lay snoozing. Since his master's death three months earlier, Bengel had taken up residence in Miller's apartment. Although Miller had never been overly fond of the cat, or vice versa, they both had become more tolerant of each other.

Miller exhaled a long breath. Now instead of three old bachelors living beneath the same roof, there were only two. And the two left had formed a truce while mourning the loss of their dear friend.

But what of Antonini's niece, Miss Jenny Blake? The idea of moving wasn't one Miller wished to contemplate, but Miss Blake's arrival made the thought a possibility. How would the girl feel about having a single man living in her house? Or worse yet, would his presence damage the young woman's reputation? Moreover, he wasn't overly fond of women.

He removed his glasses, cleaning them on his sleeve before returning them to his face. At his feet, the white cat stretched lazily before opening his eyes and pinning Miller with his dual-colored stare. There were times when Miller believed Bengel had the ability to read minds and that he was as devious as his Romany name suggested. Antonini had named the cat for the devil who appeared as the evil genius or hero in the Russian gypsy tales he loved.

Miller squatted to stroke the animal's snowy fur. "Your new mistress," he said. "I wonder what she'll be like."

Bengel snubbed Miller's show of affection and began washing his pale pink paws. It appeared that the devil cat was not only preening himself for Miss Blake's arrival, but, unlike Miller, was anticipating it.

Jenny Blake was pleased with the beautiful day. There had been no signs of rain, such as swallows flying low on the water or toads hopping home. The weather in all its glory was an omen and one Jenny needed, especially when she considered the magnitude of her new undertaking.

She stood at the stern of the canal boat that had been her home for the past two-and-a-half days. From the moment she had stepped foot on the towboat *Destiny*, she had been fascinated by everything she had encountered: from the family who owned the barge, to the boat's small crew, to the green waterway that was the C & O Canal; by the locks they had passed through; and even with the mules that pulled the boat along the towpath.

Nights on board the boat were Jenny's favorite time. At the end of the day, which began at daybreak and ended at sunset, Mister Kelly—a silent man who hadn't said a day's worth of words since the boat had departed Shepherdstown, West Virginia—would tie up alongside four or five other barges for the night. Almost always there was someone aboard one of the anchored boats adept with a harmonica or some other musical instrument.

The soft melodies played by the musicians served as a pleasant backdrop for conversation and socializing among the boaters. During those moments when frogs croaked along with the music and the water slapped gently against the hulls, Jenny regretted her somber child-

hood beneath the watchful eye of her God-fearing Nana
Blake. No music or nonsensical conversation was allowed in the Blake household. It was no wonder that her
father had left the farm to work in the coal mines, never
to return, leaving behind his mother, his young wife, and
baby daughter.

Although Jenny believed that the captain wasn't a
man who would ever desert his family, he was not one
for socializing—but his very pregnant wife Meg was. It
was Meg's love of all people and her present condition
that had necessitated the need for Jenny's presence on
the already crowded boat. She had been allowed passage
from Shepherdstown only because she had agreed to
help Meg with the cooking and the tending of the two
Kelly girls and because Meg's elder sister had become
ill and could not complete the journey to Georgetown.
Eight people were on board the ninety-foot-long boat;
the Kelly family of four, a crew of a steersman and two
mule drivers, and herself.

Jenny slept in a hammock strung inside the twelve-
by-twelve cabin that served as kitchen and sitting space,
while the Kellys slept in the forward hatchway off the
cabin. The crew slept with the four mules in the bow.

The animals and their efficiency at towing the boat
amazed her, but Jenny was glad she wasn't sharing a
compartment with them. Although Kelly's mules
seemed smarter than most, they were still part horse and
part ass and smelled like the latter, in her opinion.

They were in line now at the Georgetown terminus,
waiting to unload the coal from the boat's hull. As soon
as the unloading was completed, Jenny's journey on the
C & O Canal would end. She would miss the people she
had met on her trip.

"I'm going to miss you, Meg," she said. The two
women were sitting on the roof of the low cabin, watching the children play. The two girls were buckled into
leather harnesses and tethered to the roof so they
wouldn't fall overboard.

When she first saw how the canallers controlled their

younger children, Jenny thought the restraints cruel. Then she realized that it was an accepted practice by all boatmen traveling up and down the canal. The children didn't seem to mind; in fact, they appeared to enjoy it. It gave them the freedom they wouldn't have otherwise, while giving the adults a little peace of mind. If the youngsters should stray too close to the side and fall, they could be hauled back aboard quickly by their tethers.

"I'll miss you, too." Meg's response brought Jenny back to the present. She watched Meg pat her rounded belly. "I'll be seeing you again soon, lass. Then you can give me a tour of that fine shop you'll be owning."

"I still can't believe it," Jenny said. "Me, owning my own shop."

Her upbringing on the small farm outside of Shepherdstown certainly hadn't prepared her for the position of shop owner. The only thing she knew how to sell was the apples the three Blake women harvested each year from the tiny orchard behind the house. Besides, as she glanced across the canal where two- and three-story brick buildings sprouted from the ground like rhubarb stalks, she wondered if her mother had been right in her prediction that Jenny wouldn't like the city.

"Jenny, Jenny, watch me dance." On top of the cabin, five-year-old Shannon, the youngest of the Kelly girls, clumsily practiced the steps Jenny had taught her.

The child's awkward movements reminded Jenny of herself at that age, when her Grandmother Vassily had been alive. She would sneak Jenny behind the barn and teach her the taboo gypsy dances. Dancing, and the mention of Jenny and her mother's gypsy heritage, were forbidden on the Blake farm, but that taboo no longer applied to Jenny. She was proud of her gypsy ancestry— at least, the little she knew about it.

Jenny began clapping her hands in rhythm with Shannon's steps. True Rom songs needed no additional accompaniment.

"It's much like an Irish jig," Meg offered, her hands

joining the beat. "I'll be dancing again soon after this one makes his appearance."

From one of the boats in line behind them, a harmonica picked up the rhythm.

"His? Now, how do you know that wee one is going to be a boy?" Jenny asked.

"After bearing two girls, a woman can tell. Besides, Mr. Kelly has promised me if I give him a boy child, he'll dance the jig with me himself."

"*Your* Mr. Kelly?" Jenny shot a glance toward the sober man sitting next to the tiller. She couldn't imagine the quiet head of the Kelly clan ever dancing a jig.

Meg winked at her. "Oh, he dances a different tune when it's just the two of us."

Jenny blushed.

Meg laughed. "I be forgetting, lass, that you aren't experienced in the ways of love."

"And won't be," Jenny insisted. "I'll give my heart to no man, or give him anything else that belongs to me."

"Ah, lass, you don't always have a say in such matters."

"Yes, you do. Or *I* do. If you'd witnessed my mother's heartbreak after my father deserted us, you'd know why I intend to have a say in such matters. His leaving turned her into a very bitter woman."

Jenny loved her mother, but she wouldn't miss the bitterness the woman carried around like a club, striking down any chance for happiness. Jenny had lived in the shadow of her mother's heartbreak for so long it was a wonder she had any sunshine left in her heart. But surprisingly enough, she did. From now on, she intended to enjoy life.

"Jenny, Jenny, come dance with me," Shannon insisted, taking Jenny's hand in her small one and pulling her toward the center of the cabin's roof.

"I'll be dancing out with no man," Jenny reiterated to Meg as she faced Shannon and bowed.

Soon she was caught up in the vigorous rhythmic

dance, and all thoughts of men and heartbreak were forgotten.

After leaving the boat and crossing the canal, Jenny paused. She turned, waving one last time to Meg Kelly and her two girls before her feet carried her over the path toward Thomas Jefferson Street and the location of her new home.

"I won't be nervous," she told herself, although she felt as quivery as a tree in a storm. A soft breeze lifted the brim of the straw leghorn she'd secured to her head with pins before leaving the boat. "After all, it isn't every day a girl becomes a shop owner, especially in a town as large as this one."

Several passersby looked at her oddly, making Jenny stiffen her spine and walk a little straighter. She had to quit talking to herself. It was a habit she had acquired out of necessity, to keep from going absolutely daft during the times she spent alone walking the grassy meadows that abutted her Grandmother Blake's small farm. Besides, talking to yourself was better than not talking at all, she had decided long ago. She refused to become one of those silent, reticent people like her mother and grandmother.

Only halfway to her destination and her shoulder already ached from the weight of her carpetbag. Everything she owned, or everything she deemed worthy of the trip south, was packed inside the shabby bag. She juggled the valise to the other arm. "Not too much farther," she said, soliciting another peculiar look from a fashionably dressed lady and gentleman who approached her.

Thinking now was as good a time as any to try a little old-fashioned friendliness, she called out to the couple. "Morning to you. How are you on such a fine day?"

Instead of returning her greeting, the twosome quickened their steps.

"Well, a fine how-do-you-do to you, too," Jenny

whispered after they had passed. "I reckon city folk don't believe in talking to strangers." Or maybe they lived by the same rules her mother and grandmother lived by—don't talk to anyone.

Dismissing the couple, she continued on her way, studying her surroundings. The footpath was dappled with shade from the overhanging trees that scattered this side of the sixty-foot-wide canal. Rows of houses several stories high were built only feet away from where she walked. Some of the buildings' lower levels contained shops, and the smell of baking bread made her stomach rumble. Stopping again to give her arms a rest, she studied the bridge that crossed the canal and read the street sign: *Thomas Jefferson Street.*

She fished inside her skirt pocket and brought out an envelope. The address of her uncle's building was printed across the front. Inside the crumpled paper she could feel the key she had received from his attorney.

"It won't be long now," she told herself. Breathless, she picked up her bag again and walked up the small incline until she reached the bridge where the path leveled off. A uniformed policeman touched his hat when he passed her before continuing up the street.

From where she stood, she could see the Potomac River. It puddled at the south end of Thomas Jefferson Street and was as silvery as a looking glass in the bright morning sun. Reluctantly Jenny averted her gaze from the pretty sight to look in the opposite direction. The cobblestone street swelled like a long wave that rolled away from her. Both sides of the roadway were studded with tall brick castles, or so they appeared to a girl who had spent most of her twenty-two years living in a one-room bungalow.

Her heart pummeled her ribs. As she stared at the row of town houses on each side of the street, there was no doubt in her mind which one had belonged to her uncle. The yellow-washed brick structure that stood in the middle of the block seemed to call out to her. Although Jenny had never met her Uncle Antonini, from the stories she had heard from her Grandmother Vassily about her older brother, it seemed fitting that her gypsy uncle would paint his home in such a sunshiny color.

No longer did her carpetbag weigh her down. On steps as light as a fairy's, Jenny turned and floated toward the front of the yellow brick building. Once there she gave the three-story structure a thorough going-over.

It was built much the same as she was—tall and narrow. But instead of two blue-gray eyes looking out on the world, it had seven: three windows on each of the top two stories and one big bay across the lower front. Studying the projecting window, Jenny saw a lopsided mouth not unlike her own.

Beside the bay was an ornately carved walnut door, the same dark brown color as her hair. Two layers of red bricks formed a fan-shaped stoop that to Jenny's imaginative mind resembled a toothy smile.

"Thank goodness my teeth aren't that color."

Jenny laughed. Her analogy amused her, or perhaps it was nervousness that invoked such thoughts. Whatever it was, Jenny felt like shouting with glee. And she did just that. "You belong to me," she told the sunny-colored building.

Overcome with her emotions, she twirled in a circle, carpetbag and all, while her free hand anchored her straw leghorn to her head. Too dizzy to spin anymore, she stumbled to a stop beside the stoop and read the sign above the door: *Grimoire*.

Now why would her uncle name his shop that? Although she wasn't familiar with the word, Jenny found nothing remotely grim about the building so far.

For another moment, she contemplated the words. Wasn't *moire* some kind of fabric? Did her uncle sell piece goods? She shrugged, dismissing the sign and its meaning, anxious to be inside her shop. Removing the key from the envelope, she inserted it in the brass keyhole, turned the key, and pushed open the door.

• • •

Miller stepped closer to the window, peering down at the strange-looking woman who had stopped in front of the building. When she gazed up at the windows, he stepped back into the shadows, fearing detection.

It didn't take a math professor to deduct that Miss Jenny Blake was different from the people who passed below. With her overly large straw hat, plain skirt, and blouse, the word *yokel* popped immediately into Miller's mind. From the top of her ridiculous-looking hat to the boots that showed beneath her too-short skirt, she looked as though she belonged on a farm and not in the city.

Although Miller couldn't make a proper judgment of her height from his lofty view, he could tell that she appeared uncommonly tall for a woman. Maybe even taller than his own five-foot-nine stature. It was too bad, he thought, that he had not taken after his mother's side of the family instead of his father's. His mother had been as long and stringy as a bean, while his father had been as short and stocky as a turnip.

But his phenotype was forgotten when he saw the woman below begin twirling in the street like a whirlwind. Was she in her cups? He rolled his eyes heavenward. ''What, my good friend, were you thinking when you left your estate to such a creature?''

Perplexed, Miller shook his head. He meant no disrespect to Antonini's memory, but what had the man been thinking to believe this niece, this hoyden he had never met, would be capable of handling such a big responsibility? The curiosities housed in Antonini's shop were probably worth a small fortune, not to mention the building, which Miller knew his old friend had owned outright. And this girl, fresh off the farm, would control all of it.

And you, too, a little voice reminded him. *She is your new landlady.*

Miller swallowed. He ran his finger around his freshly starched collar, then smoothed the lapels on his tweed jacket. He was a meticulous man who demanded order not only in his appearance, but also in his surroundings at home and in the classroom. Judging from what he had witnessed so far of Miss Blake, there was nothing remotely orderly about her appearance or deportment. How was he to live with such a creature?

Another quick glance downward proved the lady had stopped swirling like a dust devil, but she had also moved out of his line of vision. He leaned closer to the window, and his forehead thunked against the surface. The sound echoed throughout the quiet room. Miller jumped back. Had the noise given away his position? He waited a few more minutes before attempting to take another peek.

When he did look again, she had moved closer to the stoop and appeared to be reading the shop's name. Or maybe she wasn't reading it. Perhaps she couldn't read.

Pressing closer to the window and feeling like a spy who feared discovery, he continued to watch the woman. *Damn, what she was doing now?* All he could see was the jerky movement of the horrible hat she wore—it was so wide it concealed her shoulders. He glanced away from the window to the square of sunshine where Antonini's cat still lay.

Bengel, whose body was twisted like a contortionist as he bathed himself, suddenly stopped his grooming and froze in place, ears forward, all senses alert. Although Miller hadn't heard the front door open two stories below, he was certain the cat had.

Were Miller's earlier suspicions true? *Had* Bengel been grooming himself for Miss Blake's arrival? He watched the cat slip lithely to his feet then hasten on muffled paws toward the apartment's open door before streaking down the stairs.

Good manners suggested that Miller should also go down and introduce himself, but for now he would leave the formalities to Bengel.

"Go greet your new mistress," Miller chided, following Bengel and closing the door. After the cat's departure, the room felt empty. Although Miller hated to admit it, he would miss the feline's company.

He walked back to his paper-laden desk and dropped unceremoniously into the chair.

"Unlike you, you Judas cat, I've more important things to do than pay social calls. I have papers to grade."

Soon all thoughts of the cat and the new landlady were banished from his mind.

Two

~

The moment the outside door closed behind her, Jenny paused in the small entryway. She dropped her bag on the floor, allowing her eyes to adjust to the sudden dimness. That took several moments, and while she waited she unpinned her hat and hung it on the hall tree just inside the doorway. The massive piece of furniture looked as though it served not only as a place to hang coats and hats, but also as bench, umbrella stand, and cane holder. An odd assortment of the last two items filled the stand's holes. Jenny, taught to be frugal all her life, wondered why her uncle had needed so many umbrellas and walking sticks. Surely one of each would have been plenty.

Opposite the front entrance, steep stairs led upward to a windowed landing. The slanted ceiling above them suggested another flight. Although she had read and re-read the legal papers she had received from her uncle's solicitor that made her her Uncle Antonini's sole heir, until this moment she had no idea of the value of her inheritance. The building alone was fancier than anything she had imagined. Never in her mind's eye had she pictured such wealth.

She turned and glanced toward the opening on the right, which led into an adjoining chamber. The sign above read WELCOME, and Jenny supposed the space beyond had been her uncle's shop. With her first glance, it was evident that her Uncle Antonini hadn't sold piece goods. But then, she wondered, how could he part with any of the lovely, unusual pieces housed inside the room?

Light streamed through the big bay. Dust motes gilded by the sun floated softly on the slanting rays above elegant chairs and tables and the polished wooden floor.

Jenny drew in a deep breath, hoping to calm the swarm of ladybugs in her stomach. She still couldn't believe that this building and its contents belonged to her. She felt undeserving of such a gift, especially when she had never met the man who had been so generous. The realization hit her in the form of a big lump in her throat. She would never have the chance to know the man. Not usually given to worrying over life's disappointments, Jenny swallowed the lump and looked for the positive. Maybe she could still know her uncle.

By leaving her his home and possessions, he'd given her part of himself. She glanced at the collection of furniture and knickknacks that filled the long narrow room. The contents would all be a reflection of her uncle and an insight into the kind of man he was. Yes, she would get to know her uncle.

Stepping deeper into the room, she was treated to a fragrance so pleasing that she longed to put a name to it. The heavy spicy scent permeated the shop and made Jenny think of exotic and foreign places. She knew, if it had been possible for her Uncle Antonini to walk into the room, he, too, would have smelled of the same intriguing scent. Her spirits lifted more with this thought. She hadn't been inside his house for ten minutes and already she felt as though she was discovering the relative she hadn't been given the chance to know.

Somewhere above her, a door closed. The sound of lithe feet descending the wooden stairs made Jenny focus her attention back to the entrance hall. It was several moments before a cat, the color of freshly fallen snow, paused regally beside the door.

"Ah," she said, "you must be Bengel." The two studied each other for an indefinite time before Jenny moved toward him. "And what a majestic puss you are, with your jewel-like eyes."

Another first in Jenny's life. A cat with two different colored eyes. One eye was the color of an aquamarine sea while the other one captured the green of a summer pond. A shrewd intelligence lay behind the dual-colored gems. As Bengel studied her, she shifted lightly on her feet. Did the noble beast find her appearance lacking? He would, she reasoned, if he compared her meager dress to his own white mink robe.

She moved cautiously, raising her hand toward the tip of his pink nose. She waited for the cat to make the first move. It wasn't long before Bengel sniffed the ends of her fingers. Satisfied that she wasn't going to eat him, he rubbed his head and ears against her nails, eager for a good scratch.

In a soft voice, she told him, "I've been waiting to meet you. You see, I've missed my old mouser I had to leave behind."

Jenny did miss the old barn cat she had left on the farm. The feline had kept mostly to himself, making it very clear that he was a working cat and not a pet. Through their long years of acquaintance, Jenny at no time had been able to woo the old Tom onto her lap. She had longed to stroke him and garner warmth from his furry presence, but such an act had not ever occurred. Whenever she tried, he made it a point to keep a safe distance, watching her until he grew bored. Then he would leave, disappearing into the shadows, to do whatever cats of his sort did. She hoped her and Bengel's relationship would be different.

After several more getting-to-know-you strokes, Bengel became animated. He rubbed against Jenny's ankles as though she were as favored as catnip, almost tripping her when she tried to move away from him.

"Well, my gracious host," Jenny said, laughing, "would you like to show me around our home?"

Bengel seemed to understand her. Leaving her ankles, he streaked toward the back of the shop, bidding her to follow with his tail curled over his back like a furry scythe.

"I'm so happy we'll be friends," she told him.

Although she continued to talk to the cat, she was spellbound by the array of goods the shop held. Until now, Jenny hadn't considered the meaning of "curiosities." That was what the attorney had called her uncle's business—a curiosity shop. And there *was* an assortment of unusual and extraordinary things.

Jenny had never seen such an assembly of art, knickknacks, furniture, and books. She had once seen a picture of a museum in a book. Her uncle's shop reminded her of that picture, full of beautiful treasures: glass, jewelry, china, precious metals, furniture, and even a case full of rusty weapons.

She imagined his collection came from all over the world, especially when she noted the small table in the front window between two leopard-skin-covered chairs. On first viewing the table's base, she hadn't known what it was, but upon closer inspection, she recognized it. It was an elephant's foot.

"How disgusting," she told Bengel as he left her ankles to jump onto one of the chairs. "I only hope Uncle Antonini didn't kill the poor elephant to get his foot or skin that leopard you're snuggling up to."

Bengel lay on his back on the chair's seat, squirming and twisting.

"You realize that's a distant relative's hide?"

His only response was to purr instead of roar.

After several more turns around the store, Jenny was eager to explore the next level. "Come," she told Bengel, "show me the rest of the house."

The cat did seem to understand. Without hesitation, he jumped from the chair and rushed toward the entrance. Jenny followed closely until he took the steep stairs two at a time. She paused only long enough to pick up her carpetbag, then mounted the steps. Soon she reached the landing where Bengel waited.

Since she had only one key, she withdrew it from her pocket and inserted it in the apartment's lock. As soon as she cracked the door, Bengel weaseled his way inside and vanished.

Cats had a way of disappearing when you needed them the most, she thought disgustedly, although she wasn't certain why she needed Bengel's company. After all, he was only a cat. But the dwelling had been his home far longer that it had been hers. Jenny still felt like the guest.

"Here, kitty kitty," she called, peeking through the opening into the darkened apartment.

"He won't come," a deep voice informed her. "Bengel doesn't consider himself a cat."

Jenny nearly jumped out of her skin. Until now, she had believed that she and Bengel were alone in the house. She swung around to face the intruder, clutching her bag against her bosom like a shield.

The man looked harmless enough from where he stood on the staircase several steps above her. Realizing he must be the tenant, Jenny relaxed. "Would he answer to pussy?"

The stranger looked as though he had swallowed something distasteful. Instead of answering her question, he said, "I'm Miller Holbrook. I believe *your* uncle's tenant."

Recognizing the man's name from the papers she'd received from the solicitor, Jenny laughed good-naturedly. "You don't know if you were his tenant?"

Unamused by her teasing remark, he stared at her from behind his gold-rimmed spectacles. Instead of the smile she expected and hoped for, he frowned. "I assume you are Antonini Vassily's niece?"

Not to be thwarted by his cold formality, she answered, "You assume right. I'm Jenny Blake, Mr. Holbrook."

"Dr. Holbrook," he corrected.

"Well, now, aren't you something. Never met a real doctor before. In the country we call them midwives."

From beneath the brim of his hat, the doctor's face turned the color of an overripe cherry. "I'm not a medical doctor," he informed her.

"Then you don't deliver young'uns?"

He cleared his throat. "No. I deliver knowledge to young minds. I'm a math professor at Georgetown College."

"How nice," she replied.

Dr. Holbrook was certainly puffed up with his own importance, Jenny thought. She had hoped that she and her tenant could be friends, but she doubted this stodgy fellow cared about forming friendships with anyone. Least of all her, if the way he looked down his aquiline nose was any indication. But Jenny wouldn't give up on him so quickly.

"Ah, then, you're a schoolmaster?"

"You could say that."

He walked down the few remaining stairs, stopping on the landing several feet away from where she stood. Because they were of the same height, she looked him straight in the eyes. They were blue, she noted, the same color as the sky outside the window behind him.

"Now if you'll excuse me, I must be on my way. I have a class soon and I don't wish to be late."

"Oh, no, sir. I don't wish you to be late neither—either." She stepped away, allowing him room to pass. His shoulder brushed against the carpetbag she still held against her chest.

The contact made him jerk away as though he had been burned. "Pardon me," he apologized, almost running down the stairs.

Jenny followed behind him. He was halfway down the steps when she called out, "Dr. Holbrook, thank you for the information—about Bengel. I won't call him kitty anymore." Before the last words escaped her lips, the front door slammed.

"What a strange man," she said. He had shut the door

so forcefully the handrail still trembled beneath her fingers. The doctor had to be shy around strangers; that was the only explanation Jenny could come up with for his hasty retreat.

Putting her tenant from her mind, she returned to the apartment's entrance where Bengel now waited.

"I'm sorry I insulted you by calling you a cat," she apologized. "I promise it won't happen again. Now if you'd be so kind, I'm ready for my tour."

On cue, Bengel turned around and strolled back inside the apartment. Jenny followed, thinking the cat's disposition was certainly more genial than her tenant's. Did Miller Holbrook only come when he was summoned by the right title?

Miller's spit-and-polished shoes carried him up Thomas Jefferson Street to M Street. There he boarded the horse-drawn trolley that traveled east. Nearing the end of the line, he jumped off the open car and covered the remaining distance to the college on foot. Once on the school grounds, his thoughts and his heartbeat returned to normal. Almost.

He enjoyed his morning constitutional, the brisk fifteen-minute walk from the trolley line to the college that on Tuesdays and Thursdays occurred mid-morning instead of the usual early hour of eight o'clock. But today it was not only the exercise that made his mind and muscles tingle, but also the memory of his first encounter with Miss Jenny Blake.

Pussy? Even now the mention of such a vulgar word slipping from a lady's lips made Miller's face burn with embarrassment. Although he doubted Miss Blake understood the double entendre, Miller didn't doubt for a moment that such a word should not be uttered in polite society even when referring to a cat.

Midwifing? "Oh, Antonini," he worried, "what is to become of your niece?" Her clothes. The poor pitiful miss needed a female's counsel on what was considered suitable attire for a young lady. Since he couldn't qualify for the position of female, who was the woman to be?

He and his friend Antonini had had an understanding. Miller had agreed to keep an eye on the girl until she was settled. But how did an old bachelor like himself go about giving advice on the fashions and the deportment suitable for a young lady?

"I can't," he said, rolling his eyes heavenward. "I only know the girl is in dire need of advice from someone."

Miller felt the weight of his thirty years as he made his way toward the brick building where he had spent the last seven years teaching young minds.

"Antonini, you should have insisted the girl's mother travel with her." Although his friend couldn't hear him, Miller spoke as though he could. "I know you weren't in good stead with your sister's child, but a young woman needs the advice of a mother no matter how unreasonable you believed her mother and grandmother to be."

Miller stopped mumbling to himself long enough to nod at a group of passing students. It appeared that Miss Blake's arrival had brought back his worst habit—mumbling aloud to himself. It was a habit he abhorred in others and wouldn't tolerate in himself. He clamped his lips together, silencing his wayward tongue, but he couldn't still his thoughts.

The image of Miss Blake insisted on accompanying him on his morning walk. Usually Miller used this time to review his class presentations, but today he was thinking about a woman. He shook his head at the rarity of such an experience. Miller never concerned himself with women, because there was no place for them in his life. In fact, he'd never met a woman who merited more than a minute of his time. Until Miss Blake. She had already taken up nearly fifteen minutes of it; but, then again, he'd not ever been partially responsible for a female before.

Maybe helping Miss Blake become more presentable wouldn't be too difficult. She would never be a beauty with that tawny tint to her skin and that dark hair and her blue-gray eyes. If he were to consider a woman, she would have pearly skin and blond hair. When he stumbled on an uneven stone on the walkway, nearly losing his balance, he damned Jenny Blake and Antonini for bringing this confusion into his orderly life.

Then guilt replaced his condemnation. Antonini had been his friend, and by golly he would keep his promise. Miller taught mathematics daily to his students. How could helping one misplaced woman adjust to her surroundings be any different? Perhaps it was his teaching experience that had prompted Antonini to seek Miller's help with his niece. This rationalization made Miller feel better about the task assigned him. He would help Miss Blake settle in and perhaps point her in the direction of the seamstress down the street.

A few minutes later Miller arrived at his building. The hallowed halls he revered and felt comfortable in beckoned to him. As he bounded up the stone steps to his classroom, he felt prideful about his profession. Not everyone had the patience to teach others, and he imagined teaching Miss Blake would try God's patience. But Miller at no time doubted he would succeed.

Having reached this conclusion, excitement rippled through him as if he were a hunter spying his kill. Educating a new student was always a challenge, and one he enjoyed. But Miller liked his students to be receptive, and he wasn't certain how the spirited Miss Blake would react to being taught.

He felt better because he now had a plan. It wasn't the best plan he had ever had, but at least it was workable. And it was one of which his old friend would approve.

"You're a very fortunate young woman," the solicitor told Jenny.

Phineas Goldfinch sat behind her uncle's desk at the back of the shop, sipping tea from one of her uncle's Blue Willow china cups. The attorney had shown up at

Jenny's door not long after Miller Holbrook had exited
it.

From the moment the little man, with his center-
parted hair and his tiny waxed moustache that turned up
on the ends, stepped inside the building, Jenny didn't
trust him. He reminded her of the men who traveled the
countryside with their medicine shows, selling snake oil
to naive customers. Her opinion of him dropped another
notch when, instead of insisting she take the seat behind
her uncle's desk, he took it himself—as though it belonged to him!

"Young woman, your uncle left you in a very comfortable position," he told her. "He was a thrifty man
who managed his earnings well. As you can see, he had
an eye for collectibles, and some of them have proved
to be quite valuable." He paused to look around the
room. To Jenny he looked like a vulture with his claw-
like fingers and red hair, waiting for the right moment
to pounce on his unsuspecting prey. Jenny felt like that
prey.

"Since you are Vassily's sole heir, you now have the
choice of selling the building and all its contents and
returning home to Shepherdstown, to your mother and
grandmother, as a very wealthy woman—advice I
wouldn't take lightly considering your inexperience. I
know someone who—"

"Return to Shepherdstown? Not ever. I won't be returning there." Jenny hadn't meant to sound so determined, but her days away from the tiny farm had made
her realize that she could in no way go back, no matter
what her money situation was. Besides, Jenny was convinced that in a city as large as the United States capital,
she could find a job if that became necessary. On no
occasion had Jenny been one to shy away from hard
work.

Mr. Goldfinch's look told her he was displeased to
hear that she meant to stay. She fidgeted beneath his cold
stare but held his gaze. His suggestion that he knew
someone had put Jenny on the alert. His next words

convinced her that he was anxious for her to be on her way.

"You are a young woman alone. I'm not certain that it would be proper for you to remain here unchaperoned."

On the isolated farm where Jenny grew up, being proper had never troubled anyone. Since Jenny had never considered her behavior anything but the way it should be, she didn't feel she had a need to concern herself with being proper now.

"My Uncle Antonini apparently saw nothing wrong with me being here unchaperoned. He left me his shop, and I intend to run it as he would have."

"But, young lady, what do you know about running a shop?"

Not wanting the pompous little man to believe that she wasn't capable, she told him, "I know how to sell apples."

"Apples?" He nearly choked on the sip of hot tea he had taken. "I assure you, young woman, selling apples can't be compared to selling junk."

"Junk?"

Jenny had been in the shop for a little more than an hour, and already she loved everything in it, even the things she hadn't seen. In her opinion, her uncle's shop was like a treasure chest, and one didn't part with treasures just for the sport of it. Although her selling experience was sorely lacking, Jenny had always had an eye for the unusual. Besides, hadn't Phineas Goldfinch told her only moments before that her uncle's "junk" had made her a wealthy woman? At the moment, selling anything that had belonged to him was inconceivable. To reaffirm her stance, she said, "Maybe I won't sell anything. Maybe I'll keep it all."

The solicitor's cup slammed against the porcelain saucer. "Then, Miss Blake, I suggest you sign these papers, and I'll be on my way."

Jenny had hoped to have a viable link with her uncle's lawyer, but their first meeting made her realize that a business relationship between them would be impossible. They wanted different things. Or, she thought, maybe they wanted the same things, if the way he kept eyeing her uncle's ''junk'' was any indication.

She signed the papers, and then they both stood. ''I'll be checking on you in a few weeks,'' he told her.

As she was signing the papers, she had made a decision. ''Don't bother, Mr. Goldfinch. Your services are no longer needed.''

''But, young woman, an estate this large needs the advice of an expert.''

''Thank you very much, but I'll hire my own expert,'' she told him. ''Send me your bill, and I'll pay you for your services.''

The wily little man thrust her signed copy of the papers at her along with a large sealed envelope, and Jenny placed the lot on a shelf next to her.

''You listen to me, young woman. You'll be sorry you terminated my firm's services.''

''My name is not 'young woman,' it is Miss Blake,'' she informed him. ''And I assure you I'll have no regrets.''

In a huff, he moved toward the door. She followed.

Looking over his bony shoulder, he said, ''Your uncle and my father go back a long way. My father's passing left me in charge of the firm Goldfinch and Goldfinch and your uncle's estate. I assure you if Antonini Vassily were still alive, he wouldn't be pleased with your decision.''

''Regrettably for me, he isn't still alive, but I do believe he left me in possession of his estate for a good reason. Now if you'll excuse me, I have work to do.''

He jerked open the front door, letting it slam against the wall. ''You'll regret your decision,'' he threatened again, descending the two steps. ''Why, you're nothing more than a country bumpkin come to town.''

Angry, she shouted back, ''And you're nothing more than a snake-oil salesman!'' Phineas Goldfinch turned and stomped up the hill.

"Trouble, miss?" a man asked behind her, interrupting her angry thoughts.

Jenny turned to stare at the policeman who had passed her earlier. He stood several doorways down from where she stood watching the attorney's retreat.

Swallowing her humiliation, she shook her head no and managed a weak smile.

"I'm the beat policeman, and a woman alone can't be too careful," the officer said. With his nightstick swinging, he came to a stop several feet away from her.

"Alone? How did you know I'm alone?" she asked. The ruddy-faced policeman looked as formidable as he did friendly.

"Professor Holbrook told me," he answered. "He said you'd be living in your uncle's house now that he had passed on. Antonini Vassily was a fine man, and I'll miss seeing him."

"You knew my uncle?"

"Been walking this beat nigh five years now. Vassily and I exchanged a few words during that time." He winked at her and pointed toward the top of the hill. "This here is my street all the way to the river and back. Also, the canal path from Thomas Jefferson over to the next block.

"People around here call me Officer Mosey. Me or my relief is on duty around the clock. If you're ever in need of the law, all you have to do is shout. One of us will hear you and come running."

"That's good to know, Officer. My name is Jenny Blake. As you said, a girl can't be too careful."

"Are you planning to keep the shop open, then?" He stepped closer to the window and looked inside.

"Oh, yes, sir, although I admit that I don't know much about selling anything but apples."

When the policeman looked at her with a surprised expression, Jenny added, "But I'm a fast learner."

He smiled at her. "Selling is selling I imagine, and while we're on the subject, my missus has a birthday approaching. Mind if I take a look inside—maybe you have something she might like.''

"Like? Uh, well, I haven't . . ."

Jenny hadn't expected to entertain her first customer so soon, but she did welcome Officer Mosey's friendliness. After the disturbing episode with Phineas Goldfinch, she was glad for the policeman's company.

She stepped back against the open door and motioned. "Do come in," she said, uncertain what a shop owner should say to her customer, but knowing instinctively that the officer wasn't interested in buying by the peck or the bushel.

He preceded her inside the shop, and Jenny's heart pounded against her ribs; she hoped she would do and say the right thing.

Officer Mosey glanced around the room. After a moment, he said, "Your uncle has some unusual things." Then, more to himself than to her, he mumbled while crossing the room, "Not sure my Bertie would like most of them." He eyed a shelf that held wide-mouthed glass jars filled with cloudy water and carcasses of frogs and baby chicks.

Not wanting to lose her first sale—or, more importantly, not wishing to appear as ignorant as she felt in her new position of shop owner—Jenny rushed toward a glass display case that held all manner of objects that she believed would appeal more to a lady's tastes.

She leaned over the top and pointed to several things inside. "Here's a pretty dragonfly pin, and a watch chain with tassels. Lookie there," she said, "a padlock locket." Too late, she realized that she sounded more like a curious shopper than a knowing shopkeeper.

Her face colored, but Officer Mosey didn't appear to notice. Instead he moseyed over to look inside. His eyes made a quick pass over the merchandise beneath the glass before he spoke.

"Don't believe my Bertie would have much use for such gewgaws," he said. "She's a plain woman."

"Well, I'm a plain woman, too, but even I would like something as pretty as these baubles."

"Would you now?" The policeman bent over and gave the case another curious stare.

Jenny watched him, especially when his ruddy face lit up with pleasure.

"There," he said, pointing. "My Bertie would like that."

"A thimble," Jenny exclaimed, sliding open the case's back panel and lifting out the object. "And what a fine thimble it is."

Officer Mosey opened his hand, and Jenny placed the sewing implement on his palm. "How much is this fine thimble?" the policeman asked as he examined the blue-and-white-patterned surface with the utmost care.

Jenny had no idea how much the thimble was. The last time she'd purchased a thimble it had been for her mother in the dry goods store in Shepherdstown. Then she had purchased a whole dozen for fifty cents. The thimbles had been made from metal instead of blue-and-white ceramic like this one. She peered through the glass at the tiny tag that remained where the thimble had sat and could barely make out the word *Staffordshire* written on the paper. Beside the word was the number ten.

"That'll be ten—"

"Officer Mosey, come quick," a man demanded from the doorway. "There has been a collision up on M Street. They sent me to fetch you. Someone said they saw you come in here."

Outside the shop window several people rushed past.

"Gotta run, Miss Blake," Officer Mosey said, plopping the thimble down on top of the case. "I'll stop in another time." He turned and quickly followed the man who had fetched him.

"So much for my first sale," Jenny said.

She picked up the thimble and started to put it back where it belonged, but first she lifted the small paper tag. It read ten dollars instead of the ten cents she had been about to charge Officer Mosey.

"Sakes alive, I was about to give away a fortune."

Ten dollars for one thimble? The amount was beyond Jenny's comprehension, and the realization of how unprepared she was to run her uncle's shop hit her like the force of a storm.

Feeling more alone and more lost than before Officer Mosey's visit, Jenny questioned her earlier decision to release her uncle's solicitor. Maybe she would regret that decision as Goldfinch had claimed, especially since she knew nothing about running a shop in a big city.

She hadn't meant for things to get out of hand with the lawyer, but at the time of their confrontation, she couldn't tolerate the little weasel another second. And as much as she hated to admit it, he was probably right: She was nothing more than a country bumpkin who knew nothing about the big city and nothing about running a shop.

Dangnation. How was she ever going to manage her uncle's estate? She couldn't even add two and two and get four. Not only was math her biggest bugaboo, but also it was beyond her realm of thinking to imagine that one tiny thimble could cost ten dollars.

Bengel came into the room and began rubbing around her ankles. She bent over, picked him up, and held him against her chest. "You and I might be prowling the streets before this is over with," she told him. He replied with a comforting purr.

Then an idea suddenly struck her, an idea that involved the professor. An idea that might save her and the cat from starvation and keep her from making costly mistakes.

Her spirits lifted. "I'll prove you wrong, Mr. Goldfinch, if it's the last thing I ever do."

Three

Several days had passed since Jenny had fired Phineas Goldfinch. She'd strengthened her resolve to stand by her hasty decision, especially after she'd received a bill for the solicitor's services—an amount that she thought far too dear. Before she paid the attorney a red cent, she would find another one, or put into motion the plan that she had come up with on the same day she had released Goldfinch's firm.

But so far, putting that plan into motion had proved impossible. She hadn't seen hide nor hair of Miller Holbrook since their first meeting. His teaching position kept him away from home for long hours, beginning before she arose in the morning and continuing late into the night after she had retired. Jenny had not heard so much as a peep from the apartment on the third floor, and she began to wonder if the professor really did exist, or if he were nothing more than a figment of her imagination.

Fantasy or not, Jenny wouldn't worry about the professor today. She had work to do. She intended to inventory everything in the shop, using old lists that she had found inside her uncle's desk. The most recent records were dated more than a year earlier, but at least the lists gave her an idea of where to begin.

Jenny had awakened this morning anxious to get

started. The weather was delightful. Earlier, she had opened the windows in her apartment on the second floor; now she went around opening the windows inside the shop. The town houses on the block were separated by a space of a few feet. This allowed only for windows across the front and the back of the three-story building. Accustomed to the wide open spaces of the country, she would have to adjust to the crowded city.

As she propped open the back door that led into a small courtyard, she sighed. The brisk, sweet-smelling air reminded her of home and the long walks she had enjoyed through green dales.

Jenny had not expected to feel homesick when she left the farm. Maybe she was tired of being cooped up inside. Since her arrival, she had left the building once to fetch a few groceries from the corner market. She yearned to explore her new neighborhood, to walk the banks of the Potomac River, and to visit the nation's capital. Before coming to the city, she had read all she could on Washington, D.C., and wanted to explore the seat of the country's government. But so far she hadn't ventured beyond her street for fear that she might not find her way back.

"In time, I'll explore," she said, watching Bengel scuttle out the open door.

On most mornings, she and the cat enjoyed the outside together; she sipping her tea at a wrought-iron table in the courtyard, and Bengel eyeing the many birds that searched the garden soil for worms.

"Today you'll do your bird-watching alone," she told him from where she stood. "I've no time to dawdle if I'm ever to open Uncle's shop again."

Jenny had decided to begin the inventory in the small, shadowy basement beneath the house. Morning would be the best time to work in the fusty-smelling place. Her tea finished, she set aside her cup and headed toward the door beneath the staircase that led downstairs.

When she descended the steps, sunlight filtered through the row of stationary windows on the back of the house. The small square panes abutted the low ceiling. Jenny supposed at one time the area had been used as a root cellar, but now it contained the coal bin and space her uncle had used for storage.

Making her way across the narrow space to where trunks and crates were stacked, she stooped to pass beneath huge wooden beams on the low ceiling.

Once she straightened too suddenly and bumped her head. "A dwarf, not a giant like me, should be working in this tiny space, and he should be wearing a heavy coat."

She rubbed her arms. The basement felt cold and dank compared to the rest of the house. She should fetch a shawl. But instead of running up two flights of stairs to get one, she decided that once she started working, and her blood started flowing, she wouldn't feel the cold. Besides, Jenny wanted to be finished and out of the basement before she lost the sun's brightest light. With her list and pen in hand, she plopped on her knees in front of an old trunk—a trunk that looked odd even in this house of oddities.

On its top, a rug lay like a scroll beneath a rusty birdcage. She lifted the cage, then pushed the rug to the floor, sending up a cloud of dust. Coughing and choking, she waited for the air to clear. Her Uncle Antonini must have stored items in the basement that he believed to be unsalvageable, objects he had forgotten about having, because it looked as though the basement hadn't been cleaned in years.

Once the dust settled, Jenny leaned over the trunk again. Strange-looking symbols were stamped upon the leather surface. She pushed up the lid. When she saw the interior, her heart beat a wild tattoo against her ribs, and she forgot all about being cold.

The old packing case was lined in scarlet satin, and the layers of silk garments inside gleamed in the subtle light, showing as many colors as a peacock's tail. Time had not dulled the vivid shades of blue and green or the material's sun-and-moon design. Jenny had never seen such beautiful fabrics. Unable to resist touching them, she picked up each piece, then rubbed her cheek against the fine silk. She preened like a peafowl after settling the clothes against her front.

The garments had been made for a tall person, a lady not unlike herself. She had to try them on. Standing, she slipped out of her own worn clothes and into the finer ones. They fit her perfectly, as though they had been made especially for her.

But who did they belong to? Why had her uncle kept them hidden away? The tiered skirt and peasant blouse certainly merited display in his shop. She bent over the trunk again and lifted out a yellow square of silk that could have been a scarf or a shawl. Unable to resist, she pulled the pins from her hair, allowing it to fall around her shoulders; then she secured the silk around her head by tying the corners in a knot.

She was about to go in search of a mirror when a twinkling in the bottom of the trunk caught the light and her attention. Falling to her knees again, Jenny pushed aside an odd-shaped glass bottle and reached for what sparkled. When she lifted the object from the trunk, she saw it was a stone the size of a robin's egg. But instead of the robin's egg soft blue color, the gem was aquamarine and many-faceted. The jewel's color reminded her of a picture she'd once seen of a faraway sea.

Jenny picked it up, cupping it in her hands. It felt warm to her touch. Its beauty was more than she could perceive. She imagined if the jewel were real, it would be worth a king's ransom.

But of course it wasn't real, she reasoned, examining it from all angles. There was a filigree loop attached to the narrowest end that she had missed with her first inspection.

"It's a pendant," Jenny said, thrilled by her discovery.

She had fallen in love with the bauble and decided immediately the trinket was meant for her to wear. After all, if it were a valuable piece of jewelry, then her Uncle

Antonini wouldn't have stored it inside a forgotten trunk in the basement.

I need a ribbon.

A quick glance inside the trunk told her there was no ribbon or chain to be found. Her gaze searched the nooks and crannies of the basement before her eyes settled on her feet.

"A shoestring, of course."

Jenny sat down on a wobbly stool and unlaced one of her boots. Then she threaded the black cotton string through the pendant's loop and secured it around her neck.

"And now a mirror." She looked around the basement again and would have missed the looking glass in the corner altogether if she hadn't spied Bengel's white reflection in its cracked surface. He sat on a chair admiring himself. The majestic cat gazed at his reflection with eyes that were a portal to another world, and invited her to share his find.

"When did you decide to join me?" she asked, standing.

Eager to see herself dressed in the colorful silks, Jenny rushed toward the mirror. She forgot to duck. Her head slammed into a low-slung beam, causing stars to twinkle above her. The room tilted, and her knees buckled.

Several minutes later she came to on the floor. Bengel had abandoned the chair to perch on the center of her chest. Still dizzy, she saw his odd eyes swim together, merge, then take on the blue-green color of the stone Jenny had tied around her neck earlier.

She didn't move, but waited for the fuzziness to disappear. After a moment, when her head had cleared somewhat, she looked again at the furry squatter still balanced on her chest.

"Get off me, you useless piece of fluff."

Jenny pushed up on one elbow, sending Bengel sliding to the floor. With her free hand, she examined the lump on her forehead. She had read somewhere a bump

on the outside was a good sign that the injury wasn't
serious. Satisfied that she would live, her hand slid automatically to the stone still tied around her neck. Un-
mindful of her actions, she rubbed it.

Ninj felt a moment of exhilaration at the first familiar
pull that usually accompanied a summons. He jumped
up from his bed of pillows, abandoning the grapes and
goat cheese that only moments before he'd nibbled as
though it were a feast fit for the gods. When one was
incarcerated for hundreds of years without work, one did
what one could to entertain himself.

Eating had become Ninj's favorite pastime. He hoped
now that he had not gained so much weight through the
centuries that he wouldn't be able to slip beyond the
lamp's opening, if indeed a summons was forthcoming.

With bated breath, he waited. Another tug from the
force made his genie blood rumble through his veins.
Quickly he straightened his silk clothing and righted the
turban on his head. It wasn't long before Ninj felt himself being pulled in all directions before being sucked
upward.

He shouted as he embarked upon his journey, "At
last, my master summons!"

Jenny hauled herself to a standing position. Although the
room swayed with her first steps, she moved toward the
mirror, carefully dodging the unfriendly beams above
her head. Her ears popped, sounding almost like a cork
exploding from a bottle. She paused to allow her head
to clear before continuing on her way. Once she gained
the distance across the room, she straightened to her full
height and admired her reflection.

The person in the cracked mirror was no one Jenny
recognized. In the diamond-white light streaming
through the narrow windows, her skin took on a lustrous
glow similar to that of the silk clothing. The bright, vivid
colors put a sheen in her hair that before this moment
she had always thought of as dull. Of course, the twin-

kling jewel at her throat made even Bengel sit up and take notice.

He was perched again on the chair in front of the mirror, but rather than striking his earlier regal pose, his ears were flattened to his head as though the neighborhood dogs were on his trail. But instead of fleeing as she expected, the cat stood his ground, hissing at her image.

Insulted by the cat's reaction, she scolded, "Now wait a moment, my friend. I think I look quite fetching." Jenny glanced back at her reflection, and her heart lodged itself beneath the twinkling jewel.

Hers was not the only image in the mirror.

She blinked several times. Believing the bump to her head had done more damage than she first suspected, Jenny dropped shakily into the chair, sending Bengel scurrying to the floor beneath it. Hidden, the cat continued to hiss.

There had to be an explanation. Her fuzzy brain was playing tricks on her. Jenny slowly faced the mirror again, looking into its silvery depths. She saw Bengel crouched below her, and above her, or perhaps behind her, stood an image like none she had seen before.

Reflected in the mirror's depth was a giant of a man, both in height and girth, staring at her. He wore purple silk pantaloons, a wide red cummerbund, and a lavender silk shirt. His head was covered with a lavender silk turban, and in his ears were large gold hoops.

"Mine," he stated, pointing at her.

"I beg your pardon," Jenny said, jumping to her feet. She had hoped the stranger's image would be nothing more than a reflection in the glass, but her hopes were shattered as she stood facing him. "I belong to no man."

He said again in a loud thundering voice, "Mine!"

Indignant now, and a little frightened, Jenny stepped away from him. "Yours, I'm not. How dare you!"

Her response seemed to take some of the anger from him. Gone was his menacing manner. It was replaced with submissiveness.

He steepled his hands in front of his great chest and bowed in her direction. The bow caused his turban to slip lower on his forehead. "My honorable master, forgive my pointed tongue. Your summons has brought me from my prison. I am here to serve you."

"Who are you?" Jenny demanded. "And I'll not be needing your service." She still wasn't sure that she wasn't suffering from the bump to her head.

"I'm Ninj," he answered, "the jinii of the late Sultana's harem."

"Genie?" Jenny asked.

Anger creased the giant's face. *"JEE-nih-eye,"* he corrected her pronunciation. "But you, master, may call me what you wish."

"How about I call me out of here?"

Jenny spun around and rushed toward the stairs, ducking beneath the beams as she crossed the distance, her stance reminding her of Bengel's earlier crouched position. She envied his hiding place beneath the chair, but not for long: It seemed the animal was as eager to escape as she was. He streaked by her so fast his white coat resembled quicksilver.

"Halt," the genie demanded, his loud voice echoing off the low ceiling.

"I really must go!" she yelled over her shoulder, but her legs obeyed his command. She stopped dead in her tracks. "I believe I hear someone upstairs," she lied, not daring to look at him.

Jenny realized now that she should never have left the back door open. The crazy man must have come in through the courtyard when she had been going through the trunk. Hadn't her mother and grandmother warned her of the dangers of the city? Why hadn't she listened?

"Master, you must not flee. I have not come to torture you, but to serve you. You see, I am old and wish only to retire."

Did she detect a quiver in the thunderous voice? That quiver gave her the courage to face him. Besides, hadn't

he said he hadn't come to torture her? She would go
with the positive.

"Retire?" Her voice cracked. "Then why don't you?
I really don't mind. Shoo!" She waved her hands at him
as if he were nothing more than a pesky fly.

But instead of flying away, the huge man came toward
her, his large arms extended. She looked from his hands
to his face, taking in every detail. She could already feel
those sausagelike fingers closing around her neck,
squeezing the air from her.

Hoping to forestall her death and appease the stranger
at the same time, she said, "Shucks, you're not old."

He didn't look old to Jenny. In fact, he looked young.
His face and hands were smooth, unwrinkled. Beneath
his turban, his hair looked as black as pitch. His brows
and mustache were the same dark color as his hair. Even
the gold hoops in his ears weren't tarnished.

"I am centuries old," he whispered, then gulped. His
jet eyes became watery, and tears sparkled on his black
lashes.

Jenny's heart went out to the man. Instead of running
as her good sense dictated, she stepped closer, giving
him her full attention. "Things can't be so bad that they
could make a grown man—a giant man," she corrected,
"cry."

"I feel lower than a maggot's belly. You, master, are
my last hope. I have waited years for your summons."

"Really, mister, you must not call me master." She
laughed nervously. "Besides, I'm not a man."

"Of course not, mistress. My humble apologies. Are
you my new Sultana?"

"Sultana?" Did he mean insulted? No, she wasn't
that, either.

"Perhaps, then, you have a name I can call you?"

"Jenny Blake," she said. "You may call me Jenny."

"Jee-nih?" His voice sounded pleased. His lips curled
upward.

She smiled back. The man had a right friendly face,
she decided, and her fear left as quickly as it had come.

She would listen to his story, although she doubted he was a genie as he claimed to be.

"So, what brings you to my shop?" she asked.

"You. You summoned me."

"I summoned you?"

"Yes. And now that I am here, you must recognize me as your slave before I can grant you a certain wish. These two tasks completed will allow me to retire to jinni paradise."

"Come now. Slavery was abolished years ago in this country." Apparently this news didn't impress him. She decided on another approach. "You don't really expect me to believe this mumbo jumbo?"

He became indignant again. "Of course, you must believe me. I come from the Sultana's harem. It was the bad jinni who told my last mistress that my magic was no longer good. Because I could not make her the Sultan's favorite, she sentenced me to centuries of imprisonment." He sighed. "If she had not believed the trickster, I could have granted her her wish. But that is like sands blown by the desert winds. I now belong to you."

"But I don't want you." When the great man looked as though he might cry again, Jenny felt guilty. "Maybe I didn't explain myself well enough. Ninj—isn't that what you called yourself?"

"Aye, Ninj."

"Well, Ninj, what I meant to say was, I'm not in need of a genie at the moment. I already have everything I could want, thanks to my uncle's generosity."

This last thought saddened her. If this Ninj character *was* capable of granting wishes, she would be more than happy to request one—that her uncle could still be alive and standing here beside her. But since something like that would take a miracle instead of a wish, she kept her thoughts to herself.

"You need a man," he told her. "A love to last a lifetime."

"A man? Ha! That is the last thing I need or want. I

hate to tell you that no love lasts a lifetime. My mother and father were a good example of that.''

"You are wrong, Mistress Jee-nih. With my expertise, I will find you the perfect man. You will see." He grinned again, revealing pearly white teeth.

He did have a nice smile. Maybe the strange man *was* telling the truth—maybe he *was* a magic genie. His clothes certainly didn't conform with standard dress of the day, but then neither did hers at the moment.

She studied his appearance—the silk pantaloons, the cummerbund, and the silk shirt. His turban was also made of silk, but if Jenny were to imagine what she believed a real genie should look like, she would imagine a large, priceless jewel pinned to the front of his headdress. And before today, she had never seen a man wear earrings.

No, he wasn't a real genie.

But perhaps he believed he was. And if he believed that by granting her a stupid wish he could retire, she reasoned, then why not play along with him? If the granting of that wish would speed up his retirement, then the sooner she would be rid of him. She still had her inventory to finish. No, she corrected herself. She still had to *begin* her inventory.

"All right," she told him. "Grant me the man of my dreams."

"Ah, my most noble mistress." Again he steepled his hands across his wide stomach and bowed. "You will not be sorry. You will see that my magic is perfect." He kissed his fingertips and blew her a kiss. "Now, I will grant you that wish."

With a flamboyant show of flexing his arms, he closed his eyes as though he were in deep meditation. With one hand held toward the heavens, he snapped his fingers.

Bengel must have thought he was being summoned. His fright forgotten for the moment, he returned to Jenny's side.

She laughed. "Oh, Ninj, he's perfect. Bengel has already stolen my heart." She bent over and scooped up the white cat and cradled him in her arms.

Ninj opened his eyes. His dark brows arched in disapproval. "It has been centuries. We will try anew."

Not wishing to insult the man, Jenny stilled her amusement. It was apparent he had no sense of humor. "Yes, we will try anew."

With another show of deep concentration and with his arms outstretched, Ninj snapped his fingers again.

This time a shrill, piercing sound shook the structure of the house. The scream was accompanied by the flapping of wings. Or at least that was what the noise sounded like to Jenny.

With the first eerie outcry, Bengel jumped from Jenny's arms and dashed up the stairs. She covered her ears with her hands to block out the harsh sound and squeezed her eyes tightly shut. After the piercing sound stopped, Jenny opened her eyes.

To her horror, a baby elephant stood in the middle of the basement, his monstrous size threatening to lift the floor overhead.

She gasped. "You really are a genie."

"Oh, dear, oh, dear," Ninj wailed from the opposite side of the elephant's bulk.

Jenny felt like wailing herself, but she knew the man's pride had been wounded because of his bungled magic. Trying to keep her good humor and indulge him as well, she yelled to him from the bottom of the stairs, "I'm sorry, Ninj, he just won't do!"

He was weeping. She heard him weeping, but had no time for such antics. If the elephant wasn't removed from their midst soon, the house would tumble down around them. In an authoritative voice, she yelled, "Get rid of him immediately!"

"Yes, mistress. Please forgive your servant's mistake. I will get rid of him."

She thought she heard another snap, but she wasn't certain if it was Ninj's fingers or the timbers above their heads. Just before she squeezed her eyes shut again, the beast flapped its large ears. Several moments passed before Jenny dared to open her eyes.

Had she imagined it? The elephant had disappeared. She wished that Ninj had followed suit, but instead he stood opposite her, looking dejected.

"Boo hoo!" he wailed. "I am as worthless as camel dung." He made a great show of wiping his tears on his sleeves. "Now I imagine you will banish me, and it will be another hundred years before I am summoned. I will never get to retire to jinni paradise." Sobs racked his giant's body.

Genies' paradise? Jenny believed in a lot of things, like in signs, good ones and bad ones, but she didn't know there were two heavens—one for genies and one for people. Surely this was all a bad dream caused by the bump to her head. But even in dreams, she couldn't stand to see anyone cry.

"Don't worry about it," she said, "I told you I didn't want a man or a love to last a lifetime. I'm really quite happy with what I have." She sent a silent prayer heavenward, thanking the great man in the sky that what she had was still standing.

Ninj interrupted her thoughts. "You understand? I must grant you a lover's wish. If not, I will be stuck in expiation forever."

Jenny didn't know the meaning of the word *expiation*, but she did know the meaning of the word *stuck*. She had been stuck for twenty-two years on the small farm outside of Shepherdstown, and she could sympathize with the man's plight. Besides, she had always had a soft heart when it came to other people's suffering.

She tried to sound sincere. "Why don't we try again?"

"You would give this worthless piece of dung another chance?" He kowtowed to her several times. "My beautiful Mistress Jee-nih, I promise, this time I will not disappoint you."

"Ninj," she warned, "no more elephants." She plopped down on the bottom step. Bengel, believing he would be safe in her lap, returned from the top of the staircase and settled himself on her legs. She stroked the cat's fur, and he rewarded her with a gurgling purr although his odd-eyed stare never strayed from Ninj.

"Mistress Jee-nih, I will succeed this time."

Ninj seemed so humbled by her allowing him another chance, Jenny couldn't help but wish the man would succeed.

"Ninj's magic is rusty from disuse," he told her, "but you will see. With a little practice, my magic will be as good as new."

Again he assumed the position Jenny decided was his summoning stance. She closed her eyes, praying he wouldn't summon up another elephant.

When she felt Bengel stiffen in her lap and his purr cease, her eyes popped open. Relieved, she laughed.

In Ninj's large hands, he held a tiny flop-eared hare, its coat a smoky gray. The genie looked from the rabbit to her. She shook her head no, and the rabbit disappeared into thin air.

"Ah, mistress. This time I will do it right." He grinned from gold hoop to gold hoop. "I am feeling more confident already."

"Me, too," she replied, enjoying seeing Ninj in a less worrisome mood. "I can't wait to meet the man of my dreams," she added, trusting her words would give him confidence.

Again she heard him snap his fingers. Several moments later, there was a commotion at the top of the stairs. All heads turned upward.

Instead of the stuff dreams were made of, Jenny saw the reserved and studious Miller Holbrook. Her surprise at seeing him made her hand cover the gem at her throat. Unconsciously she rubbed it.

"Looks like you bungled again," she told Ninj from the side of her mouth.

But when she looked in the genie's direction, he, like the smoky gray rabbit, had disappeared into thin air.

Four

Miller stood at the top of the stairs and pinched his nose. The basement smelled like a zoo. He glanced toward the bottom of the stairs where Miss Blake sat. At least he thought it was Miss Blake. Light from the windows backlighted the feminine form, and for a moment Miller puzzled over the young woman's identity.

The clothes she wore were unlike any he had seen before. Miss Blake's apparel at their first meeting had been anything but fashionable, but at least they weren't bizarre.

The yellow rag tied around her head made him think immediately of a cleaning woman. That explained it, he reasoned. She must be cleaning house today.

"Mr. Holbrook, is that you?" the lady asked as she stood. Bengel scurried from her lap to the floor.

The sound of her throaty voice coupled with her height made Miller no longer doubt her identity.

"It is me," he responded, "and I was about to ask you the same question, Miss Blake."

"Oh, it's me all right." She twirled in a circle as he imagined young women did when they wanted a compliment. "How do you like my outfit?"

Miller didn't respond immediately. Instead, he stepped down several more stairs, pretending to need a better look.

She seemed so pleased with her appearance that he didn't have the heart to tell her what he really thought of her outlandish garb. As he moved closer to her, his earlier impression changed. Rather than a cleaning lady, Miss Blake looked like a gypsy and rightfully so. She did have some Romany blood flowing through her veins. Unsure why, he lied, "You look quite fetching, Miss Blake."

A pleased smile softened her full lips, making him believe that maybe he hadn't lied. In an exotic way, his landlady *did* look fetching.

Although Miller wasn't an expert on women or textiles, it was evident that the garments she wore were made from quality silk. The brilliant blue, green, and yellow colors buffed her complexion to a golden hue, and for a moment, Miller wondered if her skin would feel as silky as the fabrics.

He swallowed uncomfortably. Not only were the colors perfect for her, but the fit of the garments was flawless. The printed sun-and-moon fabric clung possessively to the ins and outs of her womanly body. From where he stood above her, he could see the fullness of her breasts, the shadowy crease just visible above the low neckline of the dress. As he studied her, something stirred deep inside him, displacing his usual calm.

"Do you have guests?" he asked, looking beyond her into the dimly lighted room, hoping to break the spell she seemed to have cast upon him.

"I've had several this morning," she said more to herself than to him. "Guests of the kind you can't imagine."

Miller continued his descent until he stood facing her. For the first time, he noticed the shoestring encircling her neck, and the pendant. The huge blue-green jewel sparkled when it caught the light filtering through the windows. Several moments passed while Miller studied the stone. Its brilliance held him captive just as Miss Blake's appearance had held him transfixed only moments before.

When he finally found his voice, he said, "Earlier I thought I heard you in conversation with a man."

"Oh, that would have been Ninj."

"Ninj?"

Looking around for the oddly named fellow, Miller saw no one. He and Miss Blake were completely alone in the dank, odor-filled basement except for Bengel, who now sat on the corner of an open trunk, staring at the contents.

Miss Blake informed him as though she were introducing a visiting friend, "Ninj is a genie."

For a man who wasn't normally given to laughter, her announcement made him chuckle. "A genie?"

"Yes, but you frightened him away with your appearance."

He regarded her quizzically. She must have realized what she had implied, because her face turned a rosy red.

"I mean your interruption frightened him away."

Miller gave an impatient shrug. "You're teasing me. A genie?"

Either Miss Blake was addled, or she had found her Uncle Antonini's excellent supply of schnapps and had already been tilting the bottle.

He examined her more thoroughly, looking for signs of drunkenness. *God forbid the girl, with all her other deficiencies, should be a tippler, too.*

It was then Miller spotted the slightly purple lump above her brows. "Your head. What happened?"

Her hand automatically flew to her forehead. "Oh, this." She flinched when her fingers brushed against the slight swelling. "I was so anxious to see how I looked in these clothes I found in that trunk that I hit my head on a rafter on my way to the mirror."

Miller relaxed somewhat. The girl wasn't a drinker after all. "That explains this Ninj character, this genie, you believed you saw. Your vision was nothing more than a hallucination caused from the bump to your head."

"I thought so at first, too, but no, he wasn't a vision."

She turned toward the looking glass in the corner. "After I regained consciousness, I again made my way to the mirror to see myself."

She walked toward the mirror to show him how it had happened. Miller followed, stopping behind her.

"He was right there," she said, pointing at his reflection, "where you're standing now. But he was much taller—a giant of a man."

Miller smiled to humor her. "Don't you see? What you saw wasn't real. What you believed you saw was nothing more than an illusion."

Clearly irritated, she exclaimed, "What I saw was real. He and his elephant and his rabbit."

The girl was clearly delusional. "An elephant *and* a rabbit?" Her injury was worse than Miller first suspected. She needed to be examined by a physician.

He placed his hand on her arm. "Why don't we go upstairs, Miss Blake, and I'll fetch the doctor from down the street."

She shook off his grip. "A doctor of the midwiving kind?" she asked with cold sarcasm. "I don't need an examination," she insisted. "All I need is to summon Ninj again, and you'll see for yourself that he is real."

"Miss Blake, be serious. You don't expect me to believe this gibberish. I'm a mathematician. I deal with tangibles, things that occupy space and can be perceived by the senses."

Squaring her shoulders, she said, "My feelings exactly. Ninj, the elephant, and the rabbit all occupied this space earlier. I, Dr. Holbrook, perceived them with my eyes."

"Hogwash!" His patience with the woman was running thin. He turned toward the stairs. It was as Miller first believed; the woman's brains were scrambled. How did one deal rationally with such a person, much less help her settle into normal society?

As he walked forward, his foot contacted something slippery on the floor. He looked at his spit-and-polished shoe. *Damnation.* He had stepped in something. It was huge, brown, mushy, and resembled manure.

"Damn that cat," he swore.

Behind him, he heard Miss Blake giggle. He glanced over his shoulder and saw she was doubled over with laughter.

"I guess you'll believe me now," she said, once she was able to speak without laughing. "It seems Bengel has better manners than Ninj's elephant."

Miller shot her a murderous look, and Jenny covered her mouth to muffle her merriment. Ignoring her last remark, he walked on the heel of his soiled shoe and limped toward the stairs. It seemed that the proud doctor's pride was wounded after the undignified act of stepping in dung.

At least he wasn't barefooted. There was nothing worse than stepping in cow turds and having the slippery substance squish between your toes. It was a sensation you never forgot, and even now the memory made her shudder.

Barefooted. She could not imagine the professor baring anything to anyone, physical or otherwise. He was the most restrained person she had ever known. What would it take to make him really laugh—a belly-whopping, rib-aching laugh? Not possible, she told herself, continuing to watch Miller until he disappeared through the door.

"Now where is that miserable genie?" Alone again, Jenny looked toward the soiled floor and the evidence that Ninj's elephant had been real, but she could find no sign of the animal's conjurer.

"Phew," she muttered, covering her nose. The smell alone was enough to gag a maggot and to make her more determined than ever to find the missing genie and make him tidy up after his pet.

"Here, genie, genie," she called.

She looked behind the crates and furniture stockpiled around the room. Finally her search brought her back to the trunk where earlier she had found the beautiful clothes. It was Bengel's fascination with the trunk that made Jenny drop to her knees beside it and give the contents her full attention.

He was crouched ready to pounce, facing what looked like a flask. The bottle was embedded with colored glass and stones, and Jenny wondered about its use. It was far too fine a piece for storing liquid or for using as a vase for flowers.

"Whatcha got there?" she asked, then leaned over and picked up the bottle.

Bengel jumped on the rim of the trunk, yowling his displeasure with her while his odd-eye stare followed the bottle's progression to her lap.

Against the silk of her skirt, the rough glass on the bottle's surface sparkled like precious gems in the fading light. After examining the piece thoroughly, she brought the opening to her eye and peered inside.

"It's a kaleidoscope," she told Bengel. Thrilled with her discovery, she spun the bottle with her fingers and watched the constantly changing prisms. It was magical.

The enchantment made her recall a story her Grandmother Vassily had told her once about a genie and a magic lamp. Could it be that Ninj was like the genie who had lived inside the lamp?

Shaking the bottle, then turning it upside down and thumping it on the bottom, she called, "Ninj, are you in there?" She shook the container vigorously, but Ninj was nowhere to be found.

"If you're real, stand up and show yourself," she demanded, rubbing the glass surface. In her grandmother's story, rubbing the magic lamp had made the genie appear. When Ninj still failed to materialize, Jenny, disgusted, dropped the bottle inside the trunk. "It's all yours, Bengel."

Besides, she reasoned, there was no way a man of Ninj's size could fit inside the small vessel. She'd been ridiculous to suppose he could. She'd been just as ridiculous to think that she wouldn't be the one cleaning up after the elephant.

Bengel appeared pleased to have the bottle back in his possession. He jumped inside the trunk and recommenced his vigil.

Tired of kneeling, Jenny sat on the floor and leaned against the trunk. "Where are you, Ninj?"

She glanced around the room but found no sign of the genie. Perhaps the professor was right in assuming the genie had been nothing more than something her mind had called up because of the blow to her head.

Not that Jenny wouldn't be happy to be rid of the troublesome Ninj. Already he'd taken up far too much of her time with his tricks and his tale of woe. A genie paradise indeed.

But what about the manure? She glanced toward the shadows where Miller had nearly slipped. "How did that . . . that stuff get inside the basement if there wasn't an elephant?"

She asked Bengel over her shoulder, "Did you do that?" Maybe he wasn't the well-trained cat she believed him to be. "If you did soil the floor," she scolded, "then you're a naughty, naughty kitten."

It no longer mattered who did it. What mattered was that someone had to clean up. And since Bengel wouldn't qualify for the chore, it was left to her.

Once she was finished with the objectionable task, she would put the genie incident out of her mind. Jenny still had her inventory waiting for her.

She stood and walked to the mass of dung. She held her breath, but soon she had to give in to the reflex. The odor was overpowering in the small, nearly airless space. Not that Jenny wasn't familiar with mucking out stalls. She had mucked out plenty on the farm, but there had always been fresh air to combat the stench, and always a shovel.

Her throat burned from the noxious odor, and she felt light-headed. Her hand went to her throat where the stone still hung around her neck. At least the clothes and stone were real. To reassure herself of this, she rubbed the pendant with her fingers.

Her ears popped. Bengel streaked past her as though the hounds of hell were nipping at his ankles. When she looked toward the trunk, there stood Ninj.

The giant kowtowed to her. "Mistress Jee-nih, you called?"

At first she was pleased to see him, but then she recalled all the worry he had caused her. She pointed a finger at him and with a voice that brooked no defiance, she ordered, "You worthless lump of camel dung— clean up that mess."

Taken aback by her reaction, the giant cringed. Then he looked to where her finger had moved from pointing at him to pointing to the soiled floor. He smiled contritely.

"So sorry, mistress, my elephant displeased you. His worthless hide will feel my wrath." He raised a finger to his heavily mustached lips. "You must not concern yourself with things beneath your notice. Your humble servant is here to serve."

Ninj snapped the fingers of his right hand. Without a mishap, the dung disappeared from the floor, taking the foul odor with it. The result surprised them both.

Jenny breathed a sigh of relief, and Ninj smiled, looking very pleased with himself. "See, Mistress Jee-nih, already my magic is better."

"Better, yes, but it could still be improved. Your disappearance made me look foolish in front of Dr. Holbrook." She leaned against a chest of drawers. "Where were you?"

Ninj looked distressed. "But it is you, mistress, who controls my coming and going."

"Me? I called you several times, and you didn't come."

"It is not words that summon me."

"Then what is it?" she asked, pushing away from the chest. "Tell me quick before I lose my patience."

Ninj pointed to her neck. "It is the magic at your throat."

"My throat?" Jenny clutched the stone tied on the

shoestring, rubbing its surface. "You mean this?"

"Do not—"

Ninj vanished.

"So it is the stone that summons you." Jenny massaged the gem again.

The giant Ninj returned, but looked worn and exhausted. He rubbed his hand across his forehead and swayed unsteadily on his feet. "I am too old for this expulsion."

Jenny ignored his remark. "Oh, Ninj. You *are* magic. This proves I'm not delusional, and now Dr. Holbrook will have to eat his words." She wasn't sure which discovery pleased her the most. Unable to control her excitement, she asked, "Where do you go when you disappear?"

"There," he said as he pointed to the trunk. "Where the cat was a lion in a jungle of treasures." Amusement lurked in his dark eyes. "But I showed the lion who was mightier."

"You mean Bengel?"

"I mean the absent cat who is a tormentor. I thought he was going to shake the gold from my teeth the way he jiggled my house."

"Your house?"

Ninj bowed from the waist and reached inside the trunk, lifting the glass bottle. The same bottle Jenny had returned to the leather packing case earlier.

Ninj's enormous fingers were the same size as the neck of the bottle. "I live in here," he said, handing it to her. "It has been my home since my beginnings."

Jenny looked from the bottle to Ninj. "No, you couldn't possibly fit inside that small container. Besides, I just looked for you there, and you were nowhere to be found."

"Then it was you and not the pussy who tried to relieve me of my brains?" His voice grew threatening and he wagged his finger at her. "No, no, no, Mistress Jee-nih. Don't ever shake me so again. My entrails are yet to recover from the queasiness."

Jenny swallowed. Ninj did look a little green around the edges. "I'm sorry," she apologized. "Had I known that was truly your house, I wouldn't have shaken it so hard."

"Good. Shaking is bad," he said, his body no longer taut as he stood hovering over her.

Jenny studied him before turning her gaze back to the bottle. "But how—you are so—"

"Fat," he finished for her. "Far too many centuries have passed since I became inhumed in my vessel." He tugged on his silk pajamas, looking as though he was ashamed of his rounded girth. "I have grown fat and lazy. But you will see, Mistress Jee-nih, I will soon be fit and trim again."

He laughed. His laugh was easy. "You and I, we will work together to improve our looks."

"My looks?" Jenny questioned. "What is wrong with my looks?"

She ran her hands over the silk skirt. From the first moment she had seen her image in the mirror, Jenny had believed the silk garments complemented her golden skin and dark hair. She had believed herself almost beautiful. But then, she should have known better. Her mother had always told her, "A little powder and a little paint can't make a woman what she ain't."

Rather than answering her question, Ninj said, "My Sultana was beautiful—a woman who could fire a man's blood."

Jenny responded with a surly belligerence. "Is this the same woman you told me of earlier who wanted to be the Sultan's favorite? The same woman who sentenced you to purgatory because you couldn't make her his favorite?"

Jenny didn't know why she concerned herself with a woman who had lived centuries before, but the idea that Ninj considered her not as attractive as his last mistress rankled.

"In my opinion," Jenny continued, "if your late Sultana was so good at firing a man's blood, she would have been the Sultan's favorite without your help.''

"Ah, but in my country, there are many women who live in the harem. It is difficult to be the rarest orchid among so much beautiful flora.''

"Harumph! Who would want to be the most beautiful flower in a harem? Certainly not me. I would not ever want to be imprisoned like a slave. Owned by a man. Or be a man's personal property.''

"Ah, but to be chosen to live in a harem is a great honor in my country.''

"But in my country we don't have slaves. And in my opinion, any woman who would want to be a slave to a man is cuckoo. That's why I'll never marry.''

Ninj's face clouded. "A cuckoo was a bird in the old world.'' Tears sparkled in the depths of his black eyes, and he sniffed, trying to control them. He stepped closer to her, his arm outstretched. "But, Mistress Jee-nih, you must become a love slave, or I shan't be able to retire.''

"Love slave?'' Jenny threw back her head and laughed. "I'll be no man's slave—love or otherwise.''

No longer concerned with controlling his emotions, the giant Ninj bellowed like a bull. "Oh, woe is me. Of all the women in the world who would welcome me with open arms, I had to be summoned by one like you.'' Great tears rolled down his full cheeks. "Every woman I have known wanted a man—wanted a love to last a lifetime.'' He rolled his eyes heavenward. "But, no, you want nothing to do with a man. Tell me, mistress, what's a poor jinni to do?''

Jenny's heart went out to Ninj when he dropped his face into his hands and wailed again.

"I-I wish I could help you.''

"You can.'' He peeked from between his fingers. "What about the young man I summoned earlier? Would he not do?''

"What young man?''

"The man with glass disks over his eyes. I saw him briefly. Before you commanded me to leave.''

"You mean Miller Holbrook? The professor with the

spectacles?'' She gripped the bottle tighter in her hands.
''You can't be serious. Now, if I *were* looking for a man,
which I'm not,'' she reiterated, ''it wouldn't be one like
Dr. Holbrook.''

Ninj sucked back his tears and straightened. ''Why
not, mistress?''

''If that man actually smiled, I believe his face would
crack. No, the professor is too serious a fellow for me.''

''Then tell me, Mistress Jee-nih, if you were looking
for a man, what kind would you choose?''

Jenny thought about her response. ''You know, I
don't really know. I've always been so certain that at no
time would I give my heart to any man that I never gave
much thought to the subject. But one thing is for sure,
he wouldn't be like my father.''

''And how was your father?'' Ninj asked.

''Selfish, concerned only with himself. A man who
deserts his young wife and daughter can be nothing
else.''

''Your mother, did she love him?''

''I imagine she did.'' Jenny really didn't know about
the relationship between her parents. Her father had left
them for the coal mines shortly after Jenny was born. If
he were to walk into the room today, she wouldn't know
him.

''I understand my parents met when my mother and
my Grandmother Vassily first stepped off the boat in
New York. My mother was fifteen and anxious to make
a life for herself in her new country. Richard Blake
owned a farm near Shepherdstown, West Virginia.
Maybe the promise of a home and putting down roots
made her believe she loved him.'' Jenny paused. ''My
mother and I didn't talk much.''

''Perhaps for your mother your father was her love.
We can only guess what goes on between a man and
woman, or what makes for a perfect love.''

''Well, whatever goes on between them, I don't want
any part of it.'' Jenny twisted the bottle in her hands.

"Ninj, you're obsessed with your mission. I've told you a dozen times my feeling on the subject of perfect love, on wedlock. To me, there is no such thing."

"Aheee!" Ninj thumped his forehead with his hand. "What is a jinii to do with such a woman?"

She wanted this conversation to end. She didn't want to talk about love or men. Of all the genies in the world, *if there were a lot*, why had it been her misfortune to inherit one who was bent on making her fall in love? One whose very entrance into genie paradise depended on that mission's success? Fate had dealt them both a bad blow, and Jenny wasn't sure how to deal with it. She wanted to help Ninj get to paradise, but she wasn't willing to fall in love to do it.

She glanced around the basement. The bright light of the morning had turned to a shadowy gray. There was nothing more she could do here. Still holding onto Ninj's bottle, she said, "I've work to do upstairs; do you wish to remain here, or would you prefer joining me in my uncle's shop?"

"Is it warmer up there?" Ninj rubbed his arms and looked toward the stairs. "It is so dank and cold in this earthen place. Unless of course you wish me to return to my bottle."

"No, before you do that, we have more to discuss. Besides, you've been fat and idle too—"

"Miss Blake, are you still down there?" It was Miller Holbrook. She heard him shuffling his feet on the floor at the top of the stairs.

She rolled her eyes heavenward. "Now what could he want?" She looked toward Ninj. "I hope he cleaned the manure off his shoe outside instead of tracking it all over the floor. I'm in no mood to be mucking up after him."

Miller Holbrook called to her again. "Miss Blake, I've someone here I want you to meet."

"Imagine that," she said to Ninj. "You come with me."

Jenny bent to scoop up the clothes she had removed that morning and walked toward the stairs.

"We'll be right up, Dr. Holbrook. I've someone I want you to meet, too."

Five

Miller waited inside the shop wondering who Miss Blake had found for him to meet. He hoped the blow to her head had not been serious, and he also hoped she had regained her senses and wasn't still hallucinating about a genie and an elephant.

He looked down at his shoe, still puzzling over the excrement he'd removed earlier. The amount suggested that Bengel had been using the spot in the basement for a litter box for some time. What puzzled Miller the most was how the cat had managed to get into the basement after Antonini's death. As far as Miller knew, the door was always closed.

As disgusting as the task of cleaning his soiled boot had been, the leather now looked as spiffy as it had when he had put his shoe on this morning. He picked up a large magnifying glass from the desk and peered at his foot through the circle. He was pleased to see there was no evidence at all of the mishap.

"Dr. Holbrook, how may I help you?"

Miller had been so centered on studying his shoe, he nearly jumped out of his skin when Jenny Blake called out to him upon entering the room.

Hoping he hadn't seemed startled, he turned to face her. "There you are. . . . ."

His voice trailed off when he saw the giant man

emerge from the stairs behind her. The stranger was so tall that he had to duck to get through the doorway, but upon closer inspection Miller decided it was his turban that added extra inches to his height. Still, Miller stood straighter and found he had to train his gaze upward to look the man in the eyes. The titan nodded at him, and Miller nodded back.

Now where had Miss Blake found such an oddly dressed character in the short time it had taken him to fetch the doctor? One couldn't be too careful in a big city like Washington, D.C., and Miller worried about her safety as he gave the man a good look. The newcomer was not someone you would wish to encounter unexpectedly in a dark alleyway. He stood like a pillar in his silk clothing, his massive arms folded across his chest. His beady gaze at no time strayed from Miller.

Miller's preoccupation with the strange man made him forget his reason for being there until he heard Miss Blake ask, "Who might you be?" He turned to see her walk toward the stubble-faced man in the leather apron with her hand extended. "I'm Jenny Blake."

"Most folks around here call me Axle. I work for the Metropolitan Horsecar Company."

Axle stood beside an open box filled with cigars that sat on a small table. Miller knew they were some of Antonini's best smokes. Apparently Axle knew it, too. "Don't mind if I do," he said, lifting several stogies and pocketing them in his shirt. This done, he extended his hand toward Miss Blake's.

"Miller here thought you might could use some doctoring." His gaze slid over her, taking in every curve. After a moment he winked at her and grinned. "You look as fit as a filly to me."

Miller watched the exchange and wondered if he'd made a mistake in enlisting Axle's help. The man wasn't a medical doctor but a veterinarian.

The physician Miller usually used was away on holiday and wouldn't return until the following week. So Miller had fetched the next person he thought best qualified for the position. Axle doctored the horses for the Metropolitan Horsecar Company. But Miller had forgotten one thing in his rush to get help for the delusional Miss Blake. The horse doctor was also known to be a womanizer, which was evident in the way he kept looking Miss Blake up and down as if she were a common doxy, and holding her hand far too long to be considered proper.

Wishing now he hadn't rushed into inviting the man to ogle Antonini's niece, Miller interceded. He put his hand on Miss Blake's arm and guided her toward a chair. After relieving her of the bundle of clothes and the unusual bottle, he handed the lot to the giant. She allowed Miller to lead her there without an argument, but before she sat down, she insisted, "I don't need a doctor."

"I'm beginning to think the same thing," Miller mumbled beneath his breath, "or not this one."

He glared at Axle, daring him to do anything untoward to his landlady. Axle ignored him. Chuckling, he dogged their footsteps and took his place in front of Miss Blake's chair.

"So, Miss Blake, I understand you're Vassily's niece." He held his finger beneath her chin, eyeing the bruised lump on her forehead. "Old Anton never hinted that he had such a fine specimen in his family."

"She's a lady, not a horse!" Miller reminded him.

"Oh, there's no doubt in my mind that she qualifies as a female." Axle studied her features with an intensity that almost made Miller blush.

Feeling as though he'd delivered the lamb for slaughter, Miller suddenly stepped closer.

Axle wasn't pleased. "Why don't you just step aside and let me do what you called me here to do—tend to my patient?"

"She's not your patient," Miller insisted. "You're only a horse doctor, and I sometimes wonder how good you are at that."

"Can't recall having any complaints," Axle responded. "I've doctored plenty of horses and mules in my day, but none of them have been as stubborn as you. Now would you leave me to my treating?" Axle shook his head. "You're like a dang mother hen worrying over its chick."

Affronted, Miller stepped back, but he continued to watch the doctor's every move.

"Now tell me, little lady, what happened to you?" Axle smiled at her, his gaze dropping to her bosom, the same bosom that Miller had admired earlier, before returning to her face. "May I call you Jenny? I always like to be on a first-name basis with my patients."

"And I'm sure," Miller interjected, "that horses and mules respond likewise."

Axle ignored the remark. "Tell me, Jenny, what happened to your pretty face?"

Jenny eyed Ninj over Axle's head. She looked from Ninj to Miller, who was frowning, then back to Ninj again. Amusement lit up the genie's dark eyes.

For the life of her, she couldn't figure out what had made the professor so crotchety. Not that he had been the most affable person since their first meeting. But Axle was right. Miller Holbrook was like a mother hen worrying over her chick, and she wondered when he'd become her self-appointed keeper.

Jenny was tired of these three men fawning over her. She wanted them all to disappear and thought about rubbing the stone tied at her neck with the hopes that it might grant her three wishes—to be rid of the three of them.

Instead she sat on the edge of her chair. "I bumped my head on a rafter in the basement. It knocked me out for a few seconds, but now I'm fine."

Although Ninj was living evidence that he did exist, she wasn't ready to share her discovery with the horse doctor. She had done so with Dr. Holbrook, and look where it had gotten her.

"Miller here claims you were seeing things. How about now? You still seeing things?"

"Yes, I'm still seeing things. I'm seeing you, Dr. Holbrook, and Ninj." Her eyes locked on Ninj, and the corner of his lips turned up. Jenny's reference to the genie got Miller Holbrook's full attention. Instead of staring holes through the back of Axle's head, he studied the giant with renewed interest.

Ha, Jenny thought, watching Miller's expression. *Maybe now you'll believe me when I tell you I'm not hallucinating.*

"Ninj?" Axle turned to look at him. After a moment he said, "What are you, some kind of a swami? One of those religious fellows who aims at union with the divine through meditation?"

"I am Ninj, a jin—"

"Ninj is visiting the college," Miller interrupted. "He is from northern India. He is staying with me. Upstairs."

Jenny and Ninj exchanged glances. Maybe, she thought, the disbelieving professor believed her now, but Ninj wasn't pleased with Miller's introduction.

"No," he corrected him. "Hindus are pigs of the earth. I, Ninj, I come from the great Ottoman Empire."

"That so now?" Axle looked at Miller. "Seems the professor better get his facts straight, him being a teacher and all. I take it this is the dress of your country." He laid his hand on the skirt covering Jenny's knee and stroked it. "Mighty fine duds, wouldn't you say?"

Jenny jerked away from his touch at the same time Miller's temper exploded.

"Take your hands off her!" he yelled, grabbing Axle's collar and jerking the veterinarian backward. "We've had about all the doctoring we need from you, Axle! I think you better leave."

Jenny jumped to her feet. "Gentlemen, please." Fearing at any moment the two might resort to fisticuffs, she appealed to all three men for their cooperation. "My uncle's shop is no place for a brawl." She turned toward Miller, her gaze pleading. "I'm sure Axle didn't mean any disrespect. He was only admiring the beautiful material."

"Like the devil, he was." Miller released Axle's collar. "But you're right, Miss Blake. Your uncle's shop is no place for a brawl."

Axle bristled. "You taken leave of your senses, Miller Holbrook?" He smoothed the leather apron, glaring at Miller as he did so. "Never took you for a fighting man."

"Never took you for a man who'd take advantage of a mutual friend's niece, either. In spite of your philandering ways."

"Axle," Jenny interceded before her uncle's beautiful collectibles could be destroyed by a boxing match. "Please, let me show you to the door. I really appreciate you coming over to check on my injury. But it's like I told you earlier. It was only a small bump, and I'm fine now."

"I can see you're fine. It's Holbrook here who is delusional." He turned to Miller and shook his fist in Miller's face. "I'll not forget this, Professor. Next time you won't have a lady's skirts to hide behind."

"There won't be a next time. If there is, I'll break every finger on your hand if you try to touch her again."

"You'll what?" Axle balled up his fists, ready to punch, but Ninj intervened. If he hadn't insisted on escorting the doctor to the door, Jenny was positive the two men would be going at each other like professional fighters.

Miller straightened his jacket. "By the way, Axle, I believe you have something that doesn't belong to you." He moved toward the doctor and lifted the cigars from his pocket. "Don't believe Antonini would want to share these with you after your actions toward his niece."

Axle would have said more, but Ninj towered above him, his expression dangerous.

Without another word to any of them, Axle left, slamming the front door behind him. The vibration was so great that Jenny ran to rescue a vase that tumbled from the shelf. She caught it before it hit the floor.

Several moments passed while no one said anything. It was Jenny who broke the silence.

"Well, Dr. Holbrook, do you believe me now?"

Six

Miller looked back and forth between the twosome. They both waited for his response, but he couldn't answer them.

He no longer knew what he believed—about the man who Miss Blake claimed was a genie, or his own recent behavior. In the last ten years, he couldn't recall a time when he'd lost his temper, and he could not ever recall losing it over a woman.

But seeing Axle ogle her with such disrespect had blown his mind open with rage and he wasn't certain why. Hadn't he stared at her creamy bosom in the same way when he was on the basement stairs above her? The reminder made him realize that he was no better than Axle, and Miller didn't like the comparison.

Control. He had structured his life around it. But in a matter of seconds he'd lost it over a woman's threatened honor. No, he wasn't certain what he believed anymore.

While he was pondering the mystery, Miss Blake moved toward him. Stopping only a few inches away, her voice broke into his reverie.

"Dr. Holbrook, perhaps you would like to sit down." She pressed her fingers lightly against his arm. An unidentifiable but pleasant scent enveloped her. "Ninj and I are going to have some tea. Would you care to join us?"

Absently he answered, "Yes, I think I could use a drink." He would have preferred something much stronger than tea, but didn't voice his preference. Besides, it was the middle of the day, and he didn't wish to add drinking to his growing list of vices.

It was some time later that the three of them sat at the wrought-iron table in the courtyard behind the house. Miller didn't recall Jenny leaving the shop to brew the tea, but she must have because he recognized Antonini's china cups in front of them, now filled with the steamy brew. A plate of biscuits and a jar of jam sat in the table's center. During her absence, Miss Blake had changed back into her ordinary clothes, but she still wore the garish jewel at her throat.

Miller picked up the cup and sipped the lemony drink. After he replaced the cup in the saucer, he spoke. "Miss Blake, I'm very sorry for Axle's behavior. I never should have brought him here and I wouldn't have if I'd thought the action through. I hope you'll forgive me for subjecting you to the scoundrel."

She smiled, dismissing his concern with a wave of her hand. "No damage done to me or the shop." She bit into one of the flaky biscuits, and he watched her lick a drop of jam from her lips. "I realize, Dr. Holbrook, that you had my best interests at heart. You thought I needed a doctor and so you brought one. But doesn't this town have a people doctor?"

Miller felt his embarrassment. What kind of fool must she take him for—fetching an animal doctor to tend to a lady?

"Unless, of course, you believed my earlier story about the elephant."

The fellow Ninj grinned at him, and Miss Blake grinned as well. She was teasing him, and Miller relaxed. Rather than facing her displeasure as he'd expected, she had offered him her good humor.

He smiled slightly. Maybe they could become affiliates of a sort. Such an arrangement would make his helping her to settle in easier. Maybe even pleasant.

Cheered by this turn in their relationship, he said, "I think I will have one of those biscuits."

Having declined her offer of food earlier, he suddenly felt hungry. He hadn't eaten since breakfast. Time coupled with his attack on Axle must have fueled his sudden voracious craving for food.

She picked up the plate of biscuits and held it several inches away from him. When Miller reached for the roll, she moved the plate just out of his reach.

She giggled, then passed it to him again. He reached, and when his fingers were about to close around the fluffy bread, Jenny snatched the plate from his grasp a second time.

Ninj snickered behind his hands. "Mistress Jee-nih, you are such a trickster."

"Trickster?" She acted indignant. "I'll have you know that I don't share my biscuits with just anyone."

Miller dropped his hand to his lap. Her clowning around made him feel uncomfortable. He wasn't used to such behavior from young ladies. No, he corrected, he wasn't used to keeping company with young ladies.

She pinned him with her blue-gray stare. "You can have it, but only if you agree to call me Jenny."

"Jenny?"

"After all, if we're to become friends, I think it only proper."

"Proper?"

In Miller's opinion, calling his new landlady by her given name was anything but proper. But then, he had called Antonini by his given name, and her uncle had been his landlord.

After several moments, Miller conceded. "I'll call you Jenny," he said, "if you'll do me the honor of calling me Miller."

"Agreed." She held the plate in front of him again.

Instead of helping himself immediately, he hesitated. "But you must agree to one stipulation."

Jenny's brows rose into black half moons. "And that is?"

"That we use first names only when we're alone together."

"Dr. Holbrook." She giggled again, her face lighting up with the emotion.

The sound of her throaty mirth made his skin ripple uncomfortably. His reactions to this woman baffled him.

"What are you suggesting?" she asked playfully, finishing her earlier statement.

"Suggesting?" Miller felt his face redden. Engaging in such a personal conversation with a lady was unnerving to say the least. He was as inept with this small talk as some of his students were at solving equations. Maybe he'd stepped over the lines of propriety.

"I meant you no disrespect, Miss Blake. Your reputation is my first concern."

"Jenny," she corrected. "And please take your biscuit before you choke on your own fluster." She held the plate toward him for the third time. "I've no reputation to speak of. You, Ninj, and Axle are the only ones I've met since arriving in Georgetown.

"Besides, we have more important things to worry about than my reputation." She looked at Ninj, who stared at both of them from behind his steepled fingers. "I need your help not only with Ninj's problem, but also with a problem of my own."

Surprised by her declaration, Miller took the biscuit. He wasn't certain how he, a mere mortal, could help an extraordinary genie—especially when he wasn't wholly convinced that the man wasn't a trickster, as he had accused Miss Blake of being only moments before.

Miller spread a layer of jam on both sides of the sliced biscuit, then slapped them together. He lifted the dough and jam confection to his mouth and inhaled. It smelled flaky and buttery. When he bit into the bread, it tasted like heaven.

"Did you make these?" he asked, finishing it off and reaching for another one.

"Now why would I have to do that when I have my very own magic genie?" She winked at Ninj.

Miller didn't comment. He was too busy polishing off the second biscuit.

Fascinated, Jenny watched Miller eat. He downed her biscuits with such enthusiasm, he reminded her of a man who had only just discovered the taste of food.

Was he a cook? A man alone had to learn a few domestic duties, but that didn't mean that what he prepared tasted good. Jenny prided herself on being a good cook. Perhaps if she bribed him with a few homemade meals, he would agree to help her with Ninj's plight and with her bookkeeping.

Although Miller ate with relish, he remained aloof, repressing his emotions. Like happiness. Instead of a smile being a natural reflex for him, it seemed to be an effort. And for the first time since meeting the man, she wondered what had made him so reserved.

Not that Jenny was an expert on how men should act. For the most part, she never gave them a second thought. But the few boys she recalled from back home had been full of mischief and always ready to tease the girls. Of course, Jenny had always been ready to give them a good run for their money.

Everyone who knew Jenny, other than her mother and grandmother, had claimed she had a great sense of humor. She had vowed long ago never to become as humorless as her family. Maybe it was her desire to help the professor rid himself of the qualities that she disliked in her mother and grandmother that made her look at him in a new light.

While studying him from beneath her lowered lashes, she decided that some ladies might consider the professor to be attractive. In the bright sunlight, his hair was the color of roasted chestnuts with strands of reddish-brown highlights. The severity of the style—slicked back from his high forehead—couldn't disguise his hair's thickness. Without the hair tonic, she knew it would feel as silky as the garments she'd changed from earlier.

His jaw was square, his teeth straight and white, and

a dimple creased the right side of his wide mouth. Recalling Ninj's description of his spectacles, Jenny found herself wondering how he would look without the glasses. If he would smile more often then he definitely would be considered a looker.

Jenny felt Ninj's eyes upon her. When she glanced at him, the glint in their black depths hinted that he had read her mind. The old reprobate. It was bad enough having a genie demanding that you fall in love with a man, but having one with the power to read your thoughts would be torture. Jenny sent Ninj a warning look and turned her attention back to Miller.

"How well did you know my Uncle Antonini?" she asked.

"I was his tenant for almost seven years, and we became good friends. Your uncle was an extraordinary man, and I miss him very much."

Jenny was pleased with his answer. "I didn't know him at all and I miss him."

Miller's response must have pleased Bengel as well. The feline deserted the grassy space at their feet and jumped onto Miller's lap.

Surprised, Miller looked as though he didn't know how to respond to the unexpected privilege of holding the cat. Jenny expected him to shoo the animal off his perfectly creased trousers, but instead, once the cat was comfortably settled on his legs, Miller stroked the white tiger's back. "Since your uncle's death, Bengel and I have filled the void with each other's company."

"He seems to like you," Jenny said.

Miller's fingers scratched behind the cat's ears, making him shake his head like a dog jiggling water from his shaggy coat. The caress must have satisfied the feline, because he allowed Miller to continue his ministrations.

Watching the two males, Jenny decided that maybe there was hope for the professor yet. Anyone who harbored fondness for an animal could certainly harbor the same fondness for people. Watching his fingers caress Bengel, she wondered how it would feel to have Miller scratch her behind the ears in the same fashion.

Jenny Blake, where did such a thought come from? She shot Ninj a quick look and wondered if the genie could also cast spells. Shaken by her thoughts, she tried to dismiss them, focusing instead on Bengel's rumbling purr that joined the birdsong issuing from a nearby tree.

Ninj broke into the comfortable noise as well as into Jenny's thoughts. "Are you married, Master Miller?"

She stiffened in her chair, knowing exactly where the giant was headed with his question. She tried to kick him beneath the table, but he moved his long legs out of her reach.

"Married?" Miller shifted uncomfortably. "No. I'm a bachelor and very happy with my lot. I suppose that is why Antonini and I got on so well—we both enjoyed living unattached."

Good, she thought. *He isn't interested in marriage, either.* Learning that Miller felt as she did made her feel better. Now Ninj wouldn't be trying to make a match between them. She fired him a look that said, *I hope you're satisfied now.*

But the genie wasn't to be put off so easily. "Ah, but then you have a concubine?"

Miller turned as green as the sprigs of grass in the courtyard, and she wondered if his biscuits and jam were about to make another appearance.

Although Jenny wasn't familiar with the word *concubine*, Miller's reaction told her it wasn't a word he favored. He clutched the arms of his chair. The abrupt movement chased Bengel from his lap.

"Really, Mr. Ninj." Miller ran a finger inside his collar. "I don't believe this conversation is suitable for a young lady's ears."

Ninj wasn't to be thwarted. "Why not? In my country, ladies are trained at a youthful age to please men. Surely it is so in your country?"

The word's meaning finally penetrated Jenny's brain. Although she didn't know what a concubine was, she supposed it must have something to do with breeding. Recalling her earlier use of the words *pussy* and *midwife*, and Miller's reaction to them, what else would have made the professor's face go from green to red as the strawberry jam on the table? His discomposure was so comical that Jenny almost laughed. She imagined the man was a mossback if his embarrassment was any indication.

Having grown up on a farm, Jenny knew how animals copulated. Her curiosity on reproduction had sent her in search of the same act between a man and a woman. She had found the information in a book at the small library in Shepherdstown. She accepted both acts as natural occurrences in order to reproduce. But she had on no occasion considered the act itself would be pleasing, especially with the grunting sounds the animals made while engaging one another. But perhaps Ninj knew something she didn't and could explain to her how such an experience could be pleasurable. She would ask him after the professor left.

Which wouldn't be long. Already he was preparing to take his leave. Miller stood. "I really must be going," he said.

"Please," she begged, "do sit down. We have many things to discuss, and I promise you that Ninj will not utter another word or I will banish him immediately to his bottle."

"Mistress Jee-nih, but how—"

"In time, Ninj, in time. For now you'll do as I say or I'll make you disappear."

Tears welled in the giant's dark eyes. Jenny raised her brows in warning, and Ninj quickly regained his composure.

She turned her attention back to Miller. "Please, won't you stay?"

After a moment, Miller complied. He didn't look happy with his decision, but then in Jenny's opinion he hadn't looked pleased with anything since their first meeting, except maybe with her biscuits. She offered him another one, but he declined. Even her biscuits no longer satisfied him.

Afraid that he might bolt at any moment, she immediately began telling him Ninj's story. Throughout the telling, Miller's gaze kept sliding to where Ninj sat wearing a haughty expression.

"So you see," Jenny said, "I need your help. Because he's my genie, he has to grant me a love to last a lifetime. And since I don't want to fall in love, he won't be able to retire to genie paradise. Because you're a professor and all, I thought you might be able to come up with a solution."

Miller's expression was incredulous. "You expect me to believe this nonsense? In case you haven't noticed, we're approaching the twentieth century. People no longer believe in witches and hobgoblins."

"I didn't believe it at first, either," Jenny responded, "but it's true. Besides, Ninj isn't a witch."

"No, I forgot. He's just magic." Miller lifted his hands toward the sky. "Magic, sorcery, they are all the same to me. Besides, if the great genie is as magic as he claims to be, and you don't suit his purpose for retiring, let him find another master." Miller's voice was filled with sarcasm. "Isn't that how things work in your country? If one master isn't suitable, you lop off his head? Or am I confusing master and slave?"

"Mistress, not Master," Ninj corrected. "I am Mistress Jee-nih's gift. I belong to her. In my country, I am the slave. It is written thus."

Miller looked from Ninj to Jenny again. Shaking his head, he said, "Well, he certainly has cast a spell upon you. I'm sorry, Jenny, but I still feel this man is an imposter and has you hoodwinked. He probably heard of your uncle's death, then somehow learned you were new to the city and figured you would make an easy target." Miller's lips puckered in distaste. "A man of his stature living inside a bottle as small as the one you claim he can fit into. Impossible."

Jenny jumped up from the table. "You wait right

there," she said. "I'll bring you the bottle."

Before Miller could protest, she ran inside the shop and returned in a moment with Ninj's bottle. She handed it to Miller. "This is it," she said. "He lives inside there and has for many centuries."

Miller's gaze skimmed the bottle before returning to Ninj. "You've lived in here since the days of the Ottoman Empire?" His next words were filled with contempt. "Pretty cramped and lowly quarters for someone of your importance, wouldn't you say?"

"Inside it is like a palace. Very luxurious, and the food is fit for kings." Ninj patted his belly beneath the silk sash. "It is as I told Mistress Jee-nih. I have grown fat and lazy, but that will all change now."

Miller stood and slammed the bottle back upon the table. "If it is so luxurious and like a palace inside, why don't you just stay there and leave Antonini's niece alone? I don't know what your real game is, mister, but I don't believe any of your story. I've a good mind to call the law."

"Law?" Jenny was appalled. It was apparent that Miller still didn't believe her story about Ninj. "Wait, let me show you."

Moving her hand to her throat where the stone hung, she rubbed its surface.

"No, Mistress Jee—"

Ninj disappeared into thin air.

Miller whirled in a circle before lowering himself into the chair. He bent over and searched beneath the table, then straightened and craned his neck to look behind the few shrubs that dotted the garden.

"Where is he?" he demanded.

"In there," Jenny told him, pointing to the bottle on the table.

"You expect me to believe that—that giant man is inside this tiny bottle." He picked it up and placed his eye against the opening and looked inside.

"It's as I thought, he's not in there. Remember, Jenny, I deal with facts, tangibles, and volume." He shook the bottle before replacing it upon the table. "The laws of mathematics say it is impossible for a human to fit inside a container of that size." Miller looked beneath the table again. "The man is nothing but a fraud who is trying to take advantage of your position."

"No, he's magic," Jenny insisted, feeling defeated. After everything she had told him and shown him, Miller still didn't believe her. But she wasn't ready to give up completely. Although Miller wouldn't help her with Ninj's plight, he might still help her with her uncle's books. Encouraged by this thought, she said, "The only fraud around here is my late uncle's lawyer, Phineas Goldfinch."

"Phineas Goldfinch? What does he have to do with any of this? What do you mean he's a fraud?"

Well, at least she had all his attention now. But if his response was any indication of how he would receive her next news, she knew Miller wouldn't believe her reasons for terminating Mr. Goldfinch, either.

But Jenny didn't care. She would tell him anyway. She had always acted on her own and was used to making her own decisions. She didn't need Miller Holbrook's help with Ninj or her accounts.

"I fired the solicitor several days ago," she said.

"You what? But why would you do such a foolhardy thing? The Goldfinch firm has represented your uncle for as long as I've known Antonini."

"I didn't trust him. He's ready to sell everything and send me back to Shepherdstown." She folded her arms across her chest. "I refuse to allow a man like him to have any say in my affairs."

"Surely you are mistaken. Phineas Goldfinch is a reputable man. It is this Ninj character who's a danger to you. Where the devil is he anyway? I want to give him a piece of my mind."

"As you did with Axle? Do you plan to have a fist-fight with him as well?"

Miller said nothing, but continued to scan the yard for the missing Ninj.

Maybe it was just as well the professor didn't believe her. Perhaps she didn't need his help anyway. Ninj was magic; he could help her with the shop's books. Why hadn't she thought of that before?

She rubbed the gem at her neck, making sure Miller watched her.

Again, she heard what sounded like a cork exploding from a bottle.

It was several moments before Ninj materialized. Bowing from the waist, he asked, "Mistress Jee-nih, you summoned?"

Miller stood frozen in place, never blinking an eye when Ninj reappeared. A horse clopped along the street beyond the house, and a soft breeze lifted several tendrils of Miller's slicked-back hair.

The professor's indifference to what Jenny considered to be a phenomenal event didn't surprise her in the least. After all, he was a man of few emotions. Most likely, he still didn't believe the genie was real in spite of what he'd witnessed. So when he finally spoke, his response shocked her.

"I think I believe you now," he said.

Miller's announcement made Jenny and Ninj clasp hands. Standing, they danced gleefully around the table while the professor looked on solemnly.

Seven

Miller brushed back the stray locks of hair that the
breeze had shifted earlier. He would have to use more
Bay Rum tonic in order to restrain his unruly mane. As
he stared at Jenny and Ninj, holding hands and dancing
around like children, he wished for an easy solution that
could also tame the errant pair.

He was still baffled by their merriment. In all honesty,
he couldn't recall agreeing to help them. His admission
that he thought he believed that Ninj was a genie may
have incited their response. Even if he agreed to help, he
wasn't sure how to succeed. He only knew that if
Jenny asked, he would. She was his old friend's niece,
and Miller had more or less promised Antonini that he
would watch over her.

By helping her, he would be that much closer to carrying out his own plan. If he helped Ninj with his ridiculous plight, then Miss Blake would have to agree to an
unquestionable change in her actions and dress. Wondering how such an event would ever come to pass, he
fingered Madame DeBeau's card inside his jacket
pocket. With all that had occurred today, he had forgotten he had stopped by the dressmaker's shop yesterday.
At least getting Jenny to visit the dressmaker would be
a step in the right direction. They would begin by im-
proving her wardrobe.

"Before we discuss another thing, I suggest we go inside." The two merrymakers stopped their frolicking and gave Miller their full attention. "Jenny, I'll agree to help Ninj if you will agree to help me."

"Help you?" His request had clearly caught her off guard, but instead of questioning him further, she steepled her hands as she had seen Ninj do and bowed in his direction. "Your wish is my command," she said before her spoof was replaced with another bout of laughter.

"Inside. Now!" he ordered, sounding very much like a schoolmaster rather than the professor he was. But then, these two characters made him feel as though he was dealing with children.

They preceded Miller through the door to the shop. Jenny carried Ninj's bottle; Ninj, with his overly large feet encased in silk slippers, moved with a grace that Miller believed impossible for a man of his size. Once inside the building, Miller insisted that Jenny and Ninj sit down. Miller, adopting his lecturing position, paced the floor in front of them, his hands clasped firmly behind his back.

"First of all," he began, "I want you both to promise me that Ninj's presence will not be mentioned outside of this shop. I fear that if word gets out that you, Jenny, are entertaining a genie in your home, we could find ourselves in all kinds of trouble."

What Miller should have told them, but didn't, was that they would be hauled off because there were those who would believe they were insane and in need of being locked up.

"What about Axle?" Jenny asked. "He saw Ninj."

"We'll stick to the story I told him. That Ninj is from India and is visiting the college and staying with me in my apartment."

"Hindu," Ninj said and gasped. "No, I won't claim such a lie. I'm Ninj, from the great Ottoman Empire in Constantinople."

Damn, the giant was stubborn. Miller still wasn't certain that he believed this genie nonsense, but if he let

Jenny and Ninj think that he did, it would give him more time to seek out the truth about the stranger.

Hoping to appease the giant, Miller continued, "We need to give credence to our story. No one will believe us if we say you are an Ottoman Turk from Constantinople. The place no longer exists."

Ninj's brows knit together in anger. "What do you mean my country no longer exists?" He jumped to his silk-covered feet and loomed over Miller like Goliath. "Scum-sucking pig," he shouted, "you lie!"

Miller didn't consider himself a coward, but apprehension surged through his gut as he faced the menacing giant.

It was Jenny who turned mediator. She vaulted to her feet and placed her hand on Ninj's arm. "You must not talk that way," she told him. "I'm sure Miller meant you no disrespect. Remember, he has agreed to help us, and we must listen to what he has to say."

"But—"

"No buts, Ninj. If you won't behave yourself, then I'll send you to your bottle."

After a moment, Ninj took his seat again, but his expression remained intense.

Miller swallowed. "What I should have said is that the Constantinople you knew is now called Istanbul."

With this announcement, the fierce expression left Ninj's face. He laughed, his white teeth as visible as a shark's beneath his black mustache. "Ahh, Islambol," he said, "means 'where Muslims are plentiful.'"

"Oh, they're plentiful all right," Miller agreed. "Maybe you would like to add to that population. I'd be happy to arrange passage for you on the next boat."

Jenny frowned, and Ninj shook his head. "I am unable to do that. Mistress Jee-nih is my master now. I must stay with her and help her to find a love to last a lifetime. Only then will I be able to retire to paradise. I shall never go back to Islambol."

"I don't want a love to last a lifetime," Jenny pointed out. "I'm perfectly satisfied without one. Couldn't you just go to this place and tell them you accomplished your mission and demand they admit you?''

''Sounds like a good idea to me,'' Miller threw in. ''In fact, it is the best idea I've heard since this whole crazy business began.''

''The magic does not work that way,'' Ninj replied. ''The gatekeeper, he would know. Besides, I have to have my jewel.'' He pointed to his turban. ''It is missing. Without the jewel, I will have no admittance.''

''Missing? But where is it?'' Jenny asked.

Ninj pointed to the gem tied around her neck. ''That is mine,'' he said, then touched his turban. ''It belongs here.''

Jenny clasped the jewel. ''Yours? No, you're mistaken. The gem belongs to me, and you can't have it.''

If Ninj spoke the truth, Miller thought, giving him the jewel would be an easy way to be rid of the genie. ''Give it to him,'' Miller ordered her. ''It's not very fashionable tied on a shoestring. In fact, it's quite garish-looking, if you ask me.''

''Well, I'm not asking you,'' she quickly responded. ''I love it. I found it in my uncle's trunk and I'm not parting with it. It belonged to my Uncle Antonini and now it's mine.''

Miller had at no time dealt with two more stubborn people, but he could be just as obstinate. ''Jenny, haven't you been telling me that we must help Ninj retire? Around your neck is the key to the pearly gates. Give him the blasted jewel and be done—''

''No,'' Ninj broke in. ''The stone will come to me only after I have earned it.''

''Enough of this mumbo jumbo.'' Miller rounded on Jenny, then reached to untie the string that held the stone.

She sprang to her feet. ''No, it belongs to me!'' she said.

''Give him the piece of junk.''

''It's not junk. And, no, I won't give it to him. You can't tell me what—''

"Stop it, both of you!" Ninj ordered. "This petty tiff will do none of us any good. The stone cannot be removed until my mission is complete."

"You," Miller said, "are suffering from a mind disorder if you believe that she can't remove that *thing* from around her neck if she wants to." He returned his attention to Jenny. "Remove it and show him."

"She cannot. It will stay around her neck until she meets the love I promised her. I cannot remove it. No one can."

"Don't be absurd. Here, let me at it—I'll show you." Miller grabbed the knot at her nape, and this time Jenny didn't deny him access to the cord.

He picked at the knot, but it refused to budge. "I'll cut it from her neck if I have to."

Miller moved toward Antonini's desk and searched among the papers cluttering the top for a pair of scissors or a letter opener, anything that could sever the string.

"Scissors." Holding the cutting implement in the air, he moved toward Jenny again. "We must do this," he said. "We have to know if what Ninj claims is true."

"You may tear it from my neck," Jenny said, her eyes challenging, "but I'll not relinquish it."

"Whatever you say," Miller lied.

The girl certainly had a flair for dramatics, but for the moment Miller dismissed her keenness. His main objective was to prove that Ninj was a fake. In so doing, he could rid them both from the lunatic's presence.

Very carefully he inserted one blade of the scissors between the string and Jenny's neck. His fingers accidentally brushed the pulse point at her throat, and his rapid heartbeat joined hers. He was so close to her, he could feel her warm breath against his cheek. She smelled of lemon tea and strawberry jam, and another scent, one he couldn't put a name to, but one that reminded him she was very much a woman.

For the first time since spying Jenny Blake from his third-story window, Miller really looked at her. What he saw almost took his breath away.

He knew her eyes were blue-gray, but when she lifted her heavily lashed gaze to meet his, her eyes displayed rainbow-colored reflections of violet, blue, and green. Her hair tumbled around her head like a dark brown cloud, the curly ends hanging an inch or so below her shoulders. An errant strand tangled around his fingers, almost trapping them. Beneath his fingers, her skin felt warm to the touch, its honey color suggesting many days spent in the sun.

Miller's throat went dry. His experience with women was limited to the time when he had been a much younger man—to a few quick rolls in a whore's bed to relieve his youthful urges—but never had he felt desire for a woman as he did at that moment for Jenny.

"Go ahead," she said, her lips mere inches from his own.

Their gazes met and held. Miller thought for an instant that she was giving him permission to kiss her, until he heard Ninj chuckle behind him. The sound reminded him of where and who he was, and what he was about.

With renewed determination, Miller closed the scissor handles, expecting the cutting edge to slice the string in two and release him from this tormenting closeness. But the string held fast as though it was born of steel. Careful not to nick the delicate skin of Jenny's neck, Miller tried to cut the cord again, but it refused to divide while the aquamarine stone winked at him like a living eye.

"Dull scissors," he mumbled. He slipped the blade from beneath the string and stepped back.

"You can't cut it?" she asked, her eyes wide with wonder.

Her scent clung to his clothes. He puzzled over his need to draw her back into his embrace and never let her go. Miller shook his head to clear it; he felt as though he had been bewitched. If the truth were known, he damn sure couldn't cut it, in more ways than one.

"Maybe a knife would work," Jenny offered.

"You believe me now?" Ninj asked, amused. "Only love can break the tie—until then, Mistress Jee-nih, my jewel remains yours, and I remain in your service."

"Hogwash!" Miller grumbled. "I'll fetch a knife and end this nonsense once and for all."

He left them to run upstairs and returned shortly with the kitchen tool. "We'll have that off you in a jiffy," he told Jenny.

Again he stepped next to her, but trained his thoughts on his purpose instead of the woman who stood so close to him that he could feel her breath against his arms.

Miller sawed the string, but it wouldn't break. In a fit of frustration, he removed the knife and threw it aside while shooting Ninj a killing glare.

"What do we do now?" Jenny asked, her gaze questioning.

"Now," Miller replied, taking a deep breath and exhaling audibly, "we find you a perfect love."

Jenny stared at the card that Miller had given her the afternoon before. This noon, she was on her way to Madame DeBeau's Dressmaker Shop and dreading the moment when she would come face-to-face with the highly praised woman. Miller had gone on for what seemed like hours, lauding the woman's accomplishments, until Jenny had hated her sight unseen.

Miller Holbrook drove a hard bargain. Unless she agreed to make some changes in her appearance, he wouldn't help Ninj with his plight. Because Jenny was determined to help the genie, she was now on her way to the modiste's.

She was the lamb to be sacrificed for the good of the goal. It galled her to think that she had been forced by a man to package herself in pretty wrappings . . . wrappings that would be used to entrap a man she didn't want in the first place. Not only was she to be trussed and dressed like a prized bird, but she also had to learn how to act like a lady. A lady, Miller had said, to fit the role of her newly acquired position as Antonini Vassily's great-niece.

If there was one thing Jenny was sure of, it was that

someone with her background couldn't become a proper lady overnight. She was a farm girl and claimed to be nothing more. In her opinion, it had been far easier selling apples than selling curiosities in her uncle's shop was going to be. If what Miller had said about becoming a lady was true, then she was proving to be the biggest curiosity of all.

According to the doctor, her looks and actions left a lot to be desired; or, as he had put it in his refined, stiff way of speaking, her actions and looks did not reflect those of a lady.

But then, Jenny had never had to suit anyone but herself, and she liked herself just the way she was. It would take a darn sight more than an oh-so-proper professor and fancy dresses to make her into a new person. But if change was necessary, it wasn't for the professor she'd be changing. It would be for Ninj.

Thoughts of the genie made her smile. "Lordy, he must be tired, living all those centuries."

Her conversation won her questionable looks from passersby. She had to stop talking to herself in public. As Jenny made her way up the hill, all her shortcomings rode heavily on her narrow shoulders—inadequacies she had at no time considered having until Miller and Ninj had pointed them out to her.

Miller's suggestion that she become more ladylike would also help Ninj. Once a real lady, she would be courted by many men, and when she found the one she believed suitable enough to fall in love with, she would announce her feelings to Ninj. Ninj wouldn't know that it was all a hoax unless he really could read her mind. Jenny counted on the belief that he could not. Only she would know the truth. Once Ninj had taken his leave, Jenny would be free to sever the relationship, and then her new life here could return to normal.

It was a plausible plan, and one that sounded foolproof except for the stone around her neck. Would the jewel know she was lying?

"You're being absurd," she said out loud to herself.

"How can a jewel know if I'm telling the truth or not?"

But then again the gem was supposed to be magic, and Miller had not been able to remove it from around her neck. The memory made her wonder what the infamous Madame DeBeau would think about her soon-to-be customer: the country bumpkin with the garish gem tied around her neck on a shoestring.

Not willing to dwell on the upcoming meeting overlong, Jenny took in the sights of the neighborhood that before today she hadn't seen beyond her street and the canal.

The dressmaker's shop was located on Wisconsin Avenue, and Miller had drawn her a map on how to get there. The route seemed fairly simple, but the traffic was another story. Jenny had never seen so much activity.

At the end of Thomas Jefferson, she crossed M Street, dodging the trolleys and wagons rushing past. Her effort left her breathless and left her anchoring her hat, which had nearly blown off with her quick dash. Horses neighed, their shod feet clopping against the brick pavement, and trolley bells clanged a warning for people to stay out of the way. The air smelled of horseflesh, baked bread, rotting produce, and the yeasty aroma of beer.

Swinging her reticule in rhythm with her steps, Jenny rounded the corner on Wisconsin Street and started up the hill. There were no trees edging the busy thoroughfare as there were on her street. Some of the shops had awnings jutting out from their fronts. Jenny supposed the canvas coverings protected strollers from bright sun or maybe inclement weather.

"Not too much longer," she noted after reading the numbers above an apothecary shop she had just passed. She continued several more feet and stopped in front of a store whose black, curved, and scalloped canopy reminded Jenny of a woman's eyelash. *Madame DeBeau— Modiste* was written in fancy script across the plate-glass window.

Rather than entering the double doors immediately, Jenny hung back, studying the storefront. Flowers grew in pots by the entrance. Inside the shop's big window she could see several hats decorated with silk flowers and feathers. A shapely form that resembled a woman with no head wore a dress made from delicate ecru lace.

It seemed she had arrived at her destination, but without her usual courage. She had left her confidence back at the shop with Ninj and Bengel. Now that she was here, Jenny wondered how a lady should act at a dressmaker's shop. Her clothes had always been sewn by her mother, and all were functional instead of fashionable and nowhere nearly as fine as the dummy's in the window.

"You're the dummy," she told herself, laughing nervously.

It was like Miller had said. Madame DeBeau would be working for her. Jenny could choose whatever suited her tastes, but she should heed the dressmaker's advice on the latest styles.

"I can do that," she said.

Taking a deep breath and squaring her shoulders, she pushed open the door and stepped inside.

A small silver bell attached to the door's frame tinkled, announcing her arrival to the proprietor, who at the moment was absent. This was fine with Jenny because it gave her time to study her surroundings, and on no occasion had she seen a more beautiful room.

The walls and ornate cornices were painted coral, and everything was touched with shades of the same orange-pink tint, from the lightest to the darkest tones. Jenny felt as though by stepping into the shop she, too, had taken on the same warm glow. Pink-beige lace draped the front window like an intricately spun web. The same lace spilled lavishly over tabletops, puddling on the floor like spun-sugar candy. A black high-gloss chest with books for reading served a low-lying couch with one arm that was so overflowing with lace, silk, and linen pillows that Jenny wondered where a body was supposed to sit, since the room was absent of any other furnishings.

Floor-to-ceiling mirrors on the side walls reflected the room's melon colors, along with carpets that were similar to the ones she had seen in her uncle's shop. Ninj had told her those were Persian, and she guessed that these were, too. The woven rugs were of the same shades that dominated the rest of the room, but for black and vermilion diamonds and squares that patterned the otherwise pale backgrounds. A vermilion velvet drape swagged across the lace window covering and dropped to the floor on one side of the window. Across the top, coral braid spread like a silken fan over the dense pile of the drapery fabric.

There was only one thing wrong with the room, Jenny decided. Her image reflected in the silvery depths of the mirror looked as out of place as broken crockery next to fine china. Beside the mirrored wall stood a marble sculpture of a young, nearly naked woman whose hands were shackled with chains—the only piece Jenny could identify with. She didn't belong here and wished herself a million miles away. About to leave, Jenny stopped when a lady entered the room through a curtained doorway at the partitioned wall, carrying a tea tray. She stared because the woman wore a coral uniform with a lace cap of the same color pinned to her salmon-colored hair.

"*Mademoiselle,*" the lady said, "Madame DeBeau will be with you shortly. Please have a seat." The young woman motioned to the one-armed couch with its many pillows. "Sit," she ordered, and when Jenny didn't obey, she added, "On the fainting couch."

"Fainting couch?" Although Jenny felt breathless enough to swoon, she had no intention of perching among the finery of all those pillows and sipping tea from the too-tiny china cup on the tray that the lady held mere inches from her.

"I don't believe I'll be needing that couch just yet," she told the woman with good humor. "I think I'll leave and come back—"

"Sit, sit, sit," the woman insisted as though she expected Jenny to flee and she wasn't about to let her escape. "Madame DeBeau insists all her customers have tea while they wait."

"But I don't want—"

"*Ma petite*, tea's good for you. You'll see." The shop attendant circled the couch and set the tray upon the black chest. Then she took Jenny's reticule and laid it upon the chest as well before taking her elbow and nudging her toward the couch. "Sit, sit, sit," she ordered again.

When the backs of Jenny's knees contacted the long piece of furniture, she had no choice. She dropped down on the throne of pillows, causing them to plump in every direction but a comfortable one. Jenny felt as out of place as a mother bird trying to lay eggs in the wrong nest.

"*Oui*," the woman said, "couch is very nice, *non*?" Grabbing a pink linen napkin from the tray, she spread it across Jenny's lap before she could protest. "Tea." She shoved the small delicate cup into Jenny's hands. "Drink. You will enjoy."

Trying to balance herself on the mounds of pillows as well as keep the tea inside the small bowl instead of spilling it on the linen napkin, Jenny did what the woman ordered. She brought the cup to her mouth and gulped down most of the contents. Too late, she realized that the liquid was scalding hot. It burned a fiery trail down her throat and into her stomach where it simmered for several moments before cooling.

"You like, *ma petite*?"

Unable to speak and uncertain what the woman had asked her, Jenny nodded.

"Good," the woman said. "You wait for Madame DeBeau." Then she turned and headed for the back of the shop. Soon the coral-clad lady blended in with the rest of the shop's colors and disappeared completely, leaving Jenny alone in her misery.

She didn't dare move from the stacks of pillows for

fear of spilling the remaining tea, and she didn't dare take the last swallow from the cup, fearing that her mouth and throat would melt from another scalding. Totally helpless, she felt tears pool in her eyes. She hated being in this situation, and she loathed being put there by a man. Three men, to be correct: Miller, Ninj, and the stranger who was to become her perfect love.

"I've had about enough of being ordered around."

In a fit of defiance, she slurped down the last dregs of tea. Either her throat was too numb to feel any more pain, or the liquid had cooled completely, because Jenny felt nothing but elation as she bounded up from the ridiculous bed of pillows.

She had just placed the cup and napkin back upon the tray when she heard movement behind her. Believing the coral-colored woman had returned to ward off her escape, Jenny swung around to face her, ready to do battle. In place of the lady she'd expected, she stared into the blue eyes of the modiste herself—Madame DeBeau. Her immediate disapproval of Jenny was evident in her gaze.

With tight lips, Madame DeBeau said, *"Bonjour, mademoiselle."*

Eight

Bonjour? The only French word Jenny knew was *bon bon*, and she had liked the fondant coated with chocolate very much, probably because the box of sweet confections had been a gift from her Grandmother Vassily years ago. Jenny only wished that she could feel the same sweet sentiment for the woman who was staring at her as though she were something distasteful that had been brought in on one of her customer's shoes. In all honesty, Jenny couldn't find one pleasant thing about the arrogant woman and decided she was ugly from the inside out.

Even the gorgeous gown she wore, a deep orange color with cascades of beaded black lace falling over the huge bell sleeves and ending just below the lady's hips couldn't soften the woman's hardness. She was a good two inches taller than Jenny, with an ample bosom and tiny waist. After a quick study of the woman, Jenny concluded that it was not only her attitude, but also the breadth of the sleeves of the dress she wore that made her appear so waspish. Having been stung once by the nasty little critters, Jenny knew that Madame DeBeau was a person to be avoided.

Her black hair was pulled severely back from her narrow face, and she peered at Jenny from behind spectacles that rested on a stick rather than resting on her nose.

One snap of her bony, bejeweled fingers, and the attendant appeared at her side immediately.

"Lisette," she said in a heavy French accent, "show the little *savage* to the dressing room."

Savage? Jenny stared back, stung. "I may be straight off the farm," she replied bitingly, "but I'm certainly not uncivilized."

The modiste's heavily penciled brows rose two inches higher on her forehead. Throwing her hands in the air, she muttered, "Impossible," before bolting toward the back of the shop.

The young dresser touched Jenny's arm, nudging her in the direction that the proprietor had taken, but Jenny refused to budge.

"Go, go, go," Lisette ordered, flapping her hands, shooing her along.

Jenny looked toward the front door, then back at the woman. Now was the time to run if she planned to escape. But seeing a turban atop a wooden head, similar to the one Ninj wore, kept her from fleeing. The headdress reminded her of her reason for being at the dressmaker.

The shop assistant interrupted her thoughts. "Come, *ma petite*, you will see. Madame DeBeau, she will not eat you. She will make you look good enough to eat. The professor, he will wish to sample your sweet flesh."

Moments ticked by on the case clock. *Good enough to eat?* Jenny couldn't imagine anything more distasteful than Miller Holbrook, or any man for that matter, drooling over her flesh.

"Never," she said before reluctantly following Lisette through a curtain toward the back of the shop.

Once behind the partitioned wall, Jenny found herself in a room of mirrors. A skylight above their heads let natural light into the windowless area. The polished wooden floors were bare of all carpets. She noted that at least the space had two chairs that were fit for sitting, unlike the fainting couch in the front room.

Did this mean she had moved beyond the fainting

stage to the next level? Already she felt less nervous than she had earlier. Her anxiety had dissipated, and her confidence returned somewhat. Maybe it was because she had met Madame DeBeau and knew what to expect from the woman. That knowledge gave Jenny confidence. She no longer feared the again-absent modiste.

"We must undress you." The assistant fluttered her hands, motioning Jenny toward the raised round platform in the middle of the room.

"Undress me?" Jenny shook her head. "Thank you very much, but I can undress myself," she said, stepping upon the foot-high circle. "I've done so for twenty-two years and I don't need any help now."

"*Mademoiselle* is shy, *non*?"

"No! *Mademoiselle* is not shy."

Shy? It wasn't modesty that kept her from refusing the dresser's help. Jenny's naked body had never fazed her; it was the way God had made her, and she accepted that. In fact, one of Jenny's favorite pastimes at home had been swimming nude in the nearby pond. Of course, her mother and Nana Blake would have died of shame if they had known of Jenny's secret practices.

A few moments later, she stood as naked as the day she was born.

From behind her she heard the attendant's voice. "*Ooo-la-la.* Very nice."

Her description made Jenny laugh. Beyond her own image in the mirror, she saw the dresser's, who smiled approvingly at Jenny's reflection.

"Madame DeBeau will be pleased."

"I doubt that Madame DeBeau will be pleased with anything about me, except maybe the money she'll receive from my purchases."

But instead of dwelling on the woman's imminent return, Jenny's gaze lingered on her reflection in the mirrors.

She hadn't seen herself completely naked and she was fascinated by what she saw. Her mirror back home had been a small handheld looking glass that she had bought from a passing salesman.

Nana Blake had believed that vanity was a sin and allowed no mirrors in the house. Jenny had kept hers hidden, bringing it away with her when she left the farm. She knew what she looked like with clothes on because she had seen her reflection in a window in Shepherdstown, but before today, she had never seen herself completely in the raw.

And just maybe what the shop attendant had said was true. *Ooo-la-la. Nice.*

Because of her five-foot-nine height, her legs were long and shapely. Her hips were rounded and dipped in to form a narrow waist. Full breasts rode high and firm, making her narrow shoulders appear even more narrow in her nudity. At the apex of her thighs, curls as dark as the hair on her head formed a perfect *V*. Yes, Jenny supposed she did look nice, but only she and the woman behind her would be appreciating her womanly secrets.

Spinning around for a full view, she stopped in midcircle. The attendant approached her now, carrying undergarments.

Jenny had at no time worn a corset, only a camisole and drawers, but she recognized the contraption of staves from the drawings she had seen in a lady's magazine.

Time now for the trussing, Jenny thought. Although the idea of confining herself in such a gadget was less than appealing, she reminded herself that she was doing it for Ninj. Maybe for Miller as well. She shot another look at her reflection in the mirror. Any man in his right mind, she decided, would prefer his lady true-to-life natural rather than caged in wires like a domesticated bird.

"And what is this thing?" Jenny asked, staring at the strange garment Lisette handed her.

"It is called a combination. The chemise is no longer in style. This is bodice, petticoat, and drawers all in one piece. Here," the dresser said, "put this vest on first, then we will lace you into the corset."

The combination was made of pale pink material—
but then, what other color would do in this shop of cor-
als and pinks?—with lace at the neck and knees.

"No bust improvers for you," Lisette said, giggling.
"No improvement needed there."

Jenny was pleased that something about her measured
up to what a lady should look like, but of course she
still hadn't passed Madame DeBeau's inspection.

The moment she was dressed, as though on cue, the
modiste appeared in a rustle of petticoats and swishing
beaded lace. Jenny would have bet her last dollar that
the woman had been spying on them from behind the
next wall.

Peering at Jenny through her strange glasses, she "tsk,
tsk, tsked" her way around Jenny's trussed form. "I've
much work to do," she told Lisette while continuing her
orbiting.

Lisette didn't respond. She stood away from them, her
hands clasped in front of her, her concentration centered
on her employer, awaiting her instructions. The lively,
friendly dresser of a few moments before had all but
disappeared. Madame DeBeau's coldness dominated the
room, dispelling the earlier warmth and making Jenny
shiver in her half-dressed state.

Soon the instructions came, but Madame DeBeau
gave them in French. Jenny was so fascinated by the
sound of the words that to her ears sounded like poetry
that she stood mesmerized. French was clearly the most
glorious-sounding language she had ever heard, and although she didn't like the woman who spoke it, she enjoyed listening to her.

The bell at the front of the shop rang. Lisette left the
room to answer the summons. In a few moments, she
returned.

"Madame DeBeau, you have a visitor," the attendant
said, adding something else in French.

Jenny watched the modiste. Her blue eyes lit up, and
she acted as flustered as a young girl. It certainly wasn't
the reaction Jenny would have expected from the sullen,

unfriendly woman. And it certainly wasn't as unfavorable as the one she had received from the madame. It confirmed Jenny's earlier opinion—the woman didn't like her.

"Go to the basement," she told Lisette, "and bring the dresses from the wardrobe. You know which ones." Without a glance in Jenny's direction, and without excusing herself, she quit the room.

Alone in the mirrored chamber, Jenny waited, puzzling over the strange woman's behavior. For the life of her, she couldn't understand why Madame DeBeau disliked her. Was it because she wasn't as refined as the ladies with whom Madame DeBeau usually did business? Surely she didn't call all her clients savages.

When Lisette didn't return immediately, Jenny became more curious about the madame's visitor. The longer she listened to the bits and pieces of the conversation that floated past the wall, the more convinced she became that the visitor was a man.

"Untold wealth," the madame said.

The strange voice replied, "Win confidence."

As she listened, she wondered if Madame DeBeau had a lover, or perhaps a husband. Jenny couldn't believe that a man would be attracted to such a mean-tempered woman.

Curious about the couple, Jenny moved toward the curtained doorway. The coral satin drape was so opaque that she couldn't see beyond it, but that meant that they couldn't see her, either. Confident that she wouldn't be caught snooping, she peeked through the small gap between the drape and the door's frame.

Immediately she jumped back. Madame's visitor was Phineas Goldfinch. Her fired solicitor was the last person she expected to see—or more aptly, she didn't want him to see her, dressed or otherwise.

Lisette returned from the basement, her arms loaded down with so many gowns she could hardly carry them all.

Had Lisette seen her snooping? If she did, would she

let on that she had? Jenny rushed to help her with her cumbersome load, and together they hung the dresses on several rods placed around the room. They had just finished when Madame DeBeau returned.

"Ma petite," Madame cooed, "we are ready now for the fun." She clasped her hands beneath her pointed chin.

The change in the woman's manner was so noticeable that it was almost comical. Jenny and Lisette exchanged questioning glances.

For the first time since Jenny's arrival, the modiste smiled at her, but the smile didn't reach the glassy, volcanic depths of her eyes.

But Jenny didn't have time to dwell on the smile or the change in Madame's behavior, because the dressing began in earnest. So much for Jenny's opinion about what she should wear or her insistence that she dress herself. She felt like a doll being changed at someone else's will, but what was more amazing was that most everything Madame DeBeau put on her and approved Jenny liked as well.

More than an hour passed, and Jenny was anxious for the session to end. She was getting tired of being turned this way and that, pinched in here and plumped out there, when Madame DeBeau issued another string of orders to Lisette before she flopped, very unladylike, into one of the chairs.

Jenny remained standing while Lisette took her measurements, then darted from the room. Madame continued to study her from her perch on the chair, then said, "Miss Blake, do sit down." She motioned to the seat opposite her. "We'll share some liqueur."

Sharing anything with the dressmaker was the last thing Jenny wanted to do. She was ready to don her clothes and leave.

She remained standing. "I really must be going," she said. "If Lisette will bring me my clothes—"

"Those rags you wore in here, my little cabbage, should not be considered clothing." Madame DeBeau laughed. It was a deep, throaty sound that matched her earlier beautifully spoken French.

Jenny felt her temper flare. "I'm not your little cabbage. I am a grown woman who came here today on Dr. Holbrook's recommendation to purchase a new wardrobe. Granted, my clothes may not be as fashionable as the ones you turn out, but they are serviceable, and I like them."

"Bravo, *mademoiselle*. The little cabbage has fire."

Jenny didn't like people who were cold one moment and warm the next. They were not to be trusted. She decided that the sooner she could distance herself from Madame the better she would feel.

"My clothes," she said again. "Could you please have Lisette bring them to me?"

If she had her clothes, she could leave right now. Surely, in a city as large as Washington, D.C., there was more than one capable dressmaker. Jenny intended to find one of them.

"I don't believe that you and I have any further business," she told the proprietress. She walked toward the door that Lisette had disappeared through only moments before.

Madame's next statement brought her up short. "I admired your late uncle very much."

Surprised by this declaration, Jenny stopped and faced the shopkeeper. "You knew my uncle?" she asked.

Madame DeBeau straightened in her chair, making the jet beads on her dress shimmer in the room's many mirrors. When Jenny thought about it later, she realized that the woman had probably suspected that she was about to lose a sale and decided to change her tactics.

"He helped me to furnish my house." The woman gestured toward the front room. "So many beautiful, valuable things I purchased from your uncle's shop."

Jenny studied the woman. If what she said about admiring her uncle was true, perhaps she wasn't as bad as Jenny first imagined. Not having had the chance to know her uncle personally, Jenny was interested in anyone who had known him at all. Through his acquaintances, she hoped to learn all about him.

Reluctantly she took the proffered chair, but she wasn't about to let down her defenses. "Then I can see," she said, "that you have better taste than I first believed."

Madame laughed again. "I like you, Jenny Blake. You have spirit. You will make a good businesswoman, especially dressed in my clothes." Her gaze slid over Jenny. "You know, you have a body made for fine fashion—tall and slim and rounded in the right places. And legs like a colt's."

It amazed Jenny that she had suddenly become passable in Madame's eyes, if having her legs compared to those of a male horse could be considered a compliment. She had seen enough newborn horses to know that their legs were knobby and very unstable. Maybe Madame wasn't aware of this.

"My legs," Jenny said, "are much more serviceable than a colt's, and I'm the wrong sex."

The throaty laughter filled the mirrored chamber again. "Witty, too," the modiste responded. "Now perhaps if I can persuade you to remove that awful shoestring from around your neck, you will become a successful businesswoman like me."

Jenny was tempted to tell her that she didn't want to be like her; she wanted to be like herself. Instead, she kept her lips sealed because Lisette had returned carrying a tray with thimble-sized glasses on stems and an intricately cut crystal bottle that sparkled like diamonds when the light hit it. The liquid inside the bottle was cherry red. Lisette placed the tray on the small table between the two chairs.

"Bring Miss Blake a dressing gown," Madame told the attendant. "Then see that the purple skirt and lacy waist are ready for mademoiselle to wear home when she leaves."

"But my own clothes will do," Jenny insisted.

"Not anymore. I told Lisette to burn them. Antonini

Vassily's niece can't be seen in the neighborhood dressed like a country bumpkin.''

Jenny would have argued with the modiste if it hadn't been for her statement about her uncle. The last thing she wanted to do was bring shame to her uncle's name. Compliantly she slipped her arms into the sheer floral dressing gown Lisette brought to her and settled more comfortably into the chair. She watched Madame De-Beau pour the thick red liquid into the small glasses on the tray. When she had finished, she handed one glass to Jenny and took the other one for herself.

"The shoelace," Madame DeBeau said again, taking her seat. "You must remove it." Her gaze, Jenny noticed, remained fastened on the stone.

"I can't—"

She nearly blurted out the reason the stone had to stay around her neck until she recalled Miller's insistence that Ninj's true identity be kept a secret. She would have to make up a story about the necklace.

"I won't remove it," she told the shopkeeper. "It belonged to my uncle. It was his gift to me."

Madame looked appalled by her answer, as though she might need the fainting couch in the front parlor. "Antonini Vassily gave you his shoestring to wear tied around your neck?" The woman took a sip of the red liquid as though to steady her nerves. "A man of Vassily's tastes wouldn't have demanded you wear such a crass thing."

Jenny didn't bother with a response. Instead, she took a sip of her own drink. The thick, sweet substance coated her tongue and mouth. She licked the residue from her lips. "Tastes like cherries," she said.

"Cherry Heering," the woman replied. "It is my best and favorite liqueur."

"It's liquor?" Jenny asked, surprised.

This was her first experience with the devil's brew. In Nana Blake's opinion, all spirits were the devil's own, to be avoided at all times. But Jenny wondered how anything that tasted as sweet as cherries could be considered evil. Besides, she decided as she took another sip, her Nana Blake no longer had influence over her.

"The shoestring is mine," she corrected after the long pause. "The jewel belonged to my uncle."

Madame DeBeau leaned across the space of the table and, looking through her odd spectacles, examined the gem. "It's garish-looking." Her thin brows raised in question. "A mere chunk of worthless glass?"

When Jenny didn't respond, she said, "If you insist on wearing the awful thing for sentimental reasons, remove it and I'll tie it upon a proper ribbon."

"I prefer wearing it on the shoestring," Jenny told her.

Although Jenny had not tried to remove the string after Miller's experience yesterday, she knew that now was not the time to test the stone's magic.

"If you appear about the neighborhood with that—that shoelace strung around your neck, people will laugh at you."

Jenny thought about the modiste's statement. She certainly didn't wish for people to laugh at Antonini's niece.

"Maybe," she said, "you could disguise it with another ribbon."

"I could try," Madame DeBeau replied, but appearing not at all pleased with Jenny's suggestion.

Jenny took the last trickle of liquid cherries from her glass and let it slide down her throat. Her face felt flushed, and her insides glowed with warmth.

"Would you like more, *ma petite*?" Not waiting for Jenny to respond, the modiste refilled her glass.

Because it was such a small amount and because it tasted so good, Jenny decided another drink of the devil's brew wouldn't hurt her. After all, she hadn't eaten since breakfast, and the cherry liquid seemed to fill the emptiness in her stomach. The last thing she wanted was for her stomach to roar like a lion's in the presence of the uppity Madame DeBeau.

Moments passed, and Jenny grew more relaxed. Because Madame had claimed an acquaintance with her uncle, Jenny's opinion of her changed considerably. She no longer feared the woman; in fact, after several tiny glasses of the red liquid, she found herself enjoying the French woman's company. Madame DeBeau was the first person she had ever known from Paris.

"We'll do hats next," Madame said. She stood and pulled her empty chair closer to the mirrored wall, insisting that Jenny sit there.

As Jenny made her way to the chair, the silvery walls swayed, reminding her of a house of mirrors she had visited once when a traveling carnival had passed through Shepherdstown. The room appeared distorted, much as her image did when she reached the chair and dropped upon its surface.

Once Jenny was seated, the shopkeeper disappeared. Alone, Jenny made faces at her wavy reflection.

In a few moments, Madame returned, carrying a stack of boxes. "A proper lady always wears a hat in public," she said.

"I have my own hat," Jenny informed her. "Or did you burn that, too?"

"Your hat, my young miss, was more appropriate for the fruit vendor on the corner."

Jenny giggled again. Madame DeBeau had no idea how apt her description of Jenny's hat had been. She had always worn it when she had taken apples to the market.

Madame put another glass of the liqueur in Jenny's hand, and she downed it automatically. She tried on hat after hat, and after another hour had passed, Jenny finally picked out several that both women considered acceptable.

"All those wonderful things of your uncle's—what are you going to do with them?" Madame asked her.

"I'm keeping them," Jenny responded, hiccuping. The spasm made her laugh and cover her mouth. "They belong to me. Just like Ninj-winji. Although I'm not too sure I want him."

Behind her, Madame DeBeau's image appeared as blurry as Jenny's in the mirror. "Ninj?" the woman asked.

If Jenny hadn't been seeing double, she would have sworn Madame's ears moved several inches higher on her head.

Oops! I'm not to speak of Ninj. "Winji is his name." Jenny covered her lips to stifle another chuckle, wondering how she was to get around this slip of her tongue. It came to her. "Here Winji-Winji," she called. "Oh, dear, it seems my Turk—ey has disappeared."

"You have a turkey?" The modiste appeared shocked.

Jenny jumped up from her chair and had to brace herself against the wall because the floor tilted. "I really must be going. Winji will be wondering where I am."

"This turkey, he is your pet?" Madame swallowed. "Really, dear girl, you must not tell anyone you have a pet turkey. Lisette," she called, her voice cracking, "do you have Mademoiselle's skirt and shirtwaist ready for her to wear? It must be almost closing time."

Lisette appeared from behind the petitioned wall carrying the finished and pressed garments Madame had requested.

"When Mademoiselle is dressed, call a hack to carry her home. I'm afraid she's had too much liqueur."

Lisette looked disapprovingly at her employer, or so Jenny imagined when she found the attendant's reflection in the mirror beside her.

"Part of your order will be ready within a few days," the modiste said. "We'll deliver your dresses as we finish them because the professor said you needed the clothes immediately."

Jenny nodded, then said, "Madame DeBeau, I would also like to purchase that turban I saw out front."

The entire time Jenny had been trying on hats, she had thought of nothing else. She would buy the turban for Ninj since his own was minus a jewel, and the one in the shop had both a jewel and a feather.

"You want that old rag?" Madame looked at Jenny questioningly, but signaled for Lisette to fetch the headpiece. "Please tell me you don't intend to wear it."

Lisette brought the turban from the front of the store and handed it to Jenny.

Ninj will love it, she thought, not answering Madame's question.

"I made it for a costume ball," the modiste said, "but the customer didn't pick it up." Madame looked speculative before she spoke. "You may have it, dear girl, as a token of my friendship."

Lisette rolled her eyes heavenward. "Come, *Mademoiselle* Blake," she said, "I'm sure you're as anxious to get home as I am." The dresser steered her away from Madame and proceeded to help her into the purple skirt and lacy waist.

"Lisette, don't forget to lock the doors when you leave," Madame DeBeau called from the front room where they could hear her bustling about.

"Oui," Lisette responded.

Soon the bell rang on the front door, and Jenny heard it close. It was quiet inside the tiny shop, so quiet that she could hear the clock ticking and the sound of her and Lisette's breathing.

"So thoughtless," Lisette mumbled beneath her breath. "Imagine, plying a *jeune fille* with spirits." She did up the row of buttons on the back of Jenny's waist. "If I didn't need this job so badly, I'd walk out now and not at all return."

Jenny grinned foolishly at their reflections.

Thoughtless? Her eyes locked on the turban now resting on the chair. Because Madame DeBeau had given Jenny the turban, her opinion of the modiste had changed. In her tipsy state, she believed the shopkeeper to be anything but thoughtless.

Miller paced in front of the windows of his apartment, stopping only long enough to peer down at the street.

Where in heaven's name is she?

Already the sun had dipped beyond the treetops and the row of buildings at the top of the street. Deep shadows competed for space against the sun's last light, shading the narrow street and alleyways. Jenny should have been back from the dressmaker hours ago, but there was no sign of her on the premises.

As he paced, Bengel followed him. Miller knew it was time for the cat's dinner, and that was why the animal was dogging his footsteps. Since Jenny had moved in, the animal bunked down with her and took his meals in her apartment. Miller realized he had nothing to feed the pest, then wondered how he could be hungry at a time like this anyway.

"Go on, get," he said. "Your mistress will be home to feed you soon."

A dark thought ruffled through his mind. *I hope she'll be home soon.*

Perhaps Miller had been mistaken to trust that Ninj character in the house with Jenny when he wasn't here. Perhaps Ninj was the fraud that Miller still suspected him of being. At this very moment, the giant could be holding Jenny captive somewhere, and there wasn't a darn thing he could do but wait . . . wait until he heard something from someone.

Miller didn't like the direction his thoughts had taken. He didn't want to consider that Jenny might be in danger. Since he had no way of calling the so-called genie, Miller didn't know what to believe. He only knew that Jenny wasn't home where she was supposed to be, and it was getting late. Because she was new to the city, Miller was worried.

He stalked toward the window and looked up and down the street again.

Where the devil could she be?

Nine

Before today, Jenny had never ridden in a vehicle for hire, and after this first experience, she doubted she would ever ride in another one.

Not wanting to appear uninformed as to how one should act in hired cabs, Jenny had said nothing when Lisette and the driver loaded her through the rear entrance of the horse-drawn two-wheeler. Facing forward, she surveyed the cab's interior and thought she was supposed to ride standing up since there didn't appear to be a seat in the small compartment. It was only after the door was closed and secured that the divided seat lowered, jabbing her shaky knees from behind.

Already unsteady on her feet because of the cherry liqueur that Madame DeBeau had plied her with all afternoon, thankfully she dropped down upon the seat the moment the driver urged the horse forward and into the line of traffic.

The seat was alive. Or so she believed when it slid backward, taking her with it. Determined not to be hurled from the back entrance onto the street, she braced her hands against the sedan's walls. No sooner had she gained her sea legs, or carriage legs, than the seat skidded forward again, propelling her toward the front panels of the small compartment.

"Merciful heavens," she prayed out loud, "let me survive this torment."

She belched, tasting the cherry liquid. The rocking motion of the coach coupled with the cab's almost airless space made her feel as though she might spill the contents of her stomach all over the front of her new outfit. The liquid sloshed in her stomach like water in a half-empty jug. She understood now why her Nana Blake had called liquor the devil's own brew; after the pleasure, it made you feel like hell.

The coach turned and started downhill. On the slope, the seat slid backward again, and Jenny hung on to the walls for dear life. Just when she thought the horrible ride would never end, the conveyance jerked to a stop. The carriage dipped sideways when the coachman stepped onto the street. He passed the window, heading for the rear door. She heard his knock.

"Ye be home, miss," he said. "Ye'll be needin' to stand so that I can open the door to let ye out."

"Stand?" Jenny croaked. She was uncertain that she would ever stand again, so she didn't move—until the driver's instructions finally penetrated her reasoning.

Out.

With a strength she didn't know she still possessed, Jenny pushed to her feet and turned toward the back of the carriage. The door opened, the seat divided, and Jenny tumbled out of the sedan, almost toppling the driver when she fell against him.

"Ye be all right, miss," he said, steadying them both.

"I'm sorry." She felt so ridiculous she giggled.

"Don't worry your head none, miss. I've been in me cups a few times meself."

In me cups. Although she wasn't, that was exactly how she felt. Like Alice on her wild ride in the giant, swirling teacup in Lewis Carroll's *Alice's Adventures in Wonderland*. The lingering absurdity of her own wild ride home would not soon be forgotten.

"I'll be leaving ye now, miss. Will ye be all right?" the driver asked.

"I'll be fine," she said. "How much do I owe ye—you?"

"Nothing. The lady paid your fare afore we left."

"Thank you very much, then."

She watched him mount his seat on the front of the cab and urge the horse forward.

Jenny sighed with relief. She had made it home in one piece and really was none the worse for the effort. Now that the contents of her stomach no longer shimmied, Jenny felt quite pleased with herself. The squeamishness she had suffered on the ride home had disappeared. It was replaced with a feeling of accomplishment.

Her visit to the dressmaker had been an adventure unlike any she had ever had. When she thought of everything that had occurred—from meeting the great Madame to the swilling of the devil's own brew—Jenny felt given over to light-headed silliness as she stepped up to the entrance of her uncle's shop.

It was then she realized that she had left her reticule—with her key inside—at Madame DeBeau's. How would she ever get in the house if Miller was out? She pounded on the door, hoping that he was home. Ninj was contained inside his bottle, so she couldn't expect help from that quarter. Thoughts of Ninj made her realize that she had also forgotten the turban she had meant to bring to him. Surely on the morrow when Madame DeBeau discovered the neglected items, she would send them to her.

For now, she had more important things to worry her. She knocked on the door again.

I suppose if my head wasn't attached, I would have left it behind at the dressmaker's as well, she thought. Not that she believed she would miss it all that much. She still felt light-headed from too much cherry liqueur.

Jenny looked around her; it would soon be dark. Already the gaslights glowed up and down the hill. She had been at Madame DeBeau's all afternoon. Miller would be pleased with the gowns that she had ordered, and so would Ninj. When she thought of the beautiful clothes, Lisette's "Ooo-la-la. Very nice" echoed inside Jenny's head. She sang them in time with her knock as she beat on the door again.

"Ooo-la-la, nice. Ooo-la-la, nice. Ooo—"

The door swung open. Miller stood just inside with a stern expression on his face.

She hiccuped.

His brows rose.

It seemed that she had displeased the professor again. Under the circumstances, Jenny did the next thing that popped into her mind. She finished the song's refrain.

"La-la, nice," she sang at the top of her lungs.

Miller jerked her inside and slammed the door.

"God Almighty, woman, have you no shame?"

They stood inside the small entryway, the gas fixture hissing like a snake above their heads.

Miller had watched from his upstairs window when the hack had pulled to a stop in front of the house. The longer he studied the scene unfolding in the street below, the more certain he was of Jenny's problem.

It was clear to him now that Antonini's niece had a fondness for liquor. He couldn't believe it when she had pitched forward from the rented cab, straight into the driver's arms, nearly tumbling them both to the ground.

At first he had thought the woman wasn't Jenny. Her tipsy condition, the clothes she wore, and the tiny stylish hat upon her upswept hair weren't characteristic of the Jenny that Miller knew. It wasn't until the streetlight flickered against the garish stone tied at her neck that he realized the identity of the fashionably clad lady. He'd been so happy she had returned home safely that he had rushed immediately down the stairs to greet her.

But when he had heard her singing, slurring her words, in time with the beat of her knock, Miller's worst fears resurfaced. Antonini's niece was a tippler. And if her actions were any indication, she'd been tipping bottles all afternoon.

"What tavern were you visiting?" he demanded.

"Tavern?" She looked at him in disbelief. "Surely you don't think I'm in my cups."

"What else am I to think? First, you're several hours late getting home from the dressmaker. Then, when you do arrive, you make a spectacle of yourself by stumbling into the arms of the hackney driver. To add insult to injury, you were beating on the door and singing so loud the whole neighborhood probably heard you."

Miller stepped away from the entrance and stalked deeper into the shop. He slammed to a stop, jerking around to face her. She was mere inches from his nose. As bad as her pesky cat, he thought.

"Do you expect me to believe that the actions I just witnessed are those of a teetotaler?"

Her blue-gray eyes sparkled with mischief. "I recall giving you *tea* yesterday, and you had no complaints then."

"We're not talking tea and cakes here." He leaned closer and sniffed. "Cherries?"

"Oooooooooo-la-la, yes!" she responded. "And so very nice."

She fluttered her eyes like a true courtesan, or so Miller thought. He had no idea how prostitutes kept by men of wealth and rank acted, but he decided Jenny's newly acquired skill would give them a run for their money.

He suddenly realized this Jenny didn't look like the Jenny he had come to know. In fact, she looked *ooo-la-la, nice*. Too nice, a little voice warned him.

While he'd been waiting for Jenny's return, he'd lit the gaslamps throughout the shop. But judging by the way she looked now in the golden circles of muted light, Miller wished he'd kept the rooms in total darkness.

Her new white lace blouse fit her as snugly as a glove. Beneath the weblike fabric, the satin-smooth skin of her bosom—more plump and rounded than it had been before her visit to the dressmaker—glimmered beneath the delicately woven fabric.

Miller wasn't certain if it was the suggestion of forbidden skin beneath the lace, or the way the webbing ensnared her lush breasts, showing off their perfection, that made him wish he were anywhere but here, confronting the intoxicating Miss Blake.

Intoxicated Miss Blake, his mind corrected.

She leaned toward him, her lips forming a sensual moue. "Do you like my new outfit?"

Miller fumbled with his perfectly knotted tie. "It's very nice," he said, "but how long have you had this habit?"

"Habit?"

She looked bewildered. Miller watched as she nonchalantly placed her hands on her waistline and glanced down at her lace-covered bosom. The same bosom that he'd been glancing at only moments before.

Her gaze switched back to him. "I just purchased it from Madame DeBeau, but had I known they dressed in such finery in a religious order, I might have joined up a long time ago."

"Religious order?"

Now Miller was confused. She stepped closer. He stepped back, believing if anyone were in need of an *order*, it was him. One of the monastic kind where the alluring Miss Blake wouldn't be allowed past the front door.

"Well," she said, "it is the most beautiful habit I've ever had." She giggled playfully and spun around in a circle, almost toppling a crystal lamp from a table.

First Miller reached to steady the lamp, then he reached for Jenny, who looked none too steady on her feet. His fingers encircled each lace-clad arm and held on.

"Oops, the room is spinning," she said, leaning into him.

"No," he corrected, "you are spinning."

"But you have me now." Jenny flung her arms over his shoulders, settling closer against him.

He had her all right. They were as close as two people could get with their clothes on. She pressed her full height against his comparable one. Their faces were even, her lips mere inches away from his mouth, her every breath full of the passionate red scent of cherries. Miller felt her breasts, full and rounded, against his silk vest, their tips as nubby as the pits of the missing cherries.

A rational man would have distanced himself from such temptation, but at the moment Miller wasn't rational. It had been a while since he'd held a woman, especially one who fit against him like the matching piece of a puzzle.

Their like heights allowed him to stare straight into Jenny's eyes. Smoldering in the smoky blue-gray depths was something more than the unusual color.

If she kept looking at him with that inviting gaze, with her full lips formed in a kissable pout, then he just might have to deliver what he imagined they both wanted.

"I-I think—"

He knew what she thought because he was thinking the same thing. What they both craved needed no words. Miller only knew if he didn't kiss her soon and relieve the longing, he would explode into a thousand pieces.

Jenny had triggered his long-buried desire. It surprised him that he responded to that desire without shame. After all, he was lusting after his old friend's niece, but now wasn't the time to examine conventional behavior.

Angling his head nearer, his lips made whisper-light contact with hers before he pulled back.

She sagged against him. Covering her mouth with her hand, she whispered, "I'm going to—"

"Don't," Miller cautioned, nudging her hand away.

And then he really kissed her. His mouth covered hers, and he probed the seal of her lips with his tongue. He felt her trembling against him.

With a small whimper, Jenny opened her mouth, allowing Miller to ravish a sweetness that tasted of cherries. Pulling her closer, he deepened his exploration, and felt a tightening in his lower regions. The magic of the kiss overrode everything until . . .

Jenny jerked away. "I'm going to be—sick!"

She emptied the contents of her stomach all over the front of Miller's white shirt, silk vest, and perfectly knotted tie.

Ten

"Ninj, I was mortified," Jenny explained. She covered her face with her hands and peeked through her splayed fingers. Her head throbbed as though someone were beating drumsticks against her skull.

They were in the shop. It was the morning after the "cherry incident." That was how she would always think of the disaster. Even now the memory made her feel sick to her stomach, but she wasn't sure if the queasiness was caused by the liquor still in her system or her embarrassment from having thrown up all over Miller Holbrook. Whatever the reason, there was one thing she was certain of. She wouldn't touch another cherry, liquid or otherwise, for the rest of her life.

Jenny sat behind her uncle's desk, leaning forward over its top, while Ninj lay sprawled on a pile of tapestry pillows. Earlier he had gathered them from around the shop, scattering them across the Persian carpet before lounging upon the cushioned crest. To Jenny he looked like an exotic prince reclining in a lazy, relaxed way. He was nibbling at his favorite diet of grapes, flat bread, and goat cheese that she had purchased for him at the corner market. His black eyes sparkled as he listened to her recount the events of the night before.

"Whiskey, pshaw," he said, popping a grape into his mouth and chewing with enthusiasm. "Not only does it sicken the belly, but it also befuddles and spoils the brain.''

"Well, it certainly befuddled mine," Jenny attested. She belched and belatedly covered her mouth with her hand. The eruption made her laugh and made her head ache more. "But my brain wasn't nearly as spoiled as the professor's clothing. It will be awhile before he wears those duds again, if ever."

"Ahh, but Mistress Jee-nih," he said, his dark brows raised, "you two must have been very close for him to receive the contents of your stomach."

"Close?"

Jenny had been leaning forward to afford her a better look at Ninj, but his statement made her sit back in her chair so she wouldn't have to meet his gaze. The chair tilted backward. Its high-pitched squeak sounded throughout the room, sending another stab of pain into Jenny's head.

We were *close. Too close.* Jenny didn't want to think of what had transpired between her and Miller before the "incident." Even now when she thought about it, she wasn't certain if it had really happened or if, in her slightly drunken state, she had conjured up the whole unpleasant event.

Unpleasant?

The embrace and kiss had been anything but unpleasant. In truth, it had been, "Ooo-la-la nice."

Ninj sat up. " Ooo-la-la nice?" His height allowed him to remain seated on the floor like a Buddha and still make eye contact with her above the desk. "What is this ooo-la-la nice?"

Jenny groped for an answer, wishing she hadn't spoken her thoughts aloud. After a moment, she said, "It is a French expression that I learned from the dressmaker."

The last thing Jenny wanted was for Ninj to learn about her and Miller's embrace.

"And what does this expression mean?"

His question filled her head with the sensations

evoked by their kiss. "It means . . ." She sighed. "It means that something is wonderful."

"Ahh, I see, Mistress Jee-nih!" A pleased expression lit up his face. "Maybe this cherry whiskey is not so bad as I first thought." He grinned at her.

Jenny jumped up. "It was horrible, and I won't touch the devil's brew again."

Her head felt as though it might explode as she walked around the desk and perused the books in the bookcase. At that moment she felt almost sure that Ninj did have the power to read minds. Her mind, at least.

She pressed her lips together in consternation. "Ninj, how will I ever face him? Miller was as embarrassed as I was. I only hope my blunder didn't make him change his mind about helping us with your problem."

She recalled the stricken look on Miller's face as the pinkish-red liquid spurted out of her mouth, splattering across his silk vest. If she'd had the good sense the Lord gave a dog, she would have turned away and lost the contents of her stomach on the floor, but no, she had fallen against him and quickly released the red tide. When it was over, he had held her and patted her back, and she like a ninny had planted her cheek in the pink-red circle on his chest and held on.

When they both had regained their wits, Miller had guided her to a chair, then quickly ran upstairs for water and a dampened cloth. He'd had the foresight to grab a clean shirt from his apartment before returning. Even that thought made her squirm with embarrassment. While her face should have been buried in the cool, wet rag, instead she had peeked at him from behind the wet cloth as he changed. Not only had the devil's brew almost killed her, but it had also turned her into a brazen hussy who spied on men while they changed their clothes.

"Lordy, Lordy, what am I to do?" she asked the row of books.

"Do?" Ninj asked. He had left his place on the floor and now stood behind her.

"Yes, do." She turned toward him. "How will I ever face Miller Holbrook again? What he must think of me."

"It has been my experience in dealing with enamored females to advise them to use their womanly wiles."

"Enamored! I assure you, I am *not* enamored. I'm embarrassed because I was vulgarly ill all over the front of my new friend's shirt. That, Ninj, is why I feel so awful."

"Then you must apologize," he said.

He crossed his big arms against his chest and spread his legs apart. The stance made him look more like a palace guard than a genie, or so Jenny imagined.

"Then, Mistress Jee-nih, you must forget it happened. The incident will be like the shifting sands of the desert, gone in an eye blink."

"Easy for you to say."

A loud knock sounded on the front door.

"Now who could that be?" Jenny grumbled. "Can't people read? The sign in the window says we don't open until eleven."

She looked at the clock, whose hands rested on half-past ten, then toward the front of the shop, hoping if she didn't answer the summons, whoever was there would go away. She and Ninj stood stock-still, fearing any movement would alert the party on the other side of the door to their presence.

But rather than leave, the caller moved to the window and, cupping a hand against the glass, peered inside the shop.

"Madame DeBeau," Jenny whispered. "Now what am I going to do?" Turning on Ninj, she scolded, "You aren't supposed to be here." She looked at him hopefully. "Couldn't you make us both disappear?"

"I could try," he offered, looking optimistic.

But then Jenny recalled how Ninj's tricks had sometimes gone awry. She would have a hard time explaining the appearance of an elephant in her shop. More to her-

self than to Ninj, she said, ''It might be safer facing
Madame.''

Ninj's brows puckered, and he looked as though he
might weep.

''Don't you dare cry,'' Jenny warned. ''I was only
teasing.''

The modiste waved at them through the window.

''Shucks! She's seen us.''

Madame DeBeau held up the reticule along with the
turban and called out, ''*Ma petite*, I brought your
things!''

''Now I'll have to answer the door.'' She looked from
the window to Ninj, still unsure what to do about him.

Although Miller had instructed them both that Ninj
was to be as absent as possible, Jenny wasn't certain
how well Ninj had taken to Miller's advice. It would be
wiser, she decided, to banish the genie to his bottle, especially since Ninj was so touchy about his background
and his profession. It would be easier to lie to Madame
DeBeau.

Again it was as though he had read her thoughts.
''Don't banish me, mistress,'' Ninj pleaded. ''I want to
meet this cherry hawker and give her a piece of my
mind.''

His remark helped her make the decision. ''Sorry,''
Jenny said, rubbing the stone at her neck. Ninj disappeared.

Jenny remembered the modiste had used those strange
spectacles at the shop yesterday; it was possible she
hadn't seen Ninj.

''I'm coming,'' Jenny called. Making her way to the
front door, she opened it. ''Good morning, Madame
DeBeau. How kind of you to bring my things.''

Jenny had not planned to ask the shopkeeper in, but
the nefarious woman pushed past her, nearly trampling
her in her eagerness to get inside.

''You are open,'' the woman stated. She looked toward the bookcases where Jenny and Ninj had been
standing.

Shucks! She had *seen them.* Jenny wondered how much of a lie she would have to tell.

"No, ma'am. I don't open until eleven," she said. "I'm just tidying up before the day begins."

"But, dear girl, I know I saw you in conversation with a very tall man." Madame pointed to the bookcase. "He was standing right there."

Not waiting for a response, Madame DeBeau walked to the alcove where Jenny's uncle's desk sat. Craning her neck, she searched every visible nook and cranny for Jenny's customer. Earlier, Jenny had left the back door open to allow fresh air inside. The woman even had the audacity to walk to the door and look out before she returned to where Jenny stood in the middle of the room.

There was a look of ingrained snobbery on Madame's face when she spoke. "This man, he was dressed rather oddly," she said. "In the style of the Eastern pajamas that—"

"You must be mistaken—"

At that precise moment, Madame's feet contacted the spread of pillows on the floor, and she would have tripped if Jenny hadn't rushed to assist her. The modiste swayed like an ungainly pine in the wind before regaining her balance.

Looking down her long nose and shrugging off Jenny's assistance, she chastised, "What are you doing with those pillows strewn about the middle of the floor? And food?" Her balance regained, she patted the knot of hair at the back of her head. "A body could break her neck. Do you always make a habit of eating on the floor?" She stared at Ninj's abandoned tray of food.

"I'm sorry, I wasn't expecting anyone. I was checking the inventory and finishing my breakfast at the same time. It was easier to—"

"Inventory?" Madame DeBeau was all ears. "As I said yesterday, your uncle has so many beautiful treasures. Some of them priceless, *n'est-ce pas?*"

"To me, anyway," Jenny responded.

Now that she was no longer fuzzy-headed from Madame DeBeau's liqueur, her earlier distrust of the woman had returned.

Jenny tried her best to recall the conversation that had taken place between them yesterday. She knew that Madame had claimed an acquaintance with her uncle, but other than that, most of what they had talked about remained a blur in Jenny's mind. But today it was clear that Madame was very interested in her uncle's collectibles. So interested that she walked around the room, inventorying the contents with both her eyes and her fingertips.

After a thorough inspection of the shop, she stopped and faced Jenny, who had been following closely in her footsteps. "I almost forgot my reason for coming." She handed Jenny's reticule and the turban to her. "You left these yesterday."

Their gazes met above the items. *"Ma petite,"* Madame said, bending toward Jenny and pinching her cheek. "She had too much liqueur, *non*?"

With anyone else, Jenny might have tolerated the action as being sincere concern for her. But in Jenny's opinion, Madame was mocking her rather than sympathizing.

So instead of feigning embarrassment and apologizing for her stupid behavior, Jenny replied, "No. You must be mistaken. I was fine. Really. Only tired. I rushed out without my things because the hour was so late and the hack was waiting."

Madame DeBeau looked taken aback by her response, but only for a moment. Moving away from Jenny, she advanced to the bookshelf, where a velvet-lined tray sat beside Ninj's bottle. A tiny sign with the word *amulets* was glued to the tray's front. With the long fingernail of her index finger, Madame raked through the contents.

"Silly, that these should be all the rage," she said more to herself than to Jenny. "Charms to ward off evil." She stopped her raking to look at the stone around Jenny's neck. "Is that why you refuse to take off that ridiculous stone? Is it your juju, your fetish?''

''It is neither juju nor fetish. Only a gift from a man who loved me very much.''

Madame studied her for a long moment then turned her attention back to the tray and its contents. ''And your Winji,'' she asked, ''how is he today?''

Winji? Who in the world was Winji? Again Jenny tried to recall her conversation with Madame yesterday.

The woman pinned her with her cold eyes. ''Your turkey, dear girl, your pet? You were worried that you needed to get home to look after him.''

The memory hit her like a sledgehammer. She had almost told her about Ninj. ''Oh, my turkey, Winji. You mean him?'' Jenny laughed. ''After sleeping on it, I decided to take your advice. A proper lady wouldn't keep a pet turkey in the city. So early this morning I took him to the butcher.''

''Your pet? You're going to eat it?''

''Most definitely,'' Jenny responded, smiling. ''Have you ever heard of raising a turkey for anything else?''

''But I thought . . . you said. . . . oh, it doesn't matter what I thought. I really must be going.''

It did Jenny's heart good to see Madame disconcerted. ''I'll show you—''

''No need,'' her visitor boasted. ''I know the way.''

Like a whirlwind she swirled around, almost upsetting Ninj's bottle with her rotating movement. She barely caught the container before shoving it into Jenny's hands. Then the woman rushed to the door, slamming it so forcefully that the plate-glass window shook.

Jenny sighed. ''Thank goodness she's gone.'' If she never crossed Madame DeBeau's path again, it wouldn't be too soon.

She moved back to the tray of amulets, which was now in a jumble. Carrying the tray to a table, Jenny sat down and began straightening the pieces, putting them back in some semblance of their original order. She recognized the cowrie shells and what looked like shark's teeth. Jenny could only guess what the other things in the collection were: beads with stylistic circles and dots that made them look like eyes, horn-shaped twisted coral, and open-palmed hands fashioned from metal.

While she worked, Madame's words surfaced in her mind. *Charms to ward off evil.* Madame implied that was why Jenny wore the stone around her neck. Had the modiste been warning Jenny that she might be in danger?

"Don't be ridiculous," Jenny scolded herself, dismissing the idea as ludicrous.

Just because she didn't like the woman didn't mean Madame DeBeau was a bearer of evil. Jenny rolled a shark's tooth to one corner of the tray, placing it with other ones. The only danger she was in was a result of her own foolishness. First she'd allowed that offensive woman to get her drunk, and second she'd allowed herself to be kissed by a man.

Before she came to Georgetown, she had sampled neither whiskey nor a man's kiss. Maybe living on a farm in the country didn't pose as much temptation as living in the city.

No, Jenny decided, a girl could go astray no matter where she lived. In the future, she would just have to be more careful.

Having finished straightening the amulets, she stood and carried the tray back to the bookshelf. Once there, her gaze locked on the spine of one of her Uncle Antonini's books. It was titled *The Essential Handbook of Victorian Etiquette* and was written by Professor Thomas E. Hill.

Jenny slid the book from among the others. As she leafed through the pages, she discovered it contained information on the rules of conduct that governed good society. Jenny didn't know if she qualified as a member of good society, but regardless, she needed all the help she could get when it came to proper behavior, if her actions of late were any indication.

Perhaps the book and her new wardrobe would help her to present herself as a lady who could attract a real

gentleman, the one who could be her pretend love. He
would be the man who would provide her with the
means to help further Ninj's retirement. More importantly, after all was said and done, her new self would
be better prepared to get on with her life as a shopkeeper.

It was eleven o'clock, and Jenny walked to the front
window and turned the *Open* sign outward. She was of-
ficially ready to transact business, although business
hadn't been exactly booming since she'd reopened. Most
of her patrons had been her neighbors who lived up and
down the street. Some of them shop owners themselves,
they had dropped in to welcome her to the neighborhood. The largest number of shops in the immediate
Georgetown area were located on M Street and Wisconsin Avenue and were the ones she had passed yesterday
on her way to Madame DeBeau's.

Jenny made her way to the pillows scattered across
the floor. She picked up Ninj's tray of food and set it
on her desk. Then she returned the pillows to their
proper places and wondered if she had convinced Madame that the man she thought she saw through the window did not exist. Not that Jenny really cared if the
woman believed her. She cared more that she followed
Miller's suggestion to keep Ninj as scarce as possible.

Moving to the desk, she opened one of the many recordbooks stacked there. After her encounter with Officer
Mosey and the thimble, she had made it a point to find
her uncle's ledgers and familiarize herself with the
shop's inventory.

Her uncle's inventory was vast. Matching everything
in the ledgers with the actual merchandise had proved
to be a huge task, but in the short span of time since her
arrival, Jenny was beginning to feel more confident in
her new position as shop owner.

The bell on the front door tinkled as someone stepped
inside and closed the door. Jenny left her desk and
moved toward the front of the shop. A young woman
and gentleman stood in the entrance, and the woman

glanced nervously around the interior. There was something familiar about the lady, but Jenny couldn't put her finger on the source of their acquaintance until the woman spoke.

"Mademoiselle."

"Lisette?" Jenny asked, surprised. The young dresser from Madame DeBeau's shop looked entirely different without her salmon-colored hair and coral-colored uniform. "I didn't recognize—"

"Me without my horrible wig and uniform. It is fine that you don't. I hope no one believes me to be the person I appear to be in Madame's shop. A fake person, *non*?"

"Lisette is anything but fake," the gentleman with her offered. "My Lisette is the most real and sincere person I know."

"Your Lisette?" Jenny asked.

There was evidence of a strong affection between her two visitors, and Jenny didn't have long to wait before she found out why.

"This is my fiancé, Charles Taylor," Lisette announced. "He insisted on joining me today to check on you."

"She worried about you all night," Charles said. "She was angry because that overbearing woman fed you too much alcohol."

"I thought later that I should have ridden home with you in the hack, but the driver assured me he would deliver you together in one piece."

"And he did," Jenny responded.

Although she appreciated Lisette's concern for her welfare, Jenny decided against telling her the details of what had happened after her delivery. It was bad enough that she had lost the contents of her stomach on Miller Holbrook's person, but to share that experience with anyone other than Ninj would only add to her humiliation.

"I'm sorry you worried," she said, "but I appreciate that you did."

"It's like I said earlier," Charles added. "Lisette is the kindest person in the world."

Now that Lisette's concerns were voiced, Charles left her side and wandered deeper inside the shop. "Wow! You certainly have some fascinating things in here." He eyed the elephant's-foot table in the front window. "Tell me that's not what I think it is."

"It's what you think it is," Jenny said. "I don't know anything about where it came from since I've only recently inherited my uncle's shop, but I can say having only a foot of the beast under one's roof is better than the whole elephant."

Charles laughed good-naturedly. "I get your message." He walked toward the cabinet that held an assemblage of weaponry, and Jenny turned to look at Lisette.

Yesterday in the shop, Jenny had thought the petite dresser was pretty, but today, with her golden blond hair visible beneath her smart hat, the French girl could be called a beauty. It was evident that Charles thought so because his eyes glowed with pride every time he looked at his fiancée.

"I was so afraid that Madame would see me," Lisette said, "that we crossed the street and waited until she exited your shop and was well up the street."

"Madame DeBeau returned my reticule and the turban I left behind yesterday. But I don't understand—why would you care if she saw you?"

"Maybe I express myself wrong—"

"What Lisette meant to say," Charles explained, "was that she didn't wish to see Madame. Today is Lisette's day off, and she values her time away from the woman."

"Well, I can certainly understand that," Jenny said, "but, Lisette, why do you continue to work for her if you dislike her so much?"

"Madame pays me well, and I need the experience of working with American ladies. After Charles and I are married, I want to open my own dressmaker's shop."

"You should," Jenny replied. "From what I saw yesterday, you are the one who does all the work."

"*Oui*. It is not so bad because I learn much, but I didn't approve of her giving a *jeune fille* all that liquor."

"This *filly* should not have allowed herself to be plied with all that liquor. I'm as much to blame as she is."

"*Non, mademoiselle*. Madame was at fault. Besides, you are the first one I see her give so much liqueur to. Usually it is one tiny glass per customer. Madame is stingy."

"Lisette, come quickly and look at this." Charles was examining the weaponry in the case and motioned for them both to come over. He pointed to a small-scale model of a warship that sported one hundred guns. "It is the French three-decker warship *Le Lion*." Charles leaned so close to the glass, his warm breath fogged a circle on its surface. "Isn't it something?" he asked.

"Something I do not find so fascinating." Lisette glanced at the cabinet filled with gun flasks, holsters, pistols, and a collection of ancient-looking swords. After a moment, she said, "Charles is interested in arms."

"Only *your* arms, my sweet," he teased. Lisette blushed but allowed him to lace his fingers with hers and lead her to the jewelry case. "While we're here, I want to purchase a gift for my favorite lady."

"*Non*. You must save your money, Charles."

"I am saving my money. But I planned to purchase an engagement gift for you. What better place than to buy it here from your new friend?"

"But, *mon cher* . . ."

"No buts. I've money to buy you whatever your heart desires."

Lisette rolled her eyes heavenward, but then dropped her gaze back to the case. "There," she said, pointing, "that's what you can buy me."

Both Jenny and Charles looked at the object of Lisette's desire.

"A thimble?" Charles asked, disappointed. "That is too practical for an engagement gift."

Jenny recognized the thimble as the one that Officer Mosey had wanted for his wife until he had discovered its price. But seeing the French girl's fascination with the thimble, Jenny decide to practice her salesmanship.

"A fine thimble it is," Jenny told the twosome. She opened the case, lifted the thimble, and placed it in Lisette's palm. "It is made of porcelain," Jenny explained, "with tiny blue flowers painted on its surface."

Lisette slipped the thimble onto her fingertip. "Ooo-la-la, nice. And, Charles, it fits perfectly. See?" She held out her hand to admire it. "Don't you think it is a wonderful gift for a future modiste—and a symbol of our lives being sewn together forever?"

Once Lisette said this, Jenny knew she had a sale.

"How much?" he asked.

"Ten dollars," Jenny told him.

"Non," Lisette exclaimed. "One thimble should not cost so much." She slipped it from her fingertip and handed it back to Jenny.

"We'll take it," Charles insisted. "It is a perfect engagement gift for my future wife."

"Non, mon cher."

"Yes, *ma cherie*." Charles pulled a ten-dollar bill from his pocket and slapped it down on the counter.

Jenny picked up the thimble. "I'll put it in a box for you."

Earlier she had found an assortment of different sized boxes beneath the counter. Going to retrieve one, she returned a few moments later with the smallest container she could find. It was the ideal size for the thimble; she placed it inside and handed the box to Charles, who in turn handed it to Lisette.

The purchase made, they were ready to take their leave. Jenny walked with the couple to the door and stopped when Lisette turned to face her.

"I hope we can be friends," she said. "I know how lonely it can be in a strange place."

"I can't think of anything I would like better," Jenny

responded. They said their good-byes, and she stepped back inside the shop.

Her first sale, she thought as she walked back to retrieve the ten dollars Charles had left on the counter. Already she was on her way to becoming a successful shopkeeper, and now with the prospect of a new friendship beaming brightly on the horizon, Jenny felt very pleased with the way the morning had gone.

Since it was nearing the end of the term, Miller had much to occupy his time; final exams to prepare, papers to grade, student averages to compile. School would break for the summer months in two weeks, and then the students would leave, not returning to campus until the fall term began.

Miller always looked forward to the summer break. It was his time to regroup from teaching, catch up on his reading, and maybe do a little traveling. Although endings brought with them a feeling of nostalgia, Miller knew it was the way of things.

Friendships that were formed throughout the school year would be set aside until classes reconvened. But there would be those who did not pass the first round and so not be back for the second. It bothered him when students didn't make their grades. He felt it was his failing as much as theirs. After all, he was a teacher, and it was his responsibility to teach.

His last class of the day had ended several hours earlier, and he believed his chalk talk had gone very well. His first-year Algebra students appeared to have grasped the formulas they had reviewed. Everything would have been perfect if he hadn't had last night's episode with Jenny on his conscience.

Alone in the classroom, he looked beyond the windows and watched the afternoon shadows deepen. The few trees that grew on campus had changed from emerald green to hunter in the diffused light. Miller took a deep breath. A warm spring breeze drifted gently through the open windows, carrying the fragrance of freshly mowed lawns mingled with the familiar scents of chalk dust, erasers, and leather-bound books. This was his territory, and he was the crusty old lion that ruled it.

Miller knew he should have gone home hours ago. Everyone else had left the building. But the idea of facing Jenny after yesterday's faux pas kept him planted in his chair while inventing excuses not to go home.

How had he forgotten his place and hers? He, as Antonini's friend, was supposed to be looking after the man's niece, not ravishing her. Even when she had tried to warn him that she was about to be ill, he had not listened. He had been so carried away with the moment, their embrace, the kiss, that he had failed to see the forest for the trees. Miller had thought her uttered protests were brought on by a passion that matched his own. A rational man would have listened and heeded, but last night he had been anything but rational.

"Fool!" He rested his head in palms that still smelled of chalk dust. *You knew her condition,* a voice inside his head reminded him. *The girl was in her cups, and you took advantage of her. Now it is up to you to repair the damage caused by your lust.*

But how?

Today in the revealing light of day, Miller could see that everything had been an assumption on his part. He had surmised that she had been inebriated and he had also surmised that she was enjoying their romantic interlude as much as he was. His first theory had been true, but his second one had not. Now that he was again lucid, he wondered if Jenny's sickness had been brought on by drink or by his fumbling attempts at wooing her.

If she did have a drinking problem, he would have to deal with it. The other, his taking advantage of her, would have to be dealt with, too. He would have to apologize. And because he lacked experience in dealing with females and the delicate art of lovemaking, Miller wasn't sure if an apology would be enough.

"Intense, excessive, unrestrained sexual desire," he said aloud. "To put it simply, lust."

He had been carried away by the animal desires that were natural for the male of the species. Especially when the male had gone for years without a mate. His choice, of course. He only knew that last night Jenny had brought on a powerful itch that needed a good scratching.

Rather than dwelling on that itch, Miller scratched his head. He eyed the pile of mail that he had avoided for weeks. The stack of letters was spilling over the edges of the wooden tray. His glance fell on one letter he had opened, read, and stuffed back into the pile. His old school chum was still trying to get him to join the staff at the College of William and Mary, but Miller liked teaching at Georgetown College and saw no need to make a change.

Picking up several envelopes and shuffling through them, he reflected why a woman's allure wasn't as easily understood as the study of mathematics. The study of numbers, their forms, arrangements, and sets, their relationships and properties, were easy to comprehend.

As Miller stewed over this last thought, he compared a woman's characteristics to those of numbers. They both had structure and contours. He recalled Jenny's form without any effort. She had felt fine nestled against him. Just remembering made the room grow warmer. He fanned his face with an envelope and continued his rumination. Most women preferred being placed in an arrangement, especially with a man. But not his Jenny. She claimed she was against any such grouping.

Women enjoyed sets, of being in a position or state of two referred to as relationships. Then again, this natural and logical association didn't interest Jenny. And like most women, she had the properties and attributes that could force a man to reach some kind of conclusion. But Miller was nowhere near resolving his attraction to Jenny, and at the moment, she seemed like an unsolvable equation.

As he thumbed through his mail, his focus was drawn to a linen envelope. It stood out from the others because of the fine texture of the paper. His name was written across the envelope's front in a flowing script. Without opening it, Miller knew what was inside. An invitation to the annual tea dance that was given by the dean and his wife every year at this time.

Miller hated these mandatory social functions, but his profession demanded he attend. In the past he had put in his expected appearance then left as soon as it was proper. He had on no occasion escorted a woman to these affairs because there had never been anyone with whom he would have enjoyed spending the whole evening. It was his obligation to attend, and he would, but already he was dreading the tedious evening.

Jenny. Maybe an opportunity had arrived with this invitation. Should he invite her to go with him? As he thought of the possibilities her attending such a function might provide, Miller saw his problems of late resolving. What better place than a college function for Jenny to meet a man of whom her uncle would have approved? At the same time, her introduction to a real gentleman would fit into their plans of finding her a perfect love. The same love that she needed to help Ninj with his plight. Although Jenny claimed she wouldn't give her heart to any man, maybe with a push in the right direction she would really meet that special someone, a love to last a lifetime.

The prospect was brilliant. Not only would Miller be rid of the worrisome Ninj once he retired to genie paradise, but also Miller would have been instrumental in helping Jenny settle in. Once Jenny fell in love, Miller could return to living his quiet, solitary life.

"It must be magic," he said. Feeling exuberant, he kissed the dean's invitation. "A brilliant idea, old fellow."

Miller felt so pleased with himself, he suddenly couldn't wait to get home to ask Jenny to the dance.

Scooping up papers, mail, and the invitation, he

placed them in his satchel. As he rushed out the door, he hummed a tune he had once danced to in his youth, Stephen Foster's "Jeanie With the Light Brown Hair." The almost-forgotten words resurfaced in his mind, and since he was alone on the campus, he sang the words aloud. His way.

"I dream of Jenny with the dark brown hair. . . ."

Eleven

The downstairs hall was dark when Miller entered, closing the door behind him. The hour was a little past seven, but none of the lamps in the shop had been turned on. Only the fixture on the second landing burned a yellow ring of brightness, overlapping the top stair and looking like a fallen sunbeam against the shadowed wood.

Miller paused, listening. Had Jenny gone out? Only the creaking timbers of the old house could be heard above the silence. Then he heard muted conversation and recognized Jenny's voice. She was talking with Ninj. Her soft feminine laughter, mingling with Ninj's deeper male joviality, drifted down from the second floor. As Miller stood at the bottom of the stairs eavesdropping, he felt like an interloper. Should he interrupt them to tell her his good idea or bypass them on the way to his apartment?

The stairs creaked as he moved upward. Miller still didn't trust Ninj. Genies and magic were what fairy tales were made of, stories that were designed to mislead. Although he still worried that Ninj wasn't a true genie, what other explanation was there for the giant man's comings and goings, disappearances into the tiny bottle he claimed to be his home, and lastly, the stone around Jenny's neck that Miller had tried to remove but couldn't? The occurrences he had witnessed with his own eyes were not in the realm of science, and therefore he couldn't find an explanation for them.

Just before he reached the top of the landing, he heard Jenny squeal. His heartbeat kicked into high gear. Was the man forcing himself upon her? Miller was primed to rush to the door and tear it down, but realized such an action wasn't necessary. The apartment door stood open, and from his vantage point on the stairs he could see through the living room into the bedroom, where the twosome sat on the bed.

Bedroom. Bed? A single woman of Jenny's delicate age shouldn't be entertaining a man in her boudoir, magic or otherwise. Heaven forbid that the neighbors should learn about this latest discretion. Didn't the girl have a clue about proper behavior for a young lady? It appeared that she not only liked her whiskey, but her actions suggested that she could be of easy virtue as well.

Even as the thought occurred to him, Miller denied it. Although Jenny had been a warm and cuddly partner in the kiss they had shared last night, she hadn't been the instigator. He had. Besides, he reasoned, hadn't he learned anything from his mistakes of the night before? He had believed the worst before he knew the facts. Just this afternoon he had berated himself for his misguided assumptions. Miller was finished jumping to conclusions about Jenny Blake. After all, he hardly knew the woman.

Rather than bursting into the room, he sidled up to the entrance. If Jenny or Ninj looked his way they would see him, but if they didn't, he could watch them while deciding if his intervention was needed. Bengel lounged on the bed with the twosome, his odd-eye stare settling on Miller briefly before he buried his pink-tipped nose in the ring of his body and closed his eyes.

Jenny sat leaning against the massive headboard. Her legs were crossed at the ankles, and she held a book upon her lap. To make matters worse, she was barefoot. Again he wondered if the girl knew no shame.

Ninj lounged beside her as attentive as an old and trusted dog. He had foregone his old turban for a new one that was too small for his giant-sized head, but it had a jewel in its center and a spiny feather sticking out of its crown.

Miller quickly looked at Jenny's throat, hoping the garish jewel would be absent. The stone still hung on the black shoestring, but its appearance was softened by an intertwined satin ribbon.

Gone was the lace waist and purple skirt of the night before. Today she wore a black skirt and a white blouse with rows of ruffles across the front. Identical ruffles spilled over the shoulders of the tight-fitting sleeves. She had tied her hair back at the nape, fastening it with a huge black bow. As she sat relaxed upon the bed, Jenny looked very much the part of a schoolgirl.

Jenny read aloud from the book on her lap. " 'The inferior is to be introduced to the superior; the younger to the older; the gentleman to the lady.' "

Examining his nails, Ninj listened. "I think I understand. Since I am the superior one, it is proper to give my name first. 'Ninj, I would like you to meet Dr. Holbrook.' "

"But you are the slave," Jenny reminded. "Doesn't that make you inferior?"

"Only to you, Mistress Jee-nih. I am your slave, you are my master—mistress."

"But this book also says 'Titled people should be addressed by their titles,' and isn't a titled person superior to an untitled one?"

Ninj thought about this before answering. "Again, I think I understand. If I were to introduce you to my Sultana, I would say her name before yours."

Jenny rolled her eyes heavenward. "In that case, if we used your earlier example, I would say, 'Dr. Holbrook, I would like you to meet Ninj.' "

"No, no, no," Ninj insisted indignantly. "You would say, 'Great Jinni Ninj, I would like you to meet Dr. Holbrook.' "

Miller found their conversation amusing, and he smiled.

It appeared that Jenny had found a book on etiquette. She could use a few lessons on how a person conducted herself in polite society, although Miller admitted Jenny wasn't as ignorant about such things as he had first believed. Her behavior was just unconventional, but if she agreed to accompany him to the dean's tea dance, there were a few things she needed to know. The book would make his teaching easier.

Jenny continued to read. " 'To shake hands when introduced is optional; between gentlemen it is common, and oftentimes between an elderly and a young person. It is not common between an unmarried lady and a gentleman, a slight bow between them when introduced being all that etiquette requires.' "

Jenny slapped her hand against her mouth. "I blundered," she said.

"What is this 'blundered'?" Ninj asked.

"When I met Mr. Axle the other day, I gave him my hand."

Miller stepped closer to the door.

Ninj's face held an expression of horror. He reached across the bed and grabbed Jenny's arm.

She shook off his grasp. "What are you doing?" she asked.

"You said you gave Mr. Axle your hand. I am checking to make sure you still have it."

"Oh, Ninj," she said, laughing. "That is only an expression. Surely you don't think I would cut off my hand and give it to him."

"Severing human parts is not unusual in my country."

"Well, it is very rare in mine," she responded. "Come on, don't be such a ninny. Help me to practice how a lady acts when she meets a man. The sooner I learn the art of being a true lady, the sooner I can meet my love that will last a lifetime, and the sooner you can retire."

Her statement pleased Ninj, and he grinned from ear to ear.

In spite of Miller's distrust of the genie, he couldn't help but be amused by Ninj's belief that Jenny had cut off her hand for Axle. The giant was right about human parts being severed in his part of the world. Even in America, Indians gouged out their eyes or cut off fingers after the death of a loved one. Miller could only imagine what it would have been like to have lived during the reign of the Ottoman Turks. People were barbarians, especially during the period that Ninj claimed to come from.

He continued to watch the twosome. Jenny jumped to her feet in the middle of the mattress. Ninj remained seated in his cross-legged pose, but he leaned against the headboard. Bengel had abandoned the bed for a more sturdy perch. He sat upon a table, his cat expression one of boredom.

Jenny began reading again while balancing precariously on the wobbly bedspring that supported the mattress.

Miller recalled two years earlier when the new bedspring had hit the market. Antonini had rushed out immediately and purchased one to replace his roped frame. He claimed it was as comfortable as sleeping on a cloud. But Jenny looked anything but comfortable. In fact, she looked as though she might become airborne at any moment the way the mattress quaked beneath her feet.

" 'Ladies being introduced,' " Jenny read, " 'should never bow hastily, but with slow and measured dignity.' " She looked at Ninj over the edge of the book. "We must practice," she said, motioning for him to stand. When he didn't move, she begged, "Please, Ninj, I need your help."

He eyed the mattress skeptically. "Mistress Jee-nih, do you think standing on this pillow that wiggles is a good idea?"

"Don't be silly," she said, "of course it is."

Reluctantly he got to his feet, balancing himself by hanging onto the headboard.

"Now, you be the gentleman, and I'll be the lady. Bow," she ordered. "You do know how?"

"Of course Ninj knows how to bow."

He let go of the headboard and bent forward from the waist. But only for a second. The bending action threw him off balance. To keep himself upright, Ninj marked time with his feet. For Jenny to remain standing, she also began to march. The action made them look as though they were hotfooting it over a bed of coals.

But soon the marching was replaced by bouncing. The higher they jumped, the louder they giggled. Their fun continued for several more moments before Jenny collapsed in a heap at the foot of the bed. Ninj bounced a few more times before he collapsed opposite her.

Gulping air, Ninj said, "This wiggling pillow is like a magic carpet."

"You mean a carpet that flies through the air?"

"But of course that is what Ninj means." He sat up, looking smug. "In my country everyone has a magic carpet."

Jenny pinned him with a disbelieving look.

"Well," he amended, "not everyone. But if Mistress Jee-nih wants one, I will get it for her."

"Thank you very much, but a magic carpet is the last thing I need." She patted the mattress beneath her. "I'm perfectly happy with this one. Besides, it's safer."

Jenny slid from the bed and stood. Straightening her clothing and turning toward the door, she said, "Right now, I'd like to see Miller so I can—"

Her heart slammed to the soles of her bare feet. The object of her thoughts stood in the doorway.

She couldn't understand how a man could always look so clean and pressed even at the end of a long day. His dark gray suit and white shirt looked as though he had just put them on. He wore a vest, as always; today it was blue and gray and looked like a miniature checkerboard beneath the lapels of his coat.

Before she had met Miller, she had never known a man who wore a vest or even one who wore a suit often. Most of the men she had known were farmers and usually wore their work overalls to church on Sundays. Except for the preacher. He wore a suit, but it was the same one he had worn every Sunday for as long as Jenny could remember—not like the professor, who had a different suit for every day of the week.

Jenny moved toward him, and they met in the middle of the room.

"I'm sorry," they said at the same time.

She giggled. Miller's mouth twitched at the corners before settling into its usual straight line. She puzzled over what he had to be sorry about. After all, it was she who had ruined one of his fine suits with the contents of her stomach.

He looked as though he didn't know what to say next, so Jenny pushed words at him before she lost her nerve. "I know you thought from my actions last night that I am a tippler, but I'm not. Before Madame DeBeau gave me a drink yesterday—several drinks—I had on no occasion touched any kind of whiskey."

Indignation flashed in his blue eyes. "Madame DeBeau gave you whiskey?" he asked.

Jenny nodded. "My Nana Blake didn't allow alcohol in her house. She considered it the devil's brew." Jenny felt her face turn red. "And now I know why—it sure as the devil makes you feel like hell."

A trace of a smile turned up the corners of his lips, but he remained silent.

She shouldn't have looked at those lips. They made her recall with a vivid freshness the kiss they had shared and how much she had enjoyed it. Enjoyed until the "cherry incident."

Jenny looked at the toes that peeked from beneath her skirt. They were a sight easier to look at than Miller's face. Swallowing, she willed herself not to blush any deeper, wanting to get the apology and the memory of last night behind her. "I'll buy you another suit to replace the one I ruined."

"That won't be necessary," Miller said, glancing furtively toward Ninj. "I'm the one who should be apologizing to you."

"Me?" Jenny uttered, sounding like a frog. "Whatever for?"

Miller looked again in Ninj's direction before his gaze connected with her. "Because I took advantage of your condition."

"How?"

Miller's face turned as red as hers. Had he caught some of her heat?

He continued to stumble with his words. "You know," he said, "the-the . . . uhmm . . . the—"

Suddenly Jenny grasped why Miller looked so embarrassed. It was because of the kiss.

"Oh, that," she said. "It was nothing. I'd already forgotten it." Laughing nervously, she wished that she could be anywhere but standing here talking to Miller about a kiss that made them both uncomfortable. She fidgeted in place, not knowing what to say next until a redeeming thought surfaced in her mind. "You know, with everything that happened, my sickness and all, I don't even remember it," she lied.

"You don't remember it?"

Was she imagining the crestfallen expression on his face?

Of course she was.

Miller's embarrassment was evidence enough that he, too, wished that the reprehensible act between them had never occurred. Unsure what to do next, Jenny turned away.

Then she saw the book on the bed. She darted toward it and grabbed it. Twirling to face him again, she said, "Look at what I found among my uncle's books." She walked toward him, holding up the book. Ninj left the bed and followed close behind her.

Miller perused the book's title, then read it aloud.

"*The Essential Handbook of Victorian Etiquette*. Written by the master of manners himself, Professor Thomas E. Hill."

"Do you know him?" Jenny asked.

"Can't say I've met the esteemed gentleman, but he has taught both men and women how to speak and act in a variety of situations."

"My uncle, he liked him?"

"He thought his work was brilliant," Miller said. "I heard him declare as much on many occasions."

"Well, if Uncle Antonini approved of him, then I will, too." Jenny felt excited. "I'll learn everything in his book and then I'll know how to act when I meet all these city folks."

"Speaking of meeting people." Miller fished inside his satchel and pulled out the invitation. He handed it to Jenny. "Do you think you'll be ready to attend a tea dance at the college with me in two weeks' time?"

"A tea dance? With you?"

"For the cause," Miller said, looking at Ninj then back at Jenny. He winked at her. "It will be the perfect place for you to meet the man of your dreams." He patted the giant's shoulder. "So Ninj here can retire to genie paradise."

A real dance. Jenny had never been to a dance before, not even the barn dances that were held back home. Dancing was another thing that Nana Blake didn't approve of. Of course, Jenny knew a few gypsy dances that her Grandmother Vassily had taught her, but she suspected that not many society people would be dancing gypsy dances at the college tea dance.

"But I don't know how to dance," she said.

"Ninj will teach you." The giant smiled at both of them. "Ninj knows all about dancing." His eyes took on a faraway look.

"Then it's settled," Miller said. "Ninj will teach you how to dance, and I'll escort you to the affair." He turned to leave, then paused. "I almost forgot. You will need something special to wear for the occasion."

"Something special?" Jenny asked.

"You know, one of those fancy dresses that women wear to dance in?"

Again Ninj came to the rescue. "Ninj knows all about what ladies wear to dance in." He clapped his hands with glee. "Leave it to me, Mistress Jee-nih. You will be the most enchanting dancer in the hall."

Miller looked pleased. "Now that everything is taken care of, if you'll excuse me, I have an early class in the morning."

He moved toward the hallway, and Jenny followed. "Please, Dr. Holbrook, I mean Miller," she called, "may I ask a favor of you?"

He stopped, waiting until she stood only inches from him before he responded. "Why, certainly, Jenny. What can I do for you?"

For days she had been meaning to ask Miller if he would help her with her uncle's bookkeeping, but the opportunity had always escaped her. She couldn't put it off any longer. Soon she would be receiving a bill for Madame DeBeau's services, and possibly other ones, and she didn't know anything about paying bills.

She stumbled into an explanation. "Since I fired my uncle's solicitor, Phineas Goldfinch, I'm at a loss with his accounts." Jenny gulped. She felt as nervous as a fish on a hot griddle. "I found his recordbooks downstairs, but as you can imagine, I'm more unskilled at recordkeeping than I am on how to act in society."

When Miller didn't comment, she continued. "I was hoping that because you're a doctor of mathematics that perhaps you'd know how to heal those records, or maybe you could teach me how."

Miller burst into laughter. "Oh, Jenny, what am I to do with you?" he asked, still chuckling.

The sound sent a shiver all the way to Jenny's toes. It was the first genuine laughter that she had heard from Miller. Although she didn't know why he had laughed, she liked the way it sounded and the way his blue eyes twinkled behind his spectacles. She smiled back at him, pleased.

Traces of that laugh still stuck to his mouth. "You're in luck, Jenny. The school term will be ending soon, and I'll have lots of time on my hands to help you *doctor* the books. I'd be delighted to help you."

"That's wonderful," she said.

Miller turned to leave.

"Oh, yes, and, Miller, there is one more thing."

He faced her again. "And what is that?"

"You look so nice when you smile you ought to do it more often."

As soon as the words slipped past her lips, Jenny wanted to pull them back. Miller's amusement evaporated like steam off boiling water.

The silence that followed made them both uncomfortable, and it made Jenny wonder if Miller would take back his offer to help with the bookkeeping, or, more importantly, his offer to escort her to the dance. She really wanted to go to a dance.

Undecided as to what she should do next, Miller decided for her.

"I have a suggestion," he said. "You work on your dancing, and I'll work on my smiling."

Her heart lifted as he spun around and started for the stairs.

"I will," she said, following him with her heart now in her throat.

Halfway up, he stopped and looked down at her. "I will, too," he said, his lips widening into a dazzling smile.

Then he disappeared, leaving Jenny wondering how to get her heart back to its proper place inside her chest.

Miller closed the door to his apartment and listened to the latch's familiar click. Tonight it sounded different, not as hollow and empty a sound as on some nights. Maybe it was because a seed of well-being had sprouted in his chest, filling him with unaccustomed joy.

He stood unmoving, allowing his eyes to adjust to the darkness before he moved toward the gaslight and turned it on. The brightness that filled the room reminded him of the warmth of Jenny's smile when he had left her.

He thought back to her request that he doctor her books. There was no doubt in Miller's mind that plenty of businessmen had made the same request of their accountants, but not with Jenny's innocence.

He chuckled. *Heal* her books. The way he felt at the moment, he would be more than happy to heal anything of Jenny's that needed fixing, even suffering the contents of her stomach again if it would make her feel better.

He paused in front of the oval mirror by the door and stared at his reflection. Until tonight, Miller had never thought of how others might see him. He looked past his image, recalling Jenny's words: "You look so nice when you smile you ought to do it more often."

For the first time in his life, Miller wondered how others saw him. He presumed his glasses gave him an intellectual look, but if he went around with a face like stone, one that was at no time softened by a smile, he could well understand why his students seemed to fear him, not warming up to him as they did to some of the other professors.

Miller removed his glasses and leaned closer to the mirror, willing himself to smile.

His lips slowly curved upward at the corners before broadening into a half-moon shape, revealing a keyboard of straight white teeth. His cheeks plumped, making the already deep indention on his cheek appear deeper and forcing a washboard of creases upward around his eyes. But even Miller could see the exercise softened his usual granitelike expression. He practiced several more smiles before deciding he had practiced enough when the face that stared back at him looked like a grinning jack-o'-lantern.

Shaking his head, he walked away from the mirror, reveling in the way the evening had gone. His plan was falling into place. He and Jenny would attend the dance, she would meet a gentleman who would steal her heart, the troublesome genie would be gone, and Miller's life would return to normal. He could go back to enjoying his solitude, rattling around in his skin the way he had before Jenny came into his life.

Sighing, he removed his jacket and vest, rolled up his shirtsleeves, and headed for the small alcove that served as his kitchen. A cup of tea and a cookie would taste good, he thought, and would be the perfect ending to an already perfect evening.

His and Jenny's apartments were mirror images of the other. Years before, when Antonini had changed from wood to coal, he had installed a small cooking stove in both apartments. Although Miller wasn't a cook, he could heat water for tea without much of a problem. Soon a small fire burned in the stove's belly, and he put on the water to boil.

Life was good, he thought, measuring the right amount of tea leaves into the teapot. Soon the water in the teakettle sputtered to a boil. Miller removed the kettle, poured the hot water over the tea, and set the teapot aside.

This done, he took two sugar cookies from the can where he stored them, found his favorite cup and saucer in the cupboard, then took his seat at the small kitchen table. Every night Miller went through the same routine. The motions were as natural as breathing.

Sugar cookies were his favorite, especially the ones he purchased at the corner bakery. Once a week he bought fourteen of the freshly baked treats, allowing himself two a night, no more. A man had to discipline his appetite like everything else.

Taking a bite of the first cookie, he chewed the sugary-sweet confection, swallowed it, then washed down the remains with a loud slurp of tea. Slurping was one of the many advantages of being a bachelor and living alone. No one nagged at you endlessly or corrected your bad habits.

Laughter drifted up from downstairs. He pictured

Jenny and Ninj in her kitchen enjoying a snack together. He swallowed less noisily this time, straining his ears to listen when a chair scraped across the floor.

A loud squeal, a thump, and more laughter floated past her ceiling and his floor, mingling with scraps of conversation.

One cookie finished, Miller picked up the second. He took a bite and swallowed. The cookie no longer tasted sweet, and his tea wasn't nearly as good as the lemony brew Jenny had served him that day in the garden. The newfound joy that he had experienced on returning to his apartment no longer stirred him. Instead, a persistent wistfulness occupied his chest.

What was he longing for? he asked himself. Everything he wanted or needed was right here in his own little world.

"Life is good," he said aloud as a reminder. But as he stood to clear away the remains of his snack and tidy up his kitchen, it somehow didn't seem as good as it had earlier.

He tried to shake off the unfamiliar yearnings, but when the tinny sound of Antonini's prized music box floated up, Miller's pensive thoughts settled more firmly inside his heart.

Jenny must be having her first dance lesson, he thought, trying to conquer his bout of melancholy, and for a moment he imagined holding her in his arms and stepping around the floor.

Dancing. He hadn't danced in years, and the thought only made him sink deeper into the throes of his black mood.

Disgusted with himself and the direction his thoughts had taken, Miller stalked from the kitchen and jerked to a stop at his desk. He dropped into the chair, slammed open his satchel, and attacked its contents.

Dancing and stepping around the floor.

The only steps he needed to be concerned with were the procedures that his students had used in solving the algebra problems on the test papers he began to grade.

Twelve

Jenny shot Ninj a warning look. "We'll do it, but if I take you out, you'll have to promise me that you'll behave yourself."

"When did you know of the mighty Ninj to disobey his mistress?"

She thought about his question. The genie had at no time deliberately misbehaved; the incident with the elephant and the rabbit had been a mistake. It really wasn't his disobedience Jenny feared, but his experiences. They were separated by hundreds of centuries, and Ninj couldn't be expected to act in the fashion that people considered proper today.

Shucks, she didn't trust *herself* to act properly and she had only come from a farm in Shepherdstown, West Virginia. Yet when she compared Georgetown to where she grew up, it could easily have been another world.

"I wouldn't expect you to disobey intentionally," Jenny answered as Ninj looked on, "but you aren't used to the ways of the modern world. Miller did warn us that you should be as invisible as possible."

"Ninj has an idea," he said eagerly. "You take along my bottle. If I do something that displeases you, you can banish me immediately."

"You won't protest the way you usually do?"

"But of course not, Mistress Jee-nih."

Had she taken leave of her senses for considering such an outing? Jenny knew Miller would disapprove. She had worried over that fact all through the night, but this morning, this very moment, she had reached a decision. She and Ninj would take in the sights of the city together. What could possibly happen to the two of them? Besides, if she would be attending the tea dance as the professor's escort, it was only fitting that she should know something about her new home.

With the first decision made, she was faced with the second one. How would they get where they were going, especially when they didn't know where that was?

Jenny had sworn after her last ride in a rented conveyance that she would never take another one. Back home she had driven the farm wagon back and forth to town. If she had her own carriage and horse here, she could drive them herself.

Breaking into her thoughts, Ninj asked, "Mistress Jee-nih, how are we to get where it is you want to go?"

She eyed him suspiciously. Had he read her thoughts? Instead of questioning him, she said, "I've been thinking on that myself." She winked at him. "How about that magic carpet you mentioned yesterday?"

"You want me to make?" he asked, looking hopeful.

"No, Ninj, I'm teasing you. The last thing we need is to tour Washington flying on a carpet. With all the soldiers who must be in and around the city, we would surely be a target for their weapons."

"It would take many sabers to hit a magic carpet."

"Sabers?" Jenny questioned her decision again. "The militia wouldn't use knives or swords, they would pick us off with guns."

"In my country, soldiers use sabers and axes. Better than this gun you speak of."

Jenny shivered. "Let's not talk of such gruesome things. Today is to be a fun day. All we really need is a horse."

"How about a camel? Ninj can do camels."

Jenny laughed. "A camel? In Washington? I don't think so."

"Camels are good. Ninj will show you a camel in this Washington. If you do not like him, we will send him back."

Before Jenny could protest further, Ninj had assumed his conjuring position. He closed his eyes. With his arms spread wide, his mind in deep concentration, he was about to snap his fingers.

"No, Ninj." Jenny jumped in front of him, demanding he stop. "Not here. Not again, not inside."

The elephant episode in the basement had been a horrible mistake, but a camel? In her apartment? On the second floor? Never.

"I'll banish you!" she shouted, tugging on his silk shirt. "I'll make you stay home and I'll go alone."

Ninj's eyes flew open. He glared at her from between his velvety black lashes. "You do not trust Ninj to make good magic? Camels belong outside. In the castle yard. You will see."

"I really don't think—"

He snapped his fingers. The air around them crackled as though charged with electricity. They quickly scanned the apartment's interior before dashing to the back windows.

Her hand across her heart, Jenny slumped against the frame. "Thank goodness."

Ninj stared through the window. His disheartened expression almost broke Jenny's heart. She touched him gently on the arm. "I really didn't want a camel," she said, "so don't worry about it."

Sunshine spilled across his features. Ninj's loud laughter made her hair stand on end. "My magic is only slow, Mistress Jee-nih," he said, looking through the window. He pointed to the courtyard below. Jenny's gaze followed his finger, her worst fears coming to lodge in her throat. *A camel. And Madame DeBeau was worried about a turkey?*

"*Araba,*" Ninj said, still smiling widely.

In place of the camel she expected, in the midst of her tiny yard stood a carriage. The *araba*, as Ninj had called it, was unlike any she had ever seen. It was a rig fit for royalty with two small wheels on the front and two larger ones on the back.

The early-morning sun reflected off the *araba*'s gilded and painted surface, nearly blinding her with the glare. Crimson curtains hung like veils from the conveyance's top. They blew gracefully in the soft breeze, allowing Jenny a quick look into the luxurious interior; she saw brocaded cushions, Oriental rugs, and velvet carpets richly embroidered in silver and gold. The *araba* had an air of mystery about it, and Jenny wouldn't have been surprised to see Queen Victoria herself sitting amongst the finery.

"My Sultana's *araba*," Ninj said, bringing Jenny's thoughts to the moment.

"Well, you can send it right back to the Sultana with my thanks." She rubbed her arms as if she were cold.

"You do not like the *araba*?" he asked, his bottom lip quivering.

Jenny wrinkled her nose. "It's not that I don't like it. It is beautiful, a carriage deserving of Cinderella, but it is not the kind of vehicle you and I should take through the streets of Washington." When Ninj continued to look puzzled and hurt, she said, "Besides, we have nothing to pull it."

"Ninj will fix that, too."

"Ninj, no!"

Too late. He snapped his fingers before she could stop him. Bracing his arm against the window's frame, he peered down into the yard. Even before she looked out, his expression told her his magic had worked.

"Oh, my goodness. We can't—that beast is eating my Uncle Antonini's begonias!" Jenny turned and fled the room with Ninj on her heels.

"Ah, those harem days," he reminisced behind her as she stomped down the stairs. "It will be like the outings to the resorts on the *Sweet Waters of Asia and Europe.*"

"I don't know anything about the resorts, but that cow has to go before he waters my garden and ruins it."

Jenny was out the back door like a flash of lightning.

"He is no cow," Ninj insisted. "He is an ox."

She ran toward the animal, waving her arms. "Shoo, shoo."

Not the least bit intimidated by her frantic gestures, the horned white beast lifted his head and gazed at her before he dropped his head again and continued munching on her plants.

"Ninj, do something," she ordered. "Now!"

She didn't dare banish him until he had removed the animal and carriage from the yard.

"Mistress Jee-nih, you must calm yourself." Ninj stilled her by capturing her hand. "Come, you and me. We will ride and see this city you so want to see. All will be fine."

"I'm not riding anywhere in that . . . thing."

"Give me one good reason why not. You said you needed a horse. Ox and *araba* are better than a horse."

"If Miller learned that we were parading around the city in that thing . . . I'd rather ride a camel." She hoped he would remember how horribly he had erred with his magic.

Her remark didn't faze him. "Camels are good, but this is better for my esteemed mistress. This way no man shall glance upon your face. Women in my country travel behind veils, you know."

"Women in my country travel in farm wagons"—she jabbed her finger against her chest—"or at least this one does."

"You will need guards. They must be eunuchs."

A eunuch—would that be like a unicorn? Lord in heaven. The last thing she needed was an army of horny horses running along beside this already ridiculous rig. She was beginning to believe that her first idea of a magic carpet would be preferable to this. One thing she was certain of, she didn't want Ninj practicing any more of his magic except to make this cart and ox disappear.

"No eunuchs, or unicorns, or whatever," she insisted. She crossed her arms against her chest, daring him not to obey. "Make these things disappear now."

Ninj's face crumpled into quivering wrinkles. He fought to hold back his tears. "Do not worry, Mistress Jee-nih," Ninj said, managing a tremulous smile, "that to do this will cause your humble servant much pain. It matters not that I be denied the simple pleasure of a ride in an *araba*." He shielded his face behind his large hands. "It has been long since Ninj enjoyed such an outing, but your wish is my command." A tear found its way over his cheek.

Watching the giant, Jenny felt lower than a snail passed over for escargot. Just last night she had read that French people ate snails for food. No wonder Madame DeBeau had such a nasty disposition. Jenny didn't have time to dwell on snails because Ninj began wailing like a banshee.

She couldn't stand to see him cry. And what would one small ride hurt if it gave Ninj a little pleasure? He had spent centuries locked inside that musty trunk. Because of her own desire for adventure, Jenny could understand his need to take a ride in the *araba*.

"Oh, all right," she said. "We'll go, but only for a short ride. And Miller must not know we rode in *that*." His crying stopped so fast that Jenny wondered if he had faked it. "You're a sly one, aren't you?"

"Mr. Professor, he will not know."

The smile Ninj bestowed upon her reached clear to her heart, melting her last resistance.

"Who will drive?" she asked, hoping she wouldn't be sorry for agreeing to their outing.

"Ninj will."

"You know how to drive?"

"Mistress Jee-nih, you forget." He winked at her. "Ninj is magic. He can do anything."

She didn't know about the "anything" part, but he certainly had the mysterious quality to enchant, and he knew all about the art of controlling. Chiefly her.

"You hitch up the cow-ox and I'll get my things. I'm bringing your bottle," she warned him, "in case I need it."

As Jenny rushed back inside the house, she wondered which of them was the true master.

As Ninj negotiated the wagon and ox from the small courtyard into the alley behind the house, Jenny soon learned that his driving was as rusty as his magic. Of course, the ox wasn't too keen on cooperating, but then she figured if she had been asleep for hundreds of years and was suddenly thrust into service, she wouldn't be high-stepping down the avenue, either.

Though Ninj insisted that the animal was an ox, it didn't look like any ox Jenny had ever seen. With its long horns the beast reminded her of the longhorn breed from the southwestern United States. And she couldn't imagine any cow, hornless or otherwise, being coerced into pulling a wagon.

"We will be fine," Ninj assured her from the driver's seat.

She felt so silly perched on the brocaded finery inside the wagon that she laughed. "We may be fine," she told Ninj between giggles, "but I'm not so sure how the rest of the populace will fare."

A black mutt charged the wagon, barking and nipping at the ox's hooves. Ninj cursed at the dog in Arabic. The ox veered sideways, and the wagon hit a can of garbage, tumbling it across the roadway and tossing its contents everywhere.

"We've lost him!" Jenny shouted, looking back. "The scoundrel is more interested in dinner on the ground than dinner on the hoof."

"Smart dog," Ninj replied.

They reached the end of the alleyway, and Jenny told Ninj to turn onto Thomas Jefferson Street. Without incident, they turned, and the genie sat up straighter.

"See, Ninj does know how to drive."

"We haven't encountered any traffic yet," she said, leaving her perch on the pillows to kneel beside him where he sat on the seat. "We must turn on M Street. It's a main road and very busy."

Jenny recalled the traffic she'd encountered when she had crossed the street on her way to Madame DeBeau's. She hoped the ox wouldn't shy away from other vehicles or be frightened by the constant clang of trolley bells. As they approached the top of the hill where the street ended, the noise and commotion began in earnest. Jenny, on seeing the congestion, wondered how wise she had been in allowing Ninj to talk her into this excursion, especially in his *araba*.

"Which way, Mistress Jee-nih?" As he slowed the carriage, she told him to turn right.

"We'll follow the trolley tracks. I've studied the map of the city and I believe Pennsylvania Avenue is the street we want. It runs past the President's house and the Capitol building."

Her concern mounted when they didn't move. "Ninj, did you hear me?" She waited for him to urge the ox forward.

They sat unmoving, blocking the road. Several carriages veered away from the ox, who stood halfway out in the line of traffic.

Ninj's eyebrows rose in amazement. "So many *arabas*," he said, "but not as fine as my Sultana's. There must be many Sultanas in this Washington City."

"Go!" Jenny shouted. "Or your Sultana's wagon will be destroyed with us in it."

Ninj ignored her warning.

Fearing a catastrophe, Jenny ordered, "Give me those straps now."

Her order jerked Ninj from his reverie. The giant cringed on the seat beside her. "You are going to beat me?" he asked, shaking.

"Beat you? Of course not. I'm going to drive the carriage since you won't." On her knees beside Ninj,

Jenny was able to drive the carriage, and remain hidden behind the veils. She grabbed the reins from Ninj and urged the ox forward. They turned and soon were plodding along with the rest of the traffic, but at a much slower pace.

Jenny decided driving the *araba* was no different from driving a farm wagon. The beast didn't trot, but slugged along at a snail's pace, and that was fine with her. It gave her more time to take in the sights.

Like Ninj beside her, she was in awe of the huge city that spread out in every direction. Wide sidewalks edged the paved street. Row upon row of tall buildings built from brick and stone rose in many levels toward the sky. Some had turrets similar to church steeples, and flags flew from the tops of all the structures.

People and carriages were everywhere. She saw many women and men riding bicycles, most of whom moved faster than the ox. Carriages of every description traveled the avenue. A horseless one passed and tooted his horn.

"Magic," Ninj said, watching the vehicle until it disappeared.

Jenny laughed. It seemed like magic to her as well.

As they drove by a large house sitting back from the paved road and surrounded by a grassy and treed lawn, Ninj said, "So many palaces in this place."

Jenny agreed. "And would you look at that? That must be President William McKinley's house." To Jenny, the stately mansion did resemble a palace with its circular drive leading to a columned entrance.

"This president, he is your Sultan, your ruler?" Ninj asked.

"Not a sultan, but he is the leader of our country."

"He must be a strong leader and very rich if he can own so many palaces. Where is his harem?"

"He doesn't have a harem. He has only one wife."

"One wife!" Ninj declared in disgust, crossing his arms against his big chest. "He must not be so strong after all."

Jenny didn't bother answering, for there were too many things to see that demanded her immediate attention. They continued their slow pace along the street, following the trolleys and the other traffic going in their direction.

Pedestrians looked inquiringly at their strange conveyance. One group of well-dressed ladies stared with open curiosity. Above the din, Jenny overheard bits and pieces of their conversation.

"A Moslem princess," one said.

Another, on seeing Ninj, who looked very much like the genie he was, said, "He must be her eunuch."

With this observation, they looked away as though they were embarrassed. "Imagine a man who's been . . ."

Eunuch. The same word Ninj had used earlier. Jenny would have to ask him its meaning later, but now she had too many other things to focus on.

On hearing the women's gossip, Jenny was glad that she had worn the veiled hat that had arrived at the house yesterday, along with several more outfits from Madame DeBeau. Although the crimson curtains of the carriage almost shielded her from view, the gray hat with its veil and white plume of feathers kept her true identity a secret. Not that she had to worry about being recognized. In a city of so many people, she felt confident that even the professor wouldn't recognize her if he ran into her on the busy street.

The women were forgotten when at the very end of the long avenue Jenny spied the white-domed Capitol building. She had read about Capitol Hill, where the buildings housed the workings of the United States Government. The stately structures inspired a feeling of patriotism, and she swallowed back the lump that lodged in her throat and blinked back tears.

Again, she was thankful for her veiled hat and her carriage. She surely didn't want Ninj or anyone else to see her blubbering.

Ninj wiggled excitedly on the seat, pointing. "Mistress Jee-nih, a bazaar. Can we go inside?''

Jenny looked down the length of the genie's arm; the sidewalk was lined with old broken wagons. White and black folks—country people, Jenny imagined, not unlike herself when she sold apples at Shepherdstown—displayed all kinds of herbs and roots in their wagons.

Beyond the wagons stood a building that had the name *Center Market* painted across its front. The structure was enormous. Throngs of buyers, some fashionably dressed, others less opulently garbed, came and went, their baskets loaded with the day's household selections.

''We stop, Mistress. Please.'' Ninj became dreamy-eyed. ''Ninj would like to stroll again among the carts of fruit and vegetables, sniff the spicy lamb kabobs, and sample the tasty fish and seafood caught along the Sea of Marmara and the Black Sea.''

As much as Jenny would have enjoyed browsing the stalls, she didn't dare take Ninj inside. She knew he equated this market with those of his memory, and Jenny didn't have the heart to tell him that the only fish he might sample would most likely come from the Potomac River or other rivers nearby.

''Not today, Ninj. We'll come another time. Remember, we agreed to a short ride and nothing more. We really need to head home.''

''But, Mistress Jee-nih—''

''You promised you wouldn't protest,'' Jenny warned. ''Besides, we have my dancing lessons and we can't forget I have much to learn from Professor Hill's book.''

Jenny knew her answer disappointed him, but Ninj remained true to his promise. His lips remained sealed. After a moment he said, ''You are right. We will come again. But soon.''

They turned back in the direction they had come and headed home.

The flags on the roofs of the many buildings flapped noisily in the wind. Horses neighed, trolley bells clanged, and people laughed and talked among themselves as they passed.

When they finally turned onto Thomas Jefferson Street, they both were quiet, storing their memories of the excursion. Pulling to a stop in front of the shop, Jenny jumped down from the carriage, and Ninj followed.

"You'll have to make that *araba* and ox disappear," she told Ninj, fishing in her reticule for the house key. She handed Ninj his bottle and searched frantically through the drawstring bag.

"My key, it's not here," she said. "Now where can it be? We'll have to go around back and hope that I forgot to lock the door."

They slipped through the narrow alley between her building and her neighbors' and headed toward the courtyard.

In their haste, the *araba* and ox were forgotten.

Thirteen

As Miller swung down from the trolley, his steps felt as light as air. He tipped his hat at several passing ladies, and practiced smiling at them before crossing the street and stopping on the crest of the hill.

The day was muggy with the promise of an afternoon shower. From the hilltop, the Potomac looked like a silver ribbon in the noontime sun, the banks bordering its basin like brushed emerald velvet. His poetic thoughts surprised Miller, making him smile at several people who passed before he started down the sloping hill. He was as hungry as a junebug to get home; anxious to see how Jenny's dancing lessons were progressing.

This morning he had told Dean Witty that a young lady would accompany him to the annual tea dance. The dean had seemed both pleased and surprised by Miller's announcement, or maybe shocked would be a more apt description. In all the years that Witty had been the administrator of the college, Miller had never brought an escort to any of the college functions.

The administrator had thumped Miller on the shoulder when he was leaving his office and said, "Good going, old boy. Mrs. Witty will be pleased as punch that you'll be bringing someone to this year's dance. Even as we speak, I believe that she and some of the other ladies of the college are on their way to the Center Market on a

menu-planning foray. Tell your lady friend to save
plenty of room for the fine fare served at the social. Mrs.
Witty takes great pride in the refreshments.''

Before today, Miller had considered the affair as a
boring obligation he was required to attend, and he
couldn't recall if the refreshments had been good or bad.
But with Jenny attending with him, he felt in his bones
that this year's party would be different.

Hold on there, old fellow, a voice inside his head cautioned. *You asked Jenny to the affair not for your pleasure, but so she could meet a young man of good
standing. And so you could be rid of the troublesome
genie once and for all.*

Those had been his thoughts last night, and he reiterated them today. ''To be rid of Ninj is my prime objective, and, of course, to help Jenny settle in.''

His carefree air stayed with him as he approached the
house. Miller was so wrapped up in his thoughts that he
almost missed the carriage and—cow?—parked in front
of the shop. On seeing the fairy-tale rig and beast, he
snapped to a stop. He glanced sharply around, the hairs
on the back of his neck inching upward.

The antique carriage would have been a collectible
that Antonini Vassily couldn't have passed up. But since
he was no longer alive, Miller wondered who the rig
belonged to and what it was doing parked in front of the
building.

He strained to see past the crimson curtains that
shielded the carriage's interior from prying eyes. His
overwhelming desire to see inside was stronger than any
magnetic field he had encountered. He was drawn to the
vehicle like metal shavings to a magnet.

Miller looked up and down the street, hoping to see
the rig's owner. When everyone who passed gave the
carriage only a curious glance and continued on their
way, Miller moved closer. Reaching out, he fingered the
gauzy crimson veils, expecting the timeworn material to
crumble at his touch. When it didn't, he pulled back the
filmy cloth and peered inside.

His first thought on seeing the interior was that he had entered the forbidden space of some ancient culture. Silver-and-gold brocaded pillows and Oriental carpets filled the small rose-hued space. A fragrance reminiscent of an aged and exotic perfume bearing traces of ginger and cloves lingered among the furnishings. He fancied he heard the childlike sound of feminine laughter floating past the open curtain.

Miller jerked back as if he had been burned. Was he a victim of phantasmagoria or a distempered brain? Could the laughter be the result of his smiling practice, or his jovial mood? Whatever had summoned the sound, it made his earlier cheerfulness disappear.

Miller didn't believe in magic tricks, but if the carriage wasn't meant for Antonini's business, then more than likely the genie was up to something. Foreboding tracked up and down his spine. He had told both Jenny and Ninj that the genie's presence should be kept secret. If this buggy and cow parked in front of the house meant what he believed it did, then they had deliberately ignored his instructions. Miller turned and stormed toward the front door.

After they were again inside the house, entering through the back door that Jenny had left unlatched, she had asked Ninj the meaning of the word *eunuch*. He had described in detail the process of how men became eunuchs and why.

"So the eunuchs guarded the harem?" Jenny asked, trying to imagine life in such a household.

"They do. I know hundreds who live within the gates of my Sultana's quarters."

"You *knew*," Jenny reminded him. "Your Sultana no longer exists, and I hope such cruelties are no longer practiced in Istanbul."

"It was never practiced by the Turks. Castration was forbidden in Islam. Black eunuchs were traded mostly from Africa."

"How they must have hated their lives."

To Jenny, the idea of living in bondage was awful enough, but coupled with the barbaric act wrought upon these males, such an existence must have been intolerable.

"Some maybe hated their fate," Ninj said, "but most accepted it. They lived in quarters located beyond the entrance to the harem and received a generous allowance. They wore robes of the finest silk and received other gifts throughout the year. Most dreamed of becoming *kizlar agasi*, master of the girls, or the chief eunuch. A very important position."

Jenny reflected on Ninj's words, although she wondered why anyone would want such a job. "As my Nana Blake would say, it's a sin to Moses."

"You want eunuch, Mistress Jee-nih? Ninj will call up one for you."

"Don't you dare!"

Insulted, she jumped up from the wine-colored sofa in her apartment. "It would break my heart to look upon such a person, knowing how he must have suffered at the hands of man." On a lighter note, she said, "Besides, I have you for protection."

"My mistress is a good master," Ninj said, smiling. "You have a heart." He thumped his chest. "Ninj is lucky you found him. Soon I will no longer be a slave, but free in my genie paradise. And you, Mistress Jee-nih, will have your love to protect you."

My love to protect me. Jenny wanted no part of such an arrangement, but then Ninj wasn't supposed to know her and Miller's plan.

Hoping to change the subject so she wouldn't have to pretend for Ninj's benefit, she said, "Unless we get busy with my lessons, no proper gentleman will give me a second look."

She walked toward the front windows and the table where she had left Professor Hill's book. "We've wasted most of the day already when I should have been studying how to behave in society. What shall we practice first, dancing or— Heaven forbid!" she shrieked, looking down at the street. "You forgot to get rid of the *araba* and cow." She sucked in her breath. "Oh, my goodness. There's Miller. He sees it. He's looking at it. Ninj, he wasn't supposed to know about our ride!"

Ninj came to stand beside her. "So sorry, Mistress Jee-nih, your worthless slave forgot. When your key was missing—"

"Quick, make the thing disappear."

"Mr. Professor," Ninj observed, "does not look so pleased."

"Of course he doesn't." Jenny grabbed the front of Ninj's shirt with both hands and tried shaking him. "Make that thing disappear now."

"You are unhappy with your humble servant?"

Jenny sent him a look that could have melted ice.

Ninj quaked like a tree in the wind. "Ninj can do. He will make the thing disappear." Not bothering to assume his usual conjuring position, he snapped his fingers.

They both pressed their foreheads against the window and glanced down into the street.

"See," Ninj said, turning to her and grinning, "my magic is good. The *araba* is gone."

"All I can say," Jenny said, observing Miller's fast trek to the front door, "is that you better come up with some powerful magic to convince the professor that what he saw didn't exist. Quick, let's look like we're busy." She picked up Professor Hill's book and ran toward the couch and flopped down. Swinging her legs up on the cushions, she opened the book on her lap, then pointed to the opposite end of the sofa by her feet. "Hurry, Ninj, sit."

Then she began to read aloud. " 'Each dancer will be provided with a ball-card bearing a printed programme of the dances, having a space for making engagements upon the same, with a small pencil attached.' "

Jenny went through the list of dances to be performed: a march, a quadrille, a waltz, a polka, a gallop, and so on. "It says here that several round dances will be interspersed with the quadrille, usually ending with a march prior to supper.''

She let the publication drop to her lap and looked surreptitiously at the open door as she heard Miller's steps thundering against the stairs.

Ninj remarked, "After all that dancing, I would run to supper instead of march."

"Oh, silly, it doesn't mean they march to supper. I said a march would be performed prior to supper."

"Whatever, but to speak of food has made me very hungry. Our excursion to—"

"Lunch," Jenny interrupted.

Miller's shadow darkened the doorjamb.

"I guess we could eat something."

He started to rush into the room, but as though suddenly remembering himself, he stopped short and knocked on the door.

Jenny's heart lodged in her throat. She was unsure if it was because she feared his discovery of their outing or because Miller looked so handsome in his black frock coat, matching vest, and striped gray shirt. He wore a hat of brushed black felt, and Jenny thought he looked dashingly good-looking even with his spectacles.

She hadn't seen the professor since their conversation last night about smiling, but the expression on his face as he glared at both of them clearly indicated that he hadn't taken her advice.

"Professor, I mean Miller," she corrected, standing, "won't you come in? Ninj and I were about to rustle up some lunch. Would you care to join us?"

"I'm more interested in rustling up information as to why that antique coach is parked in front of the building." He moved toward the windows, glancing briefly at Ninj as he passed.

Jenny heard the genie mumble, "*Araba.*"

As she turned around in front of where Ninj sat on the couch, she deliberately stood on his large silk-slippered feet, daring him to say another word. Ninj cringed beneath her leather-booted weight, but sat as quiet as a mouse.

"Carriage," Jenny repeated. "We saw no carriage, did we, Ninj?"

Leaving the genie, she glided to the window to stand beside Miller, who held back the drape with one hand and was searching up and down the street.

"No, *araba*," Ninj answered.

"Araba?" Miller looked suspiciously at the two.

"Arabs," Jenny answered. "Only this morning Ninj and I were having a discussion about Arabs."

"I know there was an antique carriage parked in front of the shop. I saw one in a book on ancient cultures. Old, gilded, with red veils hanging from its top. Brocaded pillows and Oriental rugs inside." He let the drape fall and turned toward Ninj, spearing him with his icy blue stare. "Not unlike a carriage that may have been used for transporting an entourage for a Sultan?"

Jenny laughed nervously. "Of course, Ninj knows nothing about such a vehicle. I told you we've been right here discussing, ah—eunuchs."

Miller's face turned as gray as the stripes on his shirt, and Jenny thought a frailer man might have collapsed. Instead, he bolted to where Ninj sat on the couch. The genie appeared oblivious to Miller's sudden appearance at his knees, instead feigning interest in the crystal teardrops hanging from the cranberry glass lamp that sat on the table beside him. With one large finger, he set the drop into motion. It pinged like a teaspoon against a glass.

Miller's voice rasped the words. "You, sir, are not suitable company for a lady. What is your game?"

Jenny flew to Miller's side. "You must not talk to Ninj that way," she warned. "He did nothing but answer my questions."

"Questions? And where did you hear the word, if not from him?"

"In the country," she began, "we, ah . . . ah, speak of eunuchs all the time. Ah . . . male animals are cas-

trated, or gelded, in order to improve the breed or to
make them more docile.'' As an afterthought, she added,
''We call it eunuchsizing.''

Miller raised his hand to silence her. ''Eunuchsizing?''

He looked at Ninj, who was no longer studying the
lamp but appeared more interested in the conversation.
The giant sat with his arms folded across his chest, his
gaze switching from one to the other as she and Miller
spoke. Beneath his black mustache, his lips curved upward with the hint of a smile.

The old reprobate, Jenny thought, *is enjoying himself.*

''In my country, we call it castration,'' Ninj offered.
His statement made Miller look as though he might explode.

''Make him disappear,'' Miller ordered. ''Now.''

''But I don't want him to disappear. Besides, we're
studying the professor's book, and later on Ninj is going
to help me with my dancing.'' Jenny pinned Miller with
her gaze. ''Last night you suggested Ninj help me, remember?''

''My brain must have been addled to have suggested
such a thing.'' Miller's features twisted in disapproval.
''I know that conveyance I saw parked out front was his
doing. It wouldn't surprise me in the least to learn that
the two of you have been riding through the streets of
Washington in that totally unsuitable carriage.''

Ninj's nostrils flared. ''*Araba* is not unsuitable. In
fact—''

''Your *facts* are wrong, is what Ninj meant to say.
Since we saw nothing in the street when you told us to
look, we can't be good judges of whether the conveyance was unsuitable or not.''

Jenny prayed Ninj would make it to genie paradise
because he certainly wouldn't get to the opposite end, if
there was such a place for genies, since he refused to
tell a lie. The genie couldn't even stretch the truth a
little. She warned him to silence with her eyes.

"Now about that lunch, are you interested?" she asked Miller, rubbing her hands together.

"Lunch. How can you eat at a time like this?"

"Easy. Open mouth, put food in, chew, and swallow." The genie rubbed his fat belly. "Ninj is good at eating."

Miller clenched his hands at his sides. "Ninj is good at opening his mouth and sticking his foot in it. And before I stick my fist in your mouth, I must decline your invitation for lunch." He turned on his heels and stomped from the room. Rather than go upstairs to his apartment, he went down, and soon the front door slammed.

After Miller's exit, Ninj responded matter-of-factly, "Maybe Mr. Professor could use a gelding like your farm animals, so as to gentle his nature."

"Maybe," was Jenny's only response.

She hated lying to Miller, especially since they had become friends of a sort and he had agreed to help Ninj. Lately her life had become so filled with falsehoods, she had a hard time telling the true from the false. One minute she was fibbing to Ninj, and in the next she was fibbing to Miller.

"Come," she said, motioning for Ninj to follow her. "We shall have that lunch I promised you."

As she made her way to the kitchen, a thought whispered through her mind. Maybe she was really only fibbing to herself.

Once outside, Miller looked where the carriage had been parked. He walked to the curb, searching the street for wheel tracks or hoof marks. Nothing. Had he imagined the strange-looking rig, and if so, why? Could it be his resentment of Ninj's ability to enchant a certain young woman that made him believe the worst?

"Absolutely not," Miller declared.

He had never been jealous in his life, and he wasn't about to allow the green-eyed monster to rule his life now. Besides, what competition could a centuries-old giant with magic powers afford? Plenty, he decided, recalling Jenny's quick defense of Ninj. Yet if the conveyance had been nothing more than a figment of Miller's imagination, his accusations directed at the genie had been unwarranted and uncalled for.

Miller turned toward the canal, believing a stroll in the fresh air might give him better insight into his problems. Since Jenny's arrival, he had twice nearly gotten into fisticuffs with another man. First Axle and now Ninj. Of course, he didn't know how much of a man the genie was in spite of his size. Maybe Ninj was one of those unfortunate males who had been made into a eunuch; but they were human, and genies weren't supposed to be human. Hell, he didn't know what and if there was such a thing as a genie except in the translation of *The Arabian Nights*.

He turned off the street and walked along the towpath beside the canal. It was hard to believe that Jenny had arrived only a week before on a boat similar to those that slugged past him now on the green water. Jenny, who before her arrival had existed only in his old friend Antonini's conversations, had appeared like a small tornado whirling into his life, cutting a path of confusion, and leaving his once-serene existence in upheaval.

He thought of her constantly. Jenny with her genie. Jenny with her straightforward way of speaking and acting that both shocked and cheered him.

Eunuchsizing. He shook his head. Without even trying, his lips turned upward into the silly grin that he'd been practicing because of Jenny's suggestion. Funny, when he thought of Jenny he smiled naturally. Perhaps, he reasoned, if he gave Ninj half a chance, the genie wouldn't be so bad, either. Just different. Miller had always prided himself on his own individuality, encouraged it in his students, so why should he think of Ninj as unsavory because he was different?

Miller wondered when he had become so narrow-minded and so judgmental of others. Maybe it was time

he set aside his suspicions of Ninj and accepted him as
he was. Jenny surely had.

He bent over and picked up a shiny rock, the same
blue-gray color as Jenny's eyes, and wondered fleetingly
how desirable was normal.

Annoyed with his thoughts, he threw the rock into the
canal. The action reminded him of when he'd skipped
rocks across water as a lad.

Miller bent over and scooped up a handful of earth,
letting the dirt sift through his fingers until all he held
were stones. In order to skip rocks, you had to have just
the right kind. Every rock-skipper knew only flat ones
would skip.

He picked out a few smooth solid stones and tossed
the others back onto the ground. Raising his arm level
with his shoulder, he snapped his wrist and let the stone
fly. Seeing it leap and spring jauntily across the surface
before sinking out of sight awakened a thrill he had long
forgotten.

He fired off the others; they darted like dragonflies
fishing before *kurplunking* into the pea green depths of
the water. He sailed another one, and it missed the
breadth of the canal altogether and hit the behind of a
mule that a boatman had just released from his towrope.
The mule began hee-hawing as though he'd been hit
with buckshot rather than nipped by one little stone.

Miller quickly did an about-face and started back in
the direction he had come. With his hands tucked in his
pockets, he ran down the towpath like an errant boy
escaping his last piece of mischief. He snickered all the
way back to Thomas Jefferson Street.

By the time he reached the house, Miller had decided
it was more fun acting like a kid than a pretentious professor. Inside his pocket his fingers closed around one
of the rocks he'd dropped inside earlier during his escape. He brought it out and examined it. He wondered
when he had become as flat and shapeless as the rock
he held in his palm. Maybe it was time he relaxed and
enjoyed life more.

One thing he had to do before anything else was to apologize to Jenny and Ninj for his earlier accusations. His previous good mood restored, Miller pushed open the front door and went inside.

Fourteen

The moment Miller closed the door, he heard music coming from Jenny's apartment. Good, he thought, she must be practicing her dancing. He paused at the bottom of the landing, listening, hoping to recognize a familiar tune, maybe a waltz or a quadrille.

The tune floating downward didn't sound the least bit familiar. In fact, the longer Miller listened, the more convinced he became that the rhythmic sound of drums, flute, and tambourine wasn't the type of music the band would play at the dean's tea dance.

Where were the sounds coming from? Miller believed he was familiar with the few interchangeable discs that Antonini had played repeatedly on his prized music box, yet today was the first time he had ever heard the strange, foreign sounds that filled the house. As he listened, the melody called to mind the images of an open bazaar in some exotic faraway land—a bazaar in the same distant place and age as the buggy he had spied out front.

Ninj.

Miller took the stairs two at a time and didn't bother to knock on the open door when he reached Jenny's apartment. The moment his foot fell over the threshold he was transported into another world. The parlor and the storm brewing outside no longer existed. In their place was an exotic room with latticed windows, marble floors, and dusty divans. Palms grew in the many pots placed about the room, and the same clove-and-spice fragrance he identified with the mystery carriage permeated the air. The streaked marble floors were covered with Oriental carpets woven from woolen threads in every color of the rainbow. He sought out Jenny but saw only Ninj, who sat on a low divan littered with brocaded pillows. A water pipe sat on the floor beside him.

The room was suited to a Sultan's needs, and Miller expected to see the ruler materialize at any moment. He glanced around the rooms and realized upon closer inspection that the apartment was the same as it had always been; only the decorations were different.

He looked toward the bedroom wanting to see Jenny propped against the headboard as she had been the night before, when she'd looked the part of a young schoolgirl. But like the bedroom, the interior of which was hidden by the same latticed screens that covered the windows, Jenny was nowhere in sight. The music played unnervingly loud, grating on Miller's nerves. He searched the apartment for Antonini's music box, which was missing from its usual place beside the door. Like the other familiar furnishings it, too, had disappeared.

"Where is she?" Miller asked, storming toward where Ninj lay sprawled upon the low, pillowed divan.

"Mistress Jee-nih is readying herself for the dance. Sit, Mr. Professor." He patted the lumpy pillows beside him. "You will be pleased with her progress."

The genie took a deep draw from the long water pipe tube and smiled knowingly at Miller through the hazy smoke he let drift from his mouth. Even Bengel, who lay sprawled at the giant's silk-slippered feet, looked as regal as a temple cat with his odd eyes that glistened like rare and priceless jewels.

"Sit," Ninj insisted again. "Let the *beledi* begin," Ninj said, clapping his hands in summons.

Uneasiness crept up Miller's spine. Had he been wrong in enlisting Ninj's help in teaching Jenny to dance? *"Beledi?* What is the *beledi*, and who the devil is performing it?"

"Sit," Ninj ordered. "You will see."

As much as Miller wanted to refuse Ninj's order, his knees bent by their own volition. Soon he sprawled among the army of pillows on the low divan beside the cat at Ninj's feet.

The music stopped for a moment, then began again in a lively four-beat rhythm. *Dum, dum, tek, tek.* The drumbeat alternated between the deeper sound of the *dum* to the higher-pitched, more metallic sound of the *tek.* Soon Miller's heart thumped in cadence with the rhythmic beat, and although he knew he should be demanding to see Jenny, he felt helpless to do so. It was as though the music and the surroundings had cast a spell, holding him a prisoner against his will.

The room grew abominably humid. When Miller complained, Ninj suggested that he remove his hat, coat, and vest, and that he loosen his collar. Even after he removed the outer garments, Miller still felt as though he had been dropped into the middle of a muggy Turkish bath. He glanced quickly at the genie, who looked cool and comfortable. But not Miller. The damp heat inside the room made him sweat in an ungentlemanly fashion and made his lenses steam over. Miller removed his glasses and would have wiped away the mist but for the sudden appearance of the dancer. With her finger cymbals ringing, she slithered briskly from behind the latticed screen, demanding his full attention. Although Miller was nearly blind without his spectacles, what he could see held him mesmerized.

He thought the dark-haired beauty seemed vaguely familiar and seemed extremely tall for an Asian woman, but when she started moving, both thoughts were forgotten.

As Salome's audience had been held spellbound by the dance of the seven veils, Miller, too, was spellbound and feared that, like John, he could be at risk for losing his head. The golden gossamer veils swirled around her

body like giant butterfly wings, both concealing and revealing the sensuous movements of the dance. She un-
dulated across the room toward them, the metallic sound
of her finger cymbals echoing throughout the room.
With an air of both mystery and pleasure, she spun to a
halt several feet away from where Miller and Ninj sat.

Miller could see that beneath her floating veils, the
gold-coined top and girdle of her costume glimmered
like reflected fire against the dewy nakedness of her
bronze-colored skin.

He ran a finger beneath his collar and released several
more buttons of his shirt. Excitement surged through
him, making Miller wonder if the heat in his body was
caused by the hot, cloying atmosphere or if it was his
reaction to the voluptuous woman.

He didn't have long to ponder this last thought because she moved on to the next stage of the dance. The
melody became much slower. After the excitement and
vitality at the beginning, he noted the cymbals were now
silent. The dancer's movements became more sensuous.

From beside him, Ninj explained, "Next is the removing of the veils. You like so far, Mr. Professor?"

Miller fumbled for his glasses, but when the blasted
steam kept forming on the lenses, he gave up the wiping
and grabbed the stem of Ninj's water pipe and took a
long drag.

"I like," he told the smiling genie.

Squinting, he followed the dancer's movements while
anticipating the removal of her veils. First she used the
veils like wings, then as a demure cover-up before swirling them into an enticing tent. All the while the veil
twirled around the dancer, she moved her hips in a
figure-eight motion. She came so close to Miller during
the unveiling that she wrapped the transparent veil about
his head before dragging the sheer cloth away. Miller
felt hotter than an egg frying on summer pavement. She
released the veil, allowing the billowy drape to waft
through the air. It fell into a golden pyramid at his feet.

"My mistress, she is good, no?" Ninj asked.

Miller nodded his head in complete agreement and continued his blurry-eyed study of the entertainer.

Jenny watched the veils fall at Miller's feet, then she went into a series of belly rolls and did a shiver and a shimmy, remembering to keep her movements deep and supple as Ninj had instructed her to do last night. Jenny had proved to be a fast learner and Ninj had said as much. She contributed her ability to learn the movements so quickly to her knowledge of the gypsy dances her Grandmother Vassily had taught her. She wasn't sure if the shiver was a reaction to Miller's unexpected presence.

She hoped her dress would meet with Miller's approval. The jingling of the coins and baubles on the top and girdle inspired her into poses she couldn't have dreamed of. When she first agreed to wear the ballgown, Ninj had assured her it was what all women dancers wore. She had eyed it skeptically, thinking it a bit flimsy for society, but then what did she know about tea dances? Now that she felt the pleasant weight of her dress on her body, she would be the first to attest that it was a lot more comfortable than the stays she had to wear with the new gowns that Madame DeBeau had sewn for her.

She did a few spirals and twists, recalling Ninj's words. "Resist the music, try to hold back, but be erotic, be captivating, be arrogant, and be poignantly theatrical."

Jenny wasn't certain she could be all those things, but instead of resisting the music as he had advised, she let it carry her away to the foreign land of Ninj's ancestors, where women danced to entertain their Sultan.

At the moment, Miller was her ruler, and he looked so pleased with her performance that she was determined to put her all into it. Was that a smile lighting up his face? The idea that he might have taken her advice made her twice as determined to dance better, especially for him. She hoped he would be pleased with her progress, especially when he accompanied her to the dean's tea dance. It was odd, but she had thought at the dance she would be partnered with a gentleman; however, this was the only dance Ninj had taught her so far. He had called it the *beledi*, which to Jenny's ears sounded as foreign as the quadrille and the gallop.

Ninj had also instructed her in some of the floor routines. These she knew were done with the slower part of the music, and now that the tempo had slowed, it was time to perform those movements.

With seeming ease, Jenny dropped to her knees, allowing her hair to trail to the floor behind her as she lowered herself in a graceful arch. Writhing—gracefully, she hoped—she turned and extended her foot while allowing her raised hip to spiral in a twist. Then she suddenly twisted out of the position and coiled back to her knees, sweeping up from the waist.

"Ayawah," Ninj exclaimed in Arabic, and soon Miller chimed in with the same words. He was pleased, and his pleasure made Jenny's heart flutter with excitement.

She had finished the slow part of the dance and was now ready for the finale. She performed all the basic movements she had learned: lively and abandoned shimmies, tossing her head and hair around, and moving closer to her audience. Out of breath, her heart pounding, her whole body slick with perspiration, Jenny did a final spin and her culminating bow.

"Yasu," Ninj called out. "Praise to Allah," he said before both men began to applaude her act.

A warm glow flowed through her as she walked toward Miller. He reached for his glasses and, jerking his shirttail from his trousers, wiped the lenses clean before setting them back on his nose.

The wide smile that Jenny noticed he'd been wearing throughout her performance had done funny things to her insides, and as she stopped in front of him, she wanted to hear his praise. Afterward, she would tell him that she noticed that he'd been practicing his smiling just as she had been practicing her dancing.

The air in the room felt somewhat cooler, and Jenny

figured it was because she was no longer dancing. Now Miller really looked at her—but not in the way she expected. His glance slid from her bare stomach up and over the hills of her breasts before locking on the stone tied around her neck.

His flushed face drained of all color. "Jenny?" he croaked.

Miller jerked his glasses off again, gave them another quick swipe with his shirttail, and fumbled to replace them on his nose. He shook his head as though to clear it. Not only had his earlier smile disappeared, it had been replaced with a choleric glare that he turned on Ninj. "What the devil is she doing dressed like Little Egypt of the Chicago World's Fair?"

"Not Egypt. My country's native dance. It is called the *beledi*." Ninj smiled proudly. "Just as you told me, I teach Mistress Jee-nih how to dance."

"Dance? I wouldn't call that vibrating dancing, and besides"—Miller looked at Jenny then quickly looked away—"it's indecent for a woman to carry on so when she is barely clothed."

Ninj winked at Miller. "It is better this vibrating when she is unclothed? Yes?"

"No," Jenny answered, fearing that Miller might take a swing at the genie at any moment.

Here she had believed that Miller was enjoying her dancing. What a fool she had been. Oh, he had liked the erotic display as much as she imagined any man would, but it hadn't been her or her dancing that had held him captivated. It was clear to her now that he hadn't realized that she was the dancer until he had put on his glasses.

This realization not only left her hurt and disappointed, but also feeling guilty, as though she were fully responsible for her unladylike behavior. But her guilt quickly turned to anger. She of all people should not have expected that Ninj would know the proper dress for a ball or what kind of dances people did now. Miller shouldn't have expected him to know, either. Ninj only did what Miller asked, after all.

While Miller looked exasperated, Ninj defended himself.

"Last night, you told me yourself, Mr. Professor. You said, 'You know, one of those fancy dance dresses that women wear to dance in.' "

"I meant a dress she could wear to a ball, not to an orgy."

"Orgy." Ninj looked indignant. "You insult me. Men's heads have rolled for less."

Jenny looked back and forth between the two. The air between them crackled with their growing anger. The last thing she wanted was for heads to roll, although at the moment it would have done her heart good to see a certain man by the name of Miller Holbrook lose his because of his insensitivity. He was as much to blame for the misunderstanding as she was, but he was too pigheaded and proper to realize it.

The heated discussion was getting them nowhere. Fearing the worst, Jenny touched the stone at her neck and rubbed. Ninj disappeared into the thick warm air, leaving her alone to face Miller's wrath.

With Ninj's departure the mugginess in the room dissipated, and the harem furnishings disappeared. Miller glanced around the apartment and blinked his eyes several times in disbelief. Jenny, too, had changed. She was no longer dressed like a hootchie-kootchie girl, but Miller knew the memory of her very womanly body spangled in gold coins and swathed in golden transparent veils would never fade from his mind.

Had he imagined the dance as he had imagined the carriage parked out front? He challenged his mental health, wondering if he could be losing his mind. For a man who had always believed in the exact, why had he suddenly turned to fantasies? It seemed since Jenny and her genie had come into his life, Miller no longer knew what was real and what was imagination.

He corrected that picture immediately. One glance in Jenny's direction told him that she was very real, and so was her anger. With both hands on her hips, she faced him. Like the rumble of the faraway storm, she was ready to turn her temper on him.

"For an educated doctor, you surely aren't very smart," she said. "No one ever taught you manners, either." She bent toward him, her nose mere inches from his as she paused to take a quick sharp breath.

"Poor Ninj. He thought he was doing what was right by teaching me to dance. It isn't his fault that the only dances he knows are from his past and from his country." Her voice raised a notch, and she whirled away from him until there was a safe distance between them. "I'm from this century and from this country, and I don't know how to do a gallop or a quadrille. Or any other kind of dance that you would think proper."

"You don't understand—"

"No, I don't. I don't understand how you can be so uncaring. Ninj did exactly what you told him to do. He taught me to dance and he found me a dress that he believed appropriate."

"Some dress. You were nearly naked—"

"It was you who was mistaken for assuming that he would teach me what you wanted him to and dress me how you believed I should be dressed. Speaking of my near nakedness, you certainly appeared to be enjoying it until you realized it was me."

Hell, he had enjoyed it, Miller admitted silently, too damn much. Because Jenny continued to lambaste him with her argument, the *too damn much* quickly disappeared.

"My Nana Blake always said, 'If you want to get a job done, do it yourself,' and for once in my life I'm about to admit she was right. You, Mr. Professor, should have been the one teaching me, not Ninj."

"Maybe I jumped to—"

"Conclusions? Yes, I would say you did. It seems where Ninj is concerned, you are good at doing that." Jenny gave an impatient shrug. "You don't believe he's magic and you weren't sincere when you said you wanted to help him with his plight."

"Believe me," Miller argued, "no one wants to be rid of that genie more than I!"

"Exactly. You only want him out of here. You don't want to help him."

She flew toward him, waving her hands in a gesture of dismissal. "Just as I want you gone now." When he didn't move, she added, "You are in my apartment, aren't you?"

"Yes, I am, but I think you and I need to discuss this like two—"

"Not only do you want him out of here, you probably wish me gone, too, so you can return to your boring, nonexistent life where you never have to smile."

"That's not—"

"True? It certainly is. And if you won't leave, then I will."

"It's going to storm . . ."

"Who's afraid of a little storm? I'm not. I bet you've never sat on an open porch and waited for an approaching storm, have you, Mr. Professor? Well, I have, and unless you've done it, you can't imagine how good such an experience makes one feel."

"No, I can't say that I—"

"You should try it sometime." Jenny rushed toward the door. "You might learn something about yourself. It makes you realize how unimportant you are in the world."

"Please wait."

Her response to his plea was the empty silence that filled the apartment after her departure.

"Damn and double damn," he swore.

The woman had him cursing like a sailor, a habit he didn't particularly admire in others and one he had almost always refrained from doing. But all that had changed with the arrival of Jenny. No longer was he the quiet, controlled gentleman he prided himself on being. Instead, he had become a hot-tempered, hot-bodied, judgmental man with no patience, a man unlike the person whose body he had inhabited for the last thirty years. Miller felt he no longer knew himself.

You probably wish I were gone, too, so you could return to your boring, nonexistent life where you never have to smile.

Recalling Jenny's words, he wondered how one could have a nonexistent life. Boring, yes, but not nonexistent. To live was to exist. Once again, Jenny's choice of words made him smile.

Jenny's departure was the last thing Miller wanted. In fact, he couldn't imagine his life without the chaos of the last couple of weeks. He had come back from his walk not to conquer his enemies, but to surrender to them. He wanted to be a friend to Jenny and Ninj. He wanted to become less judgmental of the genie and become more accepting like Jenny.

But what had he done? The complete opposite of his good intentions.

Jenny had been right about his assumptions. Miller knew Ninj's background and shouldn't have expected the genie to have an understanding of the present. Besides Miller's earlier offenses, he had another whole list to atone for. Apologizing was number one, but he couldn't decide if he should do so when Jenny returned or go after her.

His decision was made for him when a strong, moisture-laden wind surged through the open windows and thunder rolled overhead. The force of the loud clap made the windows rattle and the crystals on the cranberry lamp ping against its base; and sent Bengel, who lay curled in a ball upon the settee, scurrying beneath a cloth-draped table.

Miller raced down the front stairs. Grabbing an umbrella from the many stored in the hall tree by the front door, he dashed outside to search for Jenny.

Fifteen

Jenny was so mad that she could spit needles. As she tromped along the path of the C & O Canal, her volatile temperament matched the thunder that rumbled overhead and she welcomed its angry roar.

Her foot met a rock in the middle of the path, and she gave it a forceful kick with her boot. The stone was bigger than she thought, and she received an aching toe for her efforts. Rather than stomping out her ire on the dirt path, she was forced to hobble on her way, fettered by her own outrage.

At no time in Jenny's life had she met a man more infuriating than Miller Holbrook. His insufferable superiority had tested her endurance from their first meeting. Just when she thought that he was mellowing, he did something stupid like blame Ninj for his own short-sightedness. Why had he expected both her and Ninj to be in tune with the social niceties that were as foreign to both of them as their backgrounds were to Miller?

"The devil with society," she grumbled.

She would show him. She wouldn't go to his stupid tea dance. Let him find someone else to escort, someone who wouldn't embarrass him by being dressed for an *orgy*. Even now the word stung as its meaning conjured up all kinds of illicit pictures and made Jenny's pique grow.

She knew what orgy meant from her Bible studies, and she didn't appreciate for a minute Miller's comparison to such wild revelry. It was no wonder that she had steered clear of men for most of her adult life. They had only one thing on their minds—unrestrained sexual activity; and because they lusted for the exercise, they assumed that women must, too.

Although the dancing might have been more enticing than the gypsy steps she knew, it was still a dance to be admired because of its history. Who could forget Salome, the stepdaughter of Herod, the ruler of Galilee?

Apparently Miller Holbrook remembered the belly dancer but had forgotten the more elemental lessons he had learned in church, like treating others with the same respect that you expected from others. Perhaps Miller's problem was that his head was filled with so much book learning that there was no room left inside for the good old-fashioned sensitivity that most folks shared with others.

Jenny had walked nearly fifteen minutes before she felt the first raindrops. They pockmarked the water on the canal and the dirt of the path beneath her feet—huge, heavy drops that promised the threat of a frog-choking downpour.

When she looked around, hoping to take cover and wait out the storm, she realized that she had left the congestion and noise of the canal behind. A few towboats still slugged their way along the waterway, but it was no longer stockpiled with boats waiting to load and unload their cargo at the wharves at the Georgetown terminus.

Buildings no longer lined both sides of the canal, and the crush of people was absent. In fact, she was surprised by the peacefulness and tranquility as she slowed to a stroll. The towpath was a natural walkway close to the city, but here she felt as though she had returned to the country.

Until now, Jenny hadn't realized how much she missed wandering through the valley in West Virginia.

Here along the tree-lined waterway, the air smelled as fresh and green as the grass of home.

She spotted a small stream that trickled into the canal, with a well-worn path beside it. Intrigued, Jenny turned and followed the path.

More drops of rain fell, and she knew she had to seek cover somewhere. She passed an outcropping of granite rocks that jutted upward from the earth not far from the water's edge. Following the path, she skirted the mass of rocks and saw that the stream widened. Water spilled over the boulders from a higher pool. Trees lined both sides of the natural basin, and someone had built a shelter on the small sandy beach beneath the trees.

As she neared the pool's edge, the bottom decided to fall out of the sky. In order to reach the trees and the makeshift cover, Jenny had to tiptoe over slippery rocks and boulders that looked like a giant's stepping stones.

Soaking wet, she bolted inside the shelter as a flash of lightning lit the darkening sky. The wind picked up, chilling her to the bone in spite of the still-warm day.

Four crudely fashioned poles held up the cross work of branches that an industrious picnicker had woven together for a roof. Although her haven wasn't completely weatherproof, the trees overhead still offered some refuge from the deluge that poured down in earnest now.

A clap of booming thunder made her teeth rattle. She hoped she hadn't been foolish with her choice of cover, although she hadn't had myriad options. Many a cow had died from lightning strikes because they took shelter beneath trees to wait out a storm such as this one. She offered up a prayer to the storm god that she wouldn't soon be joining the list of dead bovines. With nothing left to do, she plopped down on the ground as far away from the wooden supports as possible and hugged her knees with her arms.

Her statement to Miller came back to haunt her. *Who's afraid of a little storm? I'm not.* That had not been the complete truth. A little storm she enjoyed, but she wasn't too keen on the big ones that spit fire like dragons and had giant tails that rumbled across the heavens when they moved.

With regard to her other statement to Miller, she realized how unimportant she was in the whole scheme of things. Right now, with the lightning popping around her, she felt as insignificant as dirt.

"It won't last long," she told herself out loud as a drop of rain dripped from the roof to trail a cool finger down the back of her neck. She shivered and hugged her knees tighter and wished she were anywhere but here, preferably back in the shop, dry and warm.

The minutes lingered damply around her. "Oh, what I'd give for a cup of hot lemon tea." She craved it like a starving man craves food. The longing was so strong that Jenny imagined she could smell the tart lemony brew above the damp scent of the woods.

Her stomach rumbled. "All that dancing must have given me a powerful appetite," she said, hoping to break up the strangling sound of the storm.

Like a frog beneath a toadstool, she waited for the rain to stop. The wait gave her plenty of time to think. She thought of food, and that made her think of Ninj. When she thought of Ninj, her thoughts automatically turned to Miller.

As she sat cooling her heels, the rain cooled her anger, allowing her to look at the episode between Miller and herself more rationally. Jenny still felt that her annoyance on Ninj's behalf was warranted, but now that she was no longer miffed, she admitted that she wanted to attend the tea dance with Miller. So much so that she was willing to swallow her pride and let bygones be bygones.

For Ninj's sake, a little voice reminded her.

Her earlier desire to show Miller up no longer seemed important. If she refused to attend the dance as his escort, then not only would she be hurting herself, but also Ninj. How else was she to meet the man of her dreams?

A pretend man.

As though in defiance of her last thought, a Herculean

wind whipped beneath the flimsy roof, nearly lifting it from its twiggy rafters. The sudden forceful gust made Jenny wonder if maybe her Maker knew her intentions were less than honorable and this was His way of making her see her error. She shivered, hoping she was overreacting and that the feeble covering over her head would hold until the storm subsided.

But in order to condone her actions, she whispered, "I'm doing it for Ninj, pretending to look for the man of my dreams so that he can retire to genie heaven."

A loud pop of energy exploded behind her, making Jenny nearly jump out of her wet skin. More rumblings from heaven echoed throughout the wood.

She covered her ears with her hands and buried her face on her knees. "All right, all right," she said contritely, hoping to placate the thunder god. "Suppose I was looking for this man, a real one. What would he look like?"

Jenny mused over this for several moments before a picture formed in her mind. The image was of a man close to her own height. He would have thick hair the color of roasted chestnuts. His jaw would be square, his teeth straight and white, and a dimple would crease his right cheek. If he wore spectacles, when he took them off his eyes would be blue as a summer sky.

Her fantasizing brought a warm tingling to her depths. The man would always wear suits, crisp-collared shirts, and silk vests, and he would smell like sun-dried laundry. When he kissed her, his kiss would do funny things to her insides, just as thinking about such a fellow was doing.

The earlier voice returned to haunt her. *Like kiss you and make you lose the contents of your stomach?*

"It wasn't his kiss," she defended herself, "but that awful cherry concoction. Oh, Lordy." She groaned aloud, pressing the palms of her hands against her eyes. "My mind created an exact likeness of Miller. But why? I don't want any part of the professor."

You could have fooled me.

Jenny ignored this last thought, trying to understand why her mind had conjured up Miller's image. After much deliberation, she decided it was because he was the only man she knew other than Ninj, and Ninj wasn't really a man. Since she never had a father, it was only natural that the so-called man of her dreams would resemble Miller. There. Her deduction made sense, and the conclusion made her feel better.

Comfortable with herself now, she raised her head and watched the last remnants of the storm. Soon the rain stopped and the sun came out in full summer force. She had been spared an untimely death by lightning, and this knowledge made her spirits soar as she stood and stepped from beneath the makeshift shelter.

Her little world was saturated. The ground under her boots squished when she moved, and the leaves on the distant trees looked like diamonds where the sun bounced off their slick wet surfaces. She inhaled deeply, enjoying the scent of summer rain.

Jenny looked around the wooded area, seeing it for the first time. On a hot day, the pond above the rocks would be perfect for a swim, if folks swam in the city. No signs were posted forbidding the exercise. This water looked to be as good as the swimming hole back home. She was glad she had stumbled on this little piece of Eden in the middle of the big city.

But now it was time to leave. "I'll come again," she told the giant's stepping stones as she traversed their damp surfaces. With her eyes focused on the slippery ground, she jumped down from the last rock and was rounding the large outlying boulder when she bumped into rock-hard flesh. Two strong arms surrounded her, steadying her, while the man's umbrella poked its spiny tips into her backside. She wiggled closer to him to escape one extra-sharp point.

As she looked straight into Miller Holbrook's summer blue eyes, she asked, "How did you find me?"

"Jenny," he said, not bothering to answer her question, "I've been worried sick about you out in this storm."

His concern coupled with his nearness brought back her earlier tingly feeling.

Jenny knew she had to look like a sodden mess, but she hadn't expected to see the meticulous professor looking like a half-drowned rat. His once perfectly creased trousers were soaked, and both his jacket and pants were a rumpled mass of wrinkles. His always shiny shoes were caked in mud, and his starched white shirt was plastered to his chest. His hair still dripped from too many raindrops, and as he continued to hold her, she watched one errant drop journey down his eagle nose. Without giving it a thought, she reached up and flicked the dewdrop away.

"And you had an umbrella," she teased.

"It would have taken a tent to keep a person dry in that downpour, but none of that matters now. I found you, you're safe, and we'd best go home and get out of our clothes."

The implication of his words made them both blush, but it was Jenny who giggled and made the uneasiness fade. "Naked twice in one day," she teased. "What would Washington society say about that?"

Miller cleared his throat, which suddenly felt parched. The thought of Jenny naked brought to mind the dancer in gold whose dewy skin reflected the color of her costume. After a moment, he croaked out a response. "Our social leaders don't know what they've been missing."

"Why, Mr. Professor," Jenny said, using Ninj's title for him, "you don't mean you liked my dancing?"

Miller felt the line of his mouth relax. "I liked it— what I could see of it."

His reference to his near blindness made them both laugh.

Jenny watched the corners of his lips lift with pleasure. "Why, sir," she said, "I do believe you've been practicing your smiling." Little did Miller realize that his beautiful smile almost took her breath away.

"I'm trying," he answered with a lightness in his voice that she had never heard before. He stepped away from her, tucked her hand around his arm, and began moving along the path.

"I'm sorry, Jenny, for getting so angry at Ninj. I was wrong to expect him to know what type of gown you would need for the tea dance or what kind of dances you should learn."

"I was wrong, too," Jenny admitted. "I of all people should have known that Ninj sometimes makes mistakes. I think it is because he seems so human that we forget he is from another world."

"Like a world where elephants appear in basements?"

"Exactly."

They chuckled, sharing the memory of the incident.

As they neared the wharves of Georgetown, their drenched state brought curious stares from the people they passed, but they ignored them and kept right on walking.

"You didn't answer my question," Jenny said. "How did you find me?"

"First I went to Madame DeBeau's, thinking you might have taken refuge there."

"Refuge at Madame DeBeau's? Never. If anything, I'd like to forget I ever knew the woman."

"When you weren't there, it seemed only logical that you must have gone in the opposite direction, since you really haven't been out in the city to know anyplace else to go."

If he knew about the carriage ride that she and Ninj had taken, he might not be so agreeable. But why worry about it? It was over and forgotten. She and Ninj certainly weren't going to tell him.

"So I went toward the canal," Miller said, bringing her back to the present, "and just happened to meet the beat policeman who had seen you pass earlier."

"As many people that use that towpath, how did he know it was me? I don't recall seeing anyone."

"He said you wouldn't have noticed him, but he sure noticed you. Said you were stomping the daylights out of the ground when you passed him."

"I was not," Jenny fibbed. She wondered if the officer had seen her kick the rock, too.

"Since you were so angry when you left the house, I figured you must have been the lady he saw. So I kept walking in the direction he said you went until I found you."

"Lucky for you the rain had cooled down my temper."

"Lucky for us both, wouldn't you say? I wasn't exactly in one of my calmer moods when you left."

"No, you weren't. You were sputtering like a steam engine."

"Sputtering—"

"But about the tea dance," Jenny interrupted, fearing her comment had chased away his light mood. "If Ninj can't teach me the proper dances, then who will?"

"Who better than me? I *am* a teacher," Miller responded. "But I'll admit my dancing is a bit rusty."

"Just like your smile?" Jenny said, lifting her brows.

"Just like my smile," he confirmed. "From now on, I intend to make better use of it."

His words thrilled her, making her mood suddenly buoyant.

Where her fingers rested on his sleeve, she could feel the hot heat of his arm through the cool dampness. For the first time in her life, Jenny could actually say she was enjoying the company of a man.

A soft breeze lifted the scent of his slowly drying clothes, and its sunshiny fragrance tickled her nose. Before today, Jenny had never experienced such a warm satisfying glow—a glow that came from walking out with a man. She liked the feeling. She liked Miller Holbrook as well.

"Step-step-close, step-step-close, step-step-close." Miller recited the words as he led Jenny through a waltz around the perimeter of her parlor.

As the two dancers matched their steps, her uncle's music box pinged out a metallic tune. Ninj, whom Jenny had summoned at Miller's insistence after they had both changed into dry clothes, now sat on Jenny's sofa, clapping his large hands in time with the music.

The genie was all smiles as he watched Miller and Jenny dance. The earlier incidents with the *araba* and the belly dancing were nothing more than a fleeting memory. Like the storm that had come and gone, so had their anger. With their grievances put aside, Jenny believed that the three of them could begin again and become good friends.

Jenny was enjoying the harmony, but most of all she was enjoying Miller's embrace. But then, what lady wouldn't enjoy dancing with such a fine-looking man? When he had returned from changing his clothes, he had looked as spit-and-polished as his shoes. He wore another white shirt, and a yellow silk vest that she hadn't seen before today. The buttercup shade complimented the burnished gold wires of his spectacles and the chestnut color of his still-damp hair.

The music scratched to a finish, and Miller released her. Immediately she felt the cold of the room when his hand broke contact with her waist and their fingers were no longer entwined. Jenny blamed the sudden coolness on the rainstorm. Since returning to her apartment she hadn't been able to get warm, and she worried that she might be taking a chill. All she needed was to get a cold and not be able to attend the dance with Miller.

Standing several feet away from her, Miller broke into her thoughts. "You're a quick learner," he said.

"And you're an excellent teacher."

"I am at that," he said matter-of-factly.

If he had had feathers, Jenny imagined he'd be preening them because of her compliment.

She couldn't help laughing. Never had she met a more arrogant man. Hadn't she been privy to that information on the first day they met, when he had informed her that he was Dr. Holbrook, not Mr.? Since then, Jenny had come to realize that Miller made up for this one failing in other ways: He was kind, concerned, and had gone out of his way to be nice to Ninj since their return.

"Ninj is good teacher, too." The genie had shut off the music box to join them where they stood. "My *beledi* is much better than this floating together around the room like wambling ships. Better for men to first watch their women dance and touch them later."

Miller contemplated Ninj's statement, and Jenny cringed, thinking another disagreement was brewing. Instead, Miller surprised her with his next words.

"I don't know about that, Ninj. I kind of prefer it our way." Miller's gaze locked on Jenny, and his words weakened her knees. "It's a very nice way to hold your lady while others stare on. Would you like to try it?"

The genie looked indignant. "Ninj dances with no woman except in his bed. Maybe you and Mistress Jeenih should try my kind of dancing—how did you call it, Mr. Professor—oh yes, vibrating."

"Ninj," Jenny scolded, "you must not say such things. Miller and I are friends. In our country only married couples vibrate."

Miller's eyebrows formed two half-moons above the rims of his spectacles, and his blue eyes grew large.

This time it was she who turned beet red. "I think I'll have some tea," she said, whirling away from them and darting for the small kitchen. Her ears felt as though they had been scorched, and she swore she could hear Miller chuckling above the short, sharp sounds of her teaspoon hitting the sides of her china cup.

Once she regained her composure, Jenny walked back to where the two men stood. Trying to appear more casual than she felt, she asked, "What will I wear to the dance?"

"The *beledi* dress is good," Ninj told her. "It will provide the physical setting for your external mystique—"

"I'm sorry, Ninj, but I don't believe it's Jenny's mystique we are concerned with."

It was Miller's turn to look uncomfortable, and his discomfort made the corners of Jenny's lips turn upward. He noticed it and looked even more ill-at-ease before he cleared his throat to continue. "I've already taken care of what Jenny shall wear to the dance."

"You have? But how?"

Jenny couldn't imagine any man being concerned with a woman's wardrobe, much less a man like Miller, who appeared to shy away from anything that had to do with women. Her in particular. But then she recalled that this was the new Miller.

"You remember," he said, scratching his head, "I told you I had gone to Madame DeBeau's to look for you before the storm broke? Well, while I was there among all the female frippery, I decided that it was as good a time as any to order you a dress for the dance. Especially since she already had your—uh—calculations."

"My calculations?"

Jenny covered her mouth with her hand to smother a giggle.

His brows drew together in a frown that soon disappeared, and with a wave of his hand he dismissed her remark. "You know what I mean," he said, walking to the front windows and looking out. "I also picked out a suitable color. With Madame's help, of course."

"Of course."

"Together we chose an appropriate material, and she promised that she would get right to it. The gown will be delivered to you in time for the dance. She noted the date of the affair on her calendar and seemed thrilled that you would be accompanying me."

Jenny couldn't imagine Madame DeBeau being thrilled with anything that didn't concern herself, but she didn't voice this thought to Miller. After all, he had recommended the dressmaker to her and he seemed pleased that he had taken care of the problem of what she should wear to the dance. She only hoped that Madame wouldn't send her out gowned in something completely inappropriate. After the "cherry incident," nothing Madame might do would surprise Jenny.

She did not trust the woman. The sight of Madame and her uncle's lawyer in the shop that day still trifled with her memory. She thought it strange how, with the appearance of the lawyer, Madame's attitude changed after their conversation.

It seemed Miller could read her thoughts, as she believed that Ninj could, when he said, "Madame DeBeau has a reputation to uphold. I assure you you'll be the most beautifully dressed belle at the entertainment."

His assurance, or perhaps his compliment, made Jenny's heart take wing.

"You mean, I will look ooo-la-la, nice?"

Both Miller and Ninj recognized the expression and where it had come from, so they both laughed.

Still smiling, Miller rubbed his hands together. "Now it's time we practice some more. Ninj, you start the music, and Jenny and I will step around the floor a few more times."

"Ooo-la-la, nice," Ninj repeated on his way to the music box. "I like that expression."

Jenny and Miller stood together in the middle of the room, mere inches apart. Miller encircled her waist halfway with his right arm and placed the palm of his hand lightly above her waistline. With his left hand, he held her right hand at arm's length, while Jenny placed her left arm on his right.

Their gazes locked, their breathing quickened, and Jenny felt Miller's fingers tighten against her waist. For a moment they were back in the shop the night of the "cherry incident," when he had kissed her. Time stood still, and they remembered.

Pleased with the way things were progressing, Ninj watched them from beside the music box where the metal cylinder had almost finished playing its one tune.

Soon, he thought, smiling to himself, *I will be in paradise with my very own dancing girl.*

Sixteen

"You'll do fine," Miller told Jenny, who sat across from him in the rented brougham. Watching her now, he questioned the accuracy of his statement.

From the moment they had left the house to enter the carriage Miller had rented for the evening, Jenny had been as jumpy as a bullfrog. When they had pulled away from the curb, she had kept a stranglehold on the carriage walls. With both hands braced against the vehicle's sides, she hung on as though she expected to be tossed from her seat at any moment.

Perhaps her fear came from never riding in a public conveyance before. The woman who sat across from him was so unlike the Jenny he had come to know and believed to be fearless that her actions truly surprised him.

Miller had made arrangements for them to be driven straight to the dean's house; the driver would drop them off, then return for them around midnight when the dance was over. But judging from the way Jenny was acting, they might not make it to the function.

The longer he studied Jenny's distressed condition, the more he began to question his decision to bring her tonight. Maybe she wasn't ready for such an event, although she had turned out to be a fine dancer. She learned quickly, and she had a grace and confidence about her that would be sure to turn many young men's heads. But both grace and confidence had completely disappeared the moment the door had shut them inside the small compartment.

Trying to reassure her, Miller said, "Relax, Jenny. I assure you there is no need to panic. People ride in carriages all the time."

"Panic?" Her dark, blue-gray eyes were as large as saucers. "I'm not panicking. I'm waiting."

"Waiting?" Miller looked around the interior. "For what?"

"For the seat to move."

"For the seat to move?" Miller tried to reassure her. "The seat isn't going to move."

"It did the last time." She looked nervously at the velvet cushions beneath her before her gaze met his again.

"Whatever do you mean? 'The last time' . . ."

The carriage wheel dipped into a hole, and they bounced upward before settling back on the seats. Still clinging to the walls, she wore an expression of defiance as if to say, "See? I told you so."

"A washout," he reassured her, "from the recent rains." His assurance didn't calm her, because her hands remained glued to the walls.

"Maybe," he said, "if you will tell me about this belief you have that your seat is going to move, I'll be able to understand."

"I'll try, but I'm not turning loose of these walls."

"You don't have to, if holding them makes you feel more comfortable."

Of course, Miller would have preferred that she put her arms down and try sitting with her hands in her lap like a demure young lady. Since there appeared to be no immediate hopes of Jenny releasing her grip on the walls, Miller told himself that he must not look at the more obvious roundness of her breasts or the delicate indentures beneath her arms that her long gloves didn't hide.

"Are you going to tell me or not?" he asked, hoping to take his mind off Jenny's allure.

She took a deep steadying breath. "Give me a moment," she said, trying to relax. To Miller she still looked like a bird trapped inside a cage. He hoped she wouldn't begin throwing herself against the sides to get out.

"Take your time," he soothed. "When you're ready, I'll be here to listen."

He took a steadying breath of his own and tried not to look at Jenny, but in the close confines of the brougham, not looking was damn near impossible. They were so close their knees touched, and the contact sent a stream of fire up his legs to his groin.

The gold satin material that he had chosen for her gown reflected against her bare skin in the same distracting way that Ninj's costume had. Miller realized now that he had made a mistake in his choice of color, but at the time it had seemed so perfect—especially with her earlier image still vivid in his mind. He was jerked from his reverie by Jenny's interruption.

"Miller, I'm ready to tell you now."

While he had been wool-gathering, Jenny had relaxed somewhat, although she still continued to grip the carriage walls.

"That night when I took the hack home from Madame DeBeau's, the seat moved back and forth at will. I swore then on no occasion would I ride in another rented conveyance, and so far I haven't. Until now.

"Cramped inside that tiny wardrobe space, a body could hardly breathe. Of course, I was feeling kind of poorly because I drank too much of Madame DeBeau's cherries." Jenny made a face at the memory. "The way that seat moved as though it were alive, I just knew that I was going to be tossed out the back door of that cab and get trampled by an oncoming horse."

With Jenny's confession, it suddenly dawned on him why she felt so uncomfortable and why she feared that the seat would move. He tried to cover up his amusement and explain away her misgivings at the same time.

"Now I understand," he said. "I presume your conveyance was not like this one."

Jenny shook her head.

"Interrupt me if I'm wrong. The cab you took was only large enough for one passenger. I believe you would have entered it from the back. Once inside and the door was closed, you sat facing forward on a divided seat."

"Yes, that's exactly how it was. At first I thought I was supposed to ride standing up. Of course, before that day, I'd not ridden in a vehicle for hire."

Miller no longer fought his smile. "The crank at the driver's side was what moved your seat forward."

Jenny burst into laughter and released the walls to cover her mouth with her hands. "Crank? Do you mean Madame DeBeau? After all that cherry liquor she fed me, I wouldn't put it past her."

He chuckled. "I meant the driver moved a mechanism, not Madame DeBeau. The device is helpful when ascending or descending hills to balance the load."

"The driver won't do that with this seat?" she asked. Then, realizing that she no longer gripped the walls, she started to raise her arms again but stopped midway. "You're sure?"

"I'm positive. Trust me. You don't have to hang onto the walls. Other than a few washouts like the earlier one we hit, riding in this carriage is almost like sitting on the couch in your parlor."

Jenny looked down at the plush seat. "I must say it is more comfortable than the smaller one."

"I agree," Miller said. "I've ridden in that same type of sedan and felt it was much too confining. I understand it was invented by a man from Boston, Chauncey Thomas. I daresay, he probably never rode in his own invention, or he wouldn't have thrust it on the public."

"Well, I don't know about this Chauncey fellow, but I do know I won't ride in another one. I'll walk first."

"Good. Now that we've settled that, we can sit back and enjoy the scenery."

They rode in silence, allowing Jenny to get used to the idea that she wasn't going to be thrown from the moving vehicle. After a moment, she said, "You must think me a real ninny."

"Not at all. I think you're a vision of loveliness in your new gown. I'm very proud to be escorting you to the dance."

Jenny slowly placed her gloved hands in her lap and looked across at him. His compliment had brought a light blush to her cheeks.

She held her shoulders a little higher, and the movement afforded him a better look at her lush bosom.

Although it was clear to Miller that Jenny didn't like the dressmaker, Madame DeBeau had outdone herself with the gown she had created. The modiste had even gone so far as to send a ribbon of the same golden fabric as the dress so that Jenny could disguise the black string that held Ninj's jewel around her neck.

He was so intent on admiring her that he almost didn't hear her next words.

"You aren't so bad-looking yourself," the familiar, plain-spoken Jenny said.

Now it was Miller's turn to blush, and he tried to hide his discomfiture by coughing into his hand.

"I do believe, Mr. Professor, that you and I will be the most handsome couple attending this tea dance."

The blue-gray color of her eyes reflected the gold at her neck. "What do you think about that?" she asked.

"I think, Miss Blake, that you will do Washington society proud."

The lavishness Jenny witnessed as she and Miller made their way up the broad stairs to the mansion's entry was almost more than she could comprehend. Ninj had been right when he had said there were many palaces in Washington. Country bumpkin Jenny Blake was about to enter one of them.

They stepped inside the house and waited along with other couples to present themselves to their hosts. The polished marble floors mirrored the few dark wooden chairs and tables set around the edges of the room, and fading daylight was framed within the giant arched windows on each side of the entrance door.

Jenny inhaled deeply to calm her racing heart. The heady scent emanating from the many flower vases on the tables mingled with the smell of lemon oil and the combined fragrant perfumes of the ladies present.

She dipped her head toward Miller and whispered, "Do all professors make this much money?"

"Would that it were true," he whispered. "I understand it's his wife's money that affords them such quarters. Mrs. Sophronia Parke-Witty comes from old Washington money. She is a direct descendant of one of the old-time shipping barons who made his fortune during Georgetown's maritime prosperity. The mansion was built in the early seventeen-hundreds, and I understand it has been in her family for years."

"Seventeen-hundreds. Well, it certainly doesn't look that old to me," Jenny said, awestruck. "And I thought my uncle was rich because he owned such a fine house."

"He was rich," Miller added, "but not in such an ostentatious way."

"Ostentatious?" Jenny's question came out more loudly than she anticipated and she noted the raised brows of several couples around her. She wondered about the meaning of such an important-sounding word.

Miller's brows furrowed to warn her of her error; then he put his hand at the small of her back to urge her forward in the line. They were nearing their hosts, Dean Witty and his esteemed wife, Mrs. Sophronia Parke-Witty, who waited at the top of a short set of wide marble stairs. Jenny hung onto Miller's arm as if it were a lifeline, fearing that if she didn't her knees might buckle and she would collapse. As they slowly approached the couple, she studied the woman whose kin from more than a century ago could afford such a fine house.

Something about the dean's wife seemed remotely familiar, but Jenny couldn't put a finger on the where or if of such an acquaintance. Dismissing the notion, she studied the elegant woman. Mrs. Parke-Witty was fastidiously dressed in a high-collared dove-gray gown made from layers and layers of the sheerest fabric that Jenny had ever seen. The color of her dress perfectly matched her silvery-gray upswept hair. Her huge bosom was thrust forward like a shelf, and her notably curvy hips were thrust backward. Madame DeBeau had said the hourglass figure was considered a woman's greatest asset, but to Jenny the "pigeon" silhouette reminded her of the many birds she had seen roosting beneath the eaves of houses.

Jenny was so focused on her hostess that she nearly stumbled when Miller moved them forward in the line. They stopped in front of the couple and Jenny stared into the woman's silvery-gray eyes.

"Dr. Holbrook," Mrs. Parke-Witty said, looking Jenny up and down through a monocle that hung from her neck on a diamond-encrusted chain. Jenny felt the woman's gaze linger on Ninj's stone. "I'm so happy, Miller, that you brought an escort this year."

"Mrs. Parke-Witty," Miller said as he gave a slight bow, "allow me to present Miss Jenny Blake."

With the slow and measured dignity she had practiced, Jenny bowed, too. "Pleased to meet you, ma'am," she said.

"The pleasure is all mine, my dear. For years I've been trying to get this young man interested in the fairer sex, but my efforts have been for naught. He seems to prefer his books and his own company to that of the more genteel kind."

"Oh, I'm real gentle," Jenny said, wanting Miller's friend to like her, "as long as he doesn't rile me."

The dean chuckled beside his wife, who looked as though she had suddenly sucked on a sour lemon: Her painted lips puckered, and her face wrinkled like a pleated accordion. Jenny stole a quick peek at Miller, who, she noticed, was actually biting back a smile. She figured as long as he wasn't scowling, whatever she had said couldn't have been too bad.

The dean's wife replied abruptly, "Now that Miller has found you, I hope we'll be seeing more of you in the future."

To Jenny's ears, the woman's statement didn't ring true, but before she could respond, Miller urged her forward, and their hosts turned their attention to the next couple.

As Miller ushered her deeper into the wide receiving hall, Jenny forgot the incident. There were too many other things to see, like the beautifully appointed rooms that opened off the main hall, the huge circular stairway leading to the next level, and last but not least, the many guests who filled the rooms. To Jenny they resembled a bevy of fashion dolls all dressed up in their finery. The dance was like the ball in the *Cinderella* fairy tale.

They stopped at the entrance to the great hall where couples were already dancing. A string quartet played a lively piece, and young and old couples alike promenaded around the floor. Seeing the grace and poise of the many dancers, Jenny could understand why Ninj's *beledi* wouldn't have been appropriate for such a setting—the *beledi* was too exotic for such a traditional gathering.

They moved deeper into the room, where a lady handed Jenny a dance card with a pencil and ribbon attached. Miller tied it around her wrist. Jenny would have questioned the card's use if it hadn't been for Professor Hill's etiquette book. Not that she believed for a moment that with all the beautiful girls present any gentleman would single her out for a dance. But for Ninj's sake, she hoped at least one or two would.

What sounded like a waltz, similar to the one that she and Miller had practiced, floated from the stringed instruments. Mentally Jenny counted the beats in her head—*one, two, three, one, two, three*—and beneath her gown her foot tapped the rhythm against the floor.

Miller bowed slightly toward her. "May I have the pleasure of this waltz?" he asked.

He looked so strikingly handsome in his black tailcoat and white dress shirt, his white damask vest, and matching bow tie that he almost took her breath away.

Unable to utter a response, she accepted by placing her gloved hand in his and allowing him to lead her to the floor.

Again Jenny felt the familiar warmth of his hand at her waist, the contact of her fingers resting in his gloved hand, and the heat of his body through the many layers of their clothes. Soon he whirled her around the floor in time with the music and the other graceful dancers.

At first she counted the beat inside her head, fearing she would stumble and embarrass them both, but soon she forgot everything but Miller's eyes locked with hers and his handsome mouth, turning up at the corners into a very natural smile.

Ninj lay sprawled on the nest of pillows he had carried upstairs from the shop to Jenny's apartment, where he had scattered them across the floor by the front windows. Jenny had agreed to allow him free range of her apartment instead of staying confined to his bottle, but only if *he* agreed to behave himself.

Since Miller and Jenny's departure, he was feeling very much alone. From his position by the windows, he had watched them leave for the tea dance, wishing he had been attending with them. Ninj's powers allowed him to venture out only at his master's side. Even if he had wanted to follow them to the ball, he couldn't. He was immured here until their return.

Jenny's house, like his bottle before his summons, was beginning to close in on him. The colorless unadorned walls and ceilings, the dark wooden floors, and the small windows and doors that led to nowhere were now his prison.

Ninj longed for his Sultana's harem with its flower-painted walls and ceilings, its cool marble floors, and

the latticed windows and doors that led to inner court-
yards that were abloom with flowers and alive with the
sound of gurgling fountains.

He yearned for the tile pools where a man could im-
merse his whole body in the baths while a beautiful slave
girl rubbed exotic-smelling oils into his skin. Ninj closed
his eyes and imagined nimble fingers massaging his back
and other things that needed massaging. Those things,
too, he would have when he retired.

"Ah, those halcyon days," he reminisced aloud when
Bengel came to lounge beside him. He stroked the cat's
snowy fur and stared into his odd eyes. "You, my
friend, do you, too, long for the comfort of another
pussy? Or are you like the eunuchs who reside in the
harem?

"Perhaps you are like me who dreams of another life
and cannot do anything about it."

He continued to stroke Bengel's fur. "You, the white
tiger, and me, we are much alike. This is our kismet.
Our personal destiny was shaped long ago by one more
divine than us."

Studying his manicured nails, he asked Bengel, "Do
you think that I can bathe in Mistress Jee-nih's tub?"

The idea of a bath appealed to him. Although the copper tub that sat in the small bathing room beside the
kitchen wasn't exactly Ninj's idea of a true bath, maybe
he could wash away his restlessness. Not only could he
not go out without his master, but also his powers were
limited. He was unable to use his magic for his own
fantasies, so he would have to make do with the facilities
available to him.

"And there is always food." But since his mistress
wasn't fond of the lamb Ninj loved, he had come to like
the fried fowl she made regularly. In fact, there was a
whole platter of the bird waiting for his consumption in
the kitchen. She had made it especially for him this
morning, or at least that was what she had said.

"I will miss my Jee-nih when I retire," he told Bengel. "She is a good and kind master. You, my white tiger, are a lucky beast."

He pushed upward from his pillows and settled the turban Jenny had bought him back upon his head. "I do not have the heart to tell my mistress that this new turban is much too small. She was so excited with her gift that I could be nothing but grateful. Soon I shall wear my own turban with its jewel back in place.

"Come." He motioned to Bengel. "What we men really need is a good fight to drive away our boredom. But since a battle is impossible in this city where men do not carry swords, you and I, we will eat fried fowl."

Ninj stood. At the mention of food, Bengel stood as well and began to rub against Ninj's ankles. Almost stumbling because of the cat's ministrations, he stepped over him and walked toward the small kitchen. Bengel followed close on Ninj's silk-slippered heels.

"Perhaps, my friend, you should learn to rub oil on my body the way you rub around my ankles."

Seventeen

~

As Jenny smiled her pleasure at the young man she was waltzing with, Miller confronted his displeasure from behind a potted palm. The evening was going just as he envisioned it would. Jenny's debut into society appeared to be a success, but Miller no longer appreciated the young pups and old-dog professors vying for her favor and enjoying her beauty.

And she was a beauty. There was no doubt of it in Miller's mind, or in the minds of the other unattached males attending, if the number of partners she had was any indication. After his first turn around the floor with her, the swine had been standing in line to sign their names to her dance card. At first her success had pleased him, but as the evening wore on, Miller's pleasure had turned to torment.

It had been his plan to bring Jenny to the dance so she could meet numerous young men. Miller had come knowing that as her escort all her dances wouldn't be reserved for him, which at the time seemed like a fine idea. Once here, all he needed to do was see that she had plenty of dancing partners, which definitely wasn't a problem, make sure she enjoyed herself, and the rest was up to her. It was Jenny's choice to dance with whom she pleased.

At the moment, she seemed very pleased with her

partner, who Miller recognized as one of his math students. Not only did Jenny appear to be hanging onto the young man's every word, but it also looked as though she had allowed the lad to hold her much too close. Miller's lips thinned with irritation.

He should have told Madame DeBeau to make Jenny's gown with long sleeves and a high, close-fitting collar like the one the dean's wife wore, instead of the low-cut, off-the-shoulder neckline that revealed too much bosom and too much shoulder. Even the gown's material had been a bad choice. What there was of the gold satin fabric clung to her voluptuous curves like a second skin. Ninj's jewel at her neck gave every man in the room a reason for ogling her exposed feminine charms, while pretending interest in the damn garish rock.

Tonight the stone had managed not to look so garish. With the sprinkling of aquamarine stones on her dress and the matching drops at her ears, the entire look appeared very stylish—so much so that Miller had overheard the dean's wife and her group of followers comment on the jewel's beauty. One lady had gone so far as to compare it to the Hope diamond. To Miller the only thing remotely similar about the two stones was the mystique surrounding them; or in Jenny's case, the mystique surrounding the woman.

Miller checked his pocket watch. It was slowly approaching eight o'clock, when dinner would be served. As Jenny's escort, it was his responsibility to walk her in to the meal. Not long after their first and only dance, he had begun to count the moments until the meal would be announced, knowing it would give him an excuse to join her. He was looking forward to sharing her company throughout the long supper. Already he had grown bored with the simpering females he had been forced to partner for the dancing, a duty that reminded him of why he didn't enjoy these affairs.

He left his place behind the palm and moved across the room to collect Jenny. Having decided to forego the march before dinner, she now stood in the midst of a group of elderly females. As Miller moved in and around the spectators, he noted that Jenny looked flushed from dancing and that her skin had that same dewy look it had had the night she'd danced the *beledi* for him.

Stopping behind the cluster of women, Miller waited for the right moment to interrupt.

"Such a lovely necklace," a matron said, eyeing the stone at Jenny's neck.

Miller recognized the lady. She was the wife of a professor.

"It was a gift from my uncle," Jenny told her.

Mrs. Sophronia Parke-Witty, who appeared to be holding court over the crowd, declared, "Your uncle was Antonini Vassily, the shopkeeper?"

"Yes," Jenny responded. "Did you know him?"

As always, Jenny's face lit up when someone mentioned her uncle, and Miller listened more closely as the conversation continued.

"I know Dr. Holbrook has let rooms from him for years." Her beakish nose inched up a little higher. "I can't understand why one of our own insists upon living above a shop." The other hens clucked their agreement. "But to answer your question, Miss Blake, no, I didn't know your uncle, but I knew of his business. A colleague of my husband's purchased goods from him a number of years ago."

Another woman interrupted. "That would have been Tilly Kendall, Sophronia. You remember her, don't you?"

Miller recognized the speaker as another professor's wife whose name he couldn't recall. It was clear the lady in question revered her hostess as royalty and considered herself one of the queen's confidantes.

"Trying to be what she was not," the elder continued, turning to face Jenny. "Before her husband's demise, he, too, taught at the college. I personally couldn't tolerate the woman. I understand she made purchases from your uncle's shop then told everyone they had been passed down from her family.''

Someone else added, "We all know the only family Tilly Kendall had worth speaking of was on her husband's side. Myself, I could not at all understand why such a brilliant man married such a dull creature.''

"Maybe he liked her," Jenny added.

Her response surprised even Miller, but then he took his thought back. Lately nothing about Jenny surprised him. He did wonder when she had begun defending a man when she claimed to have so little respect for the species.

Jenny continued, "You certainly can't fault this Miss Tilly for her good taste. My uncle has some beautiful pieces in his shop. A body would be right proud to claim that they had been in her family.''

"But that isn't the point, child. Surely even you must know that one doesn't make up stories about one's ancestry.''

"If a person doesn't have any ancestry to speak of, there's not a bit of telling what they might say.''

Jenny's expression took on that determined look that Miller had come to recognize and usually meant trouble.

"Besides," Jenny continued, "if her made-up story helped her to feel better about herself, what difference does a little stretching of the truth matter? Especially if that stretching doesn't hurt anyone.''

"But don't you see—''

"Speaking of seeing," the dean's wife interrupted, "did you tell Horace about our experience last week with nobility?''

"Nobility?" Jenny was all ears.

Ignoring her, the old dame said, "You're referring to that strange-looking carriage we saw on the way to the Center Market?''

Miller's own ears perked up with the mention of the carriage.

"The gilded carriage with the red veils," someone else responded. "Who could forget it?''

He looked at Jenny. Her face was drained of its earlier flush, and Miller felt his stomach muscles tighten. His worst fears were confirmed. The strange-looking vehicle parked in front of the shop that Jenny and Ninj had convinced him didn't exist *had*. And its existence along with their denial could mean only one thing.

At that moment, his and Jenny's gazes locked above the heads of the women, and she quickly looked away.

"You mean that coach," another lady added, "that carried the princess and her giant slave?"

"The eunuch," another whispered and tittered like a young girl while the rest of the matrons turned a deeper shade of rose.

"In my opinion," the more brazen in the group added, "we women would be much better off if all the menfolks were sheared!"

"Angela Hall, you forget yourself," Mrs. Parke-Witty scolded. "We have a young lady amongst us whose ears should not hear such talk."

The chastised woman looked stricken when she realized her mistake. "I'm sorry, dear—"

"Oh, don't you worry yourself none about my ears," Jenny reassured her. "In the country, animals are castrated or gelded all the time, in order to make them more docile—"

"Miss Blake," Miller interrupted, "I believe it's time for dinner."

He had managed to wedge himself into the midst of the coughing, sputtering matrons, who looked as though they would be calling for their smelling salts at any moment.

"If you'll excuse us," he said, bowing slightly. He grabbed Jenny's arm and began steering her away from the distraught women.

"Did I say something wrong?" she asked.

He paused once they were a safe distance away from the shrill, cackling hens. "A lady does not speak of . . . uh . . . shearing animals at a ball."

Jenny looked indignant. "I wasn't speaking of clip-

ping fur. . . .'' Her voice trailed off. ''Oh, my,'' she said,
covering her mouth with her hand. ''I'm as outspoken
as Ninj.''

Miller's mouth trembled with the need to smile.

Jenny blushed and hid her giggle.

''But you're a lot prettier than he is,'' Miller said,
''and I'm delighted to be escorting you to dinner. Now,
shall we join the others? I'm starving, and I'd love to
eat before they throw us out of here.''

Manners forgotten, Miller and Jenny burst out laughing. Then they worked their way toward the front of the
line of guests waiting to enter the dining room.

After downing almost the whole platter of fried fowl,
Ninj belched. Pushing back from the table, he lifted his
arms above his head and stretched. Now that his belly
no longer gnawed at his backbone, it was time for a bath.
Since Miller and Mistress Jee-nih wouldn't be home until midnight, Ninj had lots of time to soak in Jenny's tub
and still be finished before they returned from the ball.
He was anxious to hear how the evening went, although
he felt confident that all went as he had planned.

Wiping his greasy fingers on a napkin, Ninj stood.
Leaving the kitchen and Bengel, who lay snoozing on
the floor, he moved toward the small bathing room.
Once inside, he closed the door and turned the brass
knobs on the pipes as he had seen Jenny do. The metal
tubes clanked and groaned as water flowed upward from
the basement holding tank. Soon the five-foot-long copper tub was filled with enough water for him to bathe.

Of course, it couldn't compare with the *hamam* of his
country where the Turkish baths were hot steamy rooms
with many tiled pools. Here there was no round belly
stone where a man could lie down and be massaged and
washed by slaves.

Mistress Jee-nih's bathing room was not stocked with
fragrant oils, but he did find a large scored cake resem-
bling hardened tallow that had a pleasing scent. Dropping the cake into the water, Ninj saw that it floated. At

least his mistress had Turkish towels. He took several from a shelf and placed them beside the tub. Then he disrobed and settled into the tub as best as he could because of his girth. With the strange cake that had become as slippery as an eel, he washed himself. Soon the heat of the water made him drowsy. He propped his turbaned head against the wall and fell into a restful sleep.

Ninj dreamed of home: of lamb cooked on spits, of acrobats and puppet shows, and of golden-veiled dancing girls. He dreamed of all the things he would enjoy once he retired to genie paradise.

The door clicked shut behind the two black-clad figures as they eased their way into the darkened shop.

"Shush!" the shorter one cautioned the taller one when they jerked to a standstill in the entryway.

From a room at the top of the stairs, a wedge of light slanted across the landing in the otherwise darkened building.

The taller of the two dropped a key into the pocket of a baggy shirt and whispered, "There's no one here. It's like I told you earlier. The tea dance won't be over until midnight. We have several hours to search."

"But what about the Indian that Axle told us about?"

"He'll be at the dance as well. He's the professor's friend. What does it matter? I'm sure he doesn't live here anyway."

Although traces of a full moon and the gaslamps on the street partially lit the shop's interior, it was much too dark to conduct a proper search. As they moved stealthily into the shop, the intruder pulled a candle from the folds of his garments. "If we're to find anything, we'll need this."

A match striking against a flint sounded throughout the room before a hint of sulphur tainted the close air. Soon a yellow glow illuminated the room.

"I'd feel a lot better if that damn bay window was covered with drapes."

"*Mon cher,* you worry too much. We will find the bottle Monsieur Vassily mentioned in his letter, then we will be gone. No one will know we were here."

"I shouldn't have told you about the bottle. Who can believe the descendant of a gypsy anyway? Probably as worthless as those crystal balls they use to dupe fools into believing they can read the future."

"But, ah, if it is true, imagine the riches we'll have."

"I would have had plenty if that cursed niece hadn't come to town."

A loud thump above their heads stopped their heartbeats and froze them in their tracks. After a moment, the short one muttered nervously, "I thought you said they were out."

"Do you see them?" the other shrilled, displeased but nervous as well. "Do you?" She gulped.

The man looked nervously toward the stairs, and then a smile lifted one of the three holes in his stocking-cap mask. He relaxed visibly. "It was the cat," he said.

The second one looked toward the stairway where a ghostly white image of a feline stood out against the black wall. "Be thankful the puss isn't a dog," she muttered. "Now let's hurry. *Mon Dieu!* You're making me nervous because you're so jumpy. Be careful of the pillows." She headed toward the back of the shop.

The partner mumbled beneath his breath, "Pillows are the least of my worries."

"Tell me what the bottle looks like."

"How do I know what it looks like? A lamp, I suppose."

"*Encroiable!*" the lanky one grumbled, her gaze circling the room. "Look around you and tell me how many lamps you see. I can count six right here."

"How the hell am I supposed to know what a genie lamp looks like? I knew I shouldn't have told you about that damn letter."

The taller figure moved to stand beside the shorter one and encircled him with her arms. "*Mon cher,* it is for us both that I want this thing." She kissed the top of his head. "And besides, since that nobody woman fired you, she deserves whatever misfortune comes her way."

"Yes, I suppose she does. But how can we be certain such a lamp exists?" He held the candle higher and moved several items on the shelves to look behind them. "Who believes in genies anyway?"

"I wouldn't believe in them, either, if that stupid girl hadn't purchased that ratty-looking turban from my shop. Genies wear turbans, you know."

"Then when I delivered her reticule and the turban the next day, through the window I saw this giant of a man in Eastern dress. He wore a turban." As she spoke, she became more excited. "They were talking together right here where we are standing."

"Axle's Indian, I would guess."

"Maybe, but, *mon cher,* I swear on Napoleon's grave that strange man was here one moment and gone the next." She snapped her fingers. "Like that," she said, "he disappeared into thin air.

"Then later when you told me about her uncle mentioning the trunk and contents in his letter, I put two and two together and came up with one. One genie, that is." She touched her head with one hand and whispered, "I am so clever, don't you agree?" Then, recalling her hair was covered and didn't need arranging, she dropped her hand back to her side.

"You were clever to take the key from Miss Blake's reticule. That trick saved us from having to break through the door." He bent down and perused the paraphernalia stacked around the room. "My other opinion on the extent of your cleverness will be reserved until we find the lamp and this giant you claim you saw."

"We will find both, *mon cher,* I am certain we will."

She moved toward the front of the shop and fingered several vases that sat on a table among a dozen other ones.

"Eek!" she screeched, swaying on her feet. "That cat nearly tripped me. Shoo. Get away." She kicked out at

Bengel, who rubbed around her ankles. "I've never liked pussies."

From across the room, her partner chuckled. "I've always been rather fond of them myself."

"I'm not talking about the two-legged variety."

The four-legged variety, after being booted by the intruder, jumped on one of the leopard-skin chairs that sat in the bay window and began bathing himself. A horse and carriage clopped along the street. On hearing the noise, the cat twisted around, stood on his back paws, propped his front paws against the chair's back, and stretched upward to look out the window.

Madame DeBeau sucked in her breath. "I remember now," she said, no longer whispering. She rushed toward her partner, who stood near the back of the room, rummaging through papers on the desk.

"I saw it. That day I came to the shop."

Phineas Goldfinch threw down the stack of papers. "You saw what?" he asked when she stopped in front of him.

She lifted her mask, rolling it back to expose her face. "The bottle, or lamp, or whatever it's called. I'm sure I saw it. There." She pointed to the amulet tray that sat on the bookshelf. "The carafe was embedded with colored glass and stones. I remember thinking later, after I returned home, what an unusual-looking bottle it had been and that I would have liked to purchase it for my shop. *Mon Dieu!* I held a king's ransom in my hands and didn't realize it."

"Pshaw. You still don't know if such an item exists. You're only guessing."

"I'm not. I have a feeling about this, Phineas. Especially when the man I saw through the shop window had disappeared completely when I came inside."

"You're worried about one little piece that probably will turn out to be worthless—a fool's wish. Look around you, you stupid female. Antonini Vassily's collection of junk is worth a true king's ransom, and I lost it all because of that ignorant farm girl. We should be hauling everything out instead of searching for the one thing you seek.''

Ignoring his remark, Madame DeBeau tapped a long fingernail against her teeth and scanned the shop's interior again. "If the bottle isn't down here, it must be in her apartment. Come," she ordered, moving toward the entrance. "We'll search upstairs."

The brougham rocked gently as they pulled away from the mansion. Not long after sharing Mrs. Sophronia Parke-Witty's fine repast, Miller and Jenny had danced one more waltz together before bidding their hosts farewell, choosing to leave long before the appointed hour of midnight. Now they were on their way home.

The interior of the coach was in darkness, and only the glimmer from the moon overhead and the glow of the streetlamps they passed reflected occasional light into the small, close space. Jenny sat quietly on the seat across from Miller, troubled by memories of the dance that she wished she could change.

Using the title of courtesy that he had employed throughout the evening, Miller broke into her thoughts. "Miss Blake, you're very quiet. I trust that the evening fulfilled your expectations?"

He sounded so formal, so unlike the man who an hour before had pushed them through the waiting guests for a place at the front of the supper line. They had laughed together like children, and she had felt so alive and almost beautiful when he had claimed delight to be escorting her to dinner.

The more reserved Miller had returned, and although the clock had not yet struck the witching hour, for Jenny the night was no longer filled with magic. Now that Miller had had time to think about her tasteless remarks, he probably regretted the day he had invited her to the ball. Just as she doubted that Professor Thomas Hill, the century's master of manners, would wish to claim her as a student of his book.

Fortunately the darkness inside the coach hid her embarrassment and her sudden pensive mood. After a moment she answered Miller's question. "Yes, the evening met with my approval. So many of the men I danced with promised to call." With more enthusiasm than she felt, she added, "I'm looking forward to getting to know each and every one of them."

Jenny supposed that among the many men whom she had met tonight there would be one she could pretend to adore. The pretense wouldn't be easy, however. Most of them had been shallow and boring, and she questioned how she would tolerate such a person long enough to convince Ninj that she had found a perfect love.

How could those men compare to Miller? He was so much more handsome than her other dance partners that they paled by comparison. Studying his silhouette, she wondered when he had become so attractive. His appearance hadn't changed since the first day they met, yet in the last week she had begun to think of him as the most appealing man she had ever known.

Miller shifted across from her. "All those many gentlemen caught your eye, huh? That means in the ensuing weeks you'll be a very busy lady." He cleared his throat. "I'm glad for your success."

They passed a shop, and for only a second a lamp inside the window illuminated his face. That brief glimpse revealed he wasn't as pleased as he sounded, or so Jenny wanted to believe.

"I just wonder," she said, "if the gentlemen will still wish to call on me when they hear about my error." She wrung her hands in her lap. "If my big mouth has ruined Ninj's chance for retirement, I won't be able to forgive myself."

"I assure you that your little faux pas will not put off any gentleman who is worthy of your company. You are a lovely young woman and not easy to forget or ignore."

"Do you mean—" Jenny stopped in the middle of her sentence. Of course *he* didn't mean that she was lovely and not easy to forget or ignore. He was just being kind and trying to make her feel better.

Miller chuckled. "I can assure you that Mrs. So-phronia Parke-Witty and her retinue won't be forgetting you anytime soon. I thought the whole gaggle of old biddies was going to swoon when they heard your re-mark about farm animals."

She remembered the moment too well and since she couldn't take back her words, she wanted to forget them. Her face flushed with anger at herself. *How could I have been so stupid?*

"It would serve them all well," Miller said, bringing her back to the present, "if when you meet them again, you ignored the whole lot."

She laughed bitterly. "I don't think my ignoring them will be a problem. After my *fo pooh*, or whatever it was you called it, they avoided me as if I wore a quarantine sign around my neck."

"Then, my Jenny, they are the losers."

"Do you really think so?" she asked, her mulligrub mood lifting somewhat. It was important to her that Mil-ler still wanted them to be friends. She hoped the un-derstanding they had reached that day after the rainstorm hadn't been for naught. If he accepted her apology, then their friendship could continue to grow.

"I'm sorry," she said. "I know those people are your friends. I didn't mean to embarrass you."

"Jenny, Jenny."

The way he whispered her name made her feel as though he had blown his warm breath against her ear. Her heartbeat stuttered against her ribs.

"Surely by now," he continued softly, "you must know I prefer my own company to that of others, but for you it's different."

Confused by his remark, she lowered her gaze, but after a moment she raised it. "I know it's important that I learn to be a proper lady, but after my one evening spent with important people in society, I'm convinced that hobnobbing with my betters is not for me."

"Betters? They are far from your betters." Miller leaned forward on his seat and picked up her gloved hand. "Don't ever think that you aren't as good as they are, or anyone else for that matter."

Although she couldn't see his eyes, she felt them drilling into her. His stare, like his nearness, unsettled her. She dropped her gaze to her lap, but knew it would take a legion of horses to remove her hand from his.

Miller toyed with the tiny buttons at Jenny's wrist. The heat of her made the material of her glove feel as though it had been touched with a hot iron. Beneath his fingertips, her pulse beat as erratically as that of a caged and frightened bird.

For most of Miller's adult life, he had believed that women like Mrs. Sophronia Parke-Witty and her cronies were the epitome of the gentler sex, the picture of good manners and the type of woman he admired. Women who cared about those less fortunate than themselves. Women whom he had always believed were sincere. If Miller had not decided long ago not to marry, it would have been that same kind of woman he would have chosen for a wife.

He had always assumed, because of their esteemed position in society, that they were charitable women who possessed heart beneath their fancy outer wrappings. But tonight he had seen another side to those women. A side that didn't make him proud of his earlier opinion.

He had watched them look down their patrician noses and snub Jenny because she was different, just as they had condemned the poor Kendall woman because her efforts to be like them hadn't followed their set of rules. Because of Jenny's outspoken honesty and because she lacked a certain refinement, they had shunned her.

What a fool he had been. He was ashamed of the blinders he'd worn for so many years. Jenny might not have come from a well-known family, but she was warm and caring and in no way did she intentionally hurt anyone. Jenny was just Jenny, and at no time would she be anything less.

She was his dancing girl in golden veils, his drowned mermaid in the rain. Now, as she sat across from him claiming she wasn't as good as her betters, that she was sorry because she had embarrassed him in front of his friends, Miller was angry with himself. If anyone should be doing the apologizing, it was him.

"Oh, my sweet Jenny," he finally responded, "there is no need for you to apologize to me. I'm the one who is sorry for trying to make you into something that you're not."

Unconsciously his fingers had worked the buttons on her gloves loose from their loops. He rubbed his thumb across her pulse before he bent forward and lifted her hand to his mouth. Her skin smelled of soap and water beneath the tiny slit. Miller lowered his head and brushed his lips against her silky flesh.

He heard her sharp intake of breath. Or was it his? It didn't matter. What mattered was that he wanted to kiss her, to hold her in his arms as he had done that night in the shop. With his free hand he cupped his fingers around her neck and pulled her gently toward him.

"Oh, Jenny, what am I to do with you?" he whispered.

Her expression was one of dazed confusion, but she still managed a slight smile. "You could take me home and chain me indoors. Then society would be safe."

"To hell with society."

His expletive made a smile spread across Jenny's face that he swore brightened the interior.

It felt right, so he kissed the tip of her nose. Then his lips moved lower to capture her mouth, and he drank in the sweetness that was Jenny.

She closed her eyes and let the kiss happen. The one other time Miller had kissed her, Jenny had blamed her giddiness on the cherry liqueur she had consumed. But tonight it wasn't spirits that made her head light and her knees heavy. It was Miller's embrace, and it was more debilitating than the most potent devil's brew.

Giving herself up to the intoxication of his lips, she

sighed, and the air that rippled past her lips parted them, allowing him to deepen the kiss. As his tongue touched hers, she kissed him with a hunger she didn't know she possessed. The shared intimacy set her on fire, and she gave herself over to the sensation, her breath exhaling in whispered mews.

The heated joining of their tongues and Jenny's re-action sent desire rushing through Miller. His blood pounded, and he grew hard with need. His Jenny, he wanted all of her.

The carriage jerked to a stop. He tried to brace himself to keep from losing her. Their knees bumped, their noses collided, and the coach dipped sideways with the driver's descent. Reluctantly Miller released her when the man's frame darkened the small carriage window.

"This be your address, sir," the driver barked, swing-ing open the door.

With the rush of cool night air, Miller felt as if he had been splashed with icy water. His ardor cooled, and his sanity returned, making him question the wisdom of his actions. He shouldn't have kissed her again, espe-cially with such ungentlemanly passion. The last thing they needed was for him to complicate their relationship with kissing, although he'd be the first to admit that he had enjoyed it more than he could have imagined.

Still, they both were set in their ways and they both had definite goals: his was to remain a crusty old bach-elor, and hers was to keep her life free of any man. Besides, he reasoned, they were too different to be any-thing other than friends. Her sweetness didn't match his sourness, and it was best he be the one to set them back on course.

"I'm sorry," he lied, "I forgot myself."

With nothing more than a pat on her arm, Miller stepped down from the coach then turned to offer her his hand.

"Come," he said, "I'm sure our friend Ninj is anx-ious to hear of your conquests."

Conquests? Jenny wondered what conquests he referred to. Surely not the kiss they had shared, the same kiss that he had dismissed so easily with a pat on the arm.

It was apparent Miller was used to kissing females in carriages, and she wasn't used to kissing at all. Perhaps it was time she brought out Professor Hill's book again and read the section on courtship. Her throat tightened as she tried for the same careless tone that Miller had used. "I'm sure Ninj will be waiting for us by the door."

They walked in silence toward the entrance.

Jenny was about to give the second best performance of her life—convincing Ninj that she was excited about her true-love prospects.

She had given her first best performance when she, like Miller, had easily dismissed their kiss.

Eighteen

~

Madame DeBeau said, "Someone's coming. Quick, back to the bedroom."

Yanking a walking stick from where it stood propped against a corner wall, she thrust it into Phineas Gold-finch's hands. "Use it only if you have to." For her own weapon she picked up a heavy bronze statue of David from a table.

"Stupid female. I agreed to robbery, not murder."

"Shush! You aren't going to kill anyone. Only knock them senseless if need be. If we're lucky, we can sneak out when no one is looking."

They scurried into the bedroom, where Madame searched for a place to hide. "There," she said, pointing to a giant walnut wardrobe. "We can hide there."

Following her to the massive piece of furniture, Phineas grumbled, "I knew I shouldn't have allowed you to talk me into this ridiculous search."

"*Mon Dieu!* Will you please shut up?"

She jerked open the double-mirrored doors. The two-some struggled inside and pulled the doors closed behind them. Madame adjusted their masks, then they crouched together like two peas in a pod and waited.

"I could have sworn I locked up when we left." Miller pushed open the front door and allowed Jenny to precede him before closing it again.

"Perhaps Ninj opened it," Jenny said. She exhaled an exasperated sigh and peeled off her long gloves.

He paused by the shop entrance and peered into the unlit room. "You think Ninj went out?" he asked. "Lord help this city if we've turned him loose in it."

"Ninj wouldn't go out."

"He went out with you, didn't he?"

Guiltily she replied, "Only once."

Remembering that she and Ninj had been seen, she waited for him to say more about the women's conversation he had overheard at the dance, but instead he went on about Ninj.

"Maybe he decided to fly about on his magic carpet. Tour the city by air."

She shot him an annoyed look. "I already warned him about the consequences of such an adventure." She didn't elaborate because she thought it best that the *araba* incident be forgotten. "Ninj gave me his word that he would behave himself, and I trust him."

Miller sniffed the air. "Well, he's been playing with matches and candles. I can smell both inside the shop."

Bengel appeared out of the dark interior and meowed a greeting.

"He probably lit a candle to look for something down here. You know he's unfamiliar with how to light the gaslamps." She glanced upstairs. "Remember, the only lights we left on were in my apartment." Jenny started up. "Isn't that the music box I hear? He must still be awake." If so, that meant she would have to go on about how much she enjoyed the dance.

"Eating, most likely," Miller said behind her. "It's apparent he has a fondness for food. Wouldn't surprise me to see that whole platter of chicken gone. Maybe he didn't eat all of it. I've been thinking about a snack all the way home."

"After what you ate for dinner?"

At least Miller liked her fried chicken. So much so that he'd been thinking about it when they kissed, or that was what he was implying. *You can eat the platter for all I care.*

"Personally, I couldn't eat another bite, but then I don't have hollow legs."

"Where do you come up with these sayings?" Miller asked. "If my legs were hollow as you maintain, they would be less than useless, and I wouldn't be following you up the stairs."

The idea of you being elsewhere suits me just fine.

Jenny didn't bother to respond. She was tired and irritable and wanted to be left alone to sort out her thoughts. Once on the landing, she saw that the apartment door stood wide open. The music box pinged to silence as she moved toward the entrance.

"Ninj," she called, "are you here?"

When he didn't answer, she looked around the room. Bengel darted past her feet and hopped up on his favorite chair. "Where's Ninj?" she asked the cat, tossing her gloves on the couch. "Is he asleep? I won't disturb him if he is."

She prayed the genie was well into his dreams so she wouldn't have to answer questions about the ball. All she wanted to do was go to bed and sleep away her frustration.

Seeing pillows scattered across the floor in front of the windows, Jenny decided they were the reason why Ninj had been in the shop with a candle. But where was he now?

She walked toward the bedroom, and Miller followed her as far as the door. He stopped there and hung back as she went inside.

"That's strange," Jenny said. "I don't remember leaving those drawers open." She glanced toward the wardrobe, where she saw the hems of several new gowns were caught in the mirrored doors. How could she have been so careless with her new dresses? She walked to the wardrobe and was about to open the doors when she heard Ninj's voice in the other room.

"Mistress Jee-nih," he called, "you are home early.

Before midnight. You did not like the ball?''

Jenny turned away from the cabinet and followed Miller toward the kitchen's opening. When she saw Ninj, she covered her mouth to keep from laughing.

Ninj stood just beyond them with a groggy expression on his face. He still wore the new turban she had given him, but in the place of his usual garb, a giant Turkish towel surrounded his middle. The terrycloth covered him from below his armpits to just above his knees. His huge shoulders and arms were bare, as were his hairy calves and slipperless feet.

''The ball was fine, Ninj,'' Jenny assured him. ''We had a wonderful time. I met several interesting men who have promised to come calling. It won't be long now until you—''

''Lord, man,'' Miller shouted, ''what are you doing half naked?''

The genie answered, ''Ninj is bathing.''

One glance in Miller's direction made Jenny wonder if she should fetch the smelling salts for him. His face had turned the color of chalk except for a round red circle on each cheek.

Ninj bowed in Miller's direction. ''I wasn't expecting you home so early. I fell asleep in the pool.''

''Pool?'' Miller rushed toward Ninj, positioning himself in front of the giant. ''My God, man, there's a lady present.'' He ordered, ''Get dressed now!'' He spread his arms wide as though his efforts could shield the giant from Jenny's view. ''What is it with you,'' he asked, ''that makes you enjoy people in a state of undress? First it was Jenny, and now you. Are you some kind of pervert?''

''This pervert, I don't know,'' Ninj responded. ''Naked is nice especially when bathing.''

''Miller,'' Jenny interrupted, hoping to ease the tension, ''it's fine. You do remember that I know about—shearing?''

''Get dressed now,'' Miller ordered a second time. His fists were clenched at his sides, and once again

Jenny feared the worst. The last thing she felt like doing was witnessing a brawl between her friends.

"Can't," Ninj responded.

"Can't? What do you mean you can't?"

Ninj's eyes were focused beyond where Jenny and Miller stood facing him.

"Intruders in the castle," he said. "Must call the guard."

"Intruders? Guard?" Miller asked bitingly. "You're not only perverted, but you're crazy as well."

Ninj lifted his arms. Immediately Jenny recognized his conjuring position. With his arms elevated, she expected the towel that covered him to slip to the floor. Jenny wasn't prepared to see the genie in the all-together, and she knew without a doubt that Miller wasn't. But then her mind snapped back to Ninj's words. *Intruders. Guard!*

What occurred next happened so fast she wasn't sure if what she saw was real or not.

Her first thought was that Ninj had summoned a stranger when the man who stood between them no longer wore Miller's evening clothes. It wasn't until the guardsman in typical Eastern dress swung around to face her with his scimitar raised for battle that Jenny recognized Miller's face. His spectacles were gone, and she saw hostility in his dangerous blue stare. He wore a turban made from red silk and harem pants of the same material. Buttery-soft black leather boots molded his muscular calves and fit snugly to his knees. His torso was bare except for a leather vest.

She ran toward him. Why would Miller be the guard Ninj had summoned, and what reason did they have to need a guard in the first place? The only conclusion that Jenny could reach was that Ninj's magic was still rusty.

"Ninj," she exclaimed, "you've made another mistake! Change Miller back to himself. Now!"

But as she demanded Ninj's obedience, Miller advanced toward the stairs. She tried to stop him, but her effort was futile. His free arm, the one without the

Oriental sword, snaked around her. Instead of her stopping him, his viselike grip stopped her. With a terrible suddenness, he yanked her hard against him and continued his advance.

"Ninj, do something!" she yelled, beating on Miller's chest.

She noted that his body suddenly seemed more powerful in Eastern dress than it ever had been in his fancy professor suits. He still wore a vest, but this one was made of leather with leather lacings, and it gaped apart in front. The split revealed a bare chest with a pelt of reddish-brown hair.

"Let me go," she demanded. But Miller's muscular arm remained clamped around her. They moved together toward the doorway, their bodies much closer than when they had danced that evening.

When they were halfway across the room, Jenny saw the two intruders. They were dressed all in black, and on their heads were woven knit hats pulled down over their faces. Creeping out of the parlor, the shorter one held one of her uncle's walking sticks poised like a weapon, and the taller one held a bronze statue of David about to slay Goliath. The twosome were in hot pursuit of the stairs, and she and Miller were in hot pursuit of them.

"Halt!" Ninj's huge voice rang out behind them, then he ordered Miller, "Kill the foreign devils."

"Not in my apartment, he won't!" Jenny shouted.

The first shout made the two miscreants freeze in their tracks; the death threat made them spin around to face their pursuer.

Miller set Jenny aside as though she weighed no more than a leaf and advanced toward his mark. His curved sword cut and slashed the air with the skill of an experienced warrior.

"Stop this now, Ninj," Jenny ordered when he came to stand beside her.

His lips smiled with confidence. "Ninj makes good magic, no?"

"No! Ninj makes terrible magic. You must end this now."

"Scum-sucking hogs. Ninj has no use for a purloiner. Those thieving dogs would steal the robe from your back and think nothing of leaving you naked."

"You like naked," Jenny insisted, hoping to cajole Ninj into obeying her order. "I agree that thieves should be punished, but not this way."

She would have reached for Ninj's sleeve to tug on and dissuade him, but he still wore his towel. "As soon as I can dash for those stairs, I'm fetching a policeman. As far as I'm concerned, he can haul the whole lot of you off."

"*Ayawah.* Yes. I have not known such excitement for centuries." Ninj's brows rose in pleasure, his eyes focused on the one-sided fight taking place in her parlor. "Nothing like a good battle to get a man's blood boiling."

"Or flowing," Jenny muttered. "If this continues, someone's blood *will* be flowing—all over my floor."

The shorter crook cowered beside the taller one. Jenny watched the latter thrust his partner aside and quickly exchange weapons. With the walking cane in his hand, he lunged toward Miller's weapon.

Even someone as unlearned in the ways of battle as Jenny could tell that the cane-waver had some experience in sword fighting, although his weapon was no match for Miller's. The crook's hand and foot coordination was excellent. He blocked and beat off Miller's thrusts with the strongest part of his cane and might have succeeded in beating Miller if he had been using a real weapon. But Miller's sharp blade whittled down inch after inch of the wooden walking cane the way a termite whittles wood into splinters.

"If you won't stop this madness now, then I will." Jenny gave Ninj a fierce look before darting toward the stairs.

The fighters moved toward the front of the parlor.

"I'm going for the law!" Jenny shouted.

Midway down the stairs, she recalled the night after she had danced for Miller and the argument between him and Ninj. When she had rubbed the stone at her throat, Ninj had disappeared along with her dancing costume and the Turkish decorations.

Would it work now? If she rubbed the stone, would everything disappear, or would only Ninj vanish, leaving Miller defenseless against the thieves? She couldn't risk it. But once she had fetched a policeman and Miller was halfway safe, she would send Ninj to his bottle. *Maybe never to return.* Besides, she reasoned, how could she explain a Turkish-sword–wielding guard and a near-naked genie? Such an explanation would probably land her behind bars with the key thrown away forever.

Once outside, Jenny gazed up and down the street. Officer Mosey had told her that if she ever needed him all she had to do was shout.

So shout she did. She started yelling at the top of her lungs. "Thieves! Help me! Thieves! Officer Mosey, come quick!"

Her screaming got the whole street's attention. A man assured her that he would fetch the law then jogged up the street. Uncertain what to do next, Jenny flew back inside; others would have followed her if she hadn't slammed the door, barring them entrance. She could still hear scuffling on the second story so she ran up the stairs, but not before she grabbed herself a walking stick from the hall tree.

When her feet hit the top of the landing, Officer Mosey opened the front door and called out, "Stay where you are, miss. I'll take care of this."

"Thieves," she said, pointing, "in my apartment."

He stormed up the stairs and rushed past her. Now it was time to be rid of this craziness once and for all. Her hand slapped the stone around her neck, and she rubbed it. Then she followed Officer Mosey.

Inside the room, the two thieves stood together looking exhausted, their bodies entwined in a hug. By their feet, the statue of David lay like a slain warrior, and her uncle's cane lay shredded and strewn across the floor.

Miller! her heart cried out as she searched the parlor for him. At least Ninj was nowhere in sight. She spotted a dazed Miller standing in the middle of the room. He no longer wore the costume of a castle guardsman, but instead he was the picture of frazzled refinement in his evening attire.

She ran to his side. "Are you all right?" she asked, fighting the urge to fling herself into his arms, but logic won over emotion. Miller didn't want to be embraced, especially by her. If anyone was hurt, it would be the two thieves, but she had seen them standing, embracing, so she figured that they, too, were unharmed.

Jenny checked the floor for the missing weapon. "Your sword, where is it?"

Realizing what she had said, she slapped her hand against her mouth and glanced to where Officer Mosey stood beside the two thieves. No one had heard the comment, but Miller and he stared at her in disbelief.

"My sword?" he repeated.

"I mean your scimitar."

"My scimitar? I didn't have such an implement and I wouldn't know how to use it if I did." He looked toward Officer Mosey, who suddenly appeared very interested in their conversation. "I'm not a violent person," Miller reassured him.

"*Mon Dieu!* He lies. He tried to kill us, Officer. If I hadn't had experience in fencing, my little cabbage here would have been cut up for coleslaw."

On hearing the French accent, Jenny swirled around. She watched the taller intruder yank off his mask and toss it to the floor.

"Madame DeBeau?"

Madame's eyes shot daggers at Jenny, daggers that were as lethal as Miller's scimitar had been. The French woman released her partner only long enough to remove an identical mask from his face. Then she pulled the man close to her again and cuddled him against her bosom.

"Phineas Goldfinch."

"You know these people?" Officer Mosey asked.

"I know them," Jenny said, "but I don't know what they are doing in my house dressed in thieves' clothing."

"At least we're not dressed like an Arab guardsman and his shah," Madame DeBeau hissed. "I feared for my poor Phineas' life when he"—she pointed at Miller—"came after us with that evil-looking sword. I assumed because you were an educated man that you were principled."

Her accusation seemed to jolt Miller from his dazed state. He walked toward the threesome. "I fear, Madame, that it is not my reputation at stake. I, too, am curious as to why you are in this house dressed like intruders."

Officer Mosey interrupted. "Breaking and entering would be my guess." He glanced at Jenny and asked, "Does anything appear to be missing?"

"I can't say offhand, but when I first arrived home I noticed that several bureau drawers in my bedroom were open. And my wardrobe—" She remembered seeing the hems of her gowns stuck in the door. "No, I can't say I know if anything is missing until I check further."

Madame DeBeau released her hold on the lawyer. "Of course, you won't find anything missing. But, Officer, I implore you to look around this apartment for a giant of a man. He and that one"—she glared at Miller—"are a menace to society."

"The only menace here are the two of you," Miller stated. "I suggest you find yourself a good lawyer; you'll need one when Miss Blake presses charges against you."

"I beg your pardon." Madame swelled like a blowfish. "We didn't break in, we entered through the front door." She reached in her pocket and removed a key. Against her lily-white palm the brass glittered like gold.

"Stupid female," Phineas muttered, "will you please shut up?" The lawyer appeared as though he wanted to slap the passkey from Madame's hand.

Jenny rushed toward them. "That's mine, isn't it?" she asked. "I thought I had misplaced it, but you had it all along. I remember now. It was inside my reticule the day I left it at your shop." She turned toward the policeman. "The next day she returned my things, but she must have kept the key. But why?" Jenny asked, more to herself than the others.

What could she possibly have that Madame DeBeau would chance going to jail for? A woman whose business success depended upon her good name. It didn't make sense. Why would she risk losing everything?

Unless, of course, Phineas Goldfinch had put her up to it. It seemed Jenny had pegged the man right the first day she met him. He was a weasel. Most likely, he had influenced Madame against her. Jenny recalled the day in the shop when the solicitor had interrupted her fitting, and how Madame had changed after his interruption, then later had plied Jenny with drink.

Had they planned to get back at her for dismissing the Goldfinch firm? Madame had never liked her, but why would they risk all to break into her shop? Jenny was astounded. A lawyer of all people resorting to petty thievery. Although she hadn't checked the shop downstairs, everything up here appeared to be in order except for the mussed drawers in her bedroom.

"Better frisk them, Mosey," Miller said.

"I did that. First thing. Nothing on either one of them."

"Then I suggest you take them down to the station house and charge them."

"Charge us, *monsieur*? If anyone needs to be taken to jail, it is that one." She glared at Jenny. "She's harboring a man in her house. A giant of a man in a state of near undress who was standing right there, where he, in Eastern dress"—she glanced at Miller—"tried to kill us with his ancient-looking sword."

"Appears to me," Jenny said, "that you must have imbibed too much of your own cherry liquor. Sounds like you're hallucinating. I don't see the man you described or an ancient sword.'' Her next words were for Officer Mosey. ''As you can see from our clothes, we only just returned home from a dance held at Georgetown College.'' She allowed her words to register in everyone's mind before she continued. ''I do see that you two have ruined one of my uncle's walking canes. I only hope that it wasn't such a rare and valuable piece that it cannot be replaced.''

''Take them away,'' Miller ordered.

Officer Mosey, having handcuffed the twosome earlier, pushed them toward the stairs.

''You can't do this, you little tart!'' Madame threatened when she was led past Jenny. ''I'll get even with you both. You'll rue the day that you ever tangled with me and my Phineas. We're professionals—well respected in this community.''

Jenny and Miller followed Officer Mosey and his prisoners to the front door. ''Lock up now,'' Mosey told Jenny. ''You've had enough intruders for one night.'' He saw that people had gathered outside the shop, anxious to find out what had happened. ''Go on home, folks. Everything here is under control. The crooks have been apprehended.''

Jenny thanked the man who had fetched the officer, then bade everyone standing on the street good night. She closed the front door and leaned against it. From outside, they heard Madame DeBeau shout as she was hauled up the street, ''I'll see you both in court!''

''You can bet your nickels on that,'' Miller answered. ''Scalawags, the lot of them. You were right to fire that man, and I was wrong to have sent you to that woman.''

''What do you think they were looking for?'' Jenny asked. ''And why would they risk going to jail for whatever it was?''

''I'm not certain, but now I suggest that you get some rest.'' Miller took her hand and led her toward the stairs. ''Tomorrow we'll check the shop before getting in touch with Officer Mosey. He'll want to know if there is anything missing. Tomorrow, Jenny,'' he said softly.

"You'll need your rest if you're to look your best when all those gentlemen come calling."

After brushing his lips against her forehead in a platonic gesture, Miller left her.

Jenny waited until Miller's footsteps no longer echoed off the stairs before she, too, moved away from the door. She mounted the stairs slowly, stalling against the time when she would be in her bed, alone with her reflections of the evening.

Once inside her apartment, Jenny stepped over the wood shavings spread across the floor and went to the kitchen for a broom.

As she swept away the evidence of the match, she felt anxious and unsettled and wondered if her restlessness was due to the thieves or the kiss that she and Miller had shared.

Jenny swept the surface beneath the music box and stopped to turn on the cylinder. The tune that she and Miller had danced to pinged its familiar melody throughout the room. The high-pitched sound pierced her memory like a bullet striking metal—the memory of the good times she and Miller had shared were as lethal as the explosive itself.

Jenny blinked back tears. Still dressed in her finery and wanting something to do to distract her thoughts, she flipped the broom handle down until its tip rested on the floor and she could stare straight at the bound straw attached to the wood.

With a deep voice, she pretended to be the broom. "May I please have this dance?" she asked.

Jenny affected a curtsy. "Why, thank you, Dr. Holbrook. I'd be delighted to dance with you."

Soon she and the broom were twirling together around the room, her feet in perfect time with the beat of the waltz. *One, two, three. One, two, three. One, two, three.*

For a moment Jenny was back at the dean's home, enjoying the two dances that she and Miller had shared. In vivid detail, she recalled the man who only hours before had held her in his arms and smiled at her as though she was the fairest belle in attendance.

Her heart flapped like wings against her ribs when she recalled the moments inside the coach when Miller's fingers had worked loose the buttons at her wrist. Jenny glanced at her wrist, searching its surface, expecting to see a brand where Miller's lips had touched her skin beneath the tiny slit in her glove. She found no evidence of seared skin, but the memory of his kiss made the spot feel hot and tingly. Without warning, the hot tingles slipped to the juncture of her thighs.

The room became overly warm, and she felt again as she had that afternoon when she had danced the *beledi* for Ninj and Miller.

"Nonsense," she scolded. Jenny forced her attention to her one-legged partner, whose expression remained flat. "Would that my head should be made from straw like yours."

The music stopped, and so did Jenny, but she still stared absently at her partner.

Wanting to feel again the touch of Miller's lips against her own, Jenny closed her eyes. As she dipped her head slightly, the scent of straw and dust assailed her nostrils. With the longing she felt in her heart, Jenny puckered her lips, intent on kissing the broom's surface.

Just before her lips brushed against the yellow straw, Miller's words sounded inside Jenny's head. "I'm sorry. I forgot myself."

The reminder made her toss the broom backward, sending it slamming against the floor. The sound sent Bengel scurrying through the apartment door.

Above her head, Jenny heard footsteps beat a path toward the stairs. A few moments later, Miller called from the top landing, "Are you okay down there?"

Going to stand in the still-open door, Jenny shouted back, "I'm fine! I only dropped the broom!"

"Are you certain? I'll come down if you need me."

If Miller knew just how badly she needed him at that moment, would he really come down?

Lying, she responded, "Everything is under control, but thank you."

"Good," Miller answered, "then I will see you tomorrow."

Jenny heard him retreat back into his apartment, then heard the clanking of the pipes as water flowed upward.

To vent her disappointment, she slammed her apartment door. After locking it, she tramped toward the bedroom, chastising herself as she went.

"How foolish you are, Jenny Blake, for mooning over such a man."

Upstairs, Miller mooned in the same fashion that Jenny did downstairs, but his mooning consisted of an ache that wasn't as easily remedied as Jenny's.

It had been much too long since Miller had last had a woman, and Jenny had awakened his long-dormant desire. He was temporarily in a state of sleeplessness with an ache in his groin that only snow water could relieve. And since they were in the middle of summer with a short supply of snow, Miller opted for an ice-cold bath.

A few minutes later, he sat in the copper tub. As he shivered and shook with the sting of his first plunge, he wondered how many more cold baths it would take before his body would return to its normal frozen state.

His teeth chattered, and goose pimples prickled his skin. He reasoned if his heart could stand up against the shock of the icy treatments, then it wouldn't be that long before he would have the tiger under control.

"No more kissing," he said as his teeth began to chatter.

But even as he said the words, the memory of Jenny's response to his kiss made parts of him hot enough to heat the frigid bathwater.

Ninj, still inside his bottle, downed several grapes and recollected the battle between the professor and the two thieves. Mr. Professor had shown himself to be a com-

petent warrior and skillful at holding the intruders at bay.
Ninj smiled to himself—he had chosen well for his mistress. He felt confident that the professor would be as
skilled in love as he was in battle.

Although the twosome didn't know it yet, tonight had
been a turning point in their relationship. Satisfied with
the way of things, Ninj preened like a peacock. It
wouldn't be long now before a rainbow gleamed on the
horizon.

Nineteen

～

Jenny stood inside the shop determined to work off her bout with the mulligrubs. She had dressed very carefully this morning, taking more time than usual with her appearance, and if she hadn't had such a bad case of the blues, her image in the mirror she dusted might have cheered her. But not so today. Miller's rejection still weighed heavily on her heart, and try as she might, she couldn't dismiss the memory of his kiss.

Her Nana Blake had always said, "Hard work relieves us from the toils of the mind," and for once Jenny was prone to believe her. Before the day was over, she intended to clean the shop from top to bottom and would begin by sweeping the front stoop. As she grabbed the broom and headed outside, she recalled the encounter with her broomstick partner, and the recollection made her laugh. What kind of woman went around kissing a dusty broom? *A ridiculous one,* a little voice whispered inside her head.

Once outside, Jenny began to sweep. It wasn't long before the oppressive heat that had moved into the city during the night made her feel like a wilting flower. Pausing, she picked up the corner of the apron she had tied around her waist earlier and wiped the moisture from her face.

"Morning, Miss Blake."

She dropped her apron hem and greeted Officer Mosey as he walked by. "How are you this morning?"

"Hot," he responded. He removed his cap and fanned his face. "I can't remember a time when it's been this uncomfortable, but not as uncomfortable as your two intruders. After spending the night in jail, they put up bail first thing this morning. No trial date yet."

"Good," Jenny said, "they deserve to be uncomfortable." She still couldn't comprehend why Madame DeBeau and Phineas Goldfinch had broken into her shop, but then, lately nothing made sense to her. She dismissed the thought. "By the way, thanks again for your help last night."

"Just doing my job," Officer Mosey replied.

Jenny noticed that Officer Mosey's hair was damp with perspiration and clung to his head. "We could sure do with a breeze, but I reckon it would be nothing more than a hot wind stirring if there was one."

"You're probably right," he answered, dabbing his forehead with a handkerchief before replacing his cap. "Don't you be working too hard in this heat." Waving, he moved on down the street.

Jenny watched his progress then gave the steps a couple more whisks before returning inside. It was hotter indoors than it was out and not a good day for heavy cleaning.

She grumbled to Bengel, who appeared in the open door, "Even the weather seems bent on not cooperating with me." In response, the cat licked his front legs and proceeded to bathe the rest of his fur. "You have the right idea, my friend," she said, nudging the cat inside and closing the door. "A bath would feel like heaven right about now."

Determined to stay busy, Jenny grabbed a rag and began to dust the many shelves that lined the walls of the shop. In spite of the heat, she was soon engrossed in the task of moving, dusting, and replacing the assortment of collectibles, making certain as she worked that she kept everything in its original place.

"Excuse me," a woman's voice called from behind her.

Jenny was so deep into her thoughts she hadn't heard the bell ring, and she nearly jumped out of her skin with the intrusion.

"Mercy," she said, turning to face her visitor. "I'm sorry, I didn't hear you come in."

"No, I'm sorry," the woman apologized. "I should have knocked or shouted instead of sneaking up on you."

The lady looked familiar. "Have we met?" Jenny asked the newcomer. She dropped her dust rag on the counter and looped several locks of hair that had slipped from the knot on her head back behind her ears.

"We met at the college tea dance," the lady said, "but I don't expect you to remember me. I'm sure if you're like me, you met so many people that evening you don't remember half of them."

"Oh, I remember *them* all right. . . ." Her blunder and subsequent snubbing was still fresh in her mind. But suddenly she realized how her response must have sounded to the woman, and Jenny tried to smooth over her words. "Everyone looks so different when they're all dressed up in their finery."

She studied the woman. She didn't remember her in particular, but then again, would she remember anyone she had met that evening, except for Mrs. Parke-Witty and her group of hangers-on?

"My name is Seal Oak," the lady said. "My husband is an English professor at the college."

Jenny wiped her hands on her apron, unsure what the woman's visit meant. "Well, Mrs. Oak, how can I help you?"

The woman fidgeted, looking as uncomfortable as Jenny felt. "I'm not certain I know how to begin, but as my husband always says, it's best to start at the beginning." She took a deep breath. "I've come to apologize."

"Apologize?" This was the last thing Jenny expected

from her visitor, but she gave her full attention.

"Yes," Mrs. Oak admitted, "I'm ashamed of the behavior of some of the women present at the function. It wasn't until later that I heard that you had been intentionally snubbed because of your honesty, and by then you and Dr. Holbrook had departed."

Jenny felt sorry for the woman because she looked so uncomfortable. "Oh, there's no need for an apology," she said, smiling. "I reckon you fine ladies aren't used to hearing what happens to animals on a farm."

The lady waved her hand. "Fine ladies, pshaw! We're no different from you. Sophronia Witty's only claim to fame is her dead ancestors. And from what I've heard on that quarter, the revered deceased were nothing more than scalawags who got lucky. Everyone knows she likes to put on airs."

"I reckon if I lived in such a fine house, I'd put on airs, too."

"Yes, it is a fine house, but just between you and me, it's much too ostentatious for a professor. Don't you agree?"

Ostentatious. That was the same word Miller had used when they had discussed the Parke-Witty mansion at the dance. Jenny still wasn't sure of its meaning, but since she had heard it used twice, she supposed it would be okay to agree. "Yes, ma'am," she said.

Mrs. Oak relaxed visibly with Jenny's answer. "Now that that's settled, I hope we can begin again. I must say that I'm so happy the professor found you." She patted Jenny's hand where it rested on the counter. "For so many years now, Miller has preferred his own company to that of a female's. It's good to see him show an interest in a young lady."

Jenny was about to tell her that she shouldn't expect too much from the interest Miller had shown her when another woman stepped into the shop. "Mind if I browse?" she called from the doorway.

"Browse away," Jenny replied, then returned her attention to Mrs. Oak, who was looking at the lapel watch pinned to the front of her dress.

"I hope you'll forgive me for running off so soon, but today is the day of the charity luncheon. Maybe next month you'll consider joining me and some of the other wives for the event."

Not certain she was ready to mingle with the women of the college again so soon, Jenny said, "I'll have to see—I'm the only one here at the shop."

Mrs. Oak looked at her. "I do hope you'll consider going. I'll check on you later in the month." She raised her hand and wiggled her fingers as she walked toward the entrance. "For now, toodle," she called.

She was out the door before Jenny could respond. Removing her apron, she placed it on the counter and addressed the customer. "How may I help you?" she asked.

"My husband and I have just moved to Georgetown and I'm decorating our town house. I was told that Vassily Antonini had some unique things in his shop and that I should take a look."

"Whoever told you that was correct," Jenny said, smiling. "Vassily Antonini was my uncle, and I've only recently come to Georgetown myself. And yes, he does have unusual things—beautiful things. Most of our stock would be an asset to any home."

Jenny could not imagine lepoard-skin chairs or an elephant-foot table in her Grandmother Blake's house, but city homes were different from country farmhouses.

Glancing around the shop, the woman said, "What I'm looking for is a centerpiece for my dining-room table. And I think I see just what I want." She rushed across the room.

Jenny followed her to where an ornate tiered centerpiece sat. Just a few days before, she had come across the piece in her uncle's ledger. After locating it in the shop, she had given it a thorough inspection herself.

"It's perfect," the lady insisted. "I've been looking for the right epergne and I guess I've found it."

"It's a beautiful piece all right, but very expensive."

"Money is not a factor," the woman assured her. Lovingly she trailed her fingers over the silver frame. "I see it has dishes as well as candleholders."

"Yes, ma'am, it's a pretty set."

"I'll take it. If you'll hold it for me, my husband will come by at the end of the week and pay you. Do you deliver?"

"No, ma'am. It's just me here, and I have no way of making deliveries, but perhaps it is something I will think about in the future."

"That's fine, dear. If you'll wrap it so it won't break, I'll have my Harry carry it home when he comes to pay for it."

She started toward the door, then stopped. "You will save it for me, won't you? By the way, my name is Mrs. Pauly. I promise my Harry will come by at the end of the week."

"It's yours," Jenny said, "but don't you want to know how much it costs?"

The woman waved her gloved hand nonchalantly. "My husband will settle with you."

Imagine buying something without asking the price. Jenny shook her head. Would she ever get used to the ways of city folk?

Mrs. Pauly opened the door, but stopped abruptly when she met someone entering from the outside.

"Pardon me," a deep male voice said.

As the woman left, she muttered something Jenny couldn't understand, but by then she was too busy trying to breathe. She didn't have to see the man to know that Miller was about to come into the shop. Her face burned, and she quickly grabbed the dust rag she had abandoned earlier and began rubbing the top of a nearby case. Even though this was her second encounter with Miller today, she felt as nervous as a cricket on the end of a fishing line.

He stepped inside and closed the door. In his professor tweeds, he looked so handsome she felt as though her lack of breath might cause her to swoon at his feet.

"Business is booming, I see," he said.

"You could say that," she replied. Jenny hoped she didn't look as jittery as she felt. Damn the man for playing such havoc with her emotions.

"Well, you're about to have your first callers."

"Callers?"

"Yes. Several young men you met at the ball. I passed them on the street, and they asked me to announce their visit. They'll be along any moment now."

"Here? Any moment?" Her discomfort forgotten, Jenny ran to a mirror to inspect her appearance. Patting her hair, she complained, "I'm a mess."

"You look fine," Miller responded.

As Jenny glanced at his reflection in the mirror behind her, she watched his expression change from cordial to distant.

A knock sounded on the door, and Miller's distant look deepened to a scowl.

She pulled on the cotton yoke of her steel-gray, checkered dress and straightened Ninj's jewel at her neck. Her first would-be suitors were about to arrive. At least she was making progress with some of the men in her life. But more importantly, she was one step closer to helping Ninj reach his goal.

Miller sat inside the shop at Antonini's desk going over his old friend's books. It was brutally hot. The air inside the building felt so thick and heavy he could have sliced it with a letter opener. Even with the doors and windows open, not a breath of fresh air stirred.

Removing a handkerchief from his pocket, Miller dabbed at the perspiration on his upper lip. A quick glance at Vassily's books had proven he had been an excellent recordkeeper, and Miller could see from the man's journals that a list of the shop's inventory and the dates the items had been acquired were entered neatly in each column. Not only had he listed the purchase price of each item, but also the selling price if the item had been sold. Since there had been little active trading done in the store since his old friend's death, the books were pretty much up-to-date.

The records indicated that Antonini Vassily had a substantial income from investments, that he owned his property outright, and that he also had a sizable nest egg in the bank. Because of her inheritance, Jenny Blake was now a financially secure young woman, and if a dowry was a factor in her making a good match, Miller knew that her holdings would be a plus. He wondered briefly what the society ladies would say if they knew of Miss Blake's worth.

Laughter and conversation floated to him through the open door that led to the small courtyard. Earlier this morning, three young pups she had met at the dance came to call. Because of the heat, Jenny had chosen to receive her suitors on the small tree-shaded courtyard at the back of the house.

The several men calling upon her had been of Miller's association, but not of his immediate department. Although Jenny had invited him to join their little gathering, Miller had declined, using the excuse that he had work to do and would watch the shop for her.

But Miller had found concentrating on the books to be more difficult than he'd expected. Instead of tallying columns and checking entries, he sat eavesdropping, catching snatches of the conversation going on outside. It wasn't the men who interested him, but Jenny. Much to his dismay, his dreams—what little there had been of them throughout the long restless night—had been filled with her. Even his icy-cold bath hadn't expelled his need, and he had spent the better part of that time trying to get his lust under control.

The object of his thoughts spoke. "If you haven't traveled by canal boat, then you must do so. Before my trip south," Jenny told her audience of three, "I had never ridden on such a ship, although I guess a barge doesn't rank in a category of sailing vessels."

"Ship? Not hardly," one young sprat said. "It's nothing more than a wagon on water, or so I've heard."

Miller didn't recognize the man's voice, but then he hadn't expected to. The gentleman continued, "I understand the people who work the boats can be considered only a notch above the dregs of society."

Uh-oh, Miller thought. He imagined that the speaker had just slipped several notches lower in Jenny's opinion. The realization made Miller smile.

"Being in the company of muleth and mulethkinnerth lackth a thertain appeal," a second man with a lisp responded. "I'm thertain that I wouldn't relith thuch a trip."

The first whelp spoke again. "Surely the families must be as unpleasant to be around as their mules, especially with no bathing facilities available aboard their barges."

"Well, dear son," the third man in attendance responded, "I for one cannot tolerate a stroll past the sheds on the mall where they keep animals for the study of taxidermy. I daresay a ride on a barge pulled by a mule is not a must in my future."

"Wimble, old boy, you mustn't hold mules in disdain. You do recall that historians say the first gift of an animal to the Washington Zoo was a royal jackass presented to George Washington at Mount Vernon in 1785 by Charles III of Spain."

Miller wondered what if any significance there had been to such a gift, but he didn't have long to ponder on this bit of information.

"Jackass?" Jenny exploded. "I'm beginning to feel as though I'm in company with a herd of them."

Miller heard the angry scrape of a chair across the brick, and he imagined Jenny had stood.

"In defense of the family I traveled with from Shepherdstown," she continued, "I found the canallers very nice. In fact, they were both gracious and accommodating. They believe in teaching their children good manners and wouldn't allow them to belittle those less fortunate than themselves."

Miller heard a loud guffaw; then the one called Wimble added, "Perhaps there aren't any less fortunate than themselves."

"You, sir, should be ashamed of yourself. How can you speak so ill of people you don't even know?"

If the silence that followed was any indication of the uneasiness that pervaded among the group beyond the wall, Miller suspected that Jenny's admirers were dumb-struck by her defense of the commoners.

He heard several masculine throats being cleared.

"My canal boat ride was quite memorable," Jenny added, "and I plan to continue my friendship with the woman who took me into her home on that brief voyage and made me feel welcome."

The man with the lisp cleared his throat. "We didn't mean to inthult you, Mith Blake. We're only thaying that it hath been our experienth with thuch—"

"You'll forgive me," Jenny interrupted, "but I've suddenly developed a headache."

A nervous male laugh floated past the door. "But, surely, ma'am—"

"And the sooner you gentlemen take your leave, the better I will feel."

Miller heard more chairs scrape across the brick.

"We meant you no disrespect," Wimble apologized.

"It's not your rudeness that I find distasteful, but your lack of compassion. Now if you'll excuse me." Miller heard Jenny's skirts rustle. "I'm sure Dr. Holbrook will be more than happy to show you out."

Miller waited for Jenny to appear in the doorway. When she did, her gaze locked briefly with his before she darted past him and toward the stairs.

A few moments later the three pups appeared in the doorway looking sheepish.

Miller stood. "Something wrong, gentlemen?"

The threesome exchanged glances. Wimble spoke for all of them. "It seems Miss Blake developed a headache and needed to be excused."

"I see," Miller said, knowing perfectly well the rea-son for Jenny's abrupt departure, but if he disciplined them as he wanted to do, he would be admitting that he had been eavesdropping. He said, ''I can understand why she developed a headache. The heat is insufferable today.''

''Yeth, I imagine it ith the heat. The newthpaper thays that the city will be experienthing a heat wave for the next few days.''

''Unseasonably warm temperatures,'' the third fellow confirmed.

''Yes,'' Wimble agreed. ''I see no reason why we should hang about the city when we could be taking ourselves off to Father's cottage on the coast.''

''A marvelous idea, old sport,'' the third man exclaimed. ''We should have thought of that sooner.''

The three men already had forgotten the misdeed of their tactless manners. But then, Miller reasoned, these men of wealth were no different from Mrs. Sophronia Parke-Witty and her like.

''Please express our sympathy to Miss Blake and wish her a speedy recovery. Tell her that we shall call upon her again after our return from the coast.''

''I'll do that, gentlemen.'' Miller followed the men to the front door. ''Good day to you.''

As Miller stood in the foyer, he heard a combined sigh of relief on the opposite side of the entrance.

''Young pups are still wet behind the ears. The whole litter isn't fit to wipe their pedigreed paws on Jenny's shirttail.''

Jenny lay on her bed, staring at the ceiling. She didn't cry often, but today the tears slipped from the corners of her eyes, streaming down the sides of her face to pool in her ears.

For reasons unknown to herself, Jenny was homesick. Although her mother and her Nana Blake had in no way been affectionate people and had never allowed her to wallow in self-pity, their straightforward ways had helped her through the rough times. With their nononsense attitude, they had strengthened her softness, and as she lay on her back with the ceiling swimming in her vision, she longed for their solid presence.

She sucked back another wave of tears, honking like a goose as she did so. It was so hot in the apartment, her skin boiled beneath the weight of her new gown. Jenny longed for the weightlessness of her old clothes and for the sameness of her old life—the life she had left behind on the farm.

"I can go back," she told Bengel when he sniffed the salty tears seeping from her eyes.

The cat's odd stare, with one blue and one green eye, reminded her of the endless blue skies and open green fields of West Virginia.

"We could go together," she told him. "If I sell my uncle's home, I'll have enough funds to build us a house in the country with a yard so big and wide you'll never tire of wandering." She stroked his silky white fur, eliciting a soothing purr. "You could become the resident mouser. Imagine how gallant you would feel."

Rubbing her eyes with the heels of her palms, Jenny rolled over on her stomach. Ninj's bottle sat on her dressing table, and her gaze locked on the stone and cut-glass container.

If I returned to the farm, what would become of Ninj? Without my help, he won't be able to retire.

But hadn't she already failed him? There was no doubt in Jenny's mind that the gentlemen she had entertained this morning would never return because of her shameful behavior. Once again, her opinions and her frankness had chased away possible suitors who might have helped her to secure Ninj's place in paradise.

Although the genie could be a nuisance, Jenny still wanted to help him. She hoped one of her other dancing partners would come calling, and if one did, she would keep her lips sealed.

There was also Miller to consider. If she sold her uncle's house, where would he live?

Mrs. Parke-Witty's words sounded inside her head. *With his own, instead of above a shop.* The reminder made Jenny angry. If for nothing more than to keep the dean's wife from getting her way, she wouldn't sell her home and force Miller to move. But after last night, perhaps he would be happy to see her go.

Miller. Why couldn't she stop thinking about him? Even after last night's insult when he claimed he had forgotten himself when he kissed her and then apologized for doing so, the memory of their lips touching still taunted her.

She flopped back on her backside and folded her arms across her chest. "Well, I forgot myself, too, and now I intend to forget you as well, Miller Holbrook."

Frightened by her abrupt movement, Bengel jumped. The cat's white fur stood out from his body like a porcupine's quills. Several moments passed before the old tom trusted her enough to settle down against her hip again, and once he did, Jenny's thoughts shot right back to Miller.

When she left him downstairs, it had been business as usual. Although Jenny didn't expect him to act any differently, the fact that he didn't made her question if she had dreamed the kiss, along with the whole bizarre evening from the party's inception to the incident with Madame DeBeau and Phineas Goldfinch.

Together she and Miller had taken a quick inventory of the shop, and they both agreed that nothing seemed to be missing. Miller had left to report their findings to the officials.

Jenny still puzzled over the reason for the break-in, even going so far as to check the amulet tray that Madame DeBeau had been so interested in the day she had returned Jenny's things. Although she wasn't positive of the number of amulets the tray had held, it appeared the same as it had on the occasion of Madame's first visit. But until the inventory was verified, it would remain a mystery as to why the intruders were in the shop.

So when Miller had returned and announced she would soon have callers, she had acted as if she was pleased. When her guests had arrived, she had reluctantly left Miller with the books and the shop, and he had become so absorbed in the work that he had declined her invitation to join the group for tea. Jenny had assumed he wanted no part of her company and that he was glad to leave her to her own devices.

"Some devices," she said aloud, punching her pillow before flopping against it. "I've already chased away three possible suitors."

Men, she thought. They were nothing but a bother she could live without.

Since she hadn't spoken to Ninj since last night's disaster, she decided to call up his presence. Besides, the genie had a way of cheering her. He was the only true friend she had in her new home.

Before summoning him, she dabbed the corner of the quilt against her eyes to eliminate any trace of her tears. It wouldn't do to have Ninj know of her low spirits, or the reason for them. Once she thought she looked presentable, she rubbed the stone at her neck. The familiar pop that came with Ninj's entrance sounded throughout the room.

Ninj appeared. With his large hands steepled in front of his chest, he dipped his turban-covered head. "Mistress Jee-nih, you called?"

Jenny was so glad to see him. At his appearance, she felt her spirits lifting. "I've missed you," she said, noting he wore his usual genie garb in place of the huge Turkish towel.

Ninj appeared humbled. "Then you are no longer displeased with Ninj? I seem to recall that you said I made terrible magic and that the guard police should haul me off with the lot."

"Circumstances demanded that I say such things. I certainly didn't want someone murdered. I realize now that you were only doing your genie thing, and since no real harm came to anyone, can you forgive me?" When Ninj said nothing, she continued, "In fact, I do believe your guardsman saved the castle."

Her words cajoled him from his subdued mood. With

a mischievous smile, he asked, "How is our Mr. Professor after the attack?"

"Our Mr. Professor is not even aware of his part in the battle. He doesn't appear to remember a thing about the assault, or about your state of undress. I suggest we leave it forgotten."

"A mighty warrior was he," Ninj added. "He deserves a notch in his sword handle."

"I don't believe Miller is overly concerned with notched swords."

"How were your callers?" Ninj asked. "Did you find one who meets with your approval?"

"Shallow men. All of them."

"You mean lacking in depth?" His brows lifted in interest.

Realizing her mistake, Jenny corrected herself. "Hallowed men. All of them," she praised.

Ninj's mustached lip lifted several inches. "Ah, this is good. A woman should revere her man."

As in worship? Never! But instead of voicing her thoughts, Jenny asked, "How did you know I had callers?"

Ninj's knowledge of her callers surprised her. If he knew they had come and gone, did he also know that she had dismissed them? From beneath her lowered lashes, she studied the genie, waiting for his answer.

"You said last night that you met men who would come calling, did you not?"

"Yes, I did," she responded.

Jenny was still uncertain if Ninj spoke the truth. Was he capable of seeing events even if he wasn't present? If that was the case, fooling him would be impossible. She didn't wish to think of this possibility—she *couldn't* think of it—so instead she changed the subject.

"The heat is insufferable." She jumped up from the bed and walked to the window, hoping to catch a draft of cool air. "I feel like I'm going to melt."

Outside, the stone and brick buildings looked bedraggled in the close heat. The leaves of the trees curled into

themselves as though to retreat from the boiling sun
overhead that beat down with a vengeance. Not a whis-
per of wind stole past the curtains. The sky was a cobalt
blue canvas without a sign of a cloud on its surface.

Jenny blotted her forehead against her sleeve. "I can't
remember being so hot. What I'd give for a swim in the
icy creek back home."

"You are like me, Mistress Jee-nih. I, too, long for
the *Sweet Waters of Asia and Europe.*"

Jenny sighed. "Are we but sojourners here, Ninj?"

"For me, yes, Mistress Jee-nih, my stay here is but a
temporary one."

Jenny turned to look at Ninj. She forced down the
lump that suddenly clogged her dry throat. "I will miss
you, Ninj, when you retire."

He winked at her. "It will be a good miss, yes?"

"It will be a sad one."

"By then, Mistress Jee-nih, you will have found your
special someone, and he will be the center of your uni-
verse."

Although Jenny silently denied the possibility of such
a union, her heart felt heavy. Ninj's words didn't cheer
her. In helping him, she would lose him. Because she
had vowed long ago never to give her heart to any man,
Ninj's retirement would leave her alone and bereft, but
Jenny was determined that Ninj would have his wish.
She would succeed in helping him, although she would
pay dearly for her success—she would be giving up her
only friend.

It was as though Ninj recognized her dilemma and
wanted to comfort her. He said, "Ninj knows what you
need. You need a picnic."

"A picnic?" Jenny fanned her face with her hand. "I
can't imagine why you believe I need a picnic. Besides,
after the last time we went on an outing, I promised
myself I'd never go again."

"Not with me, my mistress. You and Mr. Professor
will go."

"I assure you that a picnic is the last thing the pro-

fessor will agree to attend. Besides, he's too busy with
my uncle's books to consent to such an outing.''

Oblivious to her words, Ninj clapped his hands in
delight. "And what a picnic it will be. As in the days
of yore, you will take the *araba*. I will make all the
arrangements.''

"I refuse to ride in that cart you hold in such high
esteem. And there will be no need for you to make arrangements, because there isn't going to be any picnic.''

"I can see it now. . . ." Ninj continued verbalizing his
plans. "You will stop amid a field of tulips and hya-
cinths and eat roasted lamb cooked on an open fire.
There will be fruity sherbets and all the best cheeses.
While you dine, shepherds will play on their Bulgarian
pipes, and dancing bears and fortune-tellers will perform.''

"Ninj," Jenny interrupted, "you aren't listening to
me. There will be no picnic and most assuredly no dancing bears. I fear such guests would make us their menu.''

From the doorway, Miller asked, "Did someone say
picnic?''

He had come upon them totally unexpected and now
stood by the door to her bedroom as though he were
afraid to step into her private territory. With his sudden
appearance, the hairs prickled on the back of Jenny's
neck. If she didn't know better, she might believe that
Ninj had summoned Miller by magic, especially after he
claimed an eagerness for the excursion.

"A picnic sounds like a fine idea to me," Miller said.
"It's much too hot to be inside, and I know just the
place we can cool our heels, so to speak." He wiggled
his brows like a villain from a melodrama.

Jenny propped her fists on her hips. *Ninj and his
schemes,* she thought. *I'll not let him force Miller into
doing something he doesn't want to do.*

She turned to Miller and asked, "Do you really want
to go on a picnic?''

Ninj answered for him. "Of course, Mr. Professor
wants to go. I knew he would agree the moment I came

up with the idea. And a fine idea it is, too. Ninj will make it a wonderful picnic. You will see, it will be a most memorable event.''

Miller's gaze locked on Jenny's. "Of course, I want to go,'' he answered, "and I'm sure it will be memorable. An event neither of us will forget.''

The way he studied her and the way he sounded was as unnerving as last night's caress. Jenny had difficulty breathing, so she glanced to Ninj for help.

A knowing glint sparkled in the depths of his black eyes. "Ninj will make the preparations. You need not worry about a thing.''

Though uncertain that such an outing was a good idea, Jenny hesitated to voice her concerns. Maybe this was just what she and Miller needed to put their relationship back on track—they would be friends again, enjoying each other's company and nothing more. Jenny's earlier dark mood lightened as she got caught up in the planning.

"We'll take the chicken left over from yesterday,'' she said.

"Sounds good to me. You know how I love chicken.''

"Ninj doesn't cook fowl.''

Miller lifted his eyebrows. "Please tell me that you didn't eat the whole platter.''

"No, I left the platter,'' Ninj said, grinning from ear-ring to earring, "but the fried fowl flew the coop.''

"Coop? In the shape of your stomach. Whoever heard of a picnic without fried chicken?'' Miller asked.

"Don't worry yourself. Ninj will surprise you both with a feast fit for a king.''

"Then it's settled,'' Jenny said. "Ninj will make the preparations—but I must warn you, Ninj. No bears.''

"Bears.'' Miller looked thoughtful. "I never developed a taste for bear meat.''

Excitement rippled throughout the room as the threesome discussed preparations for the outing.

"We'll wait until later this afternoon to depart,'' Miller informed them. "It will be cooler then.''

The sheer joy of such an adventure made Jenny feel like a child again. "We'll go back to the spot I found close to the canal; it has a swimming hole!"

"A perfect place," Miller assured her. "Nothing like a little fun and relaxation to make you forget the heat, and yourself."

I agree. Ninj grinned like a fat cat, pleased with his part in the scheme. Rubbing his big hands together, he said to the excited adults, "Now, if you two will excuse me, I have work to do."

Later in the day, when the sun rested atop the trees on the rise of the hill, Jenny and Miller set out. Waving good-bye to Ninj and Bengel, who stood side-by-side on the front stoop, Jenny and Miller headed toward the canal.

The day was still hot, the air without a breeze. Miller carried a big picnic basket that Jenny had found in the basement. The prospect of sharing Ninj's meal kept their steps light. They were both looking forward to sitting beside the cool stream-fed pond.

"We could have taken the *araba*," Jenny teased when she saw the small beads of perspiration that had blossomed on Miller's upper lip. At least he had removed his vest.

"Thank you very much," Miller replied lightly, "but I don't favor riding in a veiled cart pulled by an ox." He looked so indignant that Jenny laughed.

They turned off Thomas Jefferson Street and traveled the same route that Jenny had taken the day of the storm. There weren't many people about, and she decided that everyone had decided to stay home and not waste their energy on outdoor exercise. Even the few mules she saw trudging along the towpath seemed hot and wilted.

It wasn't long before they reached the stream that trickled into the canal. Turning up the well-worn path that bordered it, Jenny soon spotted the granite rocks she remembered from her last visit. She and Miller edged around the boulders to get to the higher pool and to the makeshift shelter on the sandy beach where Jenny had waited out the storm.

Once at the pool's edge, Jenny stopped. Miller, who had been concentrating on keeping his footing on the rocks, slammed into her back and almost toppled them both into the water. The picnic basket flew out of his grasp and hit the water with a splash. Like a leaf caught in the current, it dipped and swirled before it slipped over the pool's edge and headed back the way they had come.

Miller jumped into the calf-high water to retrieve the hamper, and Jenny grabbed his coat sleeve.

"Look," she said when he tried to shake free of her grasp so he could chase their lunch. "There," she said, "beneath the trees."

He all but ignored her. "I'm more concerned with our lunch at the moment. If I've come all this way to eat, I sure don't favor my meal floating out to sea."

Jenny insisted again, pointing. "Over there. Look."

The picnic hamper forgotten, Miller's gaze followed the direction in which her fingertip was aimed, toward the slope of land on the opposite side of the pond.

The shelter made from twigs and branches was nowhere to be seen. In its place was a white canvas tent that in Jenny's opinion looked as though it had been transported from the East and dropped down on the sandy beach.

The canvas roof of the tent was supported by four poles, the side flaps rolled up and fastened. Snowy white curtains like gauzy veils hung to the ground beneath the tent's tapered top, adding an aura of mystery to the interior. Atop the roof's point a red banner fluttered, which seemed impossible when there was no sign of a breeze.

There was only one person Jenny knew who could be responsible for such a feat.

She and Miller exchanged knowing glances. "Ninj," they said together.

Jenny's laughter bubbled up inside her. "He did say that he would make all the preparations."

Miller stepped from the water back onto the rocks. "I only hope he stashed an emergency supply of food inside that tepee, because what we brought with us is on its way to China."

"I'm sure Ninj thought of everything. Especially food, knowing his preoccupation with it."

Jenny started forward, then hesitated. "Are we being bold for assuming that the tent is Ninj's doing?"

"Look around," Miller said, scanning the surrounding woods. "There isn't a soul within miles of this place. Besides, no one but a desert sheik and his entourage could afford such an outfit."

"Well, I'm not anxious to come upon his scimitar-swinging guard. Losing my head because I'm trespassing isn't my idea of a fun picnic."

"Trust me," Miller said, taking the lead as well as her hand. "You aren't going to lose your head. We'll stroll by and check out the place. If it looks uninhabited, we'll take up residence."

"Like squatters?"

"Of a sort."

Jenny allowed him to lead her toward the tent, his wet shoes squishing as he walked. Birds calling from the overhead branches and the water rushing over the nearby rocks were the only other sounds in the wood.

As they neared the exotic-looking tent, Miller paused. "Anybody home?" he called. When he heard no response, he tugged Jenny along behind him and moved closer. "This has to be Ninj's doing," he whispered. "I only hope he hasn't decided to join us."

Pausing outside the closed curtains, he hesitated, but only long enough to catch his breath. With his free hand, his fingers parted the slit where the gossamer panels met, and he peered inside.

Jenny peeked over his shoulder, expecting to see a dancing bear, or perhaps shepherds playing a tune on their Bulgarian pipes. She saw neither and expelled the breath that she had been holding.

The tent's interior reminded her of the *araba*, with its

grass mats and Oriental rugs and its tapestry and bro-caded pillows strewn across the floor.

In the center of the tent was spread a velvet cloth embroidered with gold threads. Upon the showy fabric sat a brass tray filled to overflowing with salads, caviar, olives, and cheeses. There were pastries filled with lamb, cheese, and spinach; and Turkish coffee and herb-beer to drink. For dessert, an assortment of fruit and cakes. Ninj had even gone so far as to furnish tobacco ciga-rettes and matches.

"Personally, I prefer fried chicken," Miller said, as-sessing the feast from where he stood in front of Jenny.

She tapped him playfully on the arm and moved to stand beside him. "How boring," she said. "You can have fried chicken any time, but how often can you en-joy such an exotic spread as this? I can't wait to sample each and every thing."

"I fear, my dear, if you sample each and every thing on that tray you'll die of gluttony and won't be around for fried chicken."

"But what a way to die," she teased, licking her lips and rolling her eyes heavenward. "Now, if you don't mind, I suggest we graze now and explore later."

"In case you haven't noticed, my little greedy scout, my wet shoes don't lend themselves to exploration." He marked time in place, and the *pish, pish, pish, pish* of the sodden leather sent a dragonfly winging for safety.

"You had best take off your shoes and let them dry out."

"Take them off?" Miller croaked. His blue eyes be-hind his spectacles resembled an owl's.

"Land sakes, I'm not asking you to strip naked. I promise I won't look at your bare feet, if that's what you're worried about."

"Well, no, I, uh . . . ahem."

"You are such a prude," she told him disgustedly. "If you want to, you can stand around here all night, *hemming* and *hawing*, but I'm going inside to eat. And I'll tell you right now, there's no way you're going in there with those wet shoes." Jenny pulled back the curtain and stepped inside.

Through the thin mist of fabric, she watched Miller. It took all of her control to keep from laughing. First, he bent closer to squint at her through the curtain, and then he dropped his gaze to his wet shoes. After a moment passed, he squinted at the curtain again before straightening up to pace in front of the tent. After two short strides, he stopped.

Jenny guessed his stomach won out over propriety because he stood on one leg, bent his opposite knee to untie his shoelace before removing the shoe, and then he did the same thing with the other foot. The face he pulled when his wet hose became coated with the fine sand at his feet made Jenny slap her hand against her mouth to muzzle a giggle. She had at no time met such a fussy man.

"Hose, too," she told him when he faltered.

Beneath his breath, she heard him mumble, "Women."

He jerked off the black hose, bent over, and rolled his wet trousers midway up his calf, then yanked open the curtain and stepped inside.

Jenny dropped down on the cushions and covered her face with her hands. She heard Miller move to the opposite side of the tray of food. "Can I look now?" she asked, splaying her fingers over her eyes.

Miller lay with his legs stretched out and crossed at the ankles, propped up on one arm. "Look your heart out if it makes you feel better," he grumbled. He appeared as grumpy as Ninj's absent bear.

"Can't say *I'll* feel better," she told him, "but you sure as heaven will without those sloshy shoes you were wading in."

Miller said nothing, but began to sample the various foods. *He's pouting,* she thought. They ate in silence for several more moments, then Jenny decided that she'd had enough of his behavior. She would devil him out of his dark mood.

Deliberately she made an effort to stare at his bare feet. "You have very nice feet, you know."

Miller had just popped a grape into his mouth, and she expected it to come shooting out at any moment and wondered if she should duck. His face turned as red as the pillow he was propped against, and his spectacles looked as though they might steam over. Ignoring his reaction, she purposely leaned closer to his naked feet.

"Yep," she said, "same color as your hair."

Her statement really unsettled him. Miller's gaze shot toward his feet as though he expected them to have suddenly turned chestnut brown.

Taking pity on him, she said, "The hair, silly, not your feet."

"I beg your pardon, but I don't have hair on my feet." He acted as though she had told him he had hair growing out of his ears.

"You do, too." She pointed to the tops of his toes. "Right there. It's as plain as the whiskers on your face." Jenny straightened and nonchalantly picked up a pastry and took a big bite.

Miller stroked his closely shaven chin, then peered at his feet again.

Between swallows of the rich pastry, she said, "I reckon a fellow who wears spectacles can't see the hair growing on his toes. Heck, maybe he can't even see his feet."

"And I reckon such a blind and woolly fellow like me ought to teach a perceptive lady like yourself some manners."

His remark brought her up short. She studied his face. His eyes sparkled, and the corners of his mouth twitched. Before Jenny knew what he was about, Miller jumped the tray of food, and she was pinned beneath his hard length.

"And since I'm so blind, I reckon the only way I can tell if you're the lady who needs the lesson will be to touch you." He started to tickle her. "Better count your ribs first and make sure I haven't tackled me a man."

"You wouldn't," Jenny threatened, trying to wiggle from beneath him.

"Watch me," he teased. His finger touched her ribs, and he began to play them like a keyboard. "One, two, three, four."

She tried to hold back her laughter, but it was impossible. Each jab with his finger solicited another giggle. What was it about tickling that could be both pleasant and unpleasant at the same time? But Jenny didn't have time to debate the question; she giggled and squirmed until she became breathless and weak. She tried to get in a few jabs of her own, but Miller was far better at tickling than she was.

On the bed of fine pillows, they wrestled like two recalcitrant children.

"If you poke me one more time," Jenny said between titters, "Ninj's pastry might make another showing."

"Wouldn't be the first time you decorated my shirt. Five, six, seven. Or was that nine?" Miller paused in his counting. "I forgot. Now, where was I? I have to start again. One, two, three—"

"Stop, stop," Jenny warned, "you're going to upset the food." A flailing limb, she wasn't sure whose, nearly sent the food tray toppling. When Miller reached to steady it, she bolted to her feet.

Breathing heavily, she searched frantically for the curtain's opening. Miller grabbed at her ankles, but she sidestepped his grasp.

"Where's the opening?" she moaned, stomping the ground to keep from being captured again. She dug through the filmy pleats, and when she found the opening, she darted outside.

Miller was right behind her, or almost. The sheer curtains weren't being as kind to him. Their silky, waving arms enfolded him in their embrace, and Jenny thought for sure that the tent would tumble down around him as he fought to get free.

She scanned the area. *Quick, quick,* her mind urged.

She needed a place to hide. He would be free, and then what chance would she have?

Like a bird fleeing his cage, Miller burst free, and she still hadn't found a spot to conceal herself in. The chase begin anew. Jenny darted for the cover of a thigh-high rock. Miller followed, facing her on the opposite side. She moved to one end, and he moved with her. Back and forth, back and forth, they darted, until their combined breathing came out in huge gulps.

"You win, you win," she told him, her breath coming in short gasps. She held up her arm to ward off his advance. "I take back everything I said." She paused to take a deep breath. "About your toes, feet, eyes, everything."

Miller breathed as roughly as she did. "And the remark about me being a prude?"

"That, too, that, too." Jenny dropped one hand on the rock to support her weight. "I'm sorry, I won't say you're a prude again."

"And not only do I have your word that you won't say it, you have to promise me that you won't think it, either."

"I promise." Miller faced her on the other side of the rock, looking as bedraggled as she felt. "Now may I please sit down before I collapse?"

"Be my guest." His chest heaved as he motioned with his hand toward the rock's flat top. "I'll join you."

Together they sat, side by side. Although the sun hung low over the little wood, the heat of the day still remained stored inside the rock's surface. The warm stone burned through the layers of their now sweat-dampened garments, adding to their discomfort.

Jenny gazed at the pond. *What I'd give for a nice, cold swim.* She looked at Miller, whose hair lay drooping over his forehead, his collar wilted, his jacket mussed. He had to be as hot as she was, maybe hotter.

"Why don't you take off your jacket?" she said. "You must be baking with it on."

"You're as bad as Ninj with his obsession for going without clothes."

"All right," she said, lifting her hands in case she had to ward off another attack of tickles. "I forget myself."

He reached inside his pocket and pulled out a pristine white, but rumpled, handkerchief and dabbed at his forehead. "It is bloody hot. I was just thinking how inviting that water looks and how good a swim would feel."

Did she dare? Jenny glanced at the water again then at Miller's flushed face. She used to swim back home. Her skin burned beneath the layers of clothing. It was her sticky discomfort that helped her arrive at her decision.

She stood up. "I don't know about you, but I'm going to do just that."

"Just what?" he asked, only half interested in what she had said. He continued to blot his face with the handkerchief.

"I'm going for a swim."

"You're what?" He blinked at her in startled surprise, wholly taken aback by her announcement. "You can't," he gulped.

Using Miller's earlier teasing words, Jenny responded, "Watch me."

Twenty

"Watch you? Jenny!" Miller exclaimed. "Have you lost your mind?"

Not bothering to respond, she sashayed back to the tent and disappeared behind the filmy curtains. Miller pushed away from the rock and followed her, plowing to a stop several feet away from the tent, but not daring to peer inside for fear of what he might see.

He had to talk her out of her crazy notion. He wouldn't allow her to swim—he *couldn't* allow it—but how in the name of torment could he stop such a stubborn, pigheaded woman when she had made up her mind to do something?

He dug his toes into the sand. "Jenny, it wouldn't be proper for a young woman like yourself to take a swim with a gentleman like me."

That was not what he had meant to say. She had him so befuddled his brain didn't know what his tongue was saying.

"I mean we're unchaperoned. People might get the wrong idea. Besides," he croaked, "you don't have a bathing costume."

There, he had said it. The bathing costume was the crux of the problem. It wasn't the idea of swimming so much as the idea of what Jenny might or might not wear that terrified him.

He felt the hot sand beneath his feet; the stored sun rays passed through the soles of his feet and snaked up his legs.

Inside the tent, he heard the flutter of material against her skin, the soft tug of garments being pulled over her head, then first one shoe and then the other plopping against the floor pillows.

His shirt collar felt like a ring of hot iron around his neck. Suddenly the heat that burned his feet became a conflagration of desire. It flamed upward into his groin before traveling over his torso, making his nipples sensitive against his undervest.

"Jenny, you aren't listening to me. I think you ought to reconsider. . . ."

His voice trailed off. His eyes by their own volition had found Jenny's image behind the veiled drapes. He watched her finish disrobing.

Although she was only a blur behind the curtain, Miller's mental picture of her appeared perfectly clear. Hadn't he spent the entire night tied up in knots because of the kiss they had shared, wanting more from her than a man like him had a right to ask for? Hadn't he tried to soak away his passion in an ice-cold tub of water, and afterward, when his skin rippled with goose pimples, hadn't his body still fantasized over such wonderment— Jenny naked and in his arms?

Another rustling of material against skin came from inside the tent. Miller, who believed himself to be aboveboard with women, especially with his old friend's niece, couldn't turn away. Instead, he stood with his feet planted in the sand as though they had suddenly taken root.

"I'm coming out," she told him. "If you don't want to look, then close your eyes."

"It's not that I don't—it's just that I . . ." Miller stumbled over his words like a tongue-tied youth. "I don't think going swimming is such a good idea."

Just as he spit out the words, Jenny burst through the curtains. Like a garden nymph, she sprinted toward the

pool. She wasn't completely naked, and Miller sighed
with relief, or perhaps disappointment, but whatever mo-
tivated the sigh, he could no more have willed his eyes
shut than he could have allowed someone to poke them
out without a fight.

Jenny wore her drawers and chemise and left no doubt
in Miller's mind that the body beneath the fine linen
fabric was a treasure chest of womanly secrets. His eyes
followed her trek to the water's edge. He was both intrigued and burdened by his soon-to-be mermaid.

Her legs were long, her hips rounded. Without the
proper covering of clothes, he could see that her bottom
shimmied slightly when she walked. Although her back
faced him, Miller knew her breasts would be firm and
high-perched even without the support of stays.

Her arms, shoulders, and calves were bare, and her
skin had taken on the golden glow of the setting sun.
Her hair was still in an upsweep, but several tendrils of
the dark mass had worked loose from the high-puffed
knot. The silky strands blended perfectly with the ribbon
and shoestring that held Ninj's jewel around her neck,
so much so, that you couldn't tell where hair ended and
ribbon began.

She was the forbidden apple, and Miller hungered for
her as much as Adam must have craved Eve.

"Jenny," he pleaded, "you should get dressed."

The illogical side of him hoped against hope that she
wouldn't heed his advice, while his more rational side
wrestled for control. "What if someone should come?"

"Then we'll invite them to join us," she called playfully over her shoulder.

As Jenny moved deeper into the water, Miller moved
closer to the water's edge.

"I used to swim in the creek at home," she told him,
"but there I swam in the all-together."

"All together?" A strong wave of jealousy seized
him, and he almost lost his footing. "With whom?" he
demanded.

Her laugh rippled across the water. "Not with anyone,

silly. I swam naked." She tossed the words at him as all but her shoulders and head vanished beneath the surface. "Oh, ah, it's freezing." After a moment, she *ahhh-ed* with pleasure. "It's heaven," she told him. "You must come in."

"Me?" Miller moved closer still, digesting her last piece of information. *She had swum naked.* The notion made Miller's head swim.

The water lapped at his bare toes with its wet tongue. A shudder ran along his length. He felt a deep physical excitement and questioned when he had become as perverted as he had accused Ninj of being the night before.

"You do know how to swim?" she asked. She lay on her back and floated.

From where Miller stood he had a fine view of her high-perched breasts. They poked up out of the water like two pointed islands. Her bare toes bobbed against the surface like baby turtle heads.

As the water touched her in places that Miller had dreamed of touching her last night, desire shot through him. His male parts started doing some pointing of their own, and he shifted the front of his jacket, hoping that Jenny wouldn't notice his growing discomfort.

"It will cure what ails you," she said teasingly.

Had she noticed? Her words made him think so, and he fought the urge to look down at his button fly. Damn! Between the heat outside and the heat inside, Miller expected to burst into a ball of fire at any moment.

With long graceful backstrokes, Jenny propelled herself closer to where Miller stood. "Earlier," she said, "you stated how nice a swim would be."

"I did, but—"

"I'm beginning to think that you are a prude, and I don't want to go back on the promise I made you." Jenny glided past him like a shark sizing up its prey.

"Promise? What promise?"

Miller was unable to recall her promise; in fact, he was unable to do anything but stare. His gaze dropped to the tips of her breasts. Beneath the clinging wet fabric of her chemise, he saw the tawny button shapes of her aureoles, their tiny projected nubs.

Embarrassed by his boldness, he jerked his eyes to the tiny aquamarine ribbons that laced the narrow white straps of her chemise. The ribbons were the same color as the winking stone at her neck. Her talismans, he thought, to protect her against the Evil Eye. Or a more apt explanation would be to protect her from *his* evil eyes.

"Don't you remember?" she asked. "I promised not to call you a prude again." Her feet disappeared. She stood up in the knee-deep water and faced him.

All her womanly secrets were revealed to Miller in that moment. He gaped at the contour of her breasts, the slight indentation of her belly button, and the *V* of dark hair at the apex of her thighs. What he saw was nothing more than barely visible shadows, but Miller knew if he didn't jump into the icy-cold depths of the pond, and do it fast, he was going to pop the front seam of his trousers.

"I remember your promise," Miller answered, forcing her gaze to meet his, "but I guess I'll have to prove to you I'm no bluenose."

She laughed like a sea siren, the haunting sound luring him to his destruction. Cupping her hand, she sent water spraying over him.

The temptation of her was too much for him. When Jenny dove and swam some distance away, inviting a chase, Miller knew he would take the bait.

He jerked off his jacket, tore his shirttail from his trousers, and willed his fumbling fingers to work loose the buttons on his shirt and pants. In less time than it took for the yellow butterfly that Miller saw in his peripheral vision to dart across the pond, he had discarded his outer garments. He stood in his cellulose cotton undervest and knicker drawers, thankful that Jenny now sat on a rock on the far side of the pond where she couldn't see his very evident discomfort.

He took off his spectacles and dropped them on his

clothes. With one giant thrust, Miller hit the water's surface like a skipping rock. With long strokes, he pulled himself through the water, then dove to the bottom where he swam underwater for several yards before resurfacing.

The water smarted icy-cold, but already it had begun to work its magic. His body temperature plummeted and once again he felt in control. The therapeutic water soothed him, and his earlier rock-hard need vanished like mist over a warming pond.

Miller swam several more laps before he stopped in the middle to look for Jenny. Earlier, she'd been sitting on a rock watching him. Now she was nowhere in sight, or nowhere in the range of his poor vision.

He turned in a circle, checking the shoreline. Then he felt a tweak on one of his toes. Peering through the crystal clear water toward the bottom, Miller spotted his mermaid just before she tugged him below the surface.

Like a minnow, she darted away. Miller grabbed for her ankle, but missed. When it became impossible for them to hold their breaths a moment longer, they burst through the water, gasping for air and giggling like children. Swimming on the surface, they splashed one another before the chase began anew.

"Truce," Jenny called, coming to a stop where she could stand.

Miller swam toward her. With his feet anchored to the sandy bottom, he, too, stood with his head above the water. Jenny's breath came in wispy little gasps. Her hair had come loose from its knot, and now floated around her shoulders like a mantle of seaweed.

The fiery red glow of the setting sun painted the sky a rose pink while the lengthening shadows turned the pond the color of a cardinal's belly. Miller and Jenny stared at each other, blinking water from their lashes and gasping for breath. The only other sounds were the *tap, tap, tap* of a redheaded woodpecker hunting for his wood-boring dinner and the *fee-bee, fee-bay* whistle of a Carolina chickadee. As the shadows deepened, a chorus of spring peepers began their high-pitched whistles that ended with a short trill sounding like the jingle of bells.

Feeling like a tightly wound spring, Miller said the only thing that occurred to him. "Frogs."

"You forget, I'm a country girl," Jenny responded, with a look of wonderment on her face. "I hadn't realized until now how much I've missed hearing all the evening noises. Too bad we can't bottle the sound and take it home."

"Not only are you a mermaid," Miller said, "but a forest nymph as well." He smiled, feeling more relaxed. "I have at no time had the pleasure of knowing such a creature."

"Creature?" Jenny laughed and the sound echoed off the surrounding trees. The sound sent a ground critter noisily shuffling for safety. "Should I be flattered by your compliment?"

"We are all God's creatures," Miller answered, his voice catching. He stepped closer to Jenny, knowing he was going to kiss her, knowing he had to do so.

His forward movement sent small pulsations of waves across the glassy surface of the water to wash around Jenny like a gentle caress. Suddenly, her earlier cockiness disappeared and she appeared anxious.

Not wanting her to bolt, Miller spoke softly. "The definition of creature is a living being; especially an animal."

Her eyes grew amused. "Wonderful. Now you're calling me an animal."

"I've not finished yet; a creature can also be a human being."

"Well, at least now I'm human." She played with her hands beneath the surface of the water.

"Hush," he cautioned. "My favorite meaning is the last: one who is dependent upon or subservient to another."

Miller stepped closer and lifted several strands of her

seaweed hair. "Meaning, one who is excessively eager to serve or obey."

Jenny stepped backward, shaking her head. "Well, that settles it. I'm not a creature. As you must know by now, I'm certainly not eager to obey. Anyone," she emphasized.

"Oh, my Jenny, I bet you are." He crooked his finger, motioning for her to come closer.

A playful smile lit up her face and she shook her head no.

"Come, sweet Jenny," he whispered. "It's time you learned that I'm no prude."

She looked nervous, but he knew well that Jenny was not one to back away from a challenge.

She threw out her response. "If you want me, you'll have to catch me." Then she dove away from him.

But Miller was faster. He lunged toward her and tackled her around the ribs. Entwined, they sank beneath the water, then bobbed up a few moments later still curled together, laughing and sputtering because of the liquid they had swallowed.

Unmoving, they stood front to front. With their foreheads pressed together, each fought to catch a breath that was tempered now by their longings. Then it was as though the other had read the other's heart. They touched noses, rubbed them playfully together, before angling their lips for a kiss. Their lips touched, mouths opened, and tongues explored. They were lost in the world of sensation.

Miller's hands slid down her back and cupped her fanny. With a firm grasp, he pulled her hard against his arousal.

And he was aroused.

Jenny felt him hard and hot through the flimsy fabric of her drawers, through the suddenly heated water that surrounded them.

His hands left her bottom and traveled up her rib cage where he splayed his fingers against the sides of her breasts. With his thumbs, he teased the tips into hardness and she moaned her satisfaction.

Staggering together into shallow water, they went down on their knees, still embracing. Jenny arched against him and Miller tightened his hold.

He whispered into her hair, "I want you, Jenny. I want you more than I've ever wanted any woman."

"I want you, too," she murmured, between his exploring kisses. She confirmed her want, by taking his hand and cupping it against her breast.

Together they tumbled into shallower water, giggling at their eagerness to be close. In the ankle-deep water near the pond's edge, Miller lay beside her, his chest pressing into hers. He gazed down into her face and her beauty almost took his breath away. Her hair floated around her head, spreading its glory like a crown of sea fan coral.

"You're beautiful," he whispered, before his lips touched hers.

Beautiful. Jenny had never been called that before and wondered how to respond. But her thoughts sailed away and were forgotten when Miller's lips left her mouth and he began to trail kisses down her neck.

Miller's tongue lapped at the water droplets that spotted her skin like diamonds, his breathing sketchy. He kissed the valley of her breasts before his mouth moved to her nipple, barely hidden beneath the fabric of her chemise. His lips encircled the turgid tip and he suckled.

Desire, hot and wild, shot through Jenny's body. Beneath him, she was attuned to his every movement and when he nudged her legs apart, she allowed him admittance. His hard man's body pressed against the vortex of her being and instinctively she wanted to draw him inside.

Above her, Miller's fingers fumbled with the buttons of her chemise until her breasts were bared. His eyes locked with hers, asking for permission to proceed with what they both wanted. She guided his mouth to her nipple, groaning her pleasure when he took the hardened nub between his teeth and tugged gently.

After several moments, Miller raised his head. His eyes were feverish, his lips swollen. "Let me make love to you."

She stared into his beautiful blue eyes as he waited for her answer.

Never had Jenny believed that what went on between a man and woman could be like this—this awakening, this yearning for something she couldn't put a name to. Before Miller, she hadn't thought about such things, but since his first kiss, the wonder of her feelings had resided close to her soul. Was this what her mother had felt for her father? This enormous emptiness buried deep inside a person that threatened to burst free, pushing all rational thought aside. What she felt for Miller at this moment, could it be love?

"Jenny." His voice called her back to him. "I'll understand if you say no, and I promise you, if you want to stop right now, I won't touch you again."

Not touch her? He would spare her this sweet torture by her voicing her protest. Subconsciously, hadn't this been what she had wanted from Miller the night he had kissed her in the carriage? Perhaps even before that time. Maybe it had begun when she'd been under the influence of Madame DeBeau's cherry liquor. Maybe she had blamed her light-headedness and out-of-control feeling on the devil's brew, when all the time it had been Miller's kiss that had made her head spin. Just as it was spinning now.

It felt natural, as natural and pure as their surroundings, for Miller to be making demands of her body. Just as natural as it would be for her to obey. She did like him. In truth, he was the only man she had ever truly admired. And since she never planned to marry, what better man than Miller to give her virginity to. But not here. Not in the water.

She knew if he wished to take her now, this moment, in the water, she would agree to that as well. But the look he bestowed upon her made her feel as rare and precious as a jewel, and she felt if she asked him anything, she would be rewarded with her wish.

"Can we at least go inside the tent?" she asked.

"I think that can be arranged," he answered gruffly.

Miller stood, and pulled her to her feet. Then he lifted her into the cradle of his arms and carried her toward Ninj's tent.

"Please don't drop me," she said between breathless giggles. "I don't want you to think you're deflowering a sand crab."

"If I were to drop you, my love, I'd just wash you off and then we would begin again."

They laughed. The sound of their merriment floated up to disappear into the now-darkening sky.

Once they reached the tent, Miller set her back on her feet. He found the slit in the curtains, and they slipped inside.

Ninj had thought of everything. He had gone so far as to provide them with candles and pierced tin lanterns that hung from the support poles. Since darkness was fast approaching, Miller lit the lamps with a match, and a golden glow spread throughout the veiled outdoor room, while the lanterns cast lacy shadows across the floor.

He stared at Jenny across the small space. Her teeth had begun to chatter. "You're cold," he said, searching for something to dry her with. He looked at the velvet cloth beneath the food tray. On his instructions, Jenny lifted the tray, and he whipped the cloth free like a magician. After setting the tray aside, Miller wrapped the square of black velvet around her shoulders and sponged away her chill.

Once they were no longer dripping, Miller cupped her chin in his hand. "My little sand crab hasn't changed her mind?" he asked.

Jenny shook her head no, fearing that he had changed his. "Are you afraid?" she challenged.

"Come here," he demanded, "and I'll show you just how much of a coward I'm not."

Jenny went willingly into his arms.

Their eyes remained fixed upon each other's. Miller helped peel away Jenny's wet camisole and she without his help peeled away her drawers. She helped him remove his cellulose cotton undervest before he stepped out of his knicker drawers.

The removal of their garments complete, they stood in the middle of the tent, facing each other and holding hands.

And suddenly feeling shy.

Miller said nervously, "I'm not good at this sort of thing."

"Oh, I don't know," Jenny teased. "You were pretty good in the water." Hoping to regain their earlier carefree mood, she said, "Maybe we should go for another swim and let you try your fishing skills again."

"My fishing skills?" Amusement flickered in his eyes. "Where do you come up with these sayings? These ideas?"

"Well, it seems to me, you were dangling the bait and I was nibbling."

"Dangling the bait?" The mention of dangling made his gaze drop to his swollen member. Before Jenny could look as well, he said, "Come here, my dear, and let's see how good of a landlubber I am."

Jenny couldn't resist the pun. "You mean land*lover*?

"You know what I mean."

He caressed her with his eyes, then pulled her closer. Once their naked skin touched, all traces of shyness faded.

Miller didn't know how it happened, or when it had, but the next time he came up for air after several heated kisses and exploring strokes with his tongue, they were lying on the floor of the tent, Ninj's velvet cloth beneath them.

They lay upon a velvet sky embroidered with a thousand golden threads. She was his goddess and he was her god. Their togetherness made the moment magical. As they played and caressed each other, they learned the secrets of giving and taking pleasure. Soon, when kisses and caresses no longer satisfied, they moved to fulfilling more serious needs.

Settled between her parted thighs, Miller found that their bodies meshed together perfectly. Instincts carried them toward common goals; to satisfy and be satisfied.

With Miller's first plunge into her womanly place, Jenny cried out and stiffened against him. All movement stopped. He apologized and kissed her gently and with his thumb wiped away an errant tear. She smiled, forgiving him, and wrapped her legs around his thighs to better accommodate him.

Her tight muscles accepted his stabbing length, holding him prisoner in her silken sheath. They began moving together. He thrust in and out, and she met his thrusts with an urgency that matched his.

Beneath him, Jenny moaned for release. Guided by a throbbing need that aimed for fulfillment, together they spun into a world of sensation and were hurled over the precipice to float softly back to earth.

Spent, Miller collapsed against her, but he was careful not to crush her with his weight. After the magic they had shared, Jenny had become as delicate and fragile to him as a rose. With her eyes closed, and with the corners of her mouth lifted in a satisfied smile, she resembled an angel. His angel, he thought. Bending to brush his mouth against her full lips, he hoped to convey his feelings with his kiss.

For a man who had lived most of his life keeping his emotions concealed, it was difficult for him to express everything that he felt in his heart.

Jenny's eyes fluttered opened and she stretched like a contented cat. "You're quite the fisherman, Mr. Professor. Would you care to cast your bait again?"

"You and Ninj with your insatiable appetites." Miller kissed her on the tip of the nose and rolled off her, gathering her spoon fashion against his length. "Give me a moment and I'll be more than happy to accommodate you.''

And he did, several more times during the succeeding hours.

Outside the tent, the frogs croaked hoarsely, the moths beat their smudgy wings against the curtained walls, and the half-moon resembled an old man's silvery eyebrow in the velvet black sky. Inside the tent, the new lovers were oblivious to everything except each other and the rapid beating of their hearts.

Ninj was pleased with himself. Even before the dawn blushed the sky with pink, he had been in high spirits. He had felt that way ever since Mistress Jee-nih and Mr. Professor had set out the day before for their picnic. Everything was going as planned—his retirement wouldn't be much longer in coming. Instead of forever standing outside the jeweled gates of genie paradise he would be invited inside to enjoy his old life spiced with the new.

Bengel, who had of late become his faithful companion, lay upon his favorite leopard-skin chair by the shop's front window. During the long night that man and beast had spent together, Ninj had gone back to the trunk in the basement and found the ruby-and-aquamarine-studded bracelet that had belonged to Jenny's grandmother from centuries past. It fit perfectly around the white cat's neck, and Bengel appeared as regal as the white tiger whose blood Ninj believed flowed through the feline's being.

The genie sat on the floor, propped against the companion leopard chair. He rested his turbaned head on the tawny black-spotted seat, and thought about the two lovers and his part in bringing them together.

The tent had been the perfect place for their lovers' tryst. His magic had proved powerful when he placed the tent in the leafy glade beside the natural pool. Ninj was proud of himself; proud that his powers were returning and that his magic was proving to be so strong.

Proud that he no longer summoned elephants when he wished only to summon his Mistress Jee-nih's love.

The meal he had prepared for the two lovers' picnic had been magnificent. Much better than Mistress Jee-nih's fried fowl that he had grown to like. He waited now, knowing that soon the mother sun would blush the horizon with her presence and the lovers would return. Ninj was anxious for that return. Anxious to begin the celebration that would follow the wedding feast. Anxious to be in paradise with other retired genies.

Beyond the glass window, Ninj heard the sound of footsteps approaching. Bengel, his collar of rubies and aquamarine stones reflecting the growing pink and blue of the sky, stood upon his back feet and stretched upward against the chair to peer out the window.

The front door of the shop flew open.

Ninj jumped to his feet. Had the intruders returned a second time?

The fierce white tiger left his perch, sprinting toward the entrance while Ninj waited unnoticed in the morning's gray shadows; proud that he had the power to summon a castle guard, and anxious to do so, if his mistress' castle was again under siege.

Twenty-one

⌒

Jenny slammed the door so hard it rocked the house's rafters. "I should have known better than to trust a man." Nearly trampling Bengel in her anger, she stalked toward the stairs. "Make an honest woman out of me, indeed. How dare he?"

Ninj stepped forward from inside the still-shadowy shop. "Mistress Jee-nih, you have returned."

Jenny didn't dare look long at the genie's crestfallen expression, fearing her tears would tumble free. "Why aren't you asleep?" she asked.

"Ninj is not sleepy." He looked beyond her at the door as though expecting it to open at any moment. "Mr. Professor, he is not with you?"

"No, Mr. Professor is not with me." Her answer sounded more abrupt than she intended, but the last thing she wanted was to be interrogated by Ninj. Jenny crossed her arms against her chest. "If I never set eyes upon that man again, it won't be too soon."

She swallowed back tears and pushed past Ninj, whose giant form took up most of the entrance to the shop. She flounced into the chair Bengel had deserted earlier. The loyal puss came to rub around her ankles, oozing charm and sympathy with each pass.

Scooping up the cat and burying her face in his snowy white fur, she said, "I prefer your and Bengel's company to that of men."

"Ninj is a man, Mistress Jee-nih. A man with big shoulders for you to cry upon, if you so need." The genie came to stand beside her chair. "The white tiger," he said, his fingers stroking the top of Bengel's head, "he is but a half-man not unlike a eunuch, but he, too, has a big heart. Perhaps you should tell these men creatures why you are so upset."

Creatures. Ninj's use of the word only pained Jenny more. Its utterance brought to mind too many memories—memories she didn't wish to recall. She laid her head against the chair back, but avoided his eyes. "I'm not upset," she lied, "I'm—I'm merely tired."

"Tired?"

His face brightened and Jenny swore his earrings lifted an inch higher on each side of his big head.

"Tired is good," he continued. "It means you did not get much sleep. No?" His smile widened even more beneath his silky black mustache.

"If you must know, no, I didn't sleep at all." Then deciding her words had implied exactly what she hadn't meant to, she corrected herself. "It was the swimming that tired me. Yes, that's it. I swam too much. If I hadn't swum, then I wouldn't be tired at all."

If I hadn't swum, she thought to herself, *Miller wouldn't be insisting he do the honorable thing by marrying me.*

Jenny looked at the collar encircling Bengel's throat. She fingered the jewels, saying, "The blue stones match the one at my neck."

"They are of a matching set," Ninj replied.

"Where did they come from?"

Ninj stopped scratching the cat's head and looked toward the street. Instead of answering, he said, "Here comes Mr. Professor now. Maybe he can make you feel better."

Jenny jumped up from the chair and marched toward the stairs. "He is the last person who can make me feel better. Now if you'll excuse me, Bengel and I are going to bed."

• • •

Miller felt lower than scum on a pond. He groaned. A pond was the last thing he wanted to think about. Even now, recalling what he and Jenny had shared in that small body of water made him rock-hard with desire and wild with wanting her. Rather than his hunger for her being sated, he was still ravenous for the woman he loved.

And he did love her.

He loved Jenny Blake with his heart, and his body, and his soul. He had wanted to tell her how much last night when they had made love, but words of affection had never come easy for Miller. So this morning when he had tried to put all he felt for her into words, his brain had shut down and what he had meant to say had come out all wrong.

How could he have been such a blundering fool? He had spent most of his adult life lecturing to students, yet when it came time to give the most important and meaningful speech of his life, his words had left him floundering. Miller's attempt to express himself had resulted in his alienating himself from the only person in the world he had ever really cared about. Jenny.

Miller stopped in front of the building and was about to push open the door when it opened for him. Disheartened, he faced the genie standing on the other side.

"Mr. Professor, you have returned." Ninj's greeting sounded much too cheerful. "I trust your night was pleasurable, the picnic enjoyable."

Miller shot the genie a killing look while bitterness sharpened his response. "Hell, no, it wasn't enjoyable. As far as the night being pleasant, I think it was all a dream. Any pleasure Miss Blake and I shared last night disappeared this morning like that damn tent that you conjured. It was a dream, all right—a nightmare."

"Nightmare?" The giant seemed to fold into himself. "But my magic, it is plenty strong. It should have been a night like no other. Special."

"Oh, the night was special enough. It was the morning after that was fifty times worse than the most horrible hangover." Miller stepped closer to the genie as though he meant to shove him backward. "You want to know something else, Mr. Magic Genie? At no time in my life have I suffered the aftereffects of too much alcohol, but maybe now is a good time. I'm not too old for new experiences."

"Perhaps Mr. Professor would care to tell Ninj what went wrong."

"Wrong? I've asked myself that question numerous times on the way home and I keep coming up with the same answer. My mistake was letting a woman into my life."

"Women are not all bad, Mr. Professor."

"Women are worse than bad. They are crucial in the destruction of men. You have heard about Eve, have you not?"

"You cannot be comparing my Mistress Jee-nih to—"

"Years ago, I swore I'd never get involved with a woman. My solitary, bachelor existence suited me just fine. But then *our* Jenny sails—or barges, I suppose, is a more apt description of her arrival—into my life and takes me completely by surprise."

Miller locked his hands behind his back and began to pace the small entryway, lecturing to Ninj.

"Next I find I'm beginning to like this unusual person, even though she is a woman. She makes me laugh. She makes me feel alive. I find she's living inside my head more than my brain is."

Miller held up his hand to silence Ninj when it looked as though he might be interrupted.

"It gets worse, my friend. I start practicing smiling because she tells me I should smile more. I start wanting to dance with her, hold her in my arms. I want to kiss her. Then I begin to lust for her body. Soon I'm taking ice-cold baths in the middle of the night because she is not only living in my head, she has taken up residence in my trousers."

"This is good, no?" Ninj asked, but Miller ignored him.

"I try to deny the feelings, make up excuses for them, and then I let my guard down and I become vulnerable. I let passion overrule my reason and I bed her."

He ran his fingers through his hair. "Our union is the most wonderful thing that I've ever experienced in my life. So the next morning, I want to tell her how I feel, but the words form all wrong on my tongue. In place of telling Jenny what is in my heart, I end up telling her that I'm going to make an honest woman out of her by marrying her."

"You love her then?" Ninj looked hopeful.

"And do you know what she tells me in no uncertain terms? She tells me no."

Ninj shook his head in confusion. "My Mistress Jee-nih refused your proposal?"

"I shall quote you her exact words. 'There is no way in the world that I would marry a man like you,' she said. 'One who is so wrapped up in his own importance that he can't see the forest for the trees. One who is much too serious a fellow for me, and one whose face would crack if he really laughed.'

"Then she had the audacity to call me stodgy and priggish. She ended by saying she wouldn't force a man to marry her and then end up deserted and miserable like her mother."

Pausing to catch his breath, Miller breathed out a sigh of frustration. "In more simple terms, she told me to get lost."

"Ah, now I see." Ninj nodded in understanding. "Mistress Jee-nih does not like you."

"Exactly."

"It is a shame she does not."

It was a shame, a heartbreaking shame, or so Miller felt, but his anger had left him as quickly as it had come. In its place was an engulfing emptiness. But he'd resigned himself to his fate—resigned that he would live his life without Jenny in it.

"Perhaps it is best," he said. "The two of us are too different to build a life together. All those things she accused me of being are true."

He started up the stairs, then stopped and patted Ninj's shoulder. "I guess, old friend, that your retirement will be a bit longer in coming. It seems our Jenny still hasn't found her perfect love."

Feeling like a beaten man, Miller quietly ascended the stairs.

Ninj watched him until he disappeared above the next landing.

"Yes, yes, yes," he said, dancing a jig in his silken slippers until he was too breathless to continue.

"My mistress is coming round," he told his smiling reflection in the hall mirror. "Ninj's magic is powerful."

Three days after the picnic, Jenny came downstairs to find Miller in her uncle's shop, sitting behind the desk. She had spent those three days alone, determined to ignore him. Ignoring him had been surprisingly easy, for Miller had become as scarce as fleece on a sheared lamb; therefore, she was totally unprepared to see him when she came upon him today.

He stood when he saw her. "Jenny," he said, looking uncomfortable.

Her heart dumped into her stomach and she had a hard time breathing. He looked so handsomely reserved in his professor clothes that it was difficult for her to imagine that he was the same man she had swum with and made passionate love with throughout the magical night they had spent together beside the pond.

He cleared his throat and with a flat, inflectionless voice, said, "I thought it best that I finish with these books before I leave."

Surely she hadn't heard him right. "Leave?" She searched his face. "I don't understand, where are you going?"

Miller stared at her, then beyond her through the window. "I've been thinking of relocating. An old school chum of mine has been trying for years to persuade me to join the teaching staff at the College of William and Mary in Virginia. I spoke with him by telephone the other day. He told me an opening had become available for a math instructor. Seems one of their professors died suddenly—''

"We don't have a telephone," she interrupted, then realized how silly her remark must have sounded. Telephones were in use nationwide. If Miller needed one, she was certain he could have found it. It seemed he had.

She walked toward him and stopped in front of the desk. "But what about your position here at Georgetown College? You've been employed there forever. Surely"— her voice caught—"you can't just up and leave."

He shifted uneasily on his side of the desk. "Forever is too long to stay in one place. Lately, I've been thinking a change might do me good. You know . . . new scenery, new faces."

I'm a new face.

She wanted to say the words aloud, but she kept the thought to herself. Besides, she had given up any right to voice her opinion on his comings and goings when she had thrown his proposal of marriage back into his face.

"I'm taking the train for Williamsburg late this afternoon. Tomorrow I have an interview with the dean of the college."

For the first time since entering the room, she noticed Miller's valises propped against the wall. *He really was leaving.* The knowledge made an ache blossom inside her chest. She couldn't imagine her life without Miller in it.

Grasping for anything that might change his mind, she asked, "But what about Ninj? You did promise that you would help him with his plight."

"Jenny, Jenny," he whispered.

The gentle softness in his voice made her knees go weak. The sound of her name on his lips after three long

days without hearing his voice was as potent as his
kisses. Kisses that she had denied enjoying when she
had claimed she wanted nothing more to do with the
man who had given them.

"You don't need me," he said. "What I mean is, you
don't need my help in finding a suitor. You're a lovely
and desirable woman."

His voice cracked with huskiness and the sound
tugged at Jenny's heart.

"I've seen the many calling cards left by your gentlemen admirers," Miller continued. "In no time at all,
you will find that special someone. Even if he is not the
one for you, I'm sure you can convince Ninj that he is,
and then the genie will be able to retire and you will be
able to get on with your life."

"I-I can't." Jenny could feel her throat shutting. "I
can't do it without you. Ninj will know. He'll see
through me." Jenny wrung her hands.

Please don't leave me.

A muscle ticked in his cheek. "Besides, I've done a
lot of thinking in the past few days. A single young
woman like yourself shouldn't be living under the same
roof with a crusty old bachelor like me. Such an arrangement isn't good for your reputation. If you intend to
make your home here in Georgetown and become
friends with your neighbors, they most likely would
frown upon such terms."

"You said you didn't care what people thought about
you."

"I care what they think of you."

"But you knew my uncle. You lived here with him
for years. He would want you to stay. This is your
home."

"It's your home now." His blue eyes drilled into hers
from behind his spectacles. "You'll make a fine shopkeeper, if you choose to follow in Antonini's footsteps."

Miller appeared as ill at ease as Jenny felt miserable.
He groped beneath a stack of papers on the desk as
though searching for something.

"Your uncle left you financially comfortable. You could close the shop tomorrow and live on his investments. Thanks to Antonini, you're a wealthy young woman." Not looking at her, he continued to shuffle papers. "But if you choose to keep his business going, I'm sure you will make a fine shopkeeper as well."

"I-I don't care about the money . . ."

"The books are up-to-date." He patted the stack of ledgers proudly. "I believe you'll find everything in order. Since you've admitted an aversion to working with figures, I would suggest that you hire a competent bookkeeper."

Her eyes stung. He was leaving. There was nothing she could do or say that would stop him. But then, what did she expect?

She had told him in no uncertain terms what she thought about him. Although Jenny hated herself for all the cruel things she had flung at him that morning when he had pledged to make an honest woman out of her as though he were lecturing one of his students. No one knew better than she that words once spoken could in no way be taken back—no matter how much you wished that they could.

She had hurt Miller. Sweet, sensitive Miller, who had been nothing but kind to her since her arrival in Georgetown. Her outspokenness and sharp tongue had ruined a beautiful friendship. He would never trust his feelings with her again. A proud man like Miller would never set himself up twice for a fall.

"Ah, here it is," he said, holding up a big brown envelope. "I found this. It's addressed to you and was stacked beneath a pile of books and papers on the shelf beside the desk."

"What is it?" she asked.

"It's your uncle's will, and a letter. I thought because the letter was opened, it pertained to business. I read it. I hope you don't mind. Once you read it, I think you'll understand why Madame DeBeau and Phineas Goldfinch broke into the shop."

With shaky hands, Jenny took the envelope. She glanced at it, then back at Miller. "I remember this," she said. "Phineas gave it to me the day I dismissed his firm. I was so upset I tossed it on the shelf, thinking I would read it later." She hugged the envelope to her chest. "Then I found Ninj and I forgot all about it."

"Your uncle loved you very much, Jenny. I know he regretted not having the chance to know you."

With her eyes blurring with tears, Jenny asked, "Do you regret having known me?" *Do you regret having held me, having kissed me, and making me a woman?*

He looked away from her and swallowed. It was several moments before he spoke. "Jenny, you're not making this easy. Of course I don't regret knowing you. You will always be very special to me. Even if I relocate, I'll be checking on you from time to time."

Miller fidgeted. He appeared as though he wanted to say more, but didn't know how. Finally, the words burst free. "I also want you to know that in the future, if you should learn, or discover, that you're, that you've become . . ."

"In the family way," Jenny finished for him.

"Exactly." He relaxed somewhat, but his face was flushed. "All you have to do is contact me and I'll come."

"And make an honest woman of me?"

He tugged at the knot in his tie. "Yes," he confirmed in a businesslike tone, then quickly looked away. "Well, I guess I've said everything that needs to be said. I'll be going by the college to pick up a few papers to take with me to Virginia."

"When will you be back?" she asked, fearing he might not return and dreading that he wouldn't.

Miller leaned down and picked up his valises before walking toward the front door. "Since I've nearly three months before the school term begins, I thought that after I spoke with dean, I'd go on a holiday. My friend and I talked about visiting Charleston. Possibly spending a few days at the shore."

Jenny followed him, still clutching the envelope he had given her. She wouldn't cry, she couldn't. She swallowed back the lump in her throat.

Miller opened the front door, then turned to face her again. He glanced up the stairs and then back at Jenny. Bengel ran in from outside, sprinting past their feet. Their gazes followed him into the shop and they watched him jump upon one of the leopard chairs in front of the window.

"He'll be a lot of company for you," Miller said. "He was to me before you came."

"Yes, he is good company," she admitted, staring into Miller's face.

But not as good as you. Please don't leave me. Please stay with me. Jenny's heart felt as though it might shatter. "You'll write me and let me know your plans?"

"Of course." Miller stepped outside and turned to look at her. "If you decide you want to lease the apartment, feel free to show it. Even if I don't accept the teaching position in Williamsburg, I still will find a new place to live when I return." This said, he stepped down to the pavement and continued up the street.

"Miller," she called.

He stopped, swinging again to face her. For a moment, she imagined she saw a hopeful look spread across his face, but then it was gone. "Yes?" he asked.

She wanted to apologize for all the things she had said by the pond. Although some of them were true, he was still a wonderful man. The only man she had ever truly liked, or trusted. She wanted to beg him not to leave her. Instead of saying or doing what her heart demanded, she said only, "Thank you for everything."

For several moments, he studied her. Then he gave her one of his practiced smiles. "It is I who should be thanking you."

Then he turned and walked away.

Twenty-two

Jenny stumbled back inside the house and closed the door. Leaning against it, she slid down its wooden surface and folded against its frame. With her legs spread out in front of her, she allowed her tears to flow in earnest.

They came from deep within her heart. Sobs rocked her body, rolling over her like great angry waves pounding against the shore. She gulped in big drafts of air, trying to swallow back her sorrow, but the pain remained. Her throat ached, her eyes burned, and she wondered how she would ever live without Miller. His departure had left her with an aching emptiness that had moved to the place in her chest reserved for her heart. She knew the valley of hurt would never go away.

Was this love? This debilitating ache that took over one's whole reasoning? Jenny had at no time been in love and she had nothing to compare her feelings to. She only knew that when she had watched Miller turn and walk away, she believed her heart would break into a million pieces and that her life's blood would cease flowing right there on the front stoop.

When she thought about her life stretching before her, she saw lonely days without Miller in them, days without the smile that she knew he had perfected just for her, days without his dry wit, and yes, days without his inborn stodginess that had become near and dear to her. Was love this all-absorbing passion that filled your soul with emptiness? If it was, Jenny knew she wanted no part of the emotion.

Weakened by her crying, and with her eyes feeling like dried riverbeds, Jenny lay on her side on the floor. She clutched the envelope to her heart, imagining that Miller's scent still lingered on the brown paper.

Bengel had come to stand beside her where her salty tears made elfin puddles on the wooden floor. He sniffed at the puddles and looked knowingly into her eyes. Her fingers found his snowy coat and she began to stroke him gently. He purred as though to say, "I am here for you."

Jenny's mind groped for mundane things. She stared at the blemished flooring of the old house and wondered how many footsteps had crossed the very spot where she lay. She watched dust devils floating on an errant sunbeam cast by a bright sun that was oblivious to her black mood. Her eyes trailed up the stairs leading to her landing; then her mind forded the next set of stairs and she imagined Miller's empty apartment.

Her tears began again with this thought, but soon even those ceased flowing. Feeling as though her head was stuffed with cotton and her ears were plugged with thistledown, Jenny sat up. Big wet blotches decorated the brown envelope that she still hugged to her breasts. She sniffed.

A knock sounded on the opposite side of the door. Jenny's heart thudded against her ribs. Had Miller come back? A warm glow flowed through her and she felt hope flutter anew in her chest.

She stood, chancing a look at her reflection in the hallway mirror. Her hair was mussed, her eyes red, but she didn't care about her appearance, she only cared about seeing Miller again. Still clutching the envelope to her chest, Jenny stepped to the door and flung it open. Officer Mosey stood on the opposite side. On seeing the policeman instead of Miller, Jenny's spirits sank.

"Miss Blake," the lawman said, "I was passing by and thought you and the professor would want to know the trial date has been set."

"Trial?" With everything else that had happened in the last few days, Jenny had almost forgotten about the break-in. Stammering, she asked, "Wh-when is it?"

Officer Mosey appeared uncomfortable. She knew she was a wreck. He tried not to stare at her as he continued with his message. "The judge set the day for three weeks from next Wednesday. You're still planning to conduct legal action against the intruders, aren't you?"

"Yes, sir, I am. I'll note the date on my calendar. Thank you." She started to close the door.

The policeman detained her, his expression one of concern. "Miss Blake, are you okay?" he asked.

"I'm fine, Officer Mosey. Really." Jenny tried to reassure him with a smile. "I'm just a bit under the weather. A nasty cold, but I'll be well in a few days."

He nodded in understanding. "That explains the red eyes and the sniffles. Them summer colds are the worst." He touched his walking stick to his hat and backed away. "Well, I'm sorry I bothered you," he apologized. "You get plenty of rest, and you'll soon be yourself again."

When Officer Mosey started moving up the street, Jenny stepped back inside the house and closed the door. It would take more than rest before she would be herself again, but she knew it was time to carry on. She couldn't continue her weeping forever. Her life would go on, although at the moment she wished it wouldn't.

Besides, with the mention of the trail, she wanted to see what Miller had meant when he had said the letter would explain what Madame DeBeau and Phineas Goldfinch had been searching for when they broke into the shop.

Jenny walked to one of the chairs in the front window and sat down. She pulled the papers from inside the envelope and laid all but her uncle's letter on the elephant-foot table.

She would·look at the will later, but now she would read her Uncle Antonini's letter. This man who had claimed to have loved her had left her much more than his estate. Maybe· someday she would appreciate having known Miller, her uncle's friend and tenant, but now when she thought of him, she felt only heart-numbing pain. She pushed aside the ache and began to read:

My Dearest Niece,

If you are reading this letter it means that your uncle is no longer among the living. Don't mourn me because I have had a full and rewarding life. I've only two things I regret; first, that I never married, for to live your life without love is to sentence yourself to a lifetime of loneliness.

His words brought more tears. Without Miller in her life, Jenny wondered if she, too, had sentenced herself to a lifetime of loneliness. Picking up the corner of her skirt, she dabbed her eyes dry and read on.

And secondly, I should have insisted that your Grandmother Blake allow me to become a part of your life, especially after my sister Rowena's death. But as the saying goes, "Years do not make sages; they only make old men."

As my great-niece, I have left you all my worldly possessions and hope you will accept them as a token of my love, although miles and circumstances have kept us apart. If you have a generous heart, as I suspect you do, perhaps you will choose to make your poor mother's life easier. I'm convinced our character is destined at birth, and through no fault of her own, your mother was born weak.

She thought of her mother, of the years when the two of them could have become close. They were wasted years—years that she couldn't bring back. But then her

Nana Blake had always dictated her mother's actions, even toward her own daughter. Her mother was afraid to show her any affection. Yes, her mother was weak and Jenny had been too strong to compromise.

I write this now not only because I want you to have my wealth, but also because of the information I have found on the Vassily lineage. Years ago I decided to trace our roots; you will see my research is nowhere near complete. But thanks to my modest wealth and my nomadic lifestyle, I had both the funds and the opportunity to begin. I hired Eastern scholars to search through old records that otherwise would have been closed to me. I'll relate to you now what I've learned about the Vassily name.

Many centuries have passed since our dusky, dark-haired relatives left their homeland. Scholars suggest that our people came from northern India, which at one time formed the center of the Rom nation. They fled their land around the 10th or 11th century to escape warring neighbors and a caste-status society. So began the trek of Rom tribes about the world.

Going on intuition and the stories I heard from my parents, I decided to center my research in the East. A few years back, I was contacted by one of the Eastern scholars I hired. He had been studying the 15th century Ottoman Empire around the time the Turks conquered Constantinople and changed the name to Istanbul. When checking historical records he came upon this story about a Harem slave girl—a Circassian odalisque who had been given as a gift to one of the Sultan's pashas. (The odalisque were slave women who adorned the Sultan's palace and were trained in Courtly arts, but who had not become the Sultan's concubine. A pasha was a high-ranking civil official.) For a pasha to be given an odalisque as a gift was a great honor. According to Moslem etiquette, the pasha had to free the girl and make her his wife. This particular pasha I speak of was called Hani Vassily. From this union came many chil-

dren who scattered far and wide throughout the world. Some of our family may have descended from this man, but proving it is nearly impossible.

Years later while traveling in Turkey, I came upon an old trunk in a bazaar. Upon examining its contents, I was taken by the resemblance of the woman in the photograph. She favored my sister Rowena, your Grandmother Vassily, when she was of the same age. It was for that reason that I purchased the trunk and its contents and brought them home. The man who sold me the merchandise said it had belonged to a native woman who I suppose is the lady in the photograph. Her garments match those in the trunk. Perhaps they were her wedding clothes. The unusual-looking bottle he claimed was home to a genie who I never had the pleasure of meeting.

"Ninj's bottle," Jenny said aloud.

And the jewels according to the merchant thief are priceless gems, but to me they look like the worthless baubles you can purchase in any bazaar throughout the East. I, of course, ended up paying the merchant too much money for the whole caboodle.

This, my dear niece, is all I've uncovered of our mysterious past, but I thought you might like to know about the trunk, and maybe someday if you have an interest, you'll try to find the identity of the woman in the photograph. Because of her resemblance to Rowena, I feel she could be a distant relative.

I've brought this to your attention because I know how your Grandmother Blake felt about us gypsies. How she forbid your mother any claim to her past. Only your Grandmother Vassily dared stand up to the woman. We Vassilys have very old and ancient bloodlines, and you should be proud of who you are.

Your loving uncle,
Antonini Vassily

Jenny tried to comprehend all she had read. The trunk had to be the one in the basement where she had found Ninj that day that seemed so long ago. She didn't recall seeing the photograph, but she did remember the beautiful clothes and how they had fit her as though they had been made for her.

And the jewels. She glanced at the collar encircling Bengel's neck and lightly touched the gem still tied around her own. Both pieces had come from the trunk in the basement. Did the trunk and its contents really belong to some distant relative of hers? Suddenly, she wanted to see inside the trunk again and search for the photograph her uncle had mentioned in his letter.

Jenny jumped up and ran toward the back of the shop. Throwing open the basement door, she ran down the stairs. When she reached the floor and started across the room, she remembered to duck so as not to knock her head against the low rafters.

The trunk sat in the same place. Jenny decided that the strange symbols stamped on its surface must be Arabic. She ran her fingers over them before dropping to her knees in front of the case and pushing back the lid.

The interior's fusty scent tickled her nose, but the scarlet satin lining of the old packing case was as beautiful today as it had been the first time she had seen it. The blue and green silk garments with the sun-and-moon design lay inside where she had placed them after taking them off.

Wedding clothes, her uncle had said. The idea of a woman half a world away wearing the garments on her wedding day intrigued Jenny. Could the woman have been related to her? And could that same woman have worn the garments in the ceremony when she had pledged her life and love to a man?

Beneath a layer of papers on the trunk's bottom, Jenny found the photograph that her uncle had mentioned. She sat back on her haunches and studied the faded picture.

The lady was tall and slim with the same dusky skin that she herself had, the same dark hair and eyes. Jenny tried to picture how her Grandmother Vassily would have looked at the age of this woman who appeared to be close to Jenny's age now, or maybe younger. All she had to go on was that her mother had always told Jenny that she favored the Vassilys. Could that mean that the three women looked alike?

With the pad of her thumb, she caressed the frozen image. "Am I part of you?" she asked the stranger.

Tears welled in her eyes and the photograph blurred. Jenny wiped her burning eyes on the back of her hand and continued to study the woman.

It was then she noticed the pendant that hung around the mystery lady's neck. There was no doubt that the stone that hung from a filigree chain was the same one that Jenny wore on a shoestring. And the bracelet. Although barely visible on the woman's wrist, it resembled the one that Ninj had fastened around Bengel's neck a few days before. Perhaps the jewels were a gift given to the bride by her groom on their wedding day.

Her uncle's words came back to haunt her. *"To live your life without love is to sentence yourself to a lifetime of loneliness."*

The tears came again, trembling on her eyelids and filling her throat. By allowing Miller to leave she had imposed such a penalty on herself. She dropped the picture and wept aloud, deep sobs racking her insides as she rocked back and forth.

"I've lost him," she wailed.

She swallowed the despair in her throat and unconsciously clutched the gem at her neck. Her sorrow felt like a weight that grew heavier and heavier. Burying her face in her hands, she allowed her emotions full control.

"You called, Mistress Jee-nih?" Ninj said, suddenly appearing.

Jenny didn't notice him until he touched her shoulder. She jerked her head up. With Ninj's arrival, Bengel came to sit beside her.

"Mistress Jee-nih is unhappy?" the genie asked timidly.

On seeing Ninj, her mood veered from sad to angry. "Yes," she mocked, "Mistress Jee-nih is unhappy. And it's all your fault."

"My fault?" Ninj looked puzzled. "If Ninj has made you unhappy, tell this worthless piece of camel dung how he did so."

"You with your promises of a perfect love. If you had not come into my life, I wouldn't be in this fix. I hate you, I hate you," she moaned, concealing her face in her hands.

"Fix? How can Ninj fix this fix if you don't tell him what needs fixing?"

"You're impossible," she said, raising her head to glare at him. "If you're so almighty magic, bring him back." Her fingers clutched the stone at her neck and she yanked on the string that held it. When it came loose in her hand, she threw it at Ninj. "Here, take this, I never want to see it, or you, again." She wiped her tears on her wrists.

Ninj began dancing around in a circle. He clapped his big hands. "Mistress Jee-nih, Mistress Jee-nih, it has happened," he chanted merrily. "I knew you and the Mr. Professor would help me to retire."

"Retire? It can't happen, Ninj. Not ever. Miller is gone." She lifted her head. "I let him go. I hurt him with my heartless and thoughtless words. I sent him away."

"Not true, my beautiful mistress." He continued dancing in his silken slippers, then stopped and bent toward her. "See," he said, pointing to the center of his turban.

For the first time since Ninj's appearance, Jenny really looked at the genie. He no longer wore the turban she had given him as a gift; now he wore his own, the lavender one he had worn when he had first appeared to her. And in the turban's center was the aquamarine stone.

In her anger, she had forgotten. Jenny felt her neck. Both gem and shoestring were missing.

"I did it, Mistress Jee-nih," Ninj said, looking pleased with himself. "I found you the perfect love. A love to last a lifetime."

She shook her head. "No. He's gone, Ninj. Miller has gone away. I've lost him forever."

"Not forever. I will bring him back," Ninj said matter-of-factly. "Ninj's magic is powerful. You will see, Mistress Jee-nih, I will bring Mr. Professor back."

"But—"

"No buts."

With a flamboyant show of flexing his arms, Ninj closed his eyes as though he were in deep meditation. Recognizing his now familiar summoning position, Jenny dared to hope. With one hand raised toward the heavens, he snapped his fingers.

A shrill piercing sound vibrated the walls; then a strong wind swirled through the basement, raising the heavy dust like a cloud. Jenny covered her eyes and Bengel hid beneath her skirt.

When she opened her eyes again, she saw Miller. Clutching his valises in his hands, he looked as he had earlier when he had left her standing on the stoop, but now his appearance was a little travel-worn from his magical trip.

Miller blinked and glanced around the basement. His gaze came to rest on her. "Jenny," he said, blinking again.

"It's me, Miller, I'm here, or I should say you're here."

She felt nervous and out of sorts. He had only been away from her for a short while and already he felt as distant as a stranger.

"The basement?" he asked. "How did I get here?" His glance slid to Ninj. "Your doing, I suspect. Well, I hope you know I'm about to miss my train to Williamsburg."

"Better you miss your retinue than to miss out on the love of your life. Would you not say so, Mr. Professor?"

"My retinue?"

Jenny hugged herself and laughed. "Ninj isn't familiar with trains."

"Well, I don't have time for—" Miller stopped sputtering and glanced at Jenny, then at Ninj. His stomach leaped into his chest. Had he heard Ninj say—*the love of your life?*

His eyes swept over the genie. Besides the-cat-that-swallowed-the-canary look that was plastered on his round face, there was something different about Ninj's appearance.

Then he saw it. Ninj had on the turban he had worn the first day Miller had met him, but today, it was just a bit different. Smack-dab in the middle of its lavender folds sat Jenny's aquamarine stone, glimmering like the Hope diamond.

But Miller didn't dare hope what the significance of the jewel on Ninj's turban meant. He was afraid to look at Jenny, fearing that he might see her stone still hanging around her neck.

She moved toward him and placed her hand gently on his arm. "It's true, Miller. Ninj has granted his mistress her wish." Jenny's voice faltered, but she swallowed and continued to speak. "I've found my perfect love—my love to last a lifetime."

Disbelieving, he responded, "You have?"

Her fingers touched his chin and her gaze delved deep into his eyes. "Yes, I have. It's you."

"Me?"

It seemed so natural for Miller to open his arms. Jenny came into them without hesitating. His lips found hers and he kissed her with all the pent-up emotions he'd held locked in his heart since the day she had refused his proposal by the pond.

When they had kissed their fill, Jenny leaned away from him and said, "I love you, Miller Holbrook, and I'm ready for you to make an honest woman out of me."

"My sweet Jenny." His face fell. "What a bungling fool I was that day. Surely, you must know by now that I'm not good with romantic words. What I really meant to say that morning was that I loved you, and wanted to make you my wife.''

''Shush!'' She laid her finger against his lips. ''I know now that's what you meant, but I reckon at the time I was still waging war with my own feelings. After all, I didn't plan to fall in love.'' She pressed closer to him. ''Can you ever forgive me for all the hateful things I said?''

Miller kissed the tip of her nose. ''You're forgiven. And to set the record straight, I didn't plan to fall in love, either, but—''

''Of course neither of you did,'' Ninj interjected. ''I planned it. You two were easy from the very beginning.''

''Easy?'' they both repeated.

Ninj's black eyes shone like shrewd little chips of onyx. ''Why do you think I picked you if my retirement wouldn't be assured?''

''I seem to recall, Ninj, that I'm the master and you are the slave. So that means I chose you.'' Jenny said. She turned in Miller's arms and leaned back against him. His arms encircled her and pulled her close.

''Sorry, Mistress Jee-nih, I remember you once said there were no slaves in your country.''

A soft gasp escaped her. ''You have a memory like an elephant.''

''You want elephant?'' Ninj asked. ''I will bring elephant to show you how strong Ninj's magic is.''

''No elephant, please.'' She flung her hands up in a halting gesture. ''It was you who chose us, almighty genie. Your magic is powerfully strong.''

''It is, of course,'' the genie said confidently. ''That is why I am ready to leave this world. My mission here is accomplished. Paradise waits for Ninj.''

''I hope paradise is ready for Ninj,'' Miller whispered in her ear.

Jenny squeezed Miller's hand and stepped away from him. ''Oh, Ninj, must you go?'' she asked.

"Of course, he must go." Miller looked sheepish when Jenny shot him a belligerent look.

"Mistress Jee-nih, this be our kismet. Our destinies, our fate. But you and I, because of our meeting, we will be happier in our next lives. You, with Mr. Professor; me, in genie paradise."

The genie bent over and scooped up Bengel. "And you, my white tiger, will miss Ninj as well." He removed the collar from the cat's neck and clasped it around Jenny's wrist. "A perfect fit, but then I knew it would be," he said, setting the cat back upon the floor. "The bracelet is my wedding gift to you."

Jenny glanced down at the bangle encircling her arm; the red and blue stones twinkled like stars.

"Now I must go."

For the last time, Jenny watched Ninj assume his summoning stance. She rushed toward him and threw her arms around the genie. "I love you, Ninj. I'll miss you."

"I, too, will miss you. Someday, you will see that we will both be richer for the experience." He winked at her, then snapped his fingers. He was gone.

Jenny flew into Miller's arms and wept aloud. Miller held her, hugging her close until her sobbing had ceased. He kissed her forehead and held her away from him. A surprised expression filled his face.

"What is it?" Jenny asked, looking down to where his eyes were fastened on her chest.

She saw it then. Around her neck, hanging on a filigree chain, was Ninj's jewel. An exact replica of the one the mystery woman wore in the old photograph.

Jenny bent and picked up the picture to show it to Miller. "See, they are the same," she said. She pointed to the necklace and then the bracelet on the woman's arm. They compared the woman's jewelry to hers.

"It's funny," Jenny said. "When I first saw this picture after reading my uncle's letter, I recalled that he had written that the lady might have been in her wedding dress. The same dress that's in the trunk. I tried it on the day Ninj came. You remember the dress?"

"I remember it," Miller said. "I think I fell in love with you a little that day."

She kissed him, then asked, "Do you think Ninj knew the woman in the photograph? He did say that the bracelet was his wedding gift to me."

"It's possible, but we'll probably never know." Miller picked up the pendant and flipped it over. "There is something inscribed on the back, but I can't make it out in this light."

He pulled Jenny to the windows where sunlight streamed in. Scanning the back again, he said, "Well, I'll be—"

"Tell me. What does it say?"

"There is an inscription. And a signature."

"What? Whose?"

Miller read it aloud. "It says, 'To my bride. Ninjlio Vassily.' "

Author's Note

~

Years ago I fell in love with our nation's capital when I worked in Washington, D.C., for the United States Information Agency. Like Jenny, a walk down Pennsylvania Avenue would bring tears to my eyes and a lump so large I couldn't swallow. I was humbled by all that occurred in that exciting city, where decisions are made daily that affect the world.

Washington, D.C., still has that mysterious quality to enchant with its magnificent museums, gleaming marble monuments, splashing fountains, neoclassical buildings, and tree-lined parks and thoroughfares. The city, designed by Frenchman Pierre Charles L'Enfant, more closely resembles Paris than any other American city.

While living in Washington, Georgetown was one of my favorite haunts. So when I decided I'd like to do a magic book, what better place to set it than there? Georgetown, with its history and beauty, is truly magical; its rare ambiance of antiquity and charm and its unhurried eighteenth-century atmosphere.

When I started my research I fell in love again with the city. What really surprised me was how large the capital was during the time of Jenny and Miller's story. So many of the buildings standing then are still standing today. The C & O Canal, built in the mid-eighteen-hundreds, was to be a flat water route to the western world. It is now the Chesapeake and Ohio Canal National Historical Park, a unit of the National Park System and one of the nation's most intact historic canals.

The little bits and pieces of history I wove into my story are true. I used old books with pictures of the area to describe the way the city looked back then. *The Essential Handbook of Victorian Etiquette* that Jenny referred to is a book copyrighted in 1994 by Bluewood Books and was adapted directly from material written and published by Professor Thomas E. Hill between 1873 and 1890. I did take poetic license by moving the lower ford of what is known today as Rock Creek Park closer to the limits of Georgetown for Jenny and Miller's picnic.

I loved writing this book, but there were times I felt I could have used some of Ninj's magic to finish it. I hope that with its reading you, too, will share in the magic because that is what romance is all about.

I love to hear from my readers. You can write to me c/o The Berkley Publishing Group, 375 Hudson Street, New York, New York 10014, or E-mail me at CCOTTEN/ MINDSPRING.COM.

DO YOU BELIEVE IN MAGIC?

MAGICAL LOVE

The enchanting new series from Jove will make you a believer!

With a sprinkling of fairy dust and the wave of a wand, magical things can happen—but nothing is more magical than the power of love.

___**SEA SPELL** by Tess Farraday   0-515-12289-0/$5.99

A mysterious man from the sea haunts a woman's dreams—and desires...

___**ONCE UPON A KISS** by Claire Cross
0-515-12300-5/$5.99

A businessman learns there's only one way to awaken a slumbering beauty...

___**A FAERIE TALE** by Ginny Reyes
0-515-12338-2/$5.99

A faerie and a leprechaun play matchmaker—to a mismatched pair of mortals...

___**ONE WISH** by C.J. Card
0-515-12354-4/$5.99

For years a beautiful bottle lay concealed in a forgotten trunk—holding a powerful spirit, waiting for someone to come along and make one wish...

VISIT PENGUIN PUTNAM ONLINE ON THE INTERNET:
http://www.penguinputnam.com

Payable in U.S. funds. No cash accepted. Postage & handling: $1.75 for one book, 75¢ for each additional. Maximum postage $5.50. Prices, postage and handling charges may change without notice. Visa, Amex, MasterCard call 1-800-788-6262, ext. 1, or fax 1-201-933-2316; refer to ad # 789

Or, check above books   Bill my: ☐Visa ☐MasterCard ☐Amex_____(expires)
and send this order form to:
The Berkley Publishing Group   Card#_____
P.O. Box 12289, Dept. B   Daytime Phone #_____ ($10 minimum)
Newark, NJ 07101-5289   Signature_____
Please allow 4-6 weeks for delivery.   **Or enclosed is my:** ☐ check ☐ money order
Foreign and Canadian delivery 8-12 weeks.
Ship to:
Name_____ Book Total $_____
Address_____ Applicable Sales Tax $_____
City_____ Postage & Handling $_____
State/ZIP_____ Total Amount Due $_____
Bill to: Name_____
Address_____City_____
State/ZIP_____

TIME PASSAGES

_CRYSTAL MEMORIES *Ginny Aiken* 0-515-12159-2

_A DANCE THROUGH TIME *Lynn Kurland*

    0-515-11927-X

_ECHOES OF TOMORROW *Jenny Lykins* 0-515-12079-0

_LOST YESTERDAY *Jenny Lykins* 0-515-12013-8

_MY LADY IN TIME *Angie Ray* 0-515-12227-0

_NICK OF TIME *Casey Claybourne* 0-515-12189-4

_REMEMBER LOVE *Susan Plunkett* 0-515-11980-6

_SILVER TOMORROWS *Susan Plunkett* 0-515-12047-2

_THIS TIME TOGETHER *Susan Leslie Liepitz*

    0-515-11981-4

_WAITING FOR YESTERDAY *Jenny Lykins*

    0-515-12129-0

_HEAVEN'S TIME *Susan Plunkett* 0-515-12287-4

_THE LAST HIGHLANDER *Claire Cross* 0-515-12337-4

_A TIME FOR US *Christine Holden* 0-515-12375-7

All books $5.99

VISIT PENGUIN PUTNAM ONLINE ON THE INTERNET:
http://www.penguinputnam.com

Payable in U.S. funds. No cash accepted. Postage & handling: $1.75 for one book, 75¢ for each additional. Maximum postage $5.50. Prices, postage and handling charges may change without notice. Visa, Amex, MasterCard call 1-800-788-6262, ext. 1, or fax 1-201-933-2316; refer to ad # 680

Or, check above books and send this order form to: **The Berkley Publishing Group** P.O. Box 12289, Dept. B Newark, NJ 07101-5289	Bill my: ☐Visa ☐MasterCard ☐Amex_____(expires) Card#_____ Daytime Phone #_____ ($10 minimum) Signature_____

Please allow 4-6 weeks for delivery. **Or enclosed is my:** ☐ check ☐ money order
Foreign and Canadian delivery 8-12 weeks.

Ship to:

Name_____	Book Total	$_____
Address_____	Applicable Sales Tax	$_____
City_____	Postage & Handling	$_____
State/ZIP_____	Total Amount Due	$_____

Bill to: Name_____

Address_____City_____

State/ZIP_____